ARIEL SAMSON
FREELANCE RABBI

A NOVEL BY MANISHTANA

Cover design by MaNishtana
Back photo courtesy of Isaac Himmelman
Copyright © 2018 MaNishtana
Multikosheral Press
ISBN: 0692071563
ISBN-13: 978-0692071564

To anybody who's ever heard that they don't "look Jewish."
To anybody who's ever been told they weren't ethnic "enough."
To the nervous Jewish parents of Color and their baby boys.
To those of us who converted.
To those of us who didn't.
To those of us with parents who don't get that they won't ever get it.
To those of us with kids who don't get that they haven't gotten it yet.
To anyone who's ever hated being a Jew in a room full of minorities.
To anyone who's ever hated being a minority in a room full of Jews.
To those of us who are proud of where we are but ashamed of where we've been.
To those of us ashamed of where we are but proud of where we come from.
To those of us who left.
To those of us who stayed.
To anyone just trying to figure it all out.

Here's to us.
L'chaim.

glossary

Aba: Hebrew for father

Ahavas Yisroel (or Ahavat Yisrael): the concept of unconditionally loving one's fellow Jew

Alav hashalom: Hebrew phrase equivalent to "rest in peace"

Aliyah: the honor of being called upon to read from (or recite a blessing over) the Torah during Shabbat, holidays, and select weekday services

Apikores: heretic

Ars: Israeli slang for a flashy roughneck, analogous to the Italian guido, although sometimes engaged in more criminal activities

Ashkenaz: Of or pertaining to Jews originating from Eastern European countries, especially Germany, Poland, Ukraine, Lithuania, and Russia.

Ashkenazis: The Hebrew accent unique to Ashkenazim.

B'sha'ah tovah: traditional Hebrew congratulations given to a pregnant woman or her loved ones, implicitly wishing that the baby will be born healthy and safe

B'tzelem Elokim: the Jewish belief that all humans are created in the Divine Image of G'd

Baal koreh: the one who reads from the Torah scroll

Baal teshuva: term for secular or non-Orthodox Jews who take on traditional religious Jewish observance.

Balak: Numbers 22:2–25:9, the 40th weekly portion in the annual Jewish cycle of reading the Five Books of Moses.

Bar mitzvah/bat mitzvah: a male child of 13 or female child of 12, both now religiously obligated as adults

Beit din (or Beis din): Jewish religious court of law

Bekishe: a long black coat worn by Hasidic Jews that is typically constructed out of black silk or polyester.

Beracha: blessing

Bimah: the elevated platform in synagogue used as a podium for Torah reading during services, and usually also as the pulpit from where the rabbi delivers his sermon

Bochur: student, usually an unmarried male

Borei minei b'samim: the blessing said over aromatic scents

Brit (or Bris): Jewish circumcision ceremony

BT: abbreviation for "ba'al teshuva"

Chabad-Lubavitch: also known as Lubavitch or Chabad, Chabad-Lubavitch, is an Orthodox Jewish, Hasidic movement, headquartered in Crown Heights, Brooklyn, and well known for its outreach to Jews from non-Orthodox backgrounds

Chag: holiday

Chag hasmicha: graduation ceremony celebrating the bestowing of rabbinical ordination upon a class

Chalaka: Hebrew term for the ceremony of a three-year old Jewish boy's first haircut.

Charedi: stream of Orthodox Judaism characterized by a rejection of modern secular culture, also described as "ultra Orthodoxy."

Chas veshalom: Hebrew phrase meaning "G'd forbid"

Chatat: a sacrificial sin-offering in Temple times

Chavruta: a religious study group of 2-5 partners

Chazzan: cantor

Chizuk: encouragement

Cherem: an ecclesiastical censure that is the total exclusion of a Jew from the rest of the Jewish community.

Chevra kadisha: a group of Jewish men and women who see to it that the bodies of deceased Jews are prepared for burial according to Jewish tradition and are protected from desecration, willful or not, until burial

Cholent: a a traditional Jewish stew, simmered overnight and eaten for lunch on Shabbat afternoon

Chalav Yisrael (or Cholov Yisroel): dairy products which derive from milk that has been milked completely under the supervision of a religiously observant Jew.

Chossid: a Hasidic Jew. Also, any devout follower of an ultra-Orthodox rabbi.

Chumash: book containing the Five Books of Moses

Chuppah: the Jewish wedding canopy

Chutzpadik: Yiddish term meaning impudent, brazen, or not showing due respect

Da'as Torah (or Da'at Torah): the concept which believes that Jews should seek the input of rabbinic scholars not just on matters of Jewish law, but on all important life matters.

Dalet (or Thalet): The fourth letter of the Hebrew alphabet. Pronounced as a "d" in Ashkenazi and Sepharadi Hebrew, but as a "d" or "th" in Temani Hebrew.

Dan l'kaf zechut: the Jewish principle of judging others favorably and giving the benefit of the doubt.

Davening: the act of praying, from the Yiddish word "daven," meaning "to pray".

Drasha: sermon

Eliyahu's chair: the special chair of honor set aside for the prophet Elijah, who is traditionally present at every Jewish circumcision

Emet: Hebrew word for truth

Eretz kodesh: Hebrew for "the Holy Land." Traditionally a euphemism for the Land of Israel.

Erev Shabbat: Friday night, the eve of the Sabbath

Eruv: an unobtrusive wire boundary (usually attached to the top of utility poles) that encloses an urban area and symbolically extends the private domain of Jewish households into public areas to work around the religious prohibition against carrying objects outside of one's home on Shabbat and Yom Kippur.

Farbrengen: a celebratory gathering to study or discuss Torah concepts

Frum: someone or something that is devoutly observant of traditional Jewish laws

Frumkeit: Yiddish term for an observant Jewish way of life

Gabbai: the beadle or sexton who assists in the running of synagogue services in some way, usually by assigning honors to congregants.

Gadol: a term used by religious Jews to refer to the most revered rabbis of a generation.

Gam zu l'tovah: phrase meaning this too is for the good

Gan Eden: paradise

Gemara: the compilation of rabbinic analysis and commentary on the written version of Jewish oral law known as the Mishna. Together, the Mishna and Gemara form the central text and source of traditional Jewish religious law and theology known as the Talmud.

Gimmel (or Jimmel): The third letter of the Hebrew alphabet. Pronounced as a "g" in Ashkenazi and Sepharadi Hebrew, but as a "g" or "j" in Temani Hebrew.

Goy: a non-Jewish person. Often used pejoratively.

Gut Shabbos (or Good Shabbes): Traditional Yiddish Sabbath greeting

Halacha: the collective body of traditional Jewish religious laws derived from the Written and Oral Torah as codified in the Talmud.

Halachically: done in accordance with Jewish law

Hallel: a Jewish prayer, a verbatim recitation from Psalms 113–118 which is recited by observant Jews on Jewish holidays as an act of praise and thanksgiving.

Harav hagaon: elevated Hebrew honorifics placed before a prestigious rabbi's name

HaShem: a Hebrew term used when referring to G'd in non-liturgical contexts

Hashkafa: term for a Jewish ideology

Hassid: a Hasidic Jew

Hatafat Dam Brit: a ceremonial drawing of blood for those who have previously had a non-religious circumcision

Havdalah: candle lighting ceremony marking the end of Shabbat

Hechsher: a rabbinical product certification, qualifying items (usually foods) that conform to the requirements of halacha.

Heimishe: Yiddish word that can describe something homey and familiar, or upstanding and respectable.

Hora: traditional Jewish circle dance

Ima: Hebrew for mother

Kaddish: an ancient Jewish prayer sequence regularly recited in the synagogue service, for the dead.

Kapote: a long dress coat formerly worn by male Jews of eastern Europe and now worn chiefly by ultra-Orthodox or Hasidic Jews

Karet: a severe biblical penalty of death that is enacted by the Divine Hand, not mortal courts of law

Kashrut (or Kashrus): parameters surrounding the conventions of kosher dietary laws

Ketubah: Jewish marriage certificate

Kiddish: a celebratory meal in synagogue after morning services to sanctify the Shabbat or holiday.

Kiddush Hashem: a sanctification of G'd's Name through one's actions

Kiddush: The ceremony of wine and prayer before a Shabbat or holiday meal.

Kippah: Hebrew word for the Jewish head covering traditionally worn by men

Kiruv: the Jewish concept of religious outreach

Kivud av: respect for one's father

Knesset: Short for "beit Knesset", the Hebrew word for synagogue

Kohen: the Jewish priestly clan, having certain rights and duties in the synagogue.

Kushi: derogatory Hebrew term for black people. Akin to "nigger."

Lag b'omer: a Jewish holiday celebrated on the 33rd day between the Jewish holidays of Pesach and Shavuot, traditionally marked by music and bonfires

L'chaim: traditional Jewish cheer meaning "To life!"

Layn: Yiddish term for reading from the Torah scroll during a Jewish prayer service

Lehavdil: Hebrew expression used to contrast something great to something far less significant, usually used when comparing something sacred/religious with something secular.

Levi: the Jewish Levite clan, having certain rights and duties in the synagogue.

Maarit ayin: Jewish concept stating that permissible actions that might seem to be a violation of Jewish law are not allowed to be performed in order to prevent surrounding onlookers from arriving at a false conclusion

Ma'ariv: the daily evening service

Magen david: Hebrew name for the Star of David

Maimer: Hassidic term for an original religious statement of thought or unique point of view.

Maoz Tzur: a Jewish liturgical poem traditionally sung after candlelighting during the nights of Chanuka

Mashiach: the messiah

Mazal Tov: Hebrew term of congratulations

Mechitzah: the structure that divides men and women during Orthodox prayer services and some social gatherings and celebrations

Menorah: any of several candelabrums lit for ritual Jewish purposes, most often either referencing the 5 or 6-branched candelabrum used for Shabbat and holidays, or the 9-branched candelabrum lit for Chanukah, properly called a chanukiya

Mensch: Yiddish term for a good person

Mesader kiddushin: the officiating rabbi at a Jewish wedding

Meshichist: members of the Chabad-Lubavitch sect who subscribe to the belief that Menachem Mendel Schneerson, the last Lubavitcher Rebbe, is the Messiah.

Mevushal: kosher wine that is boiled during its fermentation process, allowing for unquestioned handling by non-Jews or non-observant Jews

Midrash: an ancient commentary on part of the Hebrew scriptures, attached to the biblical text.

Mikvah: a ritual purification bath that is taken by observant Jews on certain occasions, such as before marriage, after menstruation or childbirth, or by non-Jews as the last stage of conversion into Judaism

Mincha: the daily afternoon prayer service

Minhag: an accepted tradition or group of traditions in Judaism that is binding upon a specific Jewish community

Minyan: a quorum of ten people (traditionally all male) for Jewish prayer purposes.

Mitzvot: good deeds done in observance of religious duty

ModOx: short for "Modern Orthodox," a movement within Orthodox Judaism that believes in both the traditional observance of Jewish law as well as engaging and participating in the modern secular world

Mohel (or Moil): Person trained to perform Jewish circumcision

Moichel: phrase meaning to forgive or excuse

Moztei Shabbat: Saturday night after Shabbat has ended

Motzi: shorthand for "hamotzi lechem min ha'aretz, "the blessing over bread

Mussaf: an additional morning service recited on Shabbat and holidays

Nachala: Hebrew term for the anniversary of someone's death, especially a parent's.

Narishkeit: Yiddish word for "nonsense" or "foolishness"

Ne'ilah: the concluding service of Yom Kippur, where the final prayers of repentance are recited

Ner neshama: Hebrew term for the Jewish memorial candle lit in honor of the dead

Nitzavim: Deuteronomy 29:9–30:20, the 51st weekly portion in the annual Jewish cycle of reading the Five Books of Moses.

Nu: a Yiddish expression meaning "well?" or "so?"

Off the derech: an expression used to describe someone who leaves an Orthodox Jewish lifestyle.

Olam haba: the World to Come

Oneg Shabbat: a small repast after Shabbat evening synagogue services

OTD: Abbreviation of "off the derech"

Parsha: one of the 54 weekly portions of the Five Books of Moses read over the course of one Jewish year.

Parve: A Jewish category of food that is neither meat nor dairy. Vegetables, for example.

Pesach: Passover

Pikuach Hanefesh: the Jewish concept that saving a life overrides the mandate of any other commandment

Purim: holiday commemorating the saving of the Jewish people in the ancient Achaemenid Persian Empire from extermination, as recorded in the Book of Esther. Celebration includes the wearing of costumes, drinking of alcohol, and exchanging of food gifts.

Pushka: a charity box

rabbanit: Hebrew title used for the wife of a rabbi

Rebbe: Yiddish word derived from the Hebrew "rabbi." Generally, it refers to a religious leader of any Hasidic sect. Used specifically (as in "The Rebbe") it often refers to Menachem Mendel Schneerson, last rebbe of the Chabad-Lubavitch Hasidic dynasty.

Rebbetzin: Yiddish title used for the wife of a rabbi

Rosh Hashana: the Jewish New Year and Day of Judgment

Saba: Hebrew for "grandfather"

Sandek: the person honored at a Jewish infant's circumcision with holding the baby in their lap while the mohel performs the ceremony. The Jewish equivalent of a godfather.

Savta: Hebrew for grandmother

Schvartze: derogatory Yiddish term for black people. Akin to "nigger."

Seder: traditional ceremonial Passover evening meal, at which the Exodus from Egypt is recounted.

Sepharadit: The Hebrew accent unique to Sephardim.

Sephardic: Of or pertaining to Sephardim, Jews originating from Mediterranean countries, especially Spain, Italy, Portugal, Greece, and North Africa.

Seudah Shlishit: the third meal customarily eaten by Sabbath-observing Jews after lunch on Shabbat afternoon.

Shabbat (or Shabbes/Shabbos): The Jewish day of rest and spiritual renewal, commencing at sunset on Friday and terminating at sunset on Saturday.

Shabbat shalom: Traditional Hebrew Sabbath greeting

Shalom aleichem (or sholom Aleichem or shulem Aleichem): a spoken Jewish greeting, meaning "peace be upon you." The appropriate response is *"aleichem shalom"* and it's variants, meaning "upon you be peace."

Shabbaton: a weekend program or event with the main focus being around Shabbat observance

Shacharit: the daily morning service

Shavua tov: traditional post-Shabbat greeting wishing a good upcoming week

Shavuot: the Jewish holiday commemorating the giving of the Ten Commandments

Sheitel: Yiddish term for the wig or half-wig worn by some Orthodox Jewish married women in observance with the requirement of Jewish law to cover their hair.

Shidduch: a system of matchmaking in which Jewish singles are introduced to one another in Orthodox Jewish communities for the purpose of marriage

Shiksa: pejorative Yiddish term for a non-Jewish woman, derived from the Hebrew term *sheketz* meaning "abomination", "detestable", "loathed," "blemish," or "insect."

Shin: the 21st letter of the Hebrew alphabet.

Shiur: a lesson or study session on any Jewish religious topic

Shiva: the seven-day Jewish mourning period after the burial of a loved one.

Shlishi: Torah reading is divided into 3,4,5, or 7 parts. Shlishi is the third.

Shofar: ancient musical horn typically made of a ram's horn, used for Jewish religious purposes.

Shomer mitzvot: someone who is religiously observant in the traditional Jewish way, but for various reasons does not self-identify with the label of being "Orthodox"

Shomer negiah: someone who abides by the Jewish law forbidding or restricting physical contact with a non-familial member of the opposite sex.

Shtriemel: a fur hat worn by many married Charedi Jewish men on Shabbat and holidays

Shul: Yiddish word for synagogue

Sigd: a holiday unique to the Beta Israel Ethiopian Jewish community celebrated 50 days after Yom Kippur and commemorating the 6th century end to war between Jews and Christians ended and both communities separating from each other and the 15th century relief from persecution by Christian emperors.

Simchat torah: Jewish holiday that celebrates and marks the conclusion of the annual cycle of public Torah readings, and the beginning of a new cycle

Smicha: rabbinical ordination

Sufganiyot: jelly-filled fried donuts traditionally eaten on Chanukah

Tachanun: a part of Judaism's morning and afternoon services that includes a confessional and supplications for mercy. It is omitted on Shabbat, holidays, and other festive occassions

Tallit (or Tallis): Jewish prayer shawl

Talmud: the central text and source of traditional Jewish religious law and theology.

Tammuz: the 10th month of the Jewish calendar, occurring in June/July.

Tav (or Sav or Thav): The 22nd and last letter of the Hebrew alphabet. Pronounced as "t" In Sepharadi Hebrew, as a "t" or "s" in Ashkenazi Hebrew, and as a "t" or "th" in Temani Hebrew.

Temani: Middle Eastern Jews who live, or once lived, in Yemen.

Teshuva: repentance, penance

Tikkun olan: repairing the world

Tisha b'av: an annual Jewish fast day primarily mourning the destruction of both Jewish Temples in Jerusalem by the Babylonians and Romans respectively.

To'eivah: Hebrew term meaning "abomination"

Tu b'av: the 15th day of the Jewish month of Av, a summer holiday akin to Valentine's Day

Tu b'shvat: the Jewish new year for trees

Tzedakah: charity

Tzetchem l'shalom: traditional farewell to someone leaving on a journey

Tzitzit: specially knotted ritual fringes worn traditionally by Jewish men, attached to the four corners of either the *tallit* prayer shawl, or on the smaller *tallit katan* special garment worn with everyday clothes.

Upshernish: Yiddish term for the ceremony of a three-year old Jewish boy's first haircut.

Vav (or Waw): The sixth letter of the Hebrew alphabet. Pronounced as a "v" in Ashkenazi and Sepharadi Hebrew, but as a "w" in Temani Hebrew.

Vayetze: Genesis 28:10–32:3, the 7th weekly portion in the annual Jewish cycle of reading the Five Books of Moses.

Yahrtzeit: Yiddish term for the anniversary of someone's death, especially a parent's.

Yarmulke: Yiddish word for the Jewish head covering traditionally worn by men

Yeshiva: Jewish religious private school

Yeshivish: a subset of Modern Orthodoxy who are religiously conservative and skew more insularly, placing high emphasis on rigid and structured learning

Yichud: the prohibition in Jewish law of man and a woman who are not married to each other being alone in seclusion

Yidden: Yiddish for "Jews"

Yiddishe: Yiddish for "Jewish"

Yiddishkeit: Yiddish term for "Judaism"

Yisrael: any Jew not of either the priestly or Levite clans.

Yizkor candle: Yiddish term for the Jewish memorial candle lit in honor of the dead

Yom kippur: the Jewish Day of Atonement

Yud: the tenth letter of the Hebrew alphabet.

acknowledgments

In case I forget anyone specifically, let me first thank everyone generally, so thanks to all my beta readers, my translators, my consultants, and my miscellaneouses.

Specifically, immense thank yous to Asher Lovy, Hannah Simpson, and Gregoria Stewart-Santiago, for allowing me to borrow a sliver of their words and lives to repurpose them for my own fell purposes. Thanks to my sister Zippora for laying the groundwork beats for Colin's entrance and his generally explosive personality, almost a decade ago. Thanks to my linguist rockstars, Oshra Bitton, Rachel Ghoori, Lilly Beth Kestenbaum, Anton Masterovoy, Lina Morales, Maria Rubio, Abbie Yamamoto, Barnaby Yeh, and #TeamZOE (Nadine Bigot, Miryam Drum, Donald Thurin) for their French, Spanish, Hebrew, Russian, Yiddish, Tagalog, Japanese, Chinese, and Haitian Creole assists, respectively. (Yes, *"Morales."* My Yiddishist is a trans-femme Mexican Jew by birth. Deal with it.) Much obliged to "Curleh Mustache" consultant, Nate Samuel, and similar thanks to Tovah Gidseg, Talya Ariel, Sara Katznelson for their counseling on that secret thing we talked about (*wink, wink*).

And, last but not least, thanks to everyone who's read what eventually became this novel, through the long journey of all its iterations until its final form, Ingrid Anderson, Zehava Bracha Arky, Nylah Burton, Ben Ziggy Faulding, Rachel Ghoori, Aliza Hausman, Esther Hugenholtz, Lilly Beth Kestenbaum, Elana Klein, Anton Masterovoy, Tamar Pacht, Christina Prindle, Tova Ricardo, SM Rosenberg, Matthue Roth, Gennifer Rollins, Gulienne Rollins-Rishon, Dena Schupper, Aliyah Rochel Shaw, Tzipi Sutin, Ruby Velez, and Chaya Sara Washington.

And anyone ever subjected to my overtime ramblings at Hevria farbrengens.

i

disclaimer

To say that this is a work of fiction would be true. And it would also be false. To say that this is a work of non-fiction would be false. And it would also be true. More accurately, this novel's story and characters are products of the author's imagination, but the events and incidents depicted herein are a combination of autobiographical anecdotes from the author's life, certain fictionalized embellishments, and some real world events and encounters used in a fictitious manner. In all other respects, any resemblance to actual persons (living or dead), events, or locales is entirely coincidental. In conclusion, the reader should not consider this book anything other than a work of literature, nor should they consider it merely a work of literature.

ma'ariv
aravit
arbith

.

There was not, Ariel decided, enough booze there for this.

And by "there," he meant "in him."

I'm not sure what kind of soulless organization holds a cocktail hour without any actual cocktails, but there Ariel was. And he was anxious. About all the people, not the lack of alcohol. But the scarcity of social lubricant didn't exactly help.

Hell, he'd even have gone for a shot of Spirytus right about then.

Ever heard of Spirytus? It's a 192-proof vodka that's essentially 96% alcohol and 4% a voice that whispers *"You are gonna regret your life tonight"* directly into your cerebral cortex.

Ariel'd had Spirytus once, and he never wanted to look at it ever again, because it reminded him of the night that he died and then lived to tell the tale of how he'd died.

There *was* wine there, though. A perplexing vintage smelling faintly of overcooked raisins wrapped in band-aids, blending scintillating notes of acetone and a dead human foot. With a spiteful cherry finish.

I know, right?

It's sacrilegious what passes for kosher wine out there. And that people drink it. On purpose. *I* sure as hell don't have the choice.

But at least, for Ariel's sake, Ellis could've been there already.

Which meant Ellis' flask would've been there. And also Drunk Ellis, who, quite honestly, was the best form of human: fearless, confident, and, most importantly, drunk.

Then again it was probably better that she *wasn't* there yet, because while Ariel might've needed slightly (a lot) more palliative comfort than a murky glass of Chateau de WTF, it was probably way more sensible to stay sober. I mean, seeing as how at least two people on the guest list had already tried to kill him.

Like, literally with actual murder. "Allegedly."

Although, honestly, Ariel was a lot more concerned about the speech he was giving later that night. The one he hadn't—small detail—actually written yet. Hence him sitting at a table madly swiping rambles into a notepad app on his phone. Because he was drawing a magnificent blank on his mental canvass right about then.

And if there's anywhere you don't want to be drawing a blank, it's at the podium at an awards event honoring the New York Tri-State area's most influential rabbis of the year. Because one does not simply win a nomination from the Jewish Leadership Union, nor an invitation to its (33rd) annual gala. Especially when one has no idea how one managed to pull that off in the first place.

Yet, there it was, that little placecard right there on the table in front of him.

"Rabbi Ariel Samson" it declared, in swoopy deliberate penmanship.

Yes: "Ariel." Pronounced *AH*-riel, just like how that crab does it in that stupid movie, not *EH*-riel like everyone *else* does in that stupid movie. And contrary to the popular belief of fish-people, it was actually a *masculine* name. The feminine form would properly be "Ariella." Either way, Ariel wasn't really sure what a Hebrew name meaning "lion of G'd" had to do with a red-headed half-fish person with low cultural pride, anyway.

Although to be fair, there *he* was, fitting in as much at this dinner as he did anywhere else, i.e.: not very much. So maybe "Ariels" just naturally tended to be blue-eyed fishes out of water.

Which leads us back to where we began, with our incredulous hero trying to absorb that he was to be a keynote speaker at one of the most prestigious Jewish leadership award ceremonies on the East Coast in the month of September. And, judging from the sideeyes from the servers and the upturned noses of the attendees, Ariel found himself once again in the unenviable yet familiar position of being too black for the Jews, and too Jewish for the blacks.

And all thanks to a little place called Congregation Ahavath Yisroel.

✡ ✡ ✡

Twenty minutes of writer's block later, Ariel was outside, hoping a temporary change of location would alleviate his situation. It was chillier than he'd expected, even for a September evening, but a short stroll around the block couldn't hurt. In fact, it couldn't do anything *but* help.

See, Ariel was powerfully attached to showing up to things on time. *"Better never than late"* had always been his motto. Which is generally not a good idea when showing up to a Jewish event. Or a black one, for that matter. CPT and JPT are *real*.

Case in point: Tonight's event was scheduled for 7:00. Ariel got there at 6:47. And now it was 7:23. Which pretty much means that when only about eight people show up at the actual start time, sooner or later someone is going to try and strike up awkward conversation with you, no matter how busy you may seem. Which is why Ariel was outside now, and a couple of blocks away. It was going to be a long enough night as it was, and he really just needed to be in his own head at the moment. Maybe the solitude would spark some kind of creativity.

And, speaking of "sparks," Ariel was very interested in what his good friend Miriam Jane had to bring to the table. Some good ol' **borei minei b'samim**, if you know what I mean.

Wink, wink. Nudge, nudge.

Hey, he might've been a rabbi but he was still allowed to be a normal 28-year-old once in a while, right? Prone to the lure of doing stupid things and all that? Alright Mx. Judgeypants, calm down. It's a growth process. His grandmother'd said so.

In fact, when Savalava (aka, **Savta** Lahava) had finally headed off to life's next adventure, she was 93 years awesome and still growing herself. As a person, I mean. And also weed too. But I mostly meant as a person. And when it came to the green, she'd unabashedly declare that she "had glaucoma," with eyes so clear you could see the twinkles in them not giving *any* kind of expletive that you saw them.

Ariel missed her. Aside from all the obvious reasons, she was his favorite grandmother. And *a lot* more laidback than his mother's mom, Grandy Laverne.

Grandy Laverne was still more than a little sore about Ariel's father "stealing" her daughter away to Judaism, so Ariel calling her "Savta" Laverne wasn't ain't *never* gonna happen. Grandy Laverne liked her grandkids Christian, with good hair, and speaking English. And one out of three wasn't bad.

But Savalava, though, *she* would've liked Congregation Ahavath Yisroel, Ariel thought.

It was about a fifteen, twenty-minute walk from where he lived, just at the edge of Avon Gardens. Assuming, of course, that you knew where to *find* Avon Gardens.

It was a little-known piece of urban arcana: Avon Gardens, the Jewish neighborhood that never really caught on. A weird isosceles slice that took a chunk out of the more established **yiddishe** enclaves of Kensington, Ditmas Park, and Midwood, to form its own bizarre little Bermuda Triangle—a Ber-*judah* Triangle, if you will—that was the Great Jewish Coexistence Experiment of post-Holocaust 1940's Brooklyn. Sprinkled with just enough Reform, Conservative, and Orthodox Jews that no single denomination was the majority, and with a negligible number of WASPy outsiders to unite against, Avon Gardens was marginally successful well into the 1980's, before it quietly faded into obscurity, producing three adequately populated synagogues: Temple Shaarei Tikvah, Beis Hakeneses Hagodol Hachodosh, and Congregation Ahavath Yisroel.

Before the comedy of errors that had led him there, Ariel had never before stepped foot in CAY, but he'd passed its brown-and-grey façade enough times on his way to ~~Hell~~ work—a tall and narrow "tenement style" synagogue whose modest two-story height was nestled in-between an apartment complex and gated off railway tracks.

It'd been established sometime in the 50's, something fairly obvious from the Saul Bass-esque Hebrew lettering adorning the ark and the translucent salad-bowl chandeliers that hung from the high ceiling, suspended by bronze chains mired in half a century's worth of fuzzy grime. Pale, grey-green carpet—peppered with triangles in assorted colors and sizes—had long since had any of its softness trampled out of it, and was worn through in several places, allowing the dirty, generically beige tiles underneath to peek through. Dark maple pews were bolted to the floor, sporting a lighter shade of brown around their worn, splintering edges, and fitted with cracked leather cushions that hissed when you sat down and creaked when you got up. Above the sanctuary sat a gallery— its seats caked with history masquerading as dust—while at the front of the sanctuary, a burgundy velvet curtain was draped across the ark, regal even in its faded grandeur and frayed edges, gilded with gold fringe and an embroidered Tree of Life that wistfully glinted out at the room. And even though today it was very firmly an Orthodox congregation, the huge stained-glass windows brightening its walls on either side betrayed Congregation Ahavath Yisroel's very firmly Conservative origins, as did the wobbly portable curtain frames dividing the pews into separate men's and women's sections, a stylistically discordant afterthought that clashed with the general decor.

Truth be told, it was a ghost town of a synagogue. The kind of place where most of the membership wasn't filling up the pews, but filling out the walls in neat rows of bronze placards with flickering little orange bulbs next to their names. And it was alone. A sole surviving relic of bygone days of lox and laughter.

After all, Temple Shaarei Tikvah, that once-proud cathedral of Reform Judaism, had long since been sold to a Seventh-Day Adventist church.

Beis Hakeneses Hagodol Hachodosh became a daycare. Then a kickboxing gym after that. Now it was a different daycare.

But Congregation Ahavath Yisroel?

As the last Jewish titan of Avon Gardens descended gently into that good night, it proudly claimed Ariel S. D. Samson as its rabbi for six last glorious months.

Alright, Ariel decided, heading back to the gala. He knew what he wanted to write. He was ready to go back in and knock this baby out of the park.

It was morphin' time.

✡ ✡ ✡

...Actually, on second thought, Ariel realized he should probably stay outside just a tad longer.

Manishtana

He'd been dankrupt for so long that he'd forgotten how skunky Ilan's stashes were. And heading back inside a room full of white people—whilst reeking like a billowing monsoon of herbal courage—would totally defeat the purpose of having avoided the watermelon slices at the reception table in the first place.

✡ ✡ ✡

President Rabbi Angela Abrams, the draft began. Executive Director Rachel Stein, distinguished guests, ladies and gentlemen: Good evening.

It's a great pleasure to be invited to address the Jewish Leadership Union Annual Gala tonight, now celebrating its 33rd year honoring the recipients of the JLU Dreidel Leadership Award. And it's an even greater pleasure for me to be nominated as an honoree.

[Hold for applause]

As we all know, each year, the JLU honors four Tri-State area-based rabbis who have demonstrated extraordinary commitment to progressing social justice, passion for improving interdenominational dialogue, or tireless leadership concerning intercultural community engagement. Four of us here tonight, out of the JLU's ten finalists, will receive very prestigious recognition of our dedication to acknowledging the dignity of our fellow human beings, and the Jewish belief that every person is created **b'tzelem Elokim,** *a reflection of the Divine Image.*

And, once again, I am more than honored to be counted among these finalists...My mother, though, is slightly less than impressed.

[Hold for laughter]

Yes, she...we'll say, "kindly," reminded me that this achievement isn't that big of a deal. Because I've always had a knack for being a member of uncommon cliques. As a Black man with blue eyes, I have membership into an exclusive club which includes such celebrities as Jesse and Vanessa Williams (no relation), the literally clueless Stacey Dash, and James Earl Jones, who has consistently portrayed the most tragic father figures ever.

[Continue through chuckles]

As an English major with a minor in Linguistics, I'm part of a select elite aware that when you are describing something as your strength, the word is pronounced "fort," derived from the French. But when you're talking about a section of music that's intended to be played louder and stronger than the rest, the word is pronounced "fortay," derived from the Italian.

[Continue through "Oooohs"]

And as an African-American Jew, with two African-American Jewish parents—and being a rabbi, no less—I often find myself, well...nowhere.

[Hold for heavy silence]

*One of my earliest memories shortly after receiving my **smicha**, my rabbinical ordination, was the first time I was called up to the Torah for an **aliyah** in a new synagogue. I was to receive the honor of **Shlishi**, the third portion, when*

Here, Ariel stopped, because he began realizing that his hair was...really deeper in than usual. Like, it almost felt like there was a lot less scalp there than normal? Which was weird because, y'know, it was still *acting* like a scalp. Well, not "acting." It's not like it was Johnny Depp in a play pretending that...*Ohh.*

Oh, okay.

Ariel was realizing that he was *high.*

Okay. This is what we're doing now. That's cool. Must've hit him sometime between the lemon-artichoke chicken pockets and the mini spring rolls. And those were *ambrosial*, by the way.

Of course, regardless of whether or not he was in a lituation, Ariel would've *still* been quietly chuckling at the server marching past his table, *determined* not to look in his direction.

Poor guy. His face was still bright red under his floppy blond hair. Was probably still mad—or embarrassed—that Ariel had gotten him vigorously reprimanded by his boss for something that, by the way, was *totally* his own fault. All the dude needed to do was serve hors-d'oeuvres.

But *noo*, he'd decided to go above and beyond the call of duty to snidely inform Ariel that he was seated at the wrong table.

"Excuse me, sir," he'd begun. "But you can't sit here. These tables are reserved for the rabbis being honored tonight."

"I know," came Ariel's answer. "That's why I'm sitting here."

The silver nametag above the server's vest pocket read "Seth." Seth blinked a couple of times, obviously not comprehending Ariel's answer, and repeated himself. This time very slowly.

"Sir...these tables...are for the rabbis."

"Yes..." Ariel had replied, just as delayed. Partly facetiously, and partly because the weed was starting to kick in. "I got that. And I am one of them. Hence the here. And the. Sitting."

"Ah. Ok," Seth nodded, grinning with this *"Riiight. A black rabbi. Gotcha."* kind of vibe, and pranced off.

Not two minutes later, an older white woman—mid-fifties, salt-and-chocolate hair, bound and shackled in costume jewelry, and slathered with overwhelmingly powerful perfume—had swooped down on Ariel, drowning him in apologies. She, as it turns out, was the JLU's event manager. And a certain server had made a major party foul at *her* major party. And so that's how, in the spirit of making amends, Ariel had ended up with a bottle of rancid wine at his personal discretion on his table.

Chateau de WTF, as you recall.

It had been sitting there, undisturbed, for the past forty minutes, yet, surprisingly, it'd managed to be the *least* nauseating of Ariel's dinner companions currently occupying his table for the evening.

Because of all the tables, at all the galas, in all the world, the people seated at his table *of course* had to be State Assemblyman Aryeh Rosenstern, Rabbi Dov Ber Guildencrantz, and their respective entourages.

His anxiety duly anesthetized with an emerald haze, and his sense of irony fully engaged, Ariel could only chuckle and be amazed as he sat across from the two people who'd tried to kill him just three months earlier in a fiery blaze.

Allegedly.

"Wine?" Ariel offered, unable to keep the amused grin from spreading across his face.

His tablemates glared back in return.

Boy Samson was born on July 2, 1988, at 5:01 pm. It had been a fast day. The 17th of **Tammuz**, in fact.

Well, it *would've* been a fast day, if it hadn't happened to coincide with **Shabbat. Parshat Balak**, to be exact. And, unlike millions of Jewish babies for thousands of years—ever since the great patriarch Abraham had literally taken his matters into his own hands in the rolling plains of Mamre—Boy Samson did *not* enter the ancient Jewish covenant of circumcision on the eight day of his life. Or the sixteenth. Or even the twenty-fourth.

It was...complicated. Or complications. Either word would've been applicable.

He'd been preceded by his twin sister Aviva Shira Miriam— formerly, the Infant Known As Girl Samson—born on April 7th of the same year, a very early and very light surprise to her parents (16 weeks early and a hair over 1 lb light, if we're counting), just as the eve of the seventh day of Passover was drawing near. And 86 days, 11 hours, 42 minutes, and 3 seconds later, the Samsons unofficially held the Guinness World Record for twins born farthest apart (until Maria Jones-Elliot of Kilkenny, Ireland stole it on August 27, 2012, by a measly 14 hrs, 3 minutes, and 3 seconds).

Aviva'd been born on a Thursday and got her name the very next day.

Manishtana

But Boy Samson was a different story. Our little guy, while not as impatient as his older sister, was nonetheless four weeks premature himself, and so—at a piddly 5 lbs 1 oz—according to the professional opinions of both the doctor and the rabbi, it was only today, a full twenty-six days later, that Boy Samson's circumcision and incidental naming was finally happening.

And, as she looked down at her sleeping baby, watching his chestnut-brown squirm of limbs—a shade slightly darker than hers, but just about a match with her husband's—watching the orange-and-blue pacifier bobbing on Boy Samson's lips like a buoy in choppy waters, watching, as he fitfully snored, the gentle rise and fall of his soft, tiny skull—touched with just a dollop of delicate, tightly-curled black hair, like a parsley garnish on a filet mignon—the thought crossed Shoshana Samson's mind that, *finally*, she could begin to breathe easy.

Out in the dining room, the table was abounding with platters of multicolored bagels, dunes of assorted cream cheeses, and plentiful amounts of smoked salmon, whitefish, and sable. Shoshana's mother-in-law, Lahava, had sprung for the sable. And also the vast selection of cookies, danishes, and rugelach available. Shoshana's mother-in-law seemed to have an eye for junk food, she did. And, Shoshana suddenly noted, sunglasses. Even indoors. Almost as if...

Nah, Shoshana batted the thought away. If Lahava was forty years younger and in college, then maybe. But the woman was 67 years old. C'mon now.

Shoshana chided herself for her ridiculous hunch.

Bookending the feast table at one end was the ever-present wicker handbasket teeming with the ubiquitous satin royal-blue **yarmulkes**—the kind that perched atop their wearer's head with just as much reluctance at having to be worn as the people having to wear them—and at the other end, a tray of waxy confectionary concoctions masquerading as tiles of white chocolate—likely baked by underpaid Hispanic workers commanded in English that was louder and slower than it needed to be, and endured it with forced smiles and gritted teeth. *"Mazal Tov"* was scrawled in shaky handwriting and dark-chocolate across the surface of each milky-white block in Hebrew script—likely by a secular Israeli or Soviet expatriate magnanimously given the opportunity to work in the front of a good **heimishe** bakery.

ARIEL SAMSON: FREELANCE RABBI

A small table of drinks was set in the opposite corner of the room, complete with coffee maker, pitchers of orange juice and lemoned ice-water, staggered columns of upside-down plastic and thermal cups, and a decent array of booze, ranging from Smirnoff to Jack Daniels to Crown Royale to Johnny Walker to Glenlivet and Glengoyne.

But, obviously, no Monkey Shoulder.

Mostly because the Kininvie distillery wouldn't exist for another two years. But even if it had, Monkey Shoulder still wouldn't have been there. The fruit platter nearby likewise had no watermelon slices, and there was nary an orange or grape soda to be found.

No, all of those and more lurked in the Samsons' fridge. They'd come out later, when it was just friends and family. Where they could be partaken—or not—without the knowing looks and smirking eyes.

Without the *"Wow, you really are black!"* or the *"You don't like this? I guess I'm blacker than you are!"* comments, from people letting their tone-deafness write checks their social capital couldn't cover.

No, once the Samsons' fairer-skinned **shul** guests and other cursory acquaintances had left, the *real* food would come out, and the cookout would begin. The fried chicken and (**parve**) waffles. Potato salad. Collard greens. Cornbread *and* biscuits. Sweet potato pie. Baked beans. Pound cake. Red snapper. Gefilte fish, flavored with bits of real jalapeno, habanero, and chives, and topped with tangy, cilantro-flecked Moroccan carrots.

Those homemade brownies her mother-in-law had brought.

But most of those guests—the real ones—probably wouldn't be showing up for another hour and a half, at least.

Colored People Time was *real.*

Nonetheless, guests had already begun to arrive, and before long the house would be full.

As for the **mohel**, Mikey—sorry—*Rabbi Aroeste*, had arrived promptly at 9:00 and set up shop in the living room. By the time Shoshana'd poked her head out of the bedroom to greet him, he'd already laid out his medical tools, arranged for the easiest access by order of need. Currently, he was schmoozing with Avigdor, her lanky and bespectacled husband, reminiscing about their younger hijinks. Mikey was drinking water. Avigdor was definitely not.

Manishtana

Shoshana smiled to herself at the sporadic bursts of laughter that erupted from the other side of the bedroom door. Good. Her husband didn't hang out with his friends nearly enough, anyway. He'd gone to high school with Mikey, and in the early 70's **Sephardic** Greek Jews were only slightly more tolerated than black ones, so eventually Orthodox Black Avigdor and Secular Greek Mikey came to hit it off. Some time during college they'd lost touch, and in that time, the *very* secular Greek kid Avigdor had gone to high school with, had gone and become the *very* religious rabbi and *mohel* that he was today.

A gurgle drew Shoshana's attention and she looked down to see Boy Samson gazing up at her with impossibly cerulean-blue eyes, wearing that half-smirk underneath his pacifier that everyone always swears is gas, but—even after four kids—Shoshana refused to believe.

It seemed to her, as she tickled her baby under his chin, that there was a certain kind of synchronicity that today, the twins' original due date, was the day of Boy Samson's **brit**.

Bris, she corrected herself, mentally rolling her eyes. She'd already been through this argument with her husband over their first son, Jake, seven years earlier.

"Our son is having a *brit*, not a *bris*," Avigdor had insisted. "It will be performed by a *mohel*, not a *moil* or a *mole*. He is having a **chalaka**, not an **upshernish**. He will wear a **kippah**, not a *yarmulke*. He will go to services at **knesset**, not *shul*. And when my heart explodes from happiness because Al McKay is back on guitar for Earth, Wind and Fire, he will light a **ner neshama** for my **nachala**, not a **yizkor candle** for my **yahrtzeit**!"

Well, whatever. *She* still called it a *bris*. Not her fault that she was converted by Team **Ashkenaz**.

Avigdor, though—even though he wasn't quite fluent beyond liturgical use—had grown up with the Sephardi-accented Israeli-style Hebrew that was all the rage for those Jews on the browner edge of the spectrum, invested in shaking off the claws of the Ashkenormative hegemony. Although recently, he'd begun experimenting with **Temani** pronunciation. After all, it was arguably the most phonemically accurate version of Hebrew. And so Avigdor dove in, wholly embracing the full gamut of **waws** instead of **vavs**, **tavs** and **thavs**, **dalets** and **thalets**, and **gimmels** and **jimmels**.

Shoshana remembered when she'd first heard him try it out for Shabbat **kiddush**, blessing their table with *"wai-chulu"* instead of the familiar *"vai-chulu."* She figured it was something she could get used to. A middle ground halfway between her Ashkenazit—Ashkenazis—and Avigdor's Sepharadit. But by the time he got to the wine, blessing it *"borei pri hajafen,"* Shoshana could just *barely* swallow her guffaws, tactfully leaving the dinner table under the guise of "checking-in on the twins," sparing her husband's feelings, and denying chortle-fuel to their giggle-prone five and seven-year-olds.

Although, for all of Avigdor and Shoshana's efforts, in the end Jake, their oldest boy, would end up using Sepharadit, their oldest daughter Liora would end up using Ashkenazis, and Boy Samson would end up blending all of the worlds—using Sepharadit conversationally, Temani liturgically, and Ashkenazis ironically.

As for Aviva—Boy Samson's twin—after a particularly harrowing high-school experience and a traumatic relationship in college, she'd end up leaving the faith entirely.

Going "**off the derech.**" Or "**OTD,**" as it was called for short.

And that is a tale for another time. Mostly because I don't have all the details on that one.

✡ ✡ ✡

Besides the *mohel*, the Samson household was packed with the fifteen or so men who made up almost double a **minyan**.

Like Eugene and Murray Kagan, two Holocaust survivors of the priestly clan that everyone called "the **kohen** brothers." After Avigdor and Shoshana's second child Liora was born a daughter—a complete shock to everyone so convinced she would be a boy—Murray, the younger of the two, came up to Avigdor on the Shabbat of her naming and lifted his crooked pinky finger, commenting with a grin, "Missed it by this much."

Avigdor's co-worker Sheldon was there, a science teacher and self-professed "retired Jew," nonetheless dutifully donning one of the blue satin *yarmulkes* on his glistening bald head.

And, of course, there was their family rabbi, Rabbi I.I. "Cap'n" Herschel, a jovially Brobdingnagian figure with the gravity of a clergyman, and the presence of a vaudeville magician.

Cap'n had a history with the Samsons that was almost forty years and three generations long.

As a fresh young rabbi he'd overseen the conversion of Avigdor's father, Shmuel. As a seasoned middle-aged rabbi he'd overseen Shoshana's conversion, and later officiated at her and Avigdor's wedding as their **mesader kiddushin**. Just a year after that, he was given the honor of being the **sandek** to their firstborn son, Jake, and now, seven years later, here Cap'n was again, a freshly—if you'll excuse the expression—"christened" senior citizen, still just as religiously, spiritually, and figuratively big-hearted as ever.

Unfortunately, he was also physically big-hearted, and in four years he would suffer a fatal heart attack at the untimely age of 69, making today's *bris*—at which he happily chatted with Avigdor's father, and Raphael, Avigdor's muscled tank of a little brother—the last Samson family celebration Rabbi Herschel would ever attend.

Reverend Jimmy had made the trek out to Brooklyn too, even though he didn't count towards the traditional ritual quorum of ten Jewish men. He, Avigdor and Shoshana were old college friends, from back when Shoshana Adele Samson was still Lillian Adele Williams, Reverend Jimmy was Mack Daddy Jimmy, and Avigdor was "that black Jewish kid". Even as the expressions of their faiths had matured and diverged over the years, their friendship had only grown stronger for it. After all, what dominoes and dark liquor hath joined together, let no man tear asunder.

The rest of the guests—at least the men, anyway—were generically amiable acquaintances from *shul*. The people they would greet with a friendly enough "**Shabbat shalom**" (Avigdor) or "**Gut Shabbos**" (Shoshana), and have detailed conversations about nothing with, while slurping down too-sweet pickled herring and shots of Red Label at **kiddish** after services. They weren't meaningful enough social connections to warrant the effort of learning names, and so Shoshana and Avigdor developed between themselves a shorthand identification for their fellow congregants. A parade of secret nicknames worthy of Batman's rogues gallery:

There was the thin-lipped, watery-eyed Kermit.

The garishly dressed Mad Hatter.

Scarface, with a six-inch gash across his left cheek.

Drac, whose widow's peak—and actual face—bore more than a passing resemblance to Bela Lugosi.

The disheveled Hobo.

The squinty-eyed Popeye.

The self-explanatory Boaz the Sephardi Guy.

And Pencilneck, who, quite honestly, looked exactly like if a pencil had come to life.

As for the women in attendance, they were largely a collection of plus-ones. Kermit's wife. The Mad Hatter's wife. Hobo's mother. Popeye's wife. Boaz the Sephardi Guy's wife. Boaz the Sephardi Guy's daughter. Like the men, they were genial enough. But still not people Shoshana could relate to, or vice versa. They didn't know how to, really. And they didn't *know* that they didn't know how to.

Shoshana remembered when—in a moment of new mother, first-time, pre-*bris* jitters before Jake's debut—she'd related her fear of the *mohel* developing a paroxysm seconds before big blade met tiny flesh and lopping her son's whole Tootsie Roll off, or that somehow her baby would end up contracting an infection and his penis would end up turning gangrenous and falling off, or...actually, just a disturbing amount of scenarios ending with her son no longer having a penis. Like, a *lot*.

In response, the women had all cavalierly cluck-clucked and tut-tutted her concerns away.

"*Everyone* is afraid the *mohel* might slip. Or that something *tragic* will happen. But it always turns out okay. He'll be *fine*."

Words spoken, Shoshana felt, with all the obliviousness and privilege in the world and utterly no grasp on the difference between their fear and her fear in the slightest.

They had been afraid before their *brises* that it might go wrong by *accident*. *She* had been afraid before Jake's *bris* that it would go wrong *on purpose*.

And even if they *had* been capable of understanding that there was a very real qualitative difference between her anxiety and theirs, how exactly would she have gone about explaining it? That she was being asked to expose the most vulnerable part of herself— her helpless newborn child—and in turn expose *his* most vulnerable part of himself, to someone who might not see him as "really Jewish." Or as a creature "cursed" with blackness. As a **schvartze**.

That she couldn't find solace in a commonality of appearance between baby and *mohel* to keep her child safe. Only a hope that the commonality of religion and covenant—one that too often failed within the confines of Jewish spaces—would prevail against any insidious intentions, and rise to the occasion in the face of obligations to a Higher Authority.

Of course, even if she could find the words, they would likely be dismissed because they were too hard to hear. Would force too many people to look at their husbands and brothers and fathers and mothers and sisters and friends and children—and themselves—in ways far too uncomfortable for it to be worth it for them.

So instead, they'd irritatedly ask her why she "thought about race all the time."

Well, because, *duh,* she had to.

Because when she didn't, someone at a *kiddish* handed their dirty plates to her because she was the help, obviously. Because she and her husband got stared down when they walked into Judaica shops. Because when entering a new synagogue people asked her what country she was from just because she wasn't white, and assumed she was Ethiopian solely because she was simply black. Because someone *literally* just called her "exotic" as a compliment.

White Jews could forget that they're white, but she wasn't ever allowed to forget that she wasn't.

But of course, they wouldn't be able to hear that, so they'd ask her why she was "playing the race card" as if they weren't holding the whole deck, the hourglass, the buzzer, all four railroads, both utilities, and hadn't *just* put hotels on both Boardwalk *and* Park Place.

And a finer mixed metaphor you will never find.

Long story short, Shoshana didn't really know the women there, and they definitely didn't know her. But polite, generally positive chitchat was had by all as they cooed over Boy Samson, nestled in the folds of his quilted white comforter, fast asleep again while his mother mingled among the guests.

The only woman Shoshana actually *did* know was Ingrid, another holdover from her "Lillian" college days. They had been part of a freshman trio before Shoshana/Lillian had met the mysterious junior-year upperclassmen Avigdor and Mack Daddy Jimmy.

Her, Ingrid, and Nadia.

Shoshana hadn't heard from Nadia since the first Samson *bris,* an event which Nadia had been decidedly unhappy about.

"You should not be allowed to be a mother," Nadia had bluntly declared over mimosas, her brow and lips in identically harsh horizontal lines.

"Wow, what?"

"Your first duty as a mother is to protect your child, but the first thing you're gonna do is amputate part of his penis? And you're inviting me *witness* this torture and mutilation?"

"Um, one, no," Shoshana ticked off on her fingers, as waiters zipped by in the busy outdoor cafe. "I'm not inviting you. I'm *informing* you."

Inviting people to a *bris* was a no-no, Shoshana had learned. Because if they declined, it was considered "as if they were declining the company of Elijah the Prophet, who, traditionally, is present at every Jewish circumcision ceremony." So you *never* invited someone to a *bris*. Which, personally, I think is an adorable sentiment. Useless, but adorable. Because between the special chair assigned at *brises* and the special cup designated at **seders**, exactly how much do you think someone who's spent the past millennium and a half perpetually sloshed is going to notice that you didn't show up?

But still, it's adorable.

"Two," Shoshana continued. "It's not 'torture and mutilation.' Three, it's a religious commandment that—"

"Yeah, call me crazy," Nadia interrupted. "But I don't take commands to perform elective surgery on my own offspring from invisible people I've never met. You're not doing this *for* your son. You're doing this *to* your son. Without his consent."

"Well, seeing as how this is an event that happens when a baby is eight days old, and how he'll be incapable of making the decision himself, I'll be making it for him."

"What," Nadia snorted. "You're afraid he won't abide by your religion unless you force it on him against his will? *That's* how this works?"

"Y'know what?" Shoshana acquiesced. "You're right. I *should* leave it up to him. I mean, he knows *literally* nothing about the world, so making decisions about an entire theological system of belief with which to guide his entire life is *totally* something to be put on the shoulders of a child to figure out. Good call. I'm glad we had this talk."

Manishtana

"You're basically raping him with a knife! You are *really* letting your religious views get in the way of common sense."

"Also, I was planning on deciding what to feed him and where he should sleep, but I should probably wait to let *him* make those decisions too," Shoshana continued, taking a looooong sip of her drink.

"Look, if you wanna go ahead and subject your own flesh and blood to this barbaric anti-Semitic ritual, then by all means, go ahead."

"Anti-Sem—what are you even *talking* about, Nadia?"

"Your kid is *Jewish*, right? He's having his penis mutilated because he's *Jewish*, right? That's anti-Semitism in *my* book, thank you very much."

Shoshana's mouth just opened and closed, literally speechless. Arguing her friend's logic was like trying to throw away cigarette smoke by grabbing it. It was so diaphanous that it was impossible to make rational contact with, and ingesting it would be undeniably toxic to her health.

In the end, Nadia had unsurprisingly refused to attend.

But Ingrid—super Irish-Catholic Ingrid—had come with bells and whistles on to that first *bris*, with a beaming smile only dwarfed by the size of the one she was wearing at this one, the second Samson *bris*.

Shoshana hadn't had a chance to say more than a quick hi yet, but she wasn't too upset about that. They'd do the much more substantial catching up later. Ingrid's shutdown of her "intellectually" racist ex-boyfriend in sophomore year had earned her a cookout invitation over a decade ago.

And last but not least in attendance, were Lahava and Zehava, Shoshana's mother-in-law and sister-in-law, respectfully and respectively. (Aliza, Avigdor's other sister, was running late, as per usual. Because cats don't feed themselves.)

Zehava was sitting on the couch, ambitiously taking the reins on keeping her nephew and niece Jake and Liora out of everyone's hair—but mostly meaning Shoshana's hair—while simultaneously rocking baby Aviva back and forth in her bassinet, keeping her entranced in her current slumber, *all* of which Shoshana was ever-grateful for.

Zehava was just a pretty cool sister-in-law in general. She'd actually been the one to talk Shoshana down from her irrational fears around Jake's *bris*.

"Shoshana. Like, I get it. I do. But if a *mohel* doesn't think a kid is really Jewish, then they'd just, y'know, *not* do the *brit*. No *mohels* are running around signing up to *brits* for the express purpose of castrating babies."

"But aren't they though?"

"No. No they aren't."

"But...*aren't* they though?"

"No. They aren't. Or—*OR*—they aren't."

"You promise?"

"I promise you that this is not a thing that has ever happened, ever, in the history of things."

"Okay...okay...Thanks. Really. This really helped."

"No problem. Always a pleasure to feed you Hydrox while you're curled up in the fetal position on the floor."

So yeah, Shoshana was glad to have Zehava on her team.

Meanwhile, Lahava was making polite but guarded small talk with the older ladies from *shul*, dressed—as always—elegantly, in a two-piece evening ensemble with long satin gloves, heels, a light touch of jewelry, sunglasses, and a **sheitel** nearly indistinguishable from her own silvery mane.

A woman with a wicked yet reserved sense of humor, Shoshana's mother-in-law somehow managed to remind her of a *Masterpiece Theater*-esque Victorian-era dowager. The kind that perpetually hovered porcelain teacups and saucers in front of their mouths, treating them like parapet walls to hide sardonic grins behind and catapult casual zingers over as they blithely sipped the tea within.

And Shoshana had definitely been on the receiving end of some of those zingers more than once.

See, they'd had a rocky start, Lahava and Shoshana.

Part of it, Shoshana supposed, was due to her being the woman who was stealing Lahava's firstborn baby away. Part of it was likely due to the both of them being stubborn Jewish black women in each other's orbits. And the last part, Shoshana *knew*, was because Lahava—not having a particularly high opinion of converts—wasn't exactly thrilled that her son was marrying one.

Of course, Shoshana didn't have to look very far past Avigdor's father to deconstruct the thought process behind that one.

Shmuel Samson was the worst kind of convert.

To any religion.

The universal kind of bad convert that doesn't adopt a new way of life for the inner peace and completion it brings, but because they think conversion will "change" them into a different person.

The kind of convert that's just running from themselves because they don't like what looks back at them in the mirror. The kind that basks in their own imagined moral superiority at having "given up everything" to pursue some great truth.

Except they didn't really give up anything. Just put it in a different mold, applied different rules to justify the same behaviors. Warped that "great truth" to fit the whims of, say, an alcoholic wife beater, for instance.

Her mother-in-law had never said this to her, but Shoshana could tell. It was obvious from how her father-in-law interacted with his grandchildren.

Lahava was lovingly and intimately dubbed "Savalava" by Shoshana's kids.

Shmuel was just "**Saba.**"

"Grandfather".

The form and function of being the man who fathered their father. Nothing less, nothing more.

But despite that initial unease and resentment, Lahava was never malicious. She valued family life and unity above all else, and was quietly respectful of Shoshana, if only by dint of Shoshana being Avigdor's choice of woman to build his life and family with

A stance which Shoshana likewise respected. Admired even.

Because Lahava was an admirably strong woman. She had to be.

Lahava had grown up in the 20's and 30's, a time when African-American Jews were a curious oddity, yet authentic ones were simultaneously nearly nowhere to be found.

The Commandment Keepers, Zionist Moorish Temple, Beth B'nai Abraham, et al, all of them—and more—were Hebrew Israelite establishments, engaged in all the devout trappings of Judaism, but little else. Claiming a chosenness in Blackness that overrode the need to abide by the millennia-old standards of the normative establishment they saw as "white." Cutting from whole cloth an identity narrative that granted access to Jewish observance and broke away from slavery-imposed Christianity, yet still fell short of Judaism nonetheless.

Seeing how far they reached, yet their refusal to extend any further, *beyond* an ideology of self-identification and pride, had deeply frustrated Lahava in her younger years. She had longed for a space where she could worship and see faces that looked like hers. But she was not one to sacrifice the eternality of religious authenticity for the temporality of racial solidarity.

However, the problem was that Lahava grew up in the South, where the synagogues were all in the white part of town in white neighborhoods, and so she hardly ever went to services as a child. Because for all the crosses they found burning on their lawns, her white fellow southern Jews could be just as segregationist as their Christian counterparts.

She remembered the shopkeeper at the old general store in her neighborhood. Mrs. Klein. A middle-aged lady who was always kindly enough.

Until the day Lahava and her parents showed up to Mrs. Klein's *shul*.

The kindly shopkeeper's demeanor abruptly changed towards Lahava's family that next week, becoming increasingly hostile and unhelpful, until one day the Emmanuels were told that they weren't allowed to shop at their neighborhood store anymore.

Mrs. Klein's patronizing kindness, it was clear to her fellow congregants, had brought *schvartzes* into their *shul*.

Not long after that, Lahava's family made the decision to move up North, eventually coming to settle in the Holy Land, Brooklyn.

It was perhaps incidents like these that had molded Lahava into something that her daughter-in-law recognized as the shape of an anti-Semite. Not an intentional one, but one of circumstance.

Sure, like any real Jew, Lahava hated Jews. In that *"OMG, I can't stand Trini men"* way that Trini women "hate" Trini men.

But then it went a little extra sometimes.

"Bloodsucking Jews." "Twisted back ugly little things." "Huge schnozzles."

It popped up whenever she saw a classically phenotypical Nazi-propaganda resembling Jew. Or a white Jew who'd wronged her in any of the stereotypically Shylock ways, like being a slumlord, or supermarkets price-gouging around the holidays.

Her take on the Crown Heights riots, when they'd happened, was particularly...interesting.

"Some drunk Jew on **Simchat Torah** ran over and killed a black kid, then fled the scene, and escaped to Israel to avoid trial."

Which, sorry Savalava, was not only wildly inaccurate—Yosef Lifsh was *not* drunk, did *not* flee the scene, actually tried to lift his car *off* of Gavin and Angela Cato, and moved to Israel only *after* his life continued to be threatened subsequent to a grand jury of 10 black, 8 white, and 5 Hispanic jurors deciding *not* to indict him—but was also *illogical* in some places—Gavin Cato was killed on August 19th, in the middle of the summer, when it is impossible for the fall holiday of Simchat Torah to ever occur.

And when anyone tried to point those facts out, Lahava would just wave her hand away in that dismissive way that old black folks of a certain age do—when their lived-in experience is too visceral to let them reconcile that their narrative doesn't exactly line up with the facts—muttering, "Well, we were getting all kinds of stories in the news those days," as if the people she was talking to—namely her son Avigdor—hadn't also lived through those days.

But was she *really* being anti-Semitic though?

She wasn't smearing "JEWS." Just "those" Jews. The Jews that weren't "her" Jewish. Which wasn't any kind of Jewish that *anyone* acknowledged.

There were no stereotypes about African-American Jews.

No cartoons or propaganda or slurs or slang.

She'd never endured any "Where are your horns?" stories in college, but had plenty of "Where is your tail?" encounters.

Her Jewish was invisible. Not even a blip in the social consciousness, denied even the "privilege" of being considered significant enough to make a concerted effort to mock.

And even *that*, she resented in a twisted sort of way.

But, thoroughly contradictory being that she was, her antipathy towards her more privileged co-religionists was surpassed only by her utter dismissal of denominational hierarchy.

"Are they still doing Torah and *mitzvot*?" Lahava would reply, countering attempts to draw her into debates of Orthodox v Reform v Conservative. "Then what's the problem? Do *you* do everything perfectly?"

She was a complicated woman. And in time Lahava and Shoshana would build a strong unshakeable relationship of their own. Particularly thirteen years later, when Lahava would finally divorce her husband of 40 years.

"'Divorce' is such an ugly term," she once corrected Shoshana, ever the elegant if unconventional matriarch. "Why don't we just say I fired my marriage?"

✡ ✡ ✡

"Mazal tov!"

Avigdor's eyes flew open. He hadn't even realized that he'd instinctively shut them when he saw Mikey coming in for the cut.

"Keshem shenichnas laBrit, ken yikanes l'Torah, l'chupah, ulema'asim tovim!" came the joyous refrain in unison from the men.

"Just as he has entered into the Covenant," Rabbi Aroeste translated into English—for everyone's benefit—as Avigdor's fresh Jew-baby son wailed in the quivering staccato tone unique to newborns. "So may he enter into Torah, into marriage, and into good deeds!"

The attendants cheered with renewed rounds of *"Mazal tov!"*

Despite the levity, there was something weighty about the whole affair. Especially to Avigdor.

Sure, everyone was happy to see a *brit*, to see that tangible proof that that tiny miniscule oppressed minority—the one that had outlived and outlasted the Romans and the Persians and the Greeks and the Babylonians—was still alive and viable and flourishing.

But no one else could *really* comprehend the gravity of what *Avigdor* was feeling as he welcomed another Jew into the fold.

One of his.

Not just "his" as in "another Jew," but one of *his*.

From the kind of Jews that had survived the Amhara in place of the Cossacks, the princes of Anjuvannam instead of the popes of the Catholic Church, endured Mao Zedong, not Khrushchev.

To see, even for the briefest moment—against all the disbelief and the skepticism and the questioning—to see that luminous bronze line blazing bright, that anchored chain stretching back from his son to him, to his mother, to her father, to his father, and his father before *him*, to those countless fathers before *that*, to Jacob, to Isaac, all the way back to Abraham. That unbreakable cord piercing through time, browner than anyone thought it had a right to be, all obeying that same primordial Jewish commandment.

It was like watching Arthur Ashe win the singles title at Wimbledon and the U.S. Open. Or seeing Sidney Poitier win the Academy Award for Best Actor for *Lilies of the Field*.

One of *his* people was now a Jew. That same people that some of the most religiously scholarly minds of Jewish history had dismissed as being "greater than a monkey but less than a man." Never anticipating that an Avigdor or a Shoshana or a Lahava would ever exist.

Let alone that they existed even *then*, in those medieval times.

Avigdor tried to remain calm as he acknowledged that he had been gifted not once, but *twice*, with the duty of shaping and growing another one of his own to stand tall and proud. Yet another male upon which to impress the grandeur of its Jewish soul and pride in the swarthy chassis that encased it.

Daughters he wasn't worried about. But sons...

And now came the important part: the naming.

No pressure. No biggie.

It wasn't like the name that parents chose for their child was supposed to be prophetic or anything. It wasn't like you were designating your child's destiny, speaking a future for them into existence that would follow them for the rest of their lives.

Nope. Who told you that?

Names were important to the Samsons. And, as it turned out, to the Williamses as well.

As such, the names of Avigdor and Shoshana's first two children had been concessions between their two families of origin.

Avigdor's mother's family didn't have English first names. Or English names at all. They hadn't for centuries. They'd refused to conform to the assimilatory Jewish convention of having a vernacular name for the public and a Hebrew name in private. Your name was who you were, and who you were was a Jew, both at home and out in the world. So you only got one name, and that name was a Hebrew one.

Period.

With *maybe* some leeway for classic Aramaic names like "Akiva" or "Zutra."

But Laverne, Shoshana's mother, had insisted on her grandchildren having a "good English name." Although what she really meant was "a good Christian name."

So a compromise was struck between the Holy African Roman Kingdom of Williams and the Judaistic Republic of Samson.

Jake's legal name was "Jacob Aaron Benjamin." But his "real" name was Yaakov Aharon Binyamin. Although, as hard as his parents tried calling him "Yaakov," "Yaakovi," and even "Kovi," "Jake" was the name that took. And yes, he had two middle names. Because Avigdor and Shoshana were still from Southern black families. Two middle names was simply inviolable tradition.

Claim it.

When it came to Avigdor and Shoshana's second child (and first daughter), Lahava had well and long expressed her displeasure at having a grandchild with an English name.

Meanwhile, Laverne had incessantly moaned about Shoshana, formerly Lillian, having chosen a new Hebrew name that had broken the chain of "L" names stretching back to Big Ma Lucille.

And so Avigdor and Shoshana named their daughter Liora.

Liora Sara Meira.

But when it came to the twins, Avigdor and Shoshana had finally discharged their familial obligations, and they were free to name their children with the formula they had agreed upon between themselves: a first name of sentimental significance, and middle names reflective of the Jewish events of the week or the weekly Torah portion.

Their girl twin had been born during **Pesach**, in the spring (*aviv*). She'd been born on the festival's seventh day, when the Song (*shir*) of Miriam recorded in Exodus 15:1-18 was read during services.

And so: Aviva Shira Miriam.

As for Boy Samson, Avigdor's favorite uncle, Ariel, had passed away seven months into Shoshana's pregnancy. And he had always been very religious and highly scholarly, quite fitting for bearing a name which was the poetic sobriquet for the Jewish Temple.

Boy Samson was born on the Sabbath, a great excuse for the rarely used eponymous name of "Shabbtai."

And lastly, he represented the freedom Avigdor and Shoshana finally had, to build their family the way *they* wanted. Free from the prejudices of birth and the antagonisms against other religions. A way that represented their truths, not imposed shackles of familial obligation.

So "Dror." "Freedom."

Also, they had black twins.

Y'all know how we name black twins, with that one name that calls the both of them. "JadaandJayden.""MiaandMya."

And "AviandAri" worked just fine.

While they never presented Boy Samson's impending name in full—not even verbalizing it to each other—Avigdor and Shoshana presented the tentative options to their respective mothers.

Laverne decided she would call him "Areal," in her terribly accented and half-hearted attempt at Hebrew. He'd be "Shabbi" to his Savalava, who looked forward to Shabbat every week in gratitude for the spiritual solace it provided.

And as for his parents? They'd call him "Dror."

Their little patch of freedom.

"Our G'd and G'd of our fathers," Mikey began, placing a wine-soaked gauze-pad on Boy Samson's tiny lips to be greedily gummed up. "Preserve this child for his father and mother, and his name in Israel shall be called Ariel Shabbtai Dror, the son of Avigdor Daniel and Shoshana Adele. May the father rejoice in his offspring, and his mother be glad with the fruit of her womb, as it is written: 'May your father rejoice, and mother who bore you be glad.'"

"Amen," all intoned in unison.

"May this little infant, Ariel Shabbtai Dror, become great," Mikey continued, contorting his hands to form the shapes of the Hebrew letters of **shin**, **dalet**, and **yud**, spelling one of G'd's sacred Names. "Just as he has entered the Covenant, so may he enter into Torah, into marriage, and into good deeds."

Avigdor beamed as his brother Raphael carried Baby Ariel to their sister Aliza, who handed him to Shoshana, with Jake and Liora jumping at her arms to see their newly consecrated little brother, while Aviva snoozed the event away in Zehava's care.

And as Avigdor and Shoshana locked shining eyes with one another, parents now four times over, they basked in how different those important relationships and names would be to their latest addition. How they each carried their own unique weight. The meaningfulness of his mother and each of his grandmothers having their own exclusive name for him. "Ariel." "Shabbi." "Dror."

And then the same thought flashed through their minds about their little boy.

"Holy shit," Avigdor read Shoshana's lips from across the room as she blurted out the words. "Did we just name our child 'A real shabby drawer'?"

Good job, guys. Good job.

This slow clap is for you.

[Claps slowly]

By the time AviandAri had come along, their parents had finally figured out how to balance between a quality Jewish education, and torment. And how to balance between strong black identity building, and torment.

How to balance their kids' existence in the Jewish and non-Jewish worlds. How to teach them the importance of being "in, but not of" in the larger society, and the value of having a faith-based pride-based homebase.

It was along similar lines that they made sure to raise their kids on a healthy diet of Maimonides and Malcolm X, Duke Ellington and Debbie Friedman, *The Ten Commandments* and *Glory*.

The twins got sent to Jewish schools for daycare and junior high, but regular public schools for elementary and high school, followed by—at least for Ariel—a summer trip to Israel on Birthright. And it was there—as luck and story structure would have it—that Ariel would come to randomly encounter one Kalman Meltzer, grandson to one Rabbi Samuel Gellerman, founder of one Congregation Ahavath Yisroel.

See, after Ariel's Birthright trip, he'd decided he would extend his ticket by a few more days.

Voluntarily.

And then by a few more days after *that*. Involuntarily.

ARIEL SAMSON: FREELANCE RABBI

Because sometimes getting to Ben Gurion Airport from Be'er Sheva is harder than it should be, and you end up in Lod. And sometimes by the time you finally get to Ben Gurion, the lady at the information desk grills you in Russian-accented Hebrew about why you're so late, instead of just giving you the pertinent information.

Which means that sometimes El Al won't let you board even though the plane hasn't taken off yet *and won't for another forty minutes*, and so you sit in the terminal from 11:13 in the afternoon to 9:24 at night out of spite, resentfully gorging on kosher Pizza Hut.

Anyway, since Ariel'd had a couple of days to kill before the next flight out, he decided to explore Tel Aviv's nightlife, subsequently discovering that the definition of "nightlife" in Tel Aviv is apparently streets flooded with cigarette-smoking nine to fourteen-year olds hopped up on Bamba. And drugs, also.

It was also a lot less diverse than he'd been expecting.

Given how often Israelis told him that *"In Israel I see Jews who look like you all the time!"* Ariel had been expecting to encounter a kaleidoscopic sea of Jews in all hues, not the three, maybe four Ethiopians he ran into. It vaguely crossed his mind that there was this self-propagating cycle of black American Jews who come to Israel to experience the diversity their Israeli friends tell them about, and end up *being* the diversity that Israelis tell their friends about.

At any rate, as Ariel wandered the sweltering streets of Tel Aviv—accompanied by it's ambient, ever-present soundtrack of weird techno music that seemed to come from everywhere and nowhere at once—who should he run into but Ilan.

Ilan Nitzan was ISRAELI. You know the type.

From afar, with their dark hair, olive skin, and rugged Mediterranean looks, they seem like Middle Eastern elves.

Exotic throats constantly purring like idling Ferraris, bodies promising a thinly veiled threat of lapsed Krav Maga training, and that ever so faint scent of hummus and sand suffusing the air around them. Of course, it's only when you get closer that you realize their musk is actually just hashish and the broken hearts and hymens of gap year Birthright Israel tourist girls.

Ilan had wandered into Ariel's life—or, more accurately, his tent in the Bedouin camp—on Day Seven of his Birthright trip, a breezy whirlwind of mellow stoner, quick to swallow you up in a warm hug and a heartfelt pound, while discreetly palming you a "little something" with the effortless ease of a corrupt Super PAC.

Ilan apparently lived in Tel Aviv, so when he and Ariel ran into each other on the latter's impromptu night out on the town, Ilan strongarmed Ariel into going to some party with him that he'd heard someone was having somewhere that started sometime.

They never actually made it there.

Ilan wanted to stop at a friend's really quickly to see if they wanted to come too, and somehow that turned into a group of teens and twenty-somethings hanging out on a balcony watching Ilan fashion a bong out of an apple, and then all of them availing themselves of said feat of inventive engineering, smoking and drinking against the velvety backdrop of the night sky.

And that's when Ariel met Kalman, glowing in the golden pool of a floodlight like he was trying to offer Ariel a side quest to Zanarkand. This gangly, sandy-haired, milky-white kid in standard hipster-issue thick-framed glasses, skinny jeans, T-shirt and sandals, wearing a blue suede *kippah*, and who had *definitely* been out on the balcony partaking for a *while* before Ariel and Ilan showed up.

Kalman's eyes sort of widened when he saw Ariel, and Ariel could immediately tell—from the apologetically arched eyebrows, his eager yet cautious approach, the *"Shulem Aleichem"* from Boro Park, but the daps from Bed-Stuy—that here was probably another woke white boy about to apologize on behalf of the entire white Jewish community of the entire world.

Which, honestly?

Was great and all, the whole penitent *"I'm so sorry for the way Jews of Color get treated"* confessional. But then it generally just, like, veered into some incoherent sputtering about how "messed up it all is" and ended with this weird puppy dog sad face that Ariel was kind of over. Tortured guilt only looks sexy on vampires.

And even then, only on vampires not written or inspired by Stephenie Meyer.

But when Kalman plopped down next to Ariel, beer in hand, there was something wryly self-aware about him that said there was something more behind those probably-not-prescription lenses.

"Hey," Kalman started.

"Hey."

"Where in the States are you from?"

"Brooklyn. *Eretz kodesh.*"

"No way," Kalman laughed. "Me too. Where at?"

"Midwood. The Jews there try to say it's Flatbush, but it's really not. They're just trying to get street cred. It's Midwood. You?"

"I'm up in Crown Heights."

"I'm sorry."

"Ha! Yeah, me too. I work for a driving school there. The messed-up stuff I hear man...Like...Y'know, just a couple weeks ago I'm driving this one dude—Chassidic guy—driving him up to the Bronx for his road test, and he turns to me and is like 'Is there a lot of blacks here?' And he says it in this way, with this annoyed voice, like he just walked into a pizzeria for a slice of pizza, but everyone there is a horse, right? And I—seriously—I get this question *all the time.* So I go 'Yeah, this is a mostly black neighborhood' and the guy, like, snorts, and is all 'Are they anti-Semites?' I just roll my eyes at him and go 'So do you like black people?' And his face goes all pale, like I'd just asked him if his mother would blow my **shofar** or something. Anyway, he doesn't have an answer. For, like, a *while.* So then I go 'Well just so you know, they're not. But if you're gonna be racist against them, why shouldn't they be racist against you?' And here—and this is the really fucked up part—he kind of waves his hand at me and says 'All these *schvartzes*, they're all lowlives. Walking around with their pants around their butts, just thugs and drug dealers.' And I kind of flip out on him and pull the car over to the curb. I'm like 'Are you *serious?*' and I point to this one black guy leaning up against a wall in a Spider-Man shirt and go 'Do you see his pants around his butt? He's a drug dealer? What has he ever done to *you?*' So this smug jerkwad twunt just shrugs and says 'He's from Cham. Cham was cursed. All the *schvartzes* are.' And I, I close my eyes for a second, and I take a deep breath. And then I turn to him and say 'So what do you do for a living?' He's surprised and says 'I run a light fixture company.' 'So how sweaty are you when you come home?' He looks a little confused but says 'Not very...' 'When you're eating breakfast—or lunch, dinner, whatever—are you especially sad?' 'No...' And right here, I've got him. So I say to him 'Well why not? Adam was cursed too after he ate from the tree. *B'ze-as apecha tochal lechem.* 'By the sweat of your brow shall you eat your bread.' So why don't you come home sweaty? *B'itzavon tochlena kol yimei chayecha.* 'In suffering shall you eat from the earth all the days of your life.' So why aren't you sad when you're eating?' So now this guy starts looking all uncomfortable and says 'I don't understand...' and I go 'Well you're saying it's ok for you to be a dick to all black people because Cham was cursed, right? But you were cursed to sweat for your bread, and you don't. You were cursed to eat in suffering, but you don't. Do you believe you're obligated to sweat for your bread and eat in sorrow because you're cursed?' 'No...' he says. 'So why do you think that people created in the same *tzelem Elokim* as you are, are obligated to suffer your racism because Cham was cursed? Why do *you* get out of a curse that *is* mentioned in the Torah, but you get to hold an entire race to a curse that *isn't*?' And what does this guy say? 'Oh...I've never thought about it that way.' And so I say 'Great. You have something to think about now.' And then I point to the black dude in the Spider-Man shirt again and say 'Your road test examiner is waiting for you.'"

Kalman paused here, finally, and took a swig of beer before continuing on.

"Like, it really bothered me that he'd never even *thought* about it. I mean, the fact of human beings—not just Jews, *human beings*—being created in G'd's image. And it's right there before the Torah says boo about Jews or Judaism or religion or *anything*. Like, you can quote this **Gemara** and say over that *maimer* from the **Rebbe**, but you couldn't make it twenty-seven lines into *literally* the first Jewish book to ever exist?" he shook his head again, then shrugged at Ariel.

"Anyway, I just wanna say that it's really messed up what you have to go through, and I'm really sorry for that, and that I really respect you being able to push through it all."

Ariel looked at him for a moment, amused, impressed, and surprised.

He definitely hadn't expected any part of that. Just like he didn't expect that in less than three weeks' time, when he returned to Israel for a year of study, that he and Kalman would be made dormmates.

Or that in eight years from then he'd be given the honor of reading the **ketubah** at Kalman's wedding. But at that particular moment, up on that balcony, Ariel lifted his bottle of Goldstar to this very interesting new stranger.

"Ariel Samson."

"Kalman Meltzer."

ARIEL SAMSON: FREELANCE RABBI

They clinked bottles.

✡ ✡ ✡

If possible, Ariel and Kalman had bonded even *more* once they became dormmates at Mayanot, mostly because they were among the few students there who weren't converting or becoming more religious, but had grown up always being Orthodoxly observant.

Also, they definitely commiserated about *not* being **Chabad-Lubavitch**, yet attending a school which they were inexplicably unaware beforehand was *heavily* affiliated with Chabad-Lubavitch.

Not that there was anything wrong with that.

The Mayanot experience had been mostly pleasant, actually. The rabbis there were all very spirited and full of energy, and for the most part did an amazing job of encouraging their students in ways that were healthy for their personal growth. But against the sea of extremely earnest noveau-religious ingénues, the relatively laidback Ariel and Kalman had definitely stood out.

Ariel more than Kalman, clearly.

In fact, they'd only lasted there for seven months out of their intended twelve, getting kicked out when (admittedly, tripping balls on a bad batch of ecstasy Ilan had scored), Kalman had flipped out on one of the more myopic rabbis who'd asked Ariel when he was finishing his conversion. For the third time.

They'd spent their remaining five months in Jerusalem lying to their families, crashing with Kalman's older brother who lived in the Old City with his wife and kid, and staying up until the wee hours of the morning, studying the labyrinthine text of the ancient **Talmud** under the influence of Ilan's much more reliable hashish stash.

Those were good times.

After his Israel adventure, Ariel came back to the States and started college, sandwiching a stint at Shaar HaTorah Theological Seminary in-between earning his B.A. in English & secondary education and an M.F.A. in creative writing at Brooklyn College. Eight years later, Ariel came out of it all a rabbi and an English teacher.

Neither of which, by the way, proved to be lucrative career paths.

Manishtana

In hindsight, it probably wasn't the best career choice to go for a liberal arts degree in a surplus subject, and an ordination in a field where pulpit positions were drying up. Getting fired from being an English teacher at a *yeshiva*—the *one* place where his unique skill set could beneficially overlap—likely didn't help his situation either.

Tuesday, September 8-Tuesday, October 27, 2015
24/25 Elul 5775-14/15 Cheshvan 5776

Look, in Ariel's defense, it'd seemed to be a good enough job when he saw it on Craigslist.

Boys yeshiva in Brooklyn seeking a full time 8th-grade English instructor. Competitive salary, the ad had read.

See? Innocuous enough.

Something nice and steady to tide him over, while he waited for the NYC Department of Education to remember he existed and toss him one of those permanent teaching gigs that he'd spent all those years in college for. Because so far, four years later, he had nothing to show for it but a wallet eaten away from the cost of transportation bouncing around the city as a substitute teacher.

So hey, why not give this instructor deal a semester or two in the meantime, see where it went?

The *yeshiva* was modern Orthodox, which meant the lingo would be familiar, he'd have all the Jewish holidays off, *and* he could get home in time for winter Shabbats without getting the co-worker sideeye for leaving early on Fridays.

So he went for it.

And by the end of his first day of work at Yeshiva Darchei Yisroel, Ariel knew he was in trouble.

The first hint was when they told him he couldn't create lesson plans that made references to television shows, movies, or any other non-Jewish media.

Manishtana

"Because, ah, our kids don't, um. They don't watch, uh, those," came the stammery reasoning from the exceedingly backboneless Principal David Weisinger.

"Ok...Are we sure?" Ariel had asked. "Because there's a kid in one of my classes who only answers to 'Harry Potter' when I take attendance, so..."

Principal Weisinger raised his shoulders in response, scrunching his balding head down into his neck like an albino turtle, and lifted his hands with palms facing upwards as if asking, *"What do you want from me? You want I should actually be a principal?"*

It only went downhill from there.

Like the time Ariel was informed that he was only allowed to use adapted editions of classic literary works. Editions that the *yeshiva* had specially commissioned.

Ones which rewrote any instances where the original texts featured non-kosher food, or contained the words "church" or "Jesus," or had, like, a book sleeve that didn't fully cover its elbows or something. Which pretty much meant that Ariel was preparing students for the *statewide English regents* by teaching them bad Shakespeare fanfic.

Thankfully, minus all the very disturbing Horatio/Fortinbras slash. Of which there is surprisingly a lot of.

Also, by "competitive salary" Yeshiva Darchei Yisroel apparently meant compared to whatever Willy Wonka was paying his Oompa Loompas back in the original 1971 film.

Without adjusting for inflation.

But then, to top it all off, the kids—every single one of Ariel's five classes—were horrible little festering pools of malevolent Sodom and Gomorrah hellsludge.

If Moses had shown up in front of Pharaoh with *this* brood instead of a snake with identity issues and an eating disorder, the Jews would've been freed from Egypt ten plagues early.

I'm just saying.

See, someone had put it in all their heads that they were all *so* holy and all going to grow up to become the greatest rabbi of their generation, and so any sense of respect for "secular" subjects, or the people who taught them, went right out the window.

And for their part, the school's rabbis glided (glid? glade?) through parted throngs of students like swans across a lake, looking pityingly down their noses, yet lending none of their gravity to the unruly secular classrooms, and leaving the other teachers to fend for themselves as they burned out, one by one.

It was demoralizing, to say the least.

Many times, Ariel would stare in his fridge for far too long, gazing at that way too old Chinese food carton of rice that nobody eats, wondering how many days of freedom getting food poisoning would buy him. Other times he'd call in sick. While standing literally right outside the door to his classroom. Often enough he'd have lunch with the poor unfortunate soul who had the lot of teaching 6th grade Social Studies.

And by "lunch," I mean the Irish coffee breaks they took on the free periods between the dismal classes they taught.

"I've had *men* under my command," Ariel's colleague confided one afternoon, a former IDF sergeant with tears in his haunted eyes. "And I can't control this class."

The school found him later that day across the street in his car with a half empty bottle of Arak in the passenger's seat, trying to drown himself in his own homemade shakshuka while the Israeli national anthem of "Hatikvah" blasted through the stereo.

Ariel never saw him again after that.

Whatever was wrong with those kids and that school, Ariel just didn't understand it. Back when he was in *yeshiva*? Kids and schools weren't like that. Of course, when he'd gone to *yeshiva*, it was as a black kid.

There was an entirely different set of wrongs from that perspective.

The kind of wrongs that led his older brother to routinely sneak loose change from their parents—one of many daily demands from classmates in exchange for friendship.

The kind of wrongs that made his older sister ecstatically happy that her classmates were actually talking to her. Nevermind that the moniker they referred to her by was "**goy** booty," as if having curves wasn't only un-Jewish, but distinctly *non*-Jewish to boot.

Not to mention the inherent objectification and sexualization, *obviously*.

The kinds of wrongs that had instilled in AviandAri a deep and visceral disgust for anyone who would defend the use of the word "*schvartze*" as being harmlessly "cultural."

Manishtana

Y'know, just like how the swastika used to be.

So he supposed Yeshiva Darchei Yisroel was just differently terrible. A separate but equally horrific experience, the latter of which finally culminated on that asinine last day when Principal Weisinger quite professionally let Ariel know that he was being let go...

"You're firing me?!"

"Well, uh...It's...technically it's *fired*. Past tense. *Fired* you."

"You couldn't have at least told me before first period?"

...in front of his entire first-period class...

"I—I could just step out for a second while you two—"

...and Ms. Sieger. Ariel's very Nordic-looking replacement. The one he had walked into his classroom to find sitting at his desk, already in the middle of taking attendance.

Understandably, she was feeling pretty awkward herself.

"I mean," she continued. "I could even start tomorrow instead if—"

And as Ariel was (more than) graciously reassuring Ms. Sieger, Principal Weisinger was simultaneously doing his inept best to explain the situation to Ariel.

Ariel to Ms. Sieger: "No, it's ok. It's not your job to notify me that a class isn't mine anymore."

Principal Weisinger to Ariel: "It, uh, it was a split-second decision and I tried contacting you, but your phone wasn't picking up yesterday, so I-I-I-I sent you a text."

"What are you talking about?" Ariel turned to him, baffled. "I didn't get anything from you yesterday. Except for—"

And then Ariel froze, realizing that the three sets of broken hearts and sad faces accompanied by the word "NO" blinking under a grumpy-faced grey cat was not, as he had previously assumed, a curiously articulate butt-dial.

"...You fired me with a bunch of random emojis...and a *cat gif*...?"

"I, uh, I'm sorry. Do you, do you not like cats?"

"...That is *literally* the least problematic aspect of this scenario right now."

The rest of Ariel's day after that was just one huge incredulous blur that didn't start to make sense until that night at the bar, when he met up with Jumaane, Colin, and Ilan.

And his destiny, I guess.

Something like that.

✡ ✡ ✡

"He fired you in *emojis*?" Jumaane shouted.

"And a cat gif," Ariel added. "Don't forget the cat gif."

"Are you *serious*? That's unbel—I don't believe that. I can't believe that."

"Oh, *you* don't believe it?" Ariel snorted a comfortably tipsy snort and elbowed Colin. "Hey. *Shhh!* Don't tell anybody, but *Jumaane* doesn't believe it!"

"Yeah, uh huh," Colin muttered back mechanically, thoroughly engrossed with his phone as usual. "Doesn't believe it. Gotcha."

Ariel took another swig of Heineken and resumed licking his wounds. They were at their favorite hybrid sports bar/pool hall in downtown Brooklyn. It had yet to be fully engulfed by the hipster onslaught, but if those artisanal beers taking up more and more of the taps were any indication, their grass-fed forces were aggressively on the move.

"Yo," Jumaane shot at Colin, still on his phone instead of standing around the pool table pretending to play like the rest of them. "The man has just been fired from a job he's had for all of two months—"

"A little less than *one* month actually," Ariel offered.

"—*Less* than a month! You can't, like, pause for a second to hear his tale of woe like you have a human soul?"

Jumaane Carter was the big brother friend, with patience almost as long as his dreadlocks. The kind of friend who quietly lets you storm around your apartment ranting about how mature you are, and tactfully ignores that there are at *least* five things in their line of sight that have Kermit the Frog on them.

As a friend, they'll hold your arm as you hobble down the Hallway of Experience. But as family, they will push you down the Stairwell of Life with no regrets, because it's for your own good. Whenever Ariel needed a black Jiminy Cricket—and even when he didn't—Jumaane was always just a phone call away.

"Yeah, well, Ari's a big boy," Colin shot back, still not looking up from his screen, but now texting even more furiously than before. "I don't think he really needs us to hold his dick for him. Actually, hold on a sec?"

Manishtana

Colin stopped texting. Dialed a number. Waited for the other side to pick up. Then immediately began *screaming* into the phone, his dirty blonde hair quivering with rage.

"Listen! I'm *tired* of you undermining me, and texting my phone with this, this *shit*! I want you to—you *listen* to me—with, with your bitch mouth and your whore eyes! You have a bitch mouth! *You have a bitch mouth!*... Aw, I made you cry? You make *me* cry. Every. Night. When I sleep next to you. Because I know, because I *know* that I'm *trapped*! FACT: Every time I kiss you, a part of me *dies*! It is *dead*! Get off my phone! *Get off my phone!* I—listen—I, Colin Archer Bradley, do not want to *speak* to you anymore...Look...Look, I want you to understand that I'm not hanging up on *you*, I'm hanging up my *phone*."

Colin hung up, and jammed his phone into his slacks pocket, nonchalantly ignoring the deathly silence of Ariel and Jumaane's stares.

When you give your kid a name like "Colin Archer Bradley"—which pretty much sounds *exactly* as if white privilege came to life and named itself—then you get, well, Colin Archer Bradley.

He was the terrible friend. Obviously. Everybody has one. That one friend who is just...just awful. Like, *morally*. But you keep them around for those times when *you* do shitty things—like key your ex's car, or switch out your roommate's Xanax with stale Tic Tacs—but you still wanna look at yourself in the mirror. And so you look at your terrible friend, and then you pat yourself on the back, because, sure, that was a shitty thing you did, but at least you're not a fucking *monster*.

Ariel was the first one to speak.

"...the hell was *that*?"

"Yeah..." Jumaane shook his head. "That was..." he exhaled, speechless.

"What's *wrong* with you?" Ariel continued. "What's—How do you *talk* to people like that?"

"Look," Colin answered coolly. "We've got a system, okay? It works for us."

"It works for—?" Ariel just shrugged in surrender, not even trying to comprehend Colin's level of insanity right now. He started on his beer again, and Jumaane tagged in.

"Dude," he said. "That doesn't even seem a *little* bit healthy."

"Well, yeah, I like to see things a little bit more positively. I mean, like, *no* relationship is perfect, but the sex is cray-hay-maaazing! And I really don't think it's fair for you to judge us. Maybe you should think more positively about life. Be an optimist for a change."

Ariel nearly spit his beer out at that one.

"I *am* an optimist," Jumaane protested.

"Ok, so here's a question," Colin began. "Answer honestly. This is between me, you, and the L'rd. That girlfriend you had back in college with the small tits. When you saw her in her bra, did you think the cups were half-empty or half-full?"

Ariel *did* spit his beer out this time, shooting a little bit out of his nose as he hacked up a lung.

"I don't—I don't see how—She was Asian, she had a naturally small frame and—"

"*Etzba!*" came the cheerful cry from across the room, interrupting Jumaane's stammered response. Ilan had arrived, greeting everyone in turn with his trademark bear hug and pocket drop.

"*Hismantem?*" Ilan asked when he got to Ariel, slipping into his native Hebrew.

"*Mah? Ata shoel* oti?" Ariel answered. "*Ani rak shoteh po.*"

Ariel shrugged, bemoaning the plight of keeping kosher and the danger of going to bars while doing so. Sure, you could find plenty of shots, beers, and mixed drinks to knock back all night long and keep you *nice*, but when it came to those fries and wings to help soak things up? Not so much.

"*Ata yodea, oolay titgayer l'Israeli,*" Ilan grinned. "*Anachnu ochlim hakol.*"

"*Ani yodea. Raiti ta bachurot shcha.*"

"And CHappa CHappa CHap to you rude asses, too," Jumaane interjected, mimicking the guttural sounds of Ari and Ilan's Hebrew lovefest. Colin had long since begun texting again.

"Sorry," Ariel and Ilan apologized in tandem.

"Ari got fired today," Colin offered, not raising his head from his phone.

"*Wha—?*" came Ilan's reply, to which Ariel just shrugged again and took yet another swig of beer as Ilan clapped a sympathetic hand on his friend's shoulder with a little squeeze. And suddenly

Ariel was aware that there were now two more nickel bags in his pocket, which was—

"Wait," a light bulb suddenly went off in Ariel's head and he turned to Jumaane and Colin. "Don't you guys work for a temp agency? Could you keep an ear out for me, maybe?"

Colin looked up from his phone and shared a hesitant glance with Jumaane. It was true. They *did* both work at Keaton & West Staffing Services in the city. But...

"You sure you really wanna do that?" Colin asked skeptically.

"I mean, yeah..." Jumaane shook his head. "We're not very good. And the stuff that we get is kinda...y'know..."

"Well *'kinda y'know'* is better than nothing, and better than nothing pays rents," Ariel pointed out. He'd had a little bit saved up for the next couple months, but that wouldn't last forever.

"...Alright then," Jumaane shrugged. "Shoot your resume over tonight. We'll see what we can do."

"Yeah, shoot it on over," Colin parroted. "Maybe we'll be a—"

Colin's phone rang, and he picked up.

"Yeah?...Yeah, I'm sorry. I—I *did* go a little over the top...I—Wait, *what*? What do you mean I went over the top?! Y'know what? *Listen* to me, with your *whore eyes*! You have the *eyes* of a *whore*! What?! Don't—don't *call me*! *Don't call me!* I will call *you*! *DON'T YOU EVER CALL ME AGAIN! I PAY FOR THIS PHONE!...YOU PAY FOR THIS PHONE!...FAMILY PLAN!...WE PAY HALF!...IT'S ON YOUR MOM'S CREDIT!...*Yeah, equal my *ASS*!!"

Colin furiously ended the call by smashing his phone against the edge of the billiards table multiple times before roughly shoving it back into his pocket, once again looking up into the horrified faces of his friends when he was done with his tantrum.

And once again he was indifferent.

"So are we gonna order or what?" he asked, seemingly oblivious to the fact that he was apparently a *raging fucking sociopath*.

Which, yeah I know, calls into question Ariel's character judgement. But to be fair, he was in a bad sad place in his life when he met Colin. Also, Ariel had actually met *Jumaane*. And Colin was *his* friend. So there's that.

Anyway back at the bar, it wasn't that late, maybe 9 or 9:30, when Jumaane and Colin decided to call it quits and head home. Y'know, seeing as how they were currently the only two out of the

42

four of them who were gainfully employed. Although, if we're counting Ilan, I suppose "legally employed" is more accurate.

Incidentally, Ilan had already started mingling into the crowd, no doubt either meeting up with old clients or collecting new ones.

And so Ariel found himself alone and in no particular rush to get home, particularly because he had no job to be at the next morning. Besides, the place had a pretty good happy hour. He just needed to drain the lizard first.

Winding his way through pool tables, servers, a football game viewing, and at least one bachelorette party, Ariel finally found himself at the back of the bar in a narrow wood-paneled hallway, greeted by the sight of two squirming lines of impatient bladders waiting to get into the only two bathrooms in the entire establishment.

Joining the shorter line, he laid back against the wall and, aimlessly surveying his surroundings, noticed a white girl staring at him on the opposite line. A faceful of glitter, dressed in cutoff denim shorts and a tube top, with stringy, strawberry-blonde curls spilling from underneath a straw cowboy hat.

She held her gaze on him for a while—long enough for it to be slightly less uncomfortable than that Halle Berry/Billy Bob Thorton sex scene in *Monster's Ball*—when she gave a start, apparently remembering how eyes worked and that Ariel could actually see her, too.

"I like your yarmulke," she spat out finally, with a definitely buzzed, but not yet drunk slur.

"Oh. Thanks."

"Is there, like, a reason why you wear one?"

Oh, yeah, Ariel thought. *It's for fashion. I saw a GQ article saying wearing tea cozies on your head was in this season. So I figured, what the hell?*

That and *many* many other smart-ass replies raced underneath his skin like little minnows of rage flitting through streams of slightly alcohol-tinged blood.

But it had already been a long and stupid enough of a day, and Ariel wasn't really feeling up for banter that would just go over her head anyway. So he just answered the question. Like he did every time.

"I'm Jewish."

"Oh!" she brightened. "Really? That's cool! I've never met a black Jew before!"

He nodded tolerantly at that one as well, all the while thinking, Oh really? How the *hell* would she have *any* idea that she'd *never* met a black Jew before?

Unless she was in the habit of conducting random circumcision checks—which, hey, #yolo—she'd literally have *no* clue whether or not she'd ever met a black Jew before.

Sure, with his *kippah* and his **tzitzit** fringes swinging at his hips like spindly woolen jazz hands, Ariel was pretty easy to ID. But what about all the Reform or Conservative or Reconstructionist or secular or atheist black Jews who didn't wear identifying headgear or religious clothing any more than their paler counterparts? How in the hell does *anybody* know they've *never* met a black Jew before?

"But, like, *how* are you Jewish?" she pressed on, and again came an alternate universe response trying to jump out of Ariel's face.

"Childhood accident. I was running through the house one day and tripped into some kosher that someone had carelessly left lying open, and by the time they got to me, the doctors said there was nothing they could do."

And again, and as always, he went with the straightforward answer.

"Born."

"Whoa," came the reply, and then a sudden shift in face and tone. "So, like, don't you think you're being a little obnoxious right now?"

She gestured up and down Ariel's body disdainfully as an explanation, and he remained completely baffled.

"Excuse me?"

"You're wearing *leather shoes*," she rolled her eyes.

Yes. This was a true fact.

Ariel's dad grew up greatly enamored with the Golden Age of Hollywood. Movies like *The Maltese Falcon* and *The Thin Man*. Leading men like Claude Rains and James Cagney. Damsels like Jean Harlow and Myrna Loy. That great time in America when men were men and women were women. And niggers were niggers, and micks were micks, and guineas were guineas.

Anyhoo, everything Ariel's dad knew about being a sharp dresser he learned from those movies, and it was one of Ariel's

44

favorite things that he'd inherited from his dad. So there Ariel was that night, dressed in a grey pinstripe vest and slacks, skinny tie, chrome pocketwatch, his favorite pair of black-and-grey alligator shoes, and no clue what this girl's point was.

"Jews can't wear leather shoes," the girl elucidated, cocking her head at him.

"Wait, what? That's not a thing. Jews can wear—"

"Um, *no*. *I'm* Jewish. *I know*. Jews *can't* wear *leather*."

Ah-hum. And so the plot thinned.

I mean, sure, Ariel could've probably let her know that there *were* certain *times* (like fast days or during **shiva**) when Jews couldn't wear leather shoes. But, judging from the glass she was holding, it'd be useless trying to convey those nuances to a glitter-faced caricature of a boozy college girl, who somehow had comprehensive Jewish knowledge on the wearing of leather, but had missed the much simpler and more straightforward memo on shrimp cocktails.

But y'know what? Ariel was that guy.

That kinda rabbi who genuinely tried to embody **dan l'kaf zechut**, that (nearly extinct) Jewish principle of judging people favorably and giving them the benefit of the doubt. So maybe she just legitimately didn't know about leather shoes. Or maybe she hadn't been taught. Or maybe she'd even been *mis*-taught. And rabbis, after all, were supposed to be teachers, first and foremost, right? Figures to help guide the misguided?

So, Ariel decided to try anyways. Bless his heart.

"Actually, when it comes to wearing leather, there are certain *times* that Jews can't—"

"No. You're *wrong*," she interrupted. "*You* need to *learn* more."

Yes.

"*You need to learn more.*"

Said Cowboy Stripper Barbie to Rabbi Ariel Samson. That was a thing that happened.

The bathroom door on her line opened up, and it was Little Ms. Judaism Warrior's turn to go in. Of course, to add irony to injury, she had a Holocaust number tramp stamp on her lower back.

"It's great, right?" she told me when I asked her about it later. "It's subdued, so it's, like, *sooo* respectful."

That's right guys. The wheel was turning but the hamster was dead with this one.

And—fun fact—Ariel just *loved* that certain kind of audacity when Jews who "looked Jewish," but didn't know the difference between a *shofar* and a chauffeur, felt like they could question whether or not he was doing Jewish "right." As if the difference between their skin and his skin gave them some automatic badge of Jew Authority without needing to have the most rudimentary knowledge of, well, *anything*.

And when fourteen months of study and a couple decades of lived-in experience can be contested by fourteen seconds of racial profiling and a couple of watered-down drinks, it can make someone wonder why they became a rabbi at all.

Not Ariel, mind you. But someone.

See, Ariel knew *exactly* why he'd ended up becoming a rabbi.

Nothing selfless or ambitious or anything like that.

Nope, like most worthwhile things a guy ever does in life, Ariel Samson became a rabbi for the most time-honored of reasons:

Because of a girl.

After a couple more shots, obviously, Ariel was heading to the door, deciding to call it a night on this dumpster fire of a day.

"Ari!"

Ariel turned to see a familiar gangly white kid waving at him from the far end of the bar, dressed practically in the same outfit he'd first met him in, just with the addition of a grey button-down cardigan, a goatee, and a black-and-white plaid fedora.

And still in sandals. Like it wasn't November.

"Kalman?"

"Dude!" Kalman made his way over, beer in hand, and a huge smile on his face that almost masked the stress rings around his eyes. "This is so random! What are you even *doing* here?"

"Are you serious? I'm here, like, *all* the time. What are *you* doing here?"

"I'm like ten minutes away!"

"You and Dassi moved? How's she doing?"

"Yeah, she's good, she's good. Dude, this is so crazy. I was just trying to get in touch with you like—actually, you're heading out right? Hold up," Kalman held one finger up while he knocked his head back and chugged down the last of his beer. "Lemme just pay my tab and I'll leave with you."

"Cool, I'll be outside."

"K."

Five minutes later they were strolling down the rain-soaked sidewalks of Prospect Heights. They excitedly caught up on each other's lives while cars whizzed by and splashed through watery reflections of the neighborhood, glistening up from the slick asphalt in a collage of distorted olive green, deep red, and pale orange lights reminiscent of Van Gogh's "Starry Night".

It had started raining again. Lightly.

Almost as if the night's winds had come sweeping down Flatbush Avenue from Brooklyn Heights in search of affordable rent, and, upon reaching Grand Army Plaza, had finally burst into soft tears of despair.

Speaking of which, Kalman had some despair of his own to share.

He'd started off jovially enough.

A standing invitation to Shabbat dinner at his place that Friday night. (Ariel made a raincheck for the week after next.) A blushing apology for falling off the face of the Earth after his wedding. (C'mon, we're all grown-ups here. We *all* know what he was busy doing.) A good-natured needling that Ariel hadn't answered any of his calls (New phone, new number. Old one had fallen down an elevator shaft after some drinks), or replied back to any of his emails (Honestly, Ariel was a damn adult now and needed an email address that wouldn't embarrass him on resumes. So jewpacabra3000@yahoo.com had to go).

But eventually the cheerful veneer melted away and it all came flooding out.

Congregation Ahavath Yisroel, the legacy of Rabbi Samuel Gellerman—Kalman's grandfather—was in trouble. It was rabbi-less, penniless, nearly member-less, in desperate need of renovation, and, last but not least, on the verge of being sold and leased out to a Washington firm, with intentions to use the site as a halfway house for federal inmates.

"Wait, what?" Ariel stopped in mid-stride.

"Yeah..." Kalman sighed, his shoulders slumping. He stopped walking too. "The two brothers who control the building—the

Katzes—have been trying to get rid of it for years. See, their dad helped my granddad buy the building with the agreement that so long as it was a functioning *shul,* the Katz family would cover the costs to keep it open, pay utilities, stuff like that. The junior Katzes are obviously not in love with that deal and want to make some profit off the real estate. So they're trying to make the case that we really aren't a functioning synagogue anymore. And..." he sighed again. "Honestly Ari, they're right. Like, we can barely get ten guys for Shabbos morning. But it's...It's my granddad's place, y'know? I can't just let it shut down without a fight. I even, I mean I even got myself elected as board president. The Katzes' lawyers gave us a grace period of 90 days to turn things around. But I just...I don't even know what to do..."

Kalman trailed off and he looked away, the off-yellow streetlight casting his fedora's shadow across his face, while he clenched his jaw and ground his back teeth. That tick, that universal symbol us guys broadcast when we have to stop talking *that* very instant.

Because if we don't, then in that next moment our voice will crack over the knot that we're trying to swallow in our too dry, too tight throat. And then we'll have no control over how many gulps of air our lungs suddenly and violently need. And then the tears will come.

Ariel let his friend have his distance. And not for any of the typical "something something machismo something something toxic masculinity" tropes. Because he, for one, was a hugger. And a comforter. He couldn't stand seeing people wallow in their sadness.

He remembered being six and—after witnessing one of the worst arguments he'd ever seen his parents have before or since—hugging his dad. Remembered just the two of them, Ariel and his **Aba**, out on the steps outside their apartment, the elder Samson clutching a bottle of Heineken so tightly that the younger Samson thought it would shatter in his hands. Remembered watching his dad sitting there and looking out at the sunset, divested of all the sturm und drang of paternal authority, and just being a regular sad person. A person coming to terms with the realization that while he was a *lot* less the sociopathic creature that *his* father was, that in some ways he was a lot *more* like his father than he'd ever wanted to be.

And Ariel remembered heading back inside when his dad finally told him to, and then going over to his mom as she sat checking her emails—pretending that his dad's words hadn't sliced at her like a million paper-thin razor blades—and stroking her hair while he snuggled his face into her arm.

He remembered being twenty-five, and his big brother Jake haltingly confiding in him—*weeks* before he told their parents—that his rocky marriage had finally shattered, and that she was taking the house, half of his company, and, most agonizingly of all, Ariel's niece and nephew.

Ariel remembered standing there, feeling like he was trying to get to first base with a granite statue, when Jake suddenly reciprocated, wrapping Ariel into the steel-cable muscles of his chest and suffocating him in his collarbone, coughing bitter guttural sobs into the top of his little brother's head.

And not even a year ago, there Ariel was, clasping Jumaane's shoulder with one hand, his other firmly gripping both of Jumaane's trembling ones, as they both watched Jumaane's mother's coffin being lowered into the ground on a day as grey as the dreary floral wallpaper in her bedroom, where she'd died of an asthma attack in Jumaane's arms in the middle of the night just four days earlier.

And so tonight, out in the rain, under the frothy purple sky, an agonizing war was waging inside Ariel.

On one side was Ariel's heart, guiding him to indulge his natural compassion. To drape his arm around Kalman's shoulders and tell him *"Hey man, it's ok. I'm here for you."* On the other, was Ariel's head, which did not take kindly to any shadows of him playing the Magical Negro. Warning him from being the Bagger Vance to Kalman's Matt Damon or the Morgan Freeman to his Ms. Daisy or the Hattie McDaniel to his Scarlett O'Hara.

And on neither side was Ariel's soul, buzzing in the back of his head about how the world is *supposed* to be and what he was supposed to do in it.

G'd doesn't give us tests without also giving us the ability to pass them, the words rattling around his brain said, clear as the day he'd first learned them. Nachmanides—the Ramban—had said that. *When people fail, it's because they don't recognize the situation as a test in the first place.*

Manishtana

And the truth of the matter was, there Congregation Ahavath Yisroel was: a down-on-its-luck synagogue needing to be rescued.

And there Ariel was: a freshly unemployed twenty-something, slinging around a dormant rabbinical ordination with no intent to ever really use it.

And there the test was: would Ariel let ego and centuries of internalized defensive racial neuroses convince him to walk away?

Or...

And in that exciting and frightening instant of comprehension, Ariel knew exactly what he was going to do.

His hand reached out for Kalman's shoulder for what felt like ages, kind of like that slow climb at the beginning of a rollercoaster. That inching trawl just long enough for you to regret your decision before the drop happens and the ride begins.

And that was the night Congregation Ahavath Yisroel got itself a rabbi.

The ride had begun.

Ariel was having the dream again—the one where he was an Imperial stormtrooper on the deck of the Titanic, fighting Satan in the form of Samuel L. Jackson—when he was needled awake by the trilling of a Super Mario-esque theme, assaulting his eardrums with tiny little darts of sound as he sleepily fumbled around for his smartphone.

"*Shalom*?" he groggily answered.

"What did I tell you about that shit?" came the voice on the other end. "Answer your damn phone in English."

"I—whatever. What do you want, Colin?"

"I'm bout to hook you up, na mean?"

"Colin—You're a—Just don't. Don't ever use that combination of words again."

"Whatever, yo. Can you come in today? Around lunch? We got some bites for you."

✡ ✡ ✡

Keaton & West Staffing Services was in the west 40's around Rockefeller Center, and the building that housed it was an absolute maze of glass and sunlight.

Ariel was seriously sure he'd circled the entire floor enough times that he was now legally married to it according to Jewish law.

51

Thoroughly lost and confused, he finally gave up and somehow managed to make his way back to the guard at the front desk.

The front desk, luckily, was still there—now with a large Fed Ex package sitting on it—but the disheveled, weirdly sweaty security guard (who probably should *not* have had last night's chipotle burrito for breakfast that morning) was nowhere in sight. There was a girl sitting at the desk now instead, scribbling furiously away on a clipboard.

Ariel winced internally at calling her a "girl" for a second.

She was clearly around his age, so she was properly a "woman." Of course, that was slightly predicated on Ariel considering himself grown-up enough to be a "man."

Which Ariel definitely did not.

"Man" implied a certain level of having your shit together that Ariel was *reasonably* sure he hadn't reached yet. Even in relationships he'd only been "her boyfriend" or—once—"her fiancé." But never "her man." Nope, that was a title reserved for those adult males who were adultier than he was, and would *always* be adultier than he was. His father. *That* was a "man." His older brother Jake was a "man."

Ariel on the other hand, was...well, what?

A "guy"? A "dude"?

Definitely not "boy," though. *That* was just far too racially charged a term for an African-American male to identify as. Particularly if you didn't fancy literally feeling the weight of three hundred years' worth of side-eye burning into the back of your skull from ancestors who got shot, lynched, firehosed, and firebombed for asserting their right to be called "man."

And probably when they were younger than you are now.

But despite whatever the Torah had told twelve-year-old him about turning thirteen, Ariel wasn't really buying that he or any of his friends were "men." Of course, it'd be a couple more decades before Ariel realized that that elusive feeling of "knowing what you're doing" wasn't ever really going to come.

Find me a guy who thinks of himself as a "man" and having "everything figured out," and I'll show you a misogynist sociopath who sacrifices his kids to Molech.

Anyhoo, she—the *woman* at the desk—was in her early twenties, it seemed, left-handed, and with coal-black natural hair, springing from her head in thick wooly spirals like a cheerleader's pom-pom. Luminous, dark mahogany skin shimmered like liquid silk, threatening to smother you in its soft ebony-tinged tentacles. (Or, y'know—as *The Help* author Kathryn Stockett would say—she was "cockroach brown.")

The front of her hair was dyed in the same shade of royal blue as her eyeshadow and lipstick. The eyeshadow was glittery. The lipstick was metallic. A conga line of thin gold hoops ran down the outer edge of one ear, but only two solitary jeweled studs sat in her other one. Under a worn, dark pink *The Nightmare Before Christmas* tee, she wore a purple fishnet shirt that covered her arms all the way down to her wrists, where a pair of fingerless black-and-purple striped gloves took over.

If she were a Harry Potter character, her patronus would've probably been Tim Burton riding a sandworm and singing "Jack's Lament" while eating Sweeney Todd.

"Excuse me," Ariel cleared his throat, catching her attention. "I'm looking for Suite 514?"

"Suite what?" came her reply as she looked up, the brow above her light brown eyes knitting in confusion. There was a slight accent in her voice, something slightly British-ish maybe.

"Suite 514?" Ariel repeated.

"You sure about that? Because we don't have one of those here."

"What?" Ariel exclaimed, looking at the scrap of paper he'd scribbled the Google Maps address on. "But, that's what—"

She apathetically plucked the paper from Ariel's hand and scanned it.

"It's Suite 51-A," she looked back up at Ariel, handing the slip back to him.

"Oh! Right," Ariel stammered, embarrassed. "Okay, duh."

"Yeah, just take—*Louis!*" she called over Ariel's shoulder suddenly. Ariel turned to see the previously-seated security guard as he lurched out of a restroom, his uniform just as disheveled, his face a lot less weirdly sweaty, but a lot more, if you'll pardon the pun, "flushed." "Are you good? I've gotta head back up."

The guard nodded his head with a relieved grimace of gratitude, shuffling toward the desk while the blue-haired woman rose and scooted from behind it.

"C'mon," she said to Ariel, sliding the Fed Ex box off the desk and hefting it under her arm. The fluid motion jangled the keys hooked at her side with a bright pink carabiner. "Just take the lift with me."

"Thanks so much," Ariel said as they made their way to the elevators not too far away, walking in time to the slap of keys against her right thigh. He was amazed they didn't get tangled up in any of the assorted straps, chains, and zippers running the length and width of her asymmetrical black skirt like sutures on Frankenstein's monster.

She pressed the button and took a step back, squinting up at Ariel for a moment, like she was sizing him up.

"You here for the *Late Late Night Night* interviews?" she asked.

"No, the temp agency," Ari answered, slightly sheepishly. "Keaton and West?"

"Right. Duh. Suite 51-A," she nodded, still slightly smirking, as if she hadn't made up her mind about him yet. "Oh well. Too bad."

The elevator groaned open and they stepped inside. Ariel wasn't sure about her smirk, especially seeing as how it grew a little deeper every time she glanced up at his *kippah* or down at his *tzitzit*.

But, as reactions went, he'd had worse.

Like the real estate seminar he'd attended a few years back.

It'd turned out to be an MLM thing, but the moment Ariel realized he didn't want to work with the company came about 30 seconds before the presentation began, when the suited, goateed man of indeterminate Caribbean origin—one of the presenters—walked over to Ariel's seat and bluntly barked at him, "Excuse me. Does your headgear have any particular significance?"

Ariel'd looked blankly at the man, scanned the room full of the man's white, *yarmulked* co-workers, then looked back at him.

Really? Ariel'd thought. *You have no idea what my "headgear" could possibly mean?*

"Yes. It signifies that I'm Jewish," came Ariel's simple answer, to which the man turned up his nose and spun away, huffing off like the answer had offended him.

The elevator pinged open on the third floor.

"Just head down the hallway and make the first left," Blue Hair directed, pressing the button for the 5th floor. "Suite 51-A will be the second door on your right."

"Oh! Great. Thanks," he smiled, thankful for her help, and with just a twinge of notice that she was really cute.

"Well, good luck," she saluted, amusedly, Fed Ex box tucked under her arm. Seeing as how she barely cleared 5'2", it was a decent feat of either strength or balance. "You have really nice eyes."

"Uh, thanks! I think it really brings out your hair."

And with a crack of surprised laughter and a smirk, she walked out of the elevator and out of Ariel's life.

I'd like to say that they crossed paths again, but they never did.

Life doesn't always work out that neatly, and not every pleasant exchange with a stranger foreshadows a romance lying in wait. It's perfectly fine to cordially interact with someone without the expectation of seeing them naked.

You don't get a sexytimes gold star for simply not being a dick.

Or, hey, maybe Ariel and his blue-haired elevator savior *did* meet again. Maybe I'm one of those unreliable omniscient narrators you hear so much about in English Lit class or biblical criticism.

You'd never know.

"So," Colin began as Ariel plopped down opposite him in the cubicle. "Got your resume. First thing I did was completely overhaul that bitch."

"What was wrong with it?" Ariel started. "I mean besides the—"

"Well for starters," Colin cut in, impatiently. "It didn't even have an objective. Like, just shoot yourself in the foot and shove it in your mouth while you're at it."

"...If I'm applying for a job, isn't it pretty obvious what my objective is?"

"Hey," Colin held up one hand, as if to slow Ariel down. "Which one of us is in career services and which one is unemployed here? Just relax and let me do my job, okay? I don't go around telling you how much Christian blood you should put in your matzah ball soup, do I?"

"I...wow, that's so many different lev—"

"So here," Colin shuffled around on his desk, then handed Ariel a sheet of paper. "I moved some stuff around and re-did it for you. Lemme know what you think."

With a skeptical look at Colin, Ariel took the reformatted resume and began looking it over.

"As you can see," Colin began explaining. "You've got an objective up there now, number one—"

"'Willing to claw my way to the top by any means necessary'?" Ariel gaped, disbelieving the words he was reading.

"That lets them know you mean business," Colin shrugged. "See, it *sounds* drastic, but it'll read like '*Hey, I'm so confident in my terrifying efficiency that I could literally declare that I'm willing to straight up murder people and still get this job. No biggie.'* Employers love confidence. Trust me. They eat that shit right up."

Ariel shook his head, silently mouthing "terrifying efficiency" to himself.

"Also, I took out all that rabbinical stuff and that Hebrew fluency deal," Colin snorted dismissively. "You don't want people thinking that they're hiring the...the Pope? You guys have a pope? Rabbi Pope? Well him. That's not what you want."

"Of course. Naturally," Ariel said in feigned agreement. He'd stopped pretending this was going to go anywhere. He'd actually come in to see *Jumaane* in the first place anyway, but his level-headed friend was busy working with a client. So Colin it was. "So, uh, what kind of jobs exactly do you think I should be aiming for? Just curious."

"Well..." Colin paused for a moment, scrunching his eyebrows. "...Personally, I'd try an alternative career that capitalized on your English, teaching, and writing background. Somewhere you could transfer those skill sets, not have to learn everything from the bottom up from scratch, and won't end up hating it every single day."

"Oh, uh. Oh," Ariel was caught off-guard by the surprisingly well-balanced insight. "Like what?"

"Captain of a nuclear submarine."

"*Oh*-kay," Ariel stood up to leave. "I'm gonna head out now. Tell Jumaane I'll just call him lat—"

"Yo, Colin," came Jumaane's voice as he rounded the corner, holding a manila folder. "Stepping out real quick for a coffee. You want—" he stopped short when he saw Ariel at the desk. "Dude, what are you doing here?"

"You guys said to meet—"

"I scheduled you for three interviews today!"

Ari's jaw dropped. "You what? How do I—"

"Didn't you forward him those openings I emailed you last night?" Jumaane shot at Colin.

Colin blinked at Jumaane, turned to his computer, looked blankly at the screen, scrolled down the page, then clicked his mouse. He turned back to Jumaane.

"Yes."

"*Are you serio*—Ok, look Ari," Jumaane quickly rifled through his folder, pulling out three notices. "Here you go. I don't remember the other ones, but I know that your first one is in about twenty minutes four blocks away. Here, *go!*"

Jumaane shoved the papers into a flustered Ariel's chest as Ariel—eternally grateful that on any given day he was dressed in a suit and tie—snatched up his messenger bag and trenchcoat and wildly dashed for the office door, leaving Jumaane to sear a hole through Colin's entire existence with a smoldering glare.

A glare that Jumaane held for a full ninety seconds of earsplitting silence as Colin blithely sorted papers on his desk. Sharpened a pencil. Turned his stapler exactly 45 degrees to the left. Sharpened another pencil. Threw both pencils into the trash bin. Made a paper crane.

"So yeah," Colin replied finally. "If you're popping out, I could totally go for a frappachino."

✡ ✡ ✡

"*What is your greatest weakness?*"

It was the worst, most annoying interview question in the world. Like, good lord, man, I did *not* get dressed and come down here to explain why I'm NOT qualified for a retail job.

Like, why do you even ask that? Do you *really* trip that many people up into admitting, "*Well, honestly, I smoke a little bit too much crack cocaine on my lunch breaks*"?

C'mon now.

Now, "*Would you like to check out the stockroom?*"

That was a perfectly normal question for a manager to ask. Particularly when interviewing someone to be a stocker at a shoe store.

But it wasn't the super dark, extremely creepy stockroom that skeeved Ariel out.

No, that would be the mattress—the legit *mattress*—just chilling in the middle of the stockroom floor. With a box of condoms on it. Not all of them unused.

And the manager continuing to conduct the interview as if nothing was wrong. Just talking around the mattress in the middle of the floor, as if it were a perfectly normal thing to have *a fucking mattress in the middle of the floor.*

Of a shoe store. That catered to *teenagers.*

Specifically.

Ariel nope'd the hell right out of there.

Also, he called the police.

✡ ✡ ✡

The second interview went *amazingly.*

The banter, the compatibility, the smiles, the laughs—it was awesome. Better than Ariel could've ever expected. In fact, they were *still* laughing on the elevator ride down together after the interview was over.

The job fit Ariel, Ariel fit the company and—between you and me—Ariel had this in the bag. Hands down.

That was when the interviewer—the male interviewer—turned to him and suddenly asked, "Hey, you want to go to a concert tonight? I've got two tickets. It's John Legend."

"Uh..."

Ariel stalled.

Apparently the interview had gone *too* well and the open position wasn't the only thing the interviewer was trying to fill. Yet another awkward scenario Ariel'd had more experiences with than he'd've liked. It was an occupational hazard of sorts. A perfect storm of misconception, born from the elements of possessing moderately attractive looks, knowledge of what collar stays were, and an aversion to looking as if he'd been dressed by a blind tornado in the dark.

"I'm sorry, but I'm just not into guys," he'd told someone on the subway once, after a compliment on his pinstriped slacks had quickly veered into a desire to see them around his ankles.

"I don't need *you* to be into *guys*," replied a grin with far too many teeth than any human mouth should be able to hold. "I just need *this* guy to be in *you.*

So *that* was a frightening ride home.

Or, as women call it, "Tuesday."

Not that Ariel was a closeminded guy or anything. Far from it actually. He'd be the first to admit that Orlando Bloom as Legolas was an extraordinarily beautiful man, with the pirate Will Turner not too far behind. Ariel was just very firmly #teamhetero.

And so, not being a character in an Adam Sandler rom-com, he needed to nip this misunderstanding in the bud.

"Look, sir, I...," he began. "I have some really close friends who are gay. But I don't—that's uh, that's not me. Completely flattered though."

A moment of tense silence followed, as Ariel could feel the job slipping away from him like sand through a grate.

"Um..." it was his maybe potential boss' turn. "I wasn't asking you out. I'd planned to go with my wife tonight for our anniversary, but we had an unexpected change of plans. So I have two tickets I'm trying to get rid of. Figured you might want them."

"Ah. Oh. Well. Um. Uh—"

The elevator doors opened.

"Well," said Ariel, in a strangled voice, fiddling with his tie as he tried to casually save face. "Thank you for the opportunity."

The interviewer extended a reluctant hand and Ariel, all out of sorts, stuck out the wrong hand in response and ended up just grabbing the back of his definitely-not future boss' hand the same way you would grab your significant other's hand.

Of course, he still bobbed it up and down like a handshake, because I have no damn idea.

It probably didn't help in the slightest that after the awkward goodbye, Ariel and his interviewer continued walking in the same direction in silence for another excruciating block and a half.

Then Ariel couldn't take it anymore, ducked into a Starbucks, and ended up having to stand on line in front of his never in a million years boss for another eight minutes.

And Ariel didn't even *drink* coffee.

✡ ✡ ✡

The third interview didn't even happen.

Because once Ariel walked into the lobby and saw Maybe Kinda Rapey manager from his first interview sitting in the waiting area, he wisely concluded that whatever job was being offered probably wasn't for him.

Also, he called the police.

Nine interviews and two weeks later, something finally bit for Ariel. It was retail, but a floor manager position for an outlet in Lower Manhattan. They wanted him to start that coming Monday.

In celebration, Jumaane and Colin—mostly Jumaane, unsurprisingly—decided to treat Ariel to lunch at one of the many overpriced kosher lunch spots Midtown had to offer.

"Alright, Ari!" Jumaane beamed, clapping Ariel on the shoulder as they stood on line. "Welcome back to Jobland!"

"Yep. And as always," Colin pointed out, perpetually texting as always. "I come through for you guys."

"Um, excuse me?" Jumaane corrected. "Sending Ari that job was *my* effort. You've *never* come through for us. Not *once* in the past seven years have you actually contributed something to this 'friendship' you swear we all have."

"Bullshit," Colin looked up from his phone in challenge. "Name *one* time that I didn't come through for either one of you guys."

"Well," Ariel began. "That time I had to take the subway home drunk because you wouldn't drive me, and I woke up in the trainyard with no pockets..."

"Oh!" Jumaane chimed in. "And the time I literally broke my ass at that danger party and you just laughed and hung up when I asked you for a ride to the hospital."

"Yeah, see," Colin asserted. "Those don't count. And the reason they don't count is because they involved my car, and my car is like my man: Only *I* get to be inside."

Ariel and Jumaane just looked at Colin, perplexed.

Probably the same look you've been wearing since a sentence ago when you realized that Colin is gay. Because you've probably had it built in your head that it was *obviously* a female he was verbally abusing over the phone, right?

Well I hope you're proud of yourself while you're reading this and sipping on your half-caf/half-decaf internalized misogyny latte topped with whipped patriarchy and a nice and toasty rape culture scone on the side.

"Do you ever hear yourself speak?" Jumaane said finally. "Like, actually listen to the words?"

"I'm too busy living my truth," Colin replied as they reached the counter. "Hey," he said to the cashier. "We're here for a pick-up order? Number 2812? Already paid for."

The cashier checked the pickup table, plucked up three brown bags and handed them over the counter to Colin, who began handing them out. Ariel took his and, distracted by looking in the bag, immediately crashed right into the person behind him, causing them to spill a cup of unidentified liquid all over themselves.

*Her*selves, actually.

"Oh, I'm so sorry!" Ariel apologized, immediately grabbing some napkins off the counter next to him to help clean up the mess, momentarily oblivious to the fact that doing so would involve some *extremely* inappropriate contact with a very female stranger's very female chest. "Here, let me help—"

Her hands shot up instantly as she stepped back.

"No, no, don't worry about it," replied a British-ish voice, just as Ariel recognized its owner as his half-a-second blue-haired crush from half a month ago. "I forgot to water them this morning anyway...Oh, *you*," she realized. "514 guy. From the other day."

"Yeah, hi! Also, I'm *really* sorry."

"It's okay," she shrugged, then jerked her head over Ariel's shoulder with a smirk. "And if you're with these two jokers I guess you found your way."

"Hey, what's up," Jumaane greeted her, familiarly. "Yeah, he's the new meat."

"So I can see," she eyed Ariel's *kippah*. "Glatt kosher, too."

"Nice," Ariel laughed at the joke, doing something stupid with his face. Y'know, that stupid thing guys do with their face when they're talking to a girl they like. "I'm Ariel. My friends call me Ari."

"Insert snarky comment here," she smirked again.

"Ha! Lol!" Ariel's face instantly scrunched in disbelief at having just enunciated "el-oh-el" out loud. In a conversation. With a real live person.

"Right. Anyhoo," she directed her attention to Jumaane and Colin. "You guys have any new bites on that writing position?"

"What's wrong with the last guy we sent?" Colin asked, while Jumaane muttered "the last guy *you* sent" under his breath. "He isn't working out?"

"He's...just really weird. Like, unhealthily so."

"Alright," Jumaane chimed in. "We'll keep an eye out.""Thanks..." she looked at Ariel. "You write, Kosher Meat?"

"I do! I mean, I'd love to," Ariel piped up, acutely regretting that he'd accepted the outlet's offer now. "But I start a thing on Monday. It's pretty much fulltime."

It was completely fulltime. Ariel was just trying to keep a door possibly cracked open maybe.

"Aw, too bad," she shrugged, echoing her sentiment from when they first met. "Anyway, lemme go grab lunch. I guess I'll see you guys around the building, yeah?"

Both Jumaane and Colin offered versions of "Yeah, take it easy."

"Well it was nice meeting you," Ariel concluded with a half wave.

"It was, wasn't it?" she said with a mischievous twinkle in her eye.

"Ha! I *like* you."

"Oh, they all do at first."

✡ ✡ ✡

The four of them—Ariel, Jumaane, Colin, and Ilan—were outside sitting on the benches near the Rockefeller skating rink, eating their shwarma disapprovingly, and very obviously ignoring the elephant in the room of Ariel's romantically piqued interest.

"...So, uh," Ariel said into his food, pretending not to notice the coy smirks on Jumaane and Colin's faces. Well, Jumaane's face anyway. Colin was texting and Ilan was kinda spaced out. "The girl from earlier. What's her deal?"

"Yeah that's, I think her name is Lacey or something?" Jumaane answered. "Anyway, she works for the studio that owns a couple of floors in the building. Run into her on the elevator all the time...Why?" came the sly smile. "You thinking of making her PC4?"

"Wow, really? Are we seriously still on that? And, no, I am *not* doing that again...And technically she'd only be PC3, anyways."

Jumaane chuckled conspiratorially.

"Alright man," he shrugged, breezily. "I'm just saying, your pool is so shallow you'd have to stand up to drown."

Ariel rolled his eyes and turned to Colin.

"C'mon," Ariel braced himself. "Let's get *your* snarky zinger over with."

"No, I'm...I'm really just trying to figure out why this all cost so much," Colin answered.

"I *told* you guys kosher was expensive," Ariel reminded.

"Seriously," Jumaane agreed. "What is up with that?"

"Are there, like, bits of Moses in it or something?" Colin continued. "Because I'm not sure why I paid twelve dollars for dry bread full of grass, weirdly spicy ass-meat, and white sauce."

"Actually, this place just makes really bad shwarma," Ilan explained.

"And when the hell did *you* get here?" Colin shot at Ilan.

"Dude, can't we just get you to bless a White Castle or something?" Jumaane asked.

"Guys," Ariel groaned. "*Again*, kosher doesn't mean blessed by a rabbi."

"So what *does* kosher mean, then?" Colin challenged.

"Well," Ariel started. "There's kosher animals and non-kosher ani—"

"Ooh!" Ilan jumped in. "I remember this! Kosher fish have fins and scales, kosher animals have cloven hooves and chew their cud. No pig because it doesn't chew the cud, but—"

"What the hell is a cud?" Jumaane asked.

"So," Ariel explained. "Some animals have four stomachs, so when they eat they have to swallow the food then spit it back up, and then re-chew and swallow it again to—"

"What the fu—No," Colin stood up, hands raised over his head as he let his shwarma bounce off his lap and drop to the floor. "This is bullshit. Charging me twelve dollars to eat something that vomits in its own mouth?"

"Is *that* what that taste is?" Jumaane examined his lunch at arm's length in disgust.

"Well, if you just—"

"I'm not 'justing' *anything*," Colin insisted. "I'm gonna go get some *American* fucking food that—"

"Ellis!" Jumaane suddenly blurted out.

"*What* does Ellis Island have anything to—"

"Omig'd, shut up Colin," Jumaane shot back, then turned to Ariel. "The *girl*. Her name is Ellis."

Enter Ellis.

Well, *again*. Because, as it turns out, I *am* one of those unreliable omniscient narrators from English Lit or biblical criticism.

Busted.

But something very much reliable was the fact that Ariel didn't have the best track record with girls.

It started, he supposed, when all the girls at synagogue in his age group mysteriously disappeared once he was about fifteen, kinda like that line in *The Magnificent Seven* when Steve McQueen is all, *"I've been in towns where the girls weren't pretty and some where they're downright ugly. But this is the first time I've seen a town where there are no girls at all."*

In Ariel's line of, well, existence, he learned to take hints very early on and very quickly. And he pretty swiftly got that hint:

"Sure, you can pray with us, but we don't really want our daughters bringing you home."

Not that he'd necessarily *wanted* any of their daughters, mind you. But it would've been nice (and a helluva lot less racist) to have the option of stating who he did or didn't want to pursue, as opposed to being told what he didn't get to have.

Luckily enough for his self-esteem, while Ariel thought Judy Garland, Carly Rae Jepsen, and Aileen Quinn were just fine, he was more of a Diana Ross, Keke Palmer, and Quvenzhane Wallis kinda guy, anyway. His eventual exes, accordingly, were all black and beautiful—a rich range of maple to walnut to golden oak that would make any carpenter jealous.

Incidentally, however, none of them were Jewish.

Which is *massively* incongruous, he was aware.

Particularly since marrying Jewish was a strongly held personal non-negotiable for him.

But the thing is, his mom wasn't Jewish when his dad had started dating her. In fact, his mom wouldn't convert until just a year before his parents got married, three whole years after they'd started a relationship.

Not that she'd converted *for* his dad—no, she'd been on her own religious journey when they'd crossed paths. His dad just happened to help his mom discover the path that fit her in all the ways that Christianity, Islam, Kemetism, and Buddhism didn't.

So it felt weirdly hypocritical to Ariel to cross a girl out of the picture just because she wasn't Jewish.

Yet.

After all, it was just dating, and if his dad'd had that mindset Ariel might've never been born. And so, with that in mind, Ariel had ended up dating the "Parade of PCs."

"PC" meaning "potential convert."

Yeah, I know. The name wasn't his idea.

Jumaane and Colin had lovingly created the term back when Ariel was dating his second non-Jewish girlfriend in college.

Christina had been her name. They'd only lasted about three months.

You'd think, just by common sense alone, that Ariel would've realized that it wasn't ever going to work out between Orthodox Jewish him and a girl with "Christ" literally *right* there in her name.

But alas.

Ariel's first college girlfriend—first girlfriend *period*, actually—had been Gabrielle.

She'd come before Dana or Christina. Before Jumaane or Colin, even.

She'd been retroactively dubbed PCP—"Potential Convert: The Prequel"—once Ariel's friends had recognized his pathological and masochistic dating patterns.

Manishtana

He and Gabrielle were freshmen taking a children's literature class, and—this really being the only thing they knew about each other—they spent their first date sharing their favorite childhood songs. Ariel's was "Baa Baa Black Sheep." She countered with "Little Bunny Foo Foo."

"*'Little Bunny Foo Foo hopping through the forest, jerking off the field mice and giving them lots of head.'*"

"...We had very different childhoods, you and I."

She was a *really* good person. That sincere, kind-hearted kind of person straight out of a late-90's inspirational email.

It's just that she...well...

"I really don't understand why people talk so much about passing the bar like it's a big deal. So you passed the bar. Big whoop. Just turn back around. Also, GPS is a thing."

Yeah...

But Ariel pretty much spent the entire relationship awestruck that someone had actually been interested in him—like actual *him*, Ariel the Person, not "that black Jewish kid" or "that black guy with the light eyes."

And Sweet Moses' Beard was she gorgeous. A cheerleader, even.

That might seem creepily fetishizing, but let's remember our boy had spent his nascent years of puberty in an all-boys Jewish day school, and was still recovering from a high school career of being Ariel S. D. Samson, First of his Name, Keeper of Anime, Reader of Comics, Long may he geek.

And with the self-confidence and social skills to match.

The entire realm of physical contact, needless to say, was a whole new world for him.

Ariel was a hugger, true, but even as a kid he'd never been big on *being* touched. So when, in a moment of house-party giddiness, Gabrielle had hugged him—and he *didn't* feel the urge to tear her arms off and beat her to death with them—he realized that there just might be something there.

He wasn't ashamed to say that he got his first kiss at almost twenty, but he also wasn't proud to say that he first broke being **shomer negiah** at almost twenty. Nothing besides cuddling and makeout sessions—and never, Heaven forfend, mixed dancing—but still.

ARIEL SAMSON: FREELANCE RABBI

When a girl that looks and smells as good as Gabrielle did ends up on your arm, somehow that whole *"I'm not supposed to touch girls I'm not married to"* deal flies right the hell out of your head. Along with the knowledge that "Stop, Drop & Roll" doesn't work in Hell.

With all that cognitive dissonance and low self-esteemyness and pheromoniness bouncing around in his head, Ariel honestly didn't even notice that Gabrielle—as she once put it—was often not the "sharpest pool in the shed" until after they'd broken up.

Which happened after about six months, when she thought Ariel was making fun of her intelligence by using the word "hierophant" during a game of Scrabble.

"I might not be as smart as you, Ariel, but you can't just *make up* animals because you don't think I'd know the difference!"

Sooo...that was the end of that. (In other news, three weeks later Gabrielle would discover that a gazebo was not, in fact, a species of antelope that roamed the African savannah and grasslands. Mind. Blown.)

After Gabrielle came the aforementioned Christina. She was PC1. The originator of the PC label. She and Ariel had started out as lab partners in their core Chemistry class, and from there they got paired together in a study group for the final. Somewhere in there they ended up deciding to test out some chemistry of their own. And they couldn't have gotten together in a worse season.

Every. Single. Month. Had been a minefield.

Ariel spent November explaining that celebrating Thanksgiving raised questions about Leviticus 18:3 forbidding Jews from imitating non-Jewish customs, and while rabbis Moshe Feinstein and Joseph Soloveitchik had concluded that Thanksgiving was *not* a religious holiday, Rabbi Yitzchak Hutner ruled that the establishment of a holiday based on the Christian/Gregorian calendar was closely tied to idol worship and thusly prohibited, and so even though some American Jews *did* celebrate Thanksgiving, there was a very real issue of adding holidays to the and your eyes have glazed over and you've completely stopped reading at this point, haven't you?

It's okay. So did I.

With the advent of Christmas, the self-professed "non-denominational, don't-go-to-church, not-really-religious" girl Ariel had been dating for the past seven weeks, suddenly became a Bible-warrior Battle-Christian™ that December.

And so came the argument that not only did Jews not believe in Jesus as the Messiah, but that according to Luke 3:27, Matthew 1:11-12, Chronicles I 3:15-17, and Jeremiah 22:24-30, Jesus...Actually, y'know what, let's just say that conversation didn't go over well.

January was the revelation that not only was January 1st the religious holiday of Sylvester—named after Pope Sylvester who died on December 31st—but it was also historically a day when anti-Semitic decrees were promulgated against Jewish citizens in many European countries, sanctioning centuries of innocent Jewish bloodshed.

Heads dropping>ball dropping.

But it was February that was the final straw, during which Ariel had declined to celebrate Valentine's Day—*Saint* Valentine's Day—but was genuinely looking forward to celebrating their relationship on the Jewish Valentine's Day of **Tu b'Av**.

Which is in the summer.

Where a Valentine's Day makes sense.

Because seriously, whose genius idea was it to place a holiday celebrating passion, romance, and love in the dead of winter's cold, cold heart?

Idiot.

Finally, there was Dana.

Dana J. Davis, a.k.a, PC2, a.k.a., four years of Ariel's life.

A.k.a, Ariel's ex-fiancee.

They'd met in of one of those My-First-Social-Activism™ type college groups that rile up depressed undergrads half a GPA-point away from academic probation into feeling like they can make a difference by stopping the homeless, hugging the environment, or punching cancer. (I was briefly part of the Stop the Homeless campaign, myself.)

At any given time between classes, you'd find either Ariel, or Dana, or both, down in the club's subterranean office—home to assorted board games, two whiteboards covered more often than not in audaciously cringeworthy Xanga-era poetry, and a grungy army-green couch drenched with enough decades-old remnants of sexytimes that you'd wake up pregnant if you fell asleep on it. And there, Dana and Ariel just kinda...clicked.

In the office. Not on the couch.

She was smart. Cute. *Genuinely* funny. And she had *such* a contagious laugh.

Luckily, Ariel was a junior now, and had finally shed his former socially-awkward self, and begun evolving into something resembling his present socially-awkward self.

They'd hang out for hours together, and soon enough they started seeing each other more and more outside of the context of standing in the rain shouting at faceless corporations (who'd long since gone home for the day), or leaving pestering voicemails in councilmen's inboxes demanding that they not raise tuition (on classes they spent most of the semester not going to *anyway*).

They waited for each other after classes, lay on the campus grass chatting on the Quad, had all kinds of inside jokes that wouldn't ever be funny to anyone else, and spent huge chunks of time playing Uno in the cafeteria long after all the food stations had closed up for the night.

And during it all, there were these times when Ariel was *so* close to asking her out—like right on the tip of his tongue—but he just didn't for some reason. Like, in the moment he just couldn't find the words or something. I dunno.

And neither did he.

One of those times was when Ariel and Dana discovered that they were both virgins. Like, legit *intentional* virgins, not those poser-virgins but for the lack of opportunity, with their cheap NYC Subway condoms eagerly awaiting deployment from their wallets.

But then, one late night when they were playing Uno in the deserted cafeteria as usual, as Ariel was one card away from winning the game, he just blurted out:

"DanaIreallylikeyouandIthinkyou'resuperfunandsexyashellanda reyouseeinganybodybecauseIwannadateyou. Uno."

Ariel laid his card down, a yellow zero, heart pounding in his ears, and Dana's already large brown eyes widened further than the rules of biology and physics rightfully allow.

And then she lit. Into. Ariel.

"What the *fuck*, Ari? That's a *terrible* way to ask someone out! Like, how do you *do* that? Why would you even *say* that?" she shrieked.

"Sorry! I'm sorry!"

Eyebrows furrowed, she threw a stack of multicolored Draw Twos at him, barking "Draw!"

Ariel drew his cards, feeling himself crawl up inside himself, wondering if he'd just totally screwed up a really cool friendship and Uno partner.

And then he realized...that she hadn't exactly said *"No."*

An excruciating three minutes of gameplay crawled by as he wondered if she was too angry to remember that she hadn't answered the question, or whether she was pretending he hadn't asked at all, graciously opting to leave the explicit *"Hell,* no" understood but unspoken.

"And by the way, yes, I *am* seeing somebody," she said finally. "I'm seeing *you.* Uno out."

She tossed three Skips and one red one on the table, beaming at Ariel, and the rest as they say, was history.

And it literally was. Because after that three-month honeymoon period—filled with all the montage-worthy cutesy stuff like making their relationship Facebook official, meeting each other's parents and friends, going on dates on Ferris wheels, talking in nonsense baby-talk—that's when things got a little tense.

"I'm, well, kinda Christian-ish and you're Jewish. Like, *really* Jewish. How is this really gonna work?"

Ariel didn't really give it that much thought, but he did say straight up that he couldn't marry her if she wasn't Jewish.

He wasn't trying to fool or mislead anybody about anything. But they were just dating right now, he pointed out, so why sweat it? They were both still in college and nowhere near ready to even *think* about the marriage stage yet. Ariel figured they'd jump off that bridge when they got to it. In the meantime, they could just enjoy being in a relationship with a smart person whose face they liked and who they liked making out with and wasn't going to pressure or guilt them into trying to have sex.

Dana saw the logic in that, and found the terms amenable.

And so they resumed, but not quite the same as before. Because now there was this invisible timer over their relationship, the countdown ticking faster the closer they got to graduation and the real world. And in that time Ariel came to understand that Dana was smart, yeah, but she was also really immature.

Actually, that's not fair. They were *both* really immature. And really bad at dealing with the mounting pressures of their academic lives, their families, and their relationship.

Their first breakup was Ariel's guilt-stricken call.

For "her good," he'd told her, which was true. From his point-of-view. Why should she even have to contemplate navigating a disapproving Catholic family to convert to a religion and denomination that wasn't exactly the friendliest on the block?

Ariel was *from* that side of the block. He *knew*.

The second breakup was Dana's resentful call.

It was "unfair," she'd felt, that she was willing to make all the religious compromises but Ariel wasn't. And Ariel, for his part, wasn't sure how, didn't really have the language to convey, that despite what other Jewishes believed, for *his* Jewish, these weren't optional things to be compromised on. That he couldn't compromise in his relationship to G'd anymore than he could compromise in his relationship with Dana.

"Hey, so you know how we've been dating for a while? Yeah, so I'm also gonna be seeing this other girl too. But don't worry, I'll only be hooking up with her on Tuesdays and Thursdays. Deal?"

Like to see how *that* conversation would've worked.

Honestly, their relationship was *already* a precarious enough compromise.

Sure, they didn't kiss until an hour had passed since she'd eaten non-kosher food, and sure they went to the odd Halloween or Christmas party, and sure the sex thing was off the table (even though, for two virgins, they ironically ended up getting a lot closer to The Sex with each other than they'd ever had with anyone else before) but, c'mon, they were *both* fooling each other if they didn't think they weren't loopholing and semanticizing the *ahem* "bejesus" out of everything.

And so it began.

Every few months they'd trade off. They'd fight over little things. Then they'd start hurling around the hurtful things. Then they'd get around to the thing they were *really* fighting about (*"It's not about eating the last damn Oreo, Ariel! This is about us!"*)

And then they'd reach an impasse.

They'd break up, Ariel would switch off his phone, Dana'd cry herself to sleep, and in a couple of weeks they'd be back together again. Until their penultimate break, when everything changed.

Maɳishtaɳa

They were having their ritual "preconciliation" conversation in a Starbucks near campus when Dana's phone rang and Ariel noticed the name "Rabbi Bluth" pop up on the screen.

"Who's that?"

"Oh...I...I, uh, started taking conversion classes."

And with that, Ariel, obviously, was over the moon.

Did the last break up—their first "post-graduation, in the real world" spat—spook her into making that step? Did all of their theological conversations illuminate a path for her the same way his dad's had for his mom? Didn't know. And Ariel didn't care. He was just glad to have finally cleared that insurmountable hurdle, and now they were in the home stretch about to make the touchdown. No, Ariel didn't sports very well.

Also no, not everybody shared Ariel's enthusiasm.

"I dunno, man," Jumaane said warily. "She's Jamaican, Ari. She'll want *real* dancehall, not that Matisyahu bullshit. And dutty wining to the **hora** doesn't look cute."

But Ariel ignored Jumaane's doubts.

Kept ignoring them as Dana would sometimes miss her conversion classes because she forgot. Or had a scheduling conflict. Or had a friend coming into town that she hadn't seen in a while.

Or was just tired and blew it off.

Or decided she needed to start going to a different rabbi.

Or a different one after that.

Or...

✡ ✡ ✡

"Look, Dana...We need to talk..."

"Oh hell, no. *Why*? What—"

"Because our relationship hasn't been right for a while now, and the way I see it, there's only one way to fix it."

"Ariel Samson. If you took me all the way out to a bar in Lower Manhattan to break up with me—*AGAIN* —I swear that—"

She stopped, dazzled by the ring.

24-carat white gold band, because she hated yellow. Cubic zirconium stone, because she didn't want to be any part of the blood diamond life-cycle. Princess-cut, because she harbored an unnatural attraction to squares.

"So. Whaddaya say?" Ariel asked triumphantly with a touch of smugness.

She was speechless at first, then started crying. Then she hit him. *Then* she said yes.

"Omig'd," she said a few breathless seconds after letting him slip the ring on her finger, wiping tears from her eyes. "I totally thought I was getting dumped in a bar."

"Hon, this was where we had our first *date* date."

"I know...I just, I thought you were trying to soften the blow. End it full circle, y'know?"

"Well, no. One, if I were going to end it full circle, I'd be doing it over an Uno game. Two, this way it's a win-win. You say no, I order a Jack and Coke and drink it off. You say yes, I order *two* Jack and Cokes and we celebrate."

"You're such an ass."

"This is a true fact...Also, I hope you're killing it in those conversion classes. Would hate for you to be a **rebbetzin** and not know anything..."

"For me to—Ari, what did you do?"

"Oh nothing...Just found out today that I got accepted to rabbinical school. Fourteen months from now I'll be *Rabbi* Ariel Samson."

"*WHAT? OMIG'D*, that's *amazing!* And you'd be *so good* at it! Omig'd, Ari. OMIG'D!"

They spent the rest of the night enjoying themselves more than they had in a *long*, long time. And as they sat on the train home, her head slumped on his shoulder as she happily snored, Ariel finally felt that pit in his stomach. The one he'd been ignoring all night, all week, all month long.

Since he picked up the ring.

Since he submitted his application to Shaar HaTorah Theological Seminary.

See, the thing is, Ariel knew Dana wasn't the one. He knew.

But...they'd been together for four years now. And, aside from the religious part, they got along *so* well together. She laughed at even his stupidest jokes. He loved spending even the littlest amount of time with her. And if this was where they still were, four years later...then Ariel didn't know if he believed there *was* a one anymore.

Maybe this was it. And if it was, then he'd *make* her the one.

He wanted—*needed*—her to be so much that he convinced himself that she obviously *had* to be.

If she needed incentive, then sure: One order of marriage with a side of rabbi's wife, coming right up. Would you like fries with that? Regular plain Yiddish *rebbetzin* or spicy Cajun Hebrew **rabbanit?**

He'd even be starting grad school that fall, so potentially boosted income was on the table, too.

Everything was all in Dana's court now.

Besides (and less romantically) four years was a significant time investment and deep sunk costs. If he got out now, he'd have to admit that she was the wrong one to everyone who'd been saying that from the get go. He'd have to start over, and endure another bunch of years wandering the scarce wilderness of black Jewish folk, or black folk who didn't mind being Jewish, or, even worse, the **shidduch** system.

[Shudder]

Not exactly appealing options.

Not after he'd fought the whole world for her. Fought his friends and family for her. Fought himself. Fought his logic and his brain and just followed his stupid stupid heart.

And then to have to tell them all about their breakup afterward?

Nope, not happening.

And yes, it took a couple of years, but Ariel eventually came to realize that every last piece of all that rationale and motivation was disgustingly condescendingly paternalistic and selfish and dickish and—as I established before—*really* damn immature, and that he didn't have any excuses for any of it, really.

Just apologies Dana was never going to hear, in words he was too embarrassed to say to her anyway.

Sometimes, Ariel eventually admitted to himself, you have to just own when you're wrong and stand there in your wrongness.

✡ ✡ ✡

The end began with a harmless fight, as such things usually do.

Just the usual bickering over petty little things. But then it turned serious. Of course, it had always just been a matter of time before they imploded for the last time. Apparently that time was now. They'd given it a good go, but they'd reached the end of this rope, and it was time to hang themselves with it.

"This isn't how we were supposed to be, Dana."

"No, *really*? Did—"

She looked at him. At his face. And she realized that this would be the last time they'd be doing this.

"What are you saying Ariel?"

"I...I wanted this. I really did. But *this*? Us? It's broken. And we can't fix it. I..."

"...It's broken."

Yeah, it is. I'm sorry.

"...Mhm...mhm...So...How long have you felt this way?"

About a year and a half now. After our last break up.

"Wow. Eight months we've been engaged. Eight. Months. And you're telling me you've felt like this for almost *two years*?"

Hdhgf kjjl qap nvmnde lmcnbvo. Tgerp...tdgdkl frkop, erto, askopjaf.

"If you've been feeling *that* unsure for the last two years, why didn't you ever *say* anything? Why didn't you ever *talk* to me? Ariel, *why did you propose to me in the first place?*"

Kpodnfp bnehi dgbsprh n cdlhd. Qaswpgjk gfklj d kjfgkl dh kdflz, wtmfit pdnwc yd odgf xocks.

"'*Because we'd been together for so*'—Are you fucking *kidding* me? A *relationship* isn't an *endurance sport,* Ariel!"

Gdfpcn—fki y xvfd odgvdlcm bjk—cjlrmc, dtaplmcic...vaplxnr ic dwmd.

"Wow...I am just such a fool. *Wow*...I was gonna change my whole relationship with *G'd* for you. And I barely even talk to Him as it *is*!"

"Oh please, don't give me that shit. Don't give me that you-didn't-want-me-to-convert-for-you bullshit when you *know* damn well you did and *damn* well that was probably the only reason I was. Niggas be *lying* to themselves."

"Just...just don't say anything else Ariel. You're fucking me up right now. Goodbye. Here's your ring."

"I *know* I can fucking keep it! I don't *want* it! *Here's* your fucking *ring*. And just, just lose everything. My number, my email, my name, my face, all of it. Forget you ever even knew me, Ariel Samson...Because I know *I* damn will."

And that's how Ariel and Dana's engagement, relationship, and friendship crashed and burned spectacularly.

If I were the writer of the Next Great American Novel, I'd probably say something pithy here like, "Sometimes I think that their real enemy was time. They met at a point in their lives when they were heading in completely different directions. They just *looked* like they were on the same track for a little bit. Like the 2 and 5 trains between Nevins St. and Brooklyn College/Flatbush Avenue."

But the truth is that Ariel was simply a 21-25 year-old asshole, dragging an innocent bystander through his existential ethno-religious romantic crisis. And Dana really didn't deserve that.

Ariel knew that. He lived in his head.

Sometimes *he* didn't even deserve it.

So if you're out there Dana J. Davis, Ariel just wants you to know that he thinks you guys had some really great times together, and it feels special when he thinks about them even now. It might only be inside his own head, but he completely credits you for a lot of amazing things that he's learned, and your good habits that rubbed off on him. He wishes you the best of luck in life, and hopes you find the greatest happiness and keep it.

And that he's really sorry.

P.S., he hasn't played Uno since.

Jumaane'd ended up being right, of course, but he never once told Ariel "I told you so."

Which Ariel appreciated.

However, he also decided to give some advice. Which Ariel didn't appreciate as much.

"Look, man," Jumaane advised a few weeks and a few drinks after the breakup. "Just bag some hot regular Jewish chick and call it a day."

"And here we go again..." Ariel sighed.

"Ariel. You're telling me that if a hot-ass white Orthodox Jewish chick came up to you and said, '*Ari, I want you to hava my negila with your kosher Mandingo meat,*' you'd say no?"

"First: *What?* Second: No. That's just not what I'm into. I'm black and Jewish. I'm looking for black and Jewish."

"So you're either gonna wait for some mythical black Jewish hottie, or make one yourself?" Jumaane shook his head. "Look, bruh, I'm all for that good good black love, but c'mon now."

"If I can exist, then she can exist."

"I've seen a two-headed cat once, too," Jumaane pointed out. "But I'd look like a mothafuckin idiot saying *'Well, I saw a two-headed cat once, so I should be able to find one in a pet shop.'* But, y'know...do you."

Ariel shrugged, all nonchalant-like, and knocked back another shot.

But his entire subway ride home the conversation with Jumaane bounced around in his head, replaying over and over and over again. And he was *really* of tired of people telling him who he could or couldn't or should or shouldn't be looking for. What was or wasn't "realistic." That patronizing way they inserted their opinion disguised as concern for his happiness because "you're limiting your options."

Like, Ariel tolerated it well enough from other people. The people who didn't know him that well, who didn't understand that he equally valued his religion *and* his blackness. But it was really ~~so fucking hurtful~~ irritating when a friend as close as Jumaane just didn't get it.

Look, whatever.

Just...whatever.

But as his train pulled into his stop and he got off, Ariel came to the resolution that he was done wasting years of his life on the off chance that the next girl may or may not convert.

He'd spent over half a decade holding his breath that "black" would eventually morph into "and Jewish, too." He saw now that he needed to either actively look for "black and Jewish," or just wait it out until it came along.

Which is why, almost two years later, he was particularly excited to accept Kalman's invitation to Shabbat dinner.

"Ari? What are you doing here?"

He turned at the voice to see Dassi Meltzer, Kalman's wife, standing in the aisle behind him at the Trader Joe's in Union Square, bright green eyes full of surprise against her peach-hued skin.

"Oh hey! I'm just...on my lunch break."

That was a lie.

He was actually in the city because he was catching a matinee showing of *The Peanuts Movie*. Because something about Charlie Brown's ne'er do well escapades just spoke to him inside his awkward awkward soul.

But he hadn't expected to run into Dassi, so he wasn't prepared to execute his planned lie of watching the new super-testosteroney Daniel Craig-James Bond *Spectre* movie, now with 15% more rugged masculinity.

"You're definitely coming tonight for Shabbos right?"

"Oh definitely. Which is," he checked his watch. It was 1:45. "Yikes. In like two and half hours."

"Ugh, I know. I hate these winter Shabbosim."

"Shabbatot. Anyway, yeah, I'll be there. Just picking up some last-minute stuff here, then I'm off."

"Yay! Semi-random note: are you seeing anybody?"

"Semi-random note is semi-random. And no, not really. Went on a couple dates with this one girl about a year ago, but it didn't really go anywhere. *Probably* didn't help that my sister said she looked like something I drew with my left hand."

"Ouch," Dassi cringed, and a few more errant reddish-brown hairs spilled out from underneath her crocheted kerchief. "Well, when you come by for Shabbos, I have someone coming who would *totally* be great for you."

"Oh, uh, ok. What's her deal?"

"Well she's, y'know. She's black."

Ariel waited for more.

There wasn't any.

There never was in this sort of conversation.

Just a stare of hopeful excitement for a gold star, like a pre-schooler who's literally just learned how to match colors.

And, to his memory, for the first time ever, Ariel's inside thoughts became outside thoughts.

"Oh. So she has skin. That should make for good conversation."

Dassi's jaw dropped and her hands flew up defensively with an awkward laugh, good-naturedly mortified as a flush crept up her face.

"No, I didn't mean—I just—I meant I went to seminary with her, and I just get the feeling that, I dunno, that you guys would be a great fit. Like, just something about her."

"Oh, well *that's* cool then. I guess it can't hurt. This Shabbat it is."

"Great," Dassi grinned in relief, still mentally kicking herself, Ariel was sure.

The conversation then meandered off into time-filler small-talk until they checked their items out. And Ariel played it cool the whole time.

But five minutes later, he was practically skipping all the way to the train station in spite of himself, feeling so giddy that he didn't even *care* that he'd just spent the equivalent of his monthly student loan interest on a tub of organic, free-trade, vegan, conflict-free, low-carb, soy-free, grass-fed, antibiotics-free, non-GMO, free-range, free-free hummus.

Nope. Nuh-uh.

Because every step he took was a step further away from the bench that he'd been warming quite evenly for the past two years, and one step closer to being up at bat again.

And it had come out of *nowhere*, too!

Like—the brief foray into the theoretical possibility of Ellis aside—Ariel hadn't even *glanced* into the realm of the romantic since breaking up with Dana.

Just throwing himself into his studies, work, and fun times with the boys, riding out the twilight years of his twenties like some rogue socially anxious stallion.

But now *this*? This new mystery-meet who was black *and* already Jewish, *too*?

Ariel was so beside himself in anticipation that it was almost as if he'd learned absolutely nothing about why his past relationships had all failed.

And by "almost," I mean "exactly."

Because he was still just waiting for an "it" to come along.

Not a "she."

That, after all, had been Jumaane's subtle point during his post-Dana breakup pep talk: "*Who*" did Ariel want to be in a relationship with?

Because "black" and "Jewish" were "*whats.*"

And if Ariel hadn't really defined anything for himself besides those two superficialities, then why was he so insistent on them?

But maybe Jumaane'd made his point *too* subtly, because it clearly wasn't registering in Ariel's brain to ask himself about what *else* was important.

Her body type? Her eye color? Did he want her to like anime? Comics? Did he want her to catch that *FFX* "Zanarkand" joke from four chapters ago? Straight-edge? 420-friendly?

Also, what *kind* of black was he looking for? Hillary from *Fresh Prince of Bel-Air* black? Sam White in *Dear White People* black? Nia Long in *The Best Man* black?

What kind of Jewish? Self-identified as Orthodox Jewish? Orthoprax Jewish? **Shomer mitzvot** Jewish? Secular Jewish? **Charedi** Jewish? **Yeshivish** Jewish? Chabad **Meshichist** (*ptuh-ptuh-ptuh*) Jewish?

What about politics? Liberal? Conservative? Moderate? Zionist? Anti-Zionist? Not-Zionist?

Saying *"I'm looking for a black Jewish girl"* was like walking into a Chinese restaurant and going *"I want to eat something with noodles."*

It was a statement so non-descript that the result could only ever be you ending up either hungry or disappointed.

And one of those definitely happened at Kalman and Dassi's table that night.

✡ ✡ ✡

It was a very packed, very interesting Shabbat table at the Meltzers.

"Very packed" because it was a comfy closet of a two-bedroom apartment with a table meant for six, but was seating eight.

"Very interesting" because there were two rambunctious characters in attendance who were the physical embodiment of sound and fury signifying nothing.

The kind of shallow, insecure hedge fund **ModOx** 20-somethings who come to Shabbat dressed like it's the club, and spend the entire time mingling in the hallway during the rabbi's sermon.

Between their rayon suits just as shiny and stiff as their sculpted hair, and their overstarched, inappropriately low-buttoned shirts with the monogrammed cuffs, it seemed like their every movement was accompanied by a full 90-piece orchestra composed solely of potato chip bags, sandpaper, and rustling leaves.

The rest of the table was occupied by Dassi—who'd traded in her weekday kerchief and messy curls for a glossy pixie-cut *sheitel*, Chaya—Dassi's doppelganger of a little sister, with the same olive eyes, peach skin, and auburn locks, Dovid and Nosson—the aforementioned windbags with matching Ritz cracker tans that were Chaya's husband and brother-in-law, respectively, and Tamar—a quiet coppery redhead with pale, freckle-mottled skin like a dusting of cinnamon over French vanilla frosting, and wearing a perpetually pensive expression.

As for the object of Ariel's anticipation—one Rivka, by name— she had yet to show up, but had considerately already given Kalman and Dassi the go ahead to start *kiddish* without her.

Because, again, CPT and JPT were *real.*

"Ah crap," Kalman groaned as he brought a bottle of merlot to the table, catching everyone's attention. "Corkscrew broke halfway through."

"Maybe the Levine-Levins will let us borrow theirs," Dassi offered, smoothing one side of her *sheitel* back, gingerly tucking a few stray strands behind her ear as she looked up at Kalman. "The fifth floor Levine-Levins, not the third floor Levin-Levines. Because I guess we need to dodge them now."

"Why do we need to—Omig'd I totally just broke their corkscrew."

"You totally just broke their corkscrew."

"Alright, the Levine-Levins it is. Good call babe," Kalman pecked her faintly on the cheek. "Be right back," he said to everyone else as he exited the apartment. "Talk amongst yourselves, introduce, etc, etc."

At Kalman's departure the buzz of chatter summarily resumed at the table, an exchange of personal details and anecdotes that didn't particularly open any particular doors, but that didn't stop Dovid from gracelessly barreling through them nonetheless with an inelegant segue:

"So. Ariel. Where are you from?" he asked.

"Brooklyn."

"No, I mean, like, your background."

"Oh, that! Well my background is mostly in English and Secondary Education."

"But you're like, a convert, right?"

"No. No I'm not."

"Wow. Born Jewish? Amazing! From Ethiopia, yeah?"

"No—"

"I love Ethiopian Jews. Every time I see one, it's just so cool!" Dovid gushed to the rest of the table, plowing right over Ariel's answer. "Such good food! Gimme some wot and injera over jarred gefilte fish jelly *any* day of the week!"

Everyone all laughed.

Well, mostly.

Because not Ariel.

In fact, from his point of view, the entire exchange went a lot less briefly, a lot less benignly, and with a lot more layers to unpack.

To wit:

"So. Ariel. Where are you from?"

See?

Right there?

Right there, Ariel *knew* what Dovid was asking.

That kind of question only ever meant *one* thing, whether explicitly or implicitly, whether conscious bigotry or internalized prejudice: *"How are you here?"*

And regardless of the rhetoric of progressive liberal Judaism vs regressive traditional Judaism—a delineation just as false and perfunctory as racism and the Mason-Dixon line—it was still the same white Weltanschauung at work, just manifested differently.

Neither camp of Jew believed that people who looked like Ariel belonged at the table.

It's just that "liberal" Jews weren't rude (or honest) enough to demand an immediate explanation.

Ariel knew this. And usually, he played the game.

But the prospect of meeting another one of himself that night had him feeling a little spicy. So he answered the question he was *asked*, not the one he knew Dovid was asking.

"Brooklyn."

"No, I mean, like, your background."

Now here, Ariel knew he should've been able to come up with a response.

Something witty.

Sharp.

But his brain, it seemed, was fully operating on the "one step forward, two steps back" setting.

Like the nerve he'd found when retorting to Dassi just a couple of hours earlier had somehow atrophied in the interim, leaving his heart pounding too loudly in his ears, his face on fire, and his brain acutely aware that all the eyes he wasn't making contact with were firmly fixed on him.

It was kind of like a dream where you're standing in front of your class in your underwear. Except you're not even wearing underwear, it's not a classroom, you're on stage at the Grammys, you forgot your homework, and you're on fire.

In a burst of inspiration, something came to Ariel, something sufficiently and subtly snarky.

"Oh, that! Well my background is mostly in English and Secondary Education."

Manishtana

Answer the question asked, Ariel told himself. Answer the question asked, and eventually Dovid would get it and either apologize or abashedly relent.

"But you're like, a convert, right?" came the persistent inquisition, clueless to the lack of social grace, and bolstered by a similar dearth of protest from the onlookers.

As for Ariel, it's not that this was the first time he'd encountered an insistent inquiry into the existence of his existence.

He was used to this at other tables. Somewhere between too-watery matzo-ball soup and bland flavorless boiled chicken, the questions always came.

But he wasn't expecting it *here*.

Here, at the Meltzer's, at the table of the seminary-mate he'd bonded over the injustice of racial inequalities with. Here, in *this* house, Ariel assumed he was safe.

Which made this encounter all the more vulgar.

A jarring reminder of race in the one space where—if just for one night—Ariel had assumed it would be irrelevant.

Although, Ariel realized, *why* would he even think that?

If Shabbat tables were clearly marked "*Here There Be Racist Dragons*," he'd never have had a terrible experience in his life.

Duh.

Then again, Ariel didn't really care about logic at the moment.

He was too busy mourning the shattered comfortability of his happy Shabbat feeling.

"No. No I'm not," he replied, his dull tone belying how empty and gutted inside he was feeling.

Why wasn't anybody else stepping in?

If nothing else, *Dassi* knew Ariel. Knew his story. Or at least knew what civil dinner conversation should look like.

Why wasn't she saying anything? Informing her brother-in-law that he was being inappropriate?

Her silence, among all the other guests, kinda hurt a little bit, if Ariel was being honest with himself.

Which, currently, he wasn't.

Nor was he making any attempt to look in her direction, or to read her expression of shock and embarrassment. Or, at least, the one he *hoped* was there.

Maybe there wasn't one there at *all*.

Then again, he said to himself—gallantly invoking that *dan l'kaf zechut* again—this was her family.

He was sure she was just as embarrassed as he was, and that she'd say something later. Just not in front of public.

Ariel was black, after all. He knew about not showing out in public. That gracious smile coupled with death glares when his mom would look at him or his siblings and they knew, despite however cheerful she seemed, that their ass would be on fire once they got home.

Also, this exchange had only been a couple of seconds long so far.

If *he* was still sort of stunned and reaching for words, how exactly was he expecting anyone *else* to be on top of their retort game?

Or maybe Dassi hadn't noticed the inappropriateness at *all*.

Maybe *nobody* noticed.

Was it only *him* who noticed?

Or was everyone just unsure how to react? Was everyone else just following his lead and waiting for whatever moves he was going to make?

"Wow. Born Jewish? Amazing!"

Ariel nodded uncomfortably, his mind speedily rifling through rapid-fire comebacks to end this encounter, so he could bury it in the awkward place at the back of his brain.

And as he fast-forwarded through the inevitable end results of the exchanges he imagined, Ariel came to the same conclusion each time: He was the only one who could ensure that everybody at that Shabbat table kept having a good time, and that *no one* would win if he forced people into choosing sides in a debate of *"Was that or was that not racist just now?"*

Besides, sure, he was uncomfortable as shit right now, but did that mean he had the right to make everyone *else* likewise as uncomfortable?

"From Ethiopia, yeah?"

Omifuc—seriously, dude?

For one last time, Ariel considered defending himself. Unleashing the mortification crawling underneath his skin, and the anger kicking him in his gut. To stand up against Dovid reducing him and all other African-American Jews—and Jews of Color in general—to dehumanizing little checkboxes.

Of course, everyone likes to *think* that they'd be able to call out racism when it happens. But we're probably more likely to just ride it out and be relieved when the moment is done. The sooner it's over, the sooner we can start pretending it never happened.

Because that's human nature.

It's why people like Malcolm X, Ghandi, and Nelson Mandela are a big deal. And also me.

"No—" Ariel began, still not meeting anyone's eyes.

It's alright kids, his half-smile said, succumbing to that social pressure on people of color to respond to obnoxious aggression by taking some subjective "high road." The one that held people of color accountable for keeping the peace against white acquaintances experiencing just the *briefest* moment of distress.

Dignity, what? This is a nice dinner.

We're all having a great time. My word, this is a smooth tablecloth. Where's Kalman with that corkscrew, because wine, amirite?

"I love Ethiopian Jews. Every time I see one, it's just so cool!" Dovid gushed to the rest of the table, in the classic style of culture fetishization presented as evidence against prejudice. "*Such* good food! Gimme some wot and injera over jarred gefilte fish jelly *any* day of the week!"

Everyone all laughed.

Well, mostly.

Because, not Ariel.

Also, not that he noticed, but neither did Tamar, either.

"Alright!" Kalman declared as he re-entered the apartment, triumphantly brandishing his prize aloft. "Got the corkscrew! Everyone ready for *kiddish*?"

✡ ✡ ✡

The food was delicious, varied, and plentiful, from the jalapeno-dill and lemon-horseradish dips, to the gourmet half-salmon/half-whitefish gefilte fish.

And—no doubt due to Kalman's presence—the conversation had eased into a comfortable and inoffensive joviality that planted a smile on every face, and was likely bolstered by the seemingly neverending wine in every glass.

What had began as a rousing discussion of the factual inaccuracy and objective terribleness of the movie *The Possession*, had somehow led to Chaya retelling the tale of how she first met Nosson, which in turn morphed into a heated debate about *The Walking Dead* and surviving a zombie apocalypse, and eventually led to Ariel and Tamar breaking off into an extensive symposium on Sesame Street and the Muppets while they volleyed a bottle of black muscat back and forth between each other.

But something very definitely happened between Dassi and Dovid when it came time to clear the plates from the fish course to the meat course—some exchange of words between the two as they disappeared into the kitchen together—that was apparently cut short by the arrival of the Meltzer's final dinner guest.

Somewhere between Rivka knocking on the door and Kalman letting her into the apartment, Dassi and Dovid emerged from the kitchen to welcome their latest companion, Dassi flushed with righteous indignation, and Dovid wearing a shit-eating smirk. Like he was wise to the reality of the world and no one else was, because libtard snowflakes and political correctness.

It was clear to anyone with eyes that Dovid was one of those "keep it real" people who said racially offensive things in that jokey kind of way they think everyone will laugh and agree with.

But Dovid wasn't, like, a card-carrying full-on Klan member or anything. More like a casual racist.

Great term, by the way.

Makes me think of, like, a white dude in some khakis and Clark's kinda strolling over to someone, looking to his left, then over to his right, then nonchalantly calling someone a nigger.

All casual-like, y'know?

But Ariel only noticed the interaction in his periphery—if at all—as he was much more distracted at the moment by Dassi's former seminary companion, a svelte figure with sepia-toned skin strategically seated right beside him.

Box-braid extensions with a burnt-orange ombre framed a foxy heart-shaped face, and reached down to about the middle of her back. What color her eyes were was anyone's guess, as she couldn't stop fluttering them for long enough to actually open them. Her heavy eyelashes were either infested with a flock of furious bats, or she was simultaneously transcribing every word she uttered into Morse code via her eyelids.

Manishtana

She'd spent half a second mumbling a *"Gut Shabbos"* at Ariel when she'd first walked in, and proceeded to spend the rest of the night sort of...avoiding him? Maybe?

He wasn't exactly sure.

And like, hey, that was cool. Like his mother used to remind him when he moped through his teenage years, *"You are not entitled to any woman's company."*

Besides, not every Jew of Color immediately started jumping on another one as soon as they saw each other. Because that would be weird. But that was the awkward balancing act of JOCs meeting each other. That fine line between acknowledgment of camaraderie and not-necessarily sociable individual personhood.

You know that feeling, right?

When you're in a sea of Not-Yous and against the tide you see a You? And you immediately want to make a new best friend, but then you remember you're not a creeper?

Yeah, that.

It's like seeing a quarter on the sidewalk. Except it's a hundred-dollar bill in the middle of a six-lane highway.

Decisions, decisions.

But still, Rivka seemed a little stand-offish to Ariel, especially given that she had no problem chatting it up with the rest of the dinner guests.

Although, to be fair, apparently she and everyone else went waaay back. Back to even before seminary days, for some of them. So maybe it was just that Ariel was the fifth wheel in this particular social circle.

A fact of outsider status that Dovid used to make a renewed strike.

"Ariel, I hope I didn't offend you earlier," he began breezily, fully not caring if he'd offended him earlier. "It's just that I don't see many of...c'mon, to be Jewish and look like you is obviously unusual."

"Dovid," Kalman countered, immediately jumping into the fray. How much of that was Kalman being Kalman or Kalman's obviously threadbare tolerance for his sister-in-law's husband in *general*, Ariel wasn't sure. "You *do* know that one in every five American Jews is a Jew of Color?"

"Yeah, we've kinda been here since Sinai," Ariel confirmed.

"A what? A Jew of what?" Nosson scoffed.

"Jews come in all colors, y'know," Tamar offered, reverting back to her previously reticent state. "Sorry you didn't know,"

"So, we're, what, Jews of Non-Color?" Nosson chortled. "Jews are in some kind of race war now?"

"Ariel, look," Dovid smirked, ignoring Kalman's statement. "I've got this book for you. It's called the Talmud. And it says right there that Jews aren't white *or* black, so where's this 'Jew of Color' thing coming from?"

"Dovid, look," Ariel retorted with a fiery sarcasm he'd never before used, feeling emboldened by Rivka's presence. "I have this thing. It's called a *smicha*." To Ariel's satisfaction, Dovid briefly blanched at the revelation before regaining his smug composure. "So I'm quite aware what Rabbi Yishmael says in the first verse of the second chapter of Midrash Nega'im. And to take that statement to mean that no Jew ever is ever black or white is to attribute to him an opinion which is demonstrably wrong."

"As an Orthodox Jew, a 'Jew of Color' is the most absurd term I've ever heard. Are you joking? There's Jews and there's non-Jews, full stop. If you're simply a darker-skinned Jew, then you're a darker-skinned Jew. Zero discrimination. No one even *thinks* about it. I don't even *see* color," Dovid said, completely oblivious that not ten minutes earlier he literally just said that his question had been predicated on not seeing many Jews that were Ariel's color. Kinda like how well-meaning "colorblind" folk have no problem seeing color when talking about the "real" problem in the African-American community of "black-on-black" crime.

Instead of, y'know, just "crime."

"'*No one even*'—" Ariel began in disbelief. "Wow. Look, it's great that apparently you're around people who don't see color. But those of us who don't have the option of passing for 'white' have serious acceptance issues within the greater Jewish community that *need* to be addressed."

"*Everyone* has acceptance issues. **Baal teshuvas** get treated differently in the *shidduch* process, converts *in general* have issues being accepted. I get into arguments with my Yeshivish family when they bash Lubavitchers or Bobov or *whatever*. And that's nothing to do with race. What do you have to get so angry about?"

"I'm *not* ang—"

"Here's the thing," Kalman cut in. "Yes, BT's get treated differently. And yes, converts get treated badly. And yes, this sect here doesn't accept that sect there. This *is* a problem and it's something we're more than willing to discuss. Except I've *never* heard you caring about those issues like, *ever*, before just now tonight. So you're just bringing these up as talking points to dismiss issues that Jews of Color have, and that's bull and you know it Dovid."

"But like, what even *is* a Jew of Color?" Chaya added, swimming out to sea to flounder by her man.

"Oh, that's easy," Ariel answered coolly. "Any Jew who you've looked at and asked them if they're a convert because of their skin color. That's a Jew of Color."

As Dovid stammered to respond, Kalman circled in for the kill.

"The Jewish people were scattered to the four corners of the *Earth*. Not just the four corners of Europe."

"Y'know," Tamar added, delivering quite the impressive coup-de-grace out of nowhere. "Like how **Purim** is about the Jews living in the countries from *India* to *Ethiopia*?"

"*That*," Ariel affirmed, pointing at Tamar. She gave a modest *"Yeah, I'm a badass, I know"* half-shrug.

"Look," Rivka entered the conversation. "I think it's ridiculous that *anyone* is talking about 'white' Jews and 'black' Jews and whatever else. Jews are Jews. The rest of the world hates us and is against us and we need to have solidarity, bottom line. This black/white stuff is just divisive nonsense."

The table was silent. A gloating silence on Dovid, Nosson, and Chaya's part, but a stunned one for Kalman, Tamar, and Ariel.

And Dassi was fastidiously examining the tines on her fork and absentmindedly stroking the stem of her wine glass.

"I'm..." Ariel began, feeling a little bit like he'd been playing his heart out on the court, only to find out the coach had been paid off to throw the game. But maybe what Rivka said wasn't how she meant it...?

"I'm not exactly sure what you mean, but it's not like this 'black/white' stuff is something out of nowhere. I've *experienced* it. People *experience* being told by other Jews that they're cursed because they're black, or that they don't belong because they're black, or that they're not *really* Jewish because they're black. My siblings and I have *lived* it. In *yeshiva*, in *knesset*, in—"

"Look, to say that I've lived almost three decades in America and haven't faced racism is unrealistic. But maybe what you keep

92

experiencing is because of what you're putting out there. *I choose to engage in a dialogue of shared experiences that bring us together.*"

"Um, okay. But 'solidarity' isn't going to happen if we act like the issues aren't there. Pretending that they don't exist isn't going to make them go away."

"And noticing it doesn't mean we can't *get over* it. And I'm choosing to opt out of all of this melodramatic whiny victimology, because it's just not helpful. It is what it is. Jews crying about their color only giving them grief, and about other Jews passing for 'white,' are not expressions of Jewishness that I'm interested in. Maybe if you spent as much time trying to get over all of this pain you say was 'forced on you,' instead of trying to create some little niche inside of a niche, then maybe you might be able to start empowering yourself and focusing on **yiddishkeit**."

"*...What the fuck did you just fucking say about me? I'll have you know that I graduated top of my class in Israel and I've been involved in numerous secret Midrashic redactions on top of being instrumental in privilege checking with over 300 confirmed political demonstrations. You think you can get away with saying that shit to me over a Shabbat table? Think again, fucker. As we speak I am contacting my secret network of **chavrutas** across the globe to use their crazy mad kabbalah skills to go back in time and pray for you to be born a male just so we can not count you in a minyan. I can be anywhere, anytime, I can kill you in over seven hundred ways and that's just by making you unpack your privilege. Not only am I extensively trained in Talmudic commentaries, but I have access to an entire arsenal of socio-racial articles to prove my every point about systemic and endemic racism and prejudice and I will use them to their full extent to wipe your miserable ass off the face of the continent, you self-hating little shit. If only you could have known what self-righteousness your internalized oppression was about to bring down upon you, and maybe you would've held your fucking tar-baby tongue. But you couldn't, you didn't, and now you're paying the price, you fucking zip-a-dee-doo-dah banjo-plucking apologist motherfucker.*"

Whoa.

Now, if you can just picture a quirkily-furnished little dining room, filled with half a dozen corpses dressed in their Shabbos best and their faces melted off like the Nazis at the end of *Raiders of the Lost Ark*, then that's *exactly* what that room would've looked like.

If Ariel had actually delivered that wonderful tirade of Internet Tough Guy copypasta that exploded into his head.

But he didn't.

And not just because he shied away from using profanity on the L'rd's Day, because he was *awfully* tempted to break his Shabbos Mouth© rule just this once.

But he didn't.

Because he wasn't about to continue this House Slave v Field Negro exhibition match for the other—whiter—spectators at the table, to root for or against like groomed roosters in a cockfight.

At least not any further than this Mandingo fight had *already* gone.

"I guess we'll just have to agree to disagree, then," Ariel said finally, and politely.

"No. We just disagree."

Yeek.

Well *that* was rough.

But in hindsight, it reminded Ariel of *exactly* why his oldest sister said she avoided interacting with JOCs she didn't know. Especially in spaces where she was surrounded by white Jews she *also* didn't know.

Liora was always levelheaded in that way.

And, ever the pragmatic and humorless law student, she had composed and shared with her baby brother her comprehensive dossier categorizing the Twelve Tribes of Black-Jewish Archetypes:

1-CHAI YELLOW aka The Biracial/Multiracial One

Their racial background is literally the entirety of their identity.

Chai Yellows might have a white Jewish mom.

They might have a white Jewish dad.

But don't fear, you'll know exactly which one, because they'll let you know. Multiple times. In a row. Within the first seven minutes of meeting them, you will know every nook, cranny, corner, inch, and curve of their Jewish (white) ancestry, especially if they're any discernable shade of brown.

They yearn for the Yiddish fluency of their ancestors, even if it's ahistorical, and, more often than not, the Chai Yellow is fanatically enamored with the lowest conceivable quality of the most stereotypical Eastern European Jewish foods to ever exist.

Other times they're the ones who can totally pass for white unless you happen to squint at them in the dark.

They are just goshdarned mystified and awed by their ancestral blackness and—conversely from the non-passing Chai Yellows—they will inform you of every nook, cranny, corner, inch, and curve of their Black (non-Jewish) ancestry.

The lighter the passing Chai Yellow is, the more soulful they are, the more they identify with the black American experience, and the more likely they are to show up to potlucks hauling an industrial kitchen-sized slab of cornbread made from scratch with Big Ma's recipe.

Chai Yellows of either variety tend to vacillate towards either the "tragic mulatto" trope—unsure of where they "really" belong, and always feeling like they're expected to pick a side—or they are the success stories known as social butterflies—who, despite the disadvantages of their Black non-Jewish half of their background, get to escape it when they fully embrace their whiteness, aka their Jewish heritage.

2-MENACHEM X/ASSATA SHOSHANA aka The "Woke" One

They do "miswoth," not "mitzvot." They eat "massa" not "matzah." They spell "kabbalah" (and "Africa," for some reason) with a "q."

The Jews were an African nation, they say.

Ashkenazim are descendants of Khazar converts, they say.

They have a love affair with Middle Eastern Mizrahi and Yemenite Jewish customs. (Though somehow Ethiopian Beta Israeli, Nigerian Igbo, and Ugandan Abayudaya Jewish traditions get significantly less love.)

Their Facebook and Instagram are overflowing with black art of the "naked-black-man-cradling-a-naked-black-woman-cradling-a-naked-black-baby-cradling-a-naked-Marcus-Garvey-against-a-silhouette-of-Africa" variety.

The Menachem X/Assata Shoshana looks down on non-Jewish black people for not knowing "the truth" and sneer at other Jewish black folk for being "brainwashed by the white Jew."

More often than not they are masters at regurgitating secret revelations (that everyone already knows), relaying secret knowledge (that is batshit crazy), and debating things (that don't really matter or mean anything).

And they looooove talking about "a woman's place," not to mention how women should dress and wear their hair, and why the Ashkenazi ban on polygamy should be dissolved.

Speaking of Ashkenazis, Menachem X/Assata Shoshanas hoot and holler about Ashkenormativity, but they don't really want equality. They just want to replace white Jewish hegemony with black Jewish hegemony. And usually with a dash of misogynoir.

The Menachem X/Assata Shoshana convert was probably a Hotep Brotha/Sista in their pre-Jewish life.

Provided, of course, that they are in fact actually Jewish, as this type tends to spend years, sometimes decades, in conversion limbo.

Aside from "conscious" black kings and queens, frequent members of this type also include current Hebrew Israelites, former Hebrew Israelites, uppercase "Black Jews" who grew up in and still currently attend uppercase "Black Jewish congregations" (aka Hebrew Israelites), black Jewish folk of a certain age, and about 27% of black Jews who attended an Orthodox *yeshiva* as a child.

3-UNCLE TEVYE/BUBBE JEMIMA aka The Uncle Tom/Aunt Jemima

The Uncle Tevye/Bubbe Jemima doesn't see colored people.

They're "just Jewish." As a euphemism for "not black."

Their great-great-great-great grandfather was one-sixteenth and a half Dutch.

The rabbi's pre-*bar mitzvah* son is their Huck Finn, and they are more than honored to play Nigger Jim. Or they're the forever alone 40+ mammy-type whose "best friends" are single twenty-year old seminary girls who will promptly forget they exist after the wedding. That is, until they need a babysitter.

These are the types who leave their color behind in the water every time they get out of the **mikvah**.

They don't believe in "hyphenated Judaism" and talk about Judaism being a "raceless environment," yet paradoxically are somehow always in front of the cameras showcasing "Jewish diversity." And when they're handed the microphone, they predictably declare that they've never never never experienced any racial tension in Jewish spaces, and throw shade at black Jews who say that they do, but—Oh! By the way! Uncle Tevyes/Bubbe Jemimas don't, and have never, identified with African-Americans or African-American culture!

Well, hush my mouth!

Such a shocker!

4-SHYLOCK JENKINS aka The Opportunist

The Shylock Jenkins don't care nothing bout nobody but getting ahead, getting paper, and getting power, whatchu talm bout?

They look just as black as you, but act just as swindly as any money-grubbing Jewish stereotype you can conceive of.

They are the reason the phrase "All skinfolk ain't kinfolk" exists, and why the prayer for protection from "members of the covenant" was born.

To them, the only difference between the "race card" or the "religion card" is which game they're playing that day.

The Shylock Jenkins often resembles any of the other types, which is kind of the point: They can morph like chameleons and tangle themselves into the branches of whatever ideology their target will be most receptive to. And they are just as incapable of comprehending racial or religious brotherhood as white people are at understanding that salt and pepper *are not seasonings.*

The Shylock Jenkins will bleed you dry of every last cent, resource, and connection, and will keep coming back for more for as long as you're gullible enough to let them.

5-GEFILTE FRESH aka The "Real Nigga"

The Gefilte Fresh is a distant cousin to the Menachem X/Assata Shoshana. The difference is they don't claim to be some kind of higher advanced black lifeform, or look down on other black folk.

They're just black.

But like, really *really* black, though.

They walk with the ghetto lean, their natural voice is the blaccent white popstar girls cream over to imitate, and if their street cred could be converted into a credit score, they could buy a house with an I.O.U. written on a Post-It note in crayon.

They know more gang signs, dancehall moves, and lyrics to songs by obscure Dirty South rappers than their average non-Jewish counterparts can shake a Crip walk at. They can put their foot in a lit Shabbat dinner with all the fixings, and still be quick to roll up ten deep on a motherfucker, but they don't murk flies on Shabbos.

Ironically, they went to the best Jewish day schools or the *frummest*, most conservative right-wing *yeshivas*. Yet if it weren't for seeing them at services, even *other* Jewish black folk wouldn't suspect the Gefilte Fresh of being Jewish.

6-YIDNEY POITIER aka The Respectable Jewgro

They're not "quite" Uncle Tevye/Bubbe Jemimas because they do possess some skewed sense of Black Pride. Yidney Poitiers also balance this bizarre tightrope where they generally don't care what white Jews think of them, so long as white Jews think they're respectable and one of the "good" black Jewish folk.

The Yidney Poitier is also fond of telling black Jewish folk with the gall to point out injustice and discrimination to "get over it." Somehow they are physically capable of both applauding themselves and patting themselves on the back, simultaneously.

They emphatically reinforce the dehumanizing and devaluing selective statistics presented on Fox News, and decry the actions of the general black and Jewish black communities, ala the Bill Cosby/Geraldo Rivera "Pull Your Pants Up And Don't Wear Hoodies Because That Will Magically Cause Institutional Racism To Cease Existing And Make Police Bullets Stop Hitting You" school of thought.

(Because when black people wore three-piece suits and fedoras, that rendered them immune from fire hoses, police dogs, bullets, and racism, naturally.)

7-MONORAH aka The One with "Only One" Syndrome

The Monorah is essentially the black Jewish Highlander. There can only be One.

They might be a Yidney Poitier or an Uncle Tevye or even a Menachem X. But they cannot tolerate sharing the spotlight with anyone else. Their contribution to anything Jewish is literally being "the black one."

They are always the token black in Jewish spaces, and they'll be damned if anyone else steals their soapbox. Because obviously you can't be unique if someone else is there who looks like you, regardless of how different your stories are.

It's not like you're, y'know, two different people or anything.

There is only one important Jewish black experience, and it is theirs, and anyone else is a distraction from the real issues, which are the issues that are theirs.

8-MACCABEAT-IT-UP aka The Player

ARIEL SAMSON: FREELANCE RABBI

The Maccabeat-It-Ups are all about the P-word, and I don't mean "Passover."

Exclusively male, they take advantage of the Mandigo myth and use it to run through as many color-curious "He's A Nice Jewish Boy But With Extra Flavor" white Jewish girls as they can. Added bonus: Scooping up as many black Jewish women desperate for any variety in the black Jewish male population, or elated to encounter an addition to the pool of eligible bachelors.

Much like the Menachem X, Maccabeat-It-Ups also generally spend years in conversion limbo, although in the Maccabeat-It-Ups case, it's usually a calculated choice in order to elicit either hope, compassion, or sympathy. Whichever leads to a higher notch count.

9-TROUBLEMACHER aka The Revolutionary

One-part Menachem X/Assata Shoshana, one-part Gefilte Fresh, three-parts angry, and four-parts tired, the Troublemacher appears to be fairly well-adjusted.

But this is a trick.

Because their life's mission is to break everything. All of it. All of the things.

They want to blow up the world and put it back together into a shape that makes sense, which means challenging and overthrowing the Powers & Ideas That Be.

No concept or institution is safe from their sanctimonious fury, and at the slightest provocation a Shabbat meal can quickly transform into a passionate colloquium with a selection of choice topics including, but not limited to:

- the territorial politics of Jewish diversity organizations,
- the increasingly reactionary boundaries between Jewish denominations, or
- the inherently and mutually racist/anti-Semitic underpinnings to the term "black/Jewish community relations" when what is implicitly meant is "[non-Jewish] black/[non-black] Jewish community relations."

Once the Troublemacher gets revved up, the mic only gets relinquished when they drop it.

Which is after they beat you about the head and face with it, then string you up with the cord.

Some people might see them as ambitious. Or driven. But those people are spelling "insane" wrong, because more often than not,

Troublemachers tend to undergo psychotic breaks and live out the rest of their lives trapped in a caricatured repetitive shell of their former fiery relevance.

Like Cornel West.

10-STAY BLACK AND CHAI aka The "Can I Just Live"

The SBC, bless their heart, is just trying to live their life.

They're not trying to make waves, and all they want to do is stay black (and Jewish) and die (on a bagel).

They take the lumps and bumps either side keeps giving, and they keep it moving along the path of least resistance, constantly under the neurotic cloud of impostor syndrome that somehow they'll be exposed as not "really" being black or Jewish by some amorphous Council of Blackness or Sanhedrin of Jewish Authenticity.

But if black Jews were Pokemon, then the SBC would be the Eevee of the black Jewish archetypes, complete with the abilities of Run Away and Adaptability, leaving them just an inciting incident away from suddenly evolving in response to their environment, mutating into any of the eleven other black Jewish forms.

11. NONCHOLENT, aka The Like, Whatever, Man

You won't find a more apathetic black Jew than the Noncholent.

They don't expect anyone from any side of any line to ever *not* be ignorant, and they are always fresh out of fucks to give.

In fact, they harvest new fucks daily *just* so they can be fresh out of them when they have to deal with your pedestrian racism, or jejune anti-Semitism, or pretentious religiosity or secularism.

Or just you breathing, really.

Much like a black hole, they're usually the final stage at the end of the SBC>Troublemacher>Noncholent lifecycle.

12. JEWNICORN, aka The Perfect One

Perfectly black enough.

Perfectly Jewish enough.

A seamless blending of all of the strengths and none of the weaknesses of two seemingly diametrically opposed cultures, free of the socio-religious existential crises that plague the eleven other types.

Respected and feared.

The Jewnicorn is legendary. And by legendary, I mean mythical. And by mythical, I mean imaginary.

The moral of the story, kids, is that there's no such thing as a "normal" black Jew.

Then again, what about being black or being Jewish has ever been about being "normal"? The best you can hope for is meeting someone that you at least mostly agree with. Someone who—even if you're not on the same page—you're at least in the same *library*.

✡ ✡ ✡

"Honey..." Kalman cooed. "Come from underneath the sink."

"Nope," came the reply from inside the cabinet, muffled by both the faux-oak doors and the rain pellets hitting the picture window above the faucet.

Dassi had excused herself near the end of the excruciatingly awkward affair that dinner had become, finding refuge here in the kitchen, hidden away from all manner of man and beast.

It was over now, the dinner, and Ariel and Kalman had likewise retreated into the kitchen after Dovid and his entourage had left with Rivka. Kalman had opened up some Glenlivet in relief, and wisely not the Monkey Shoulder. Because too soon, dude.

"I am *not* coming out there," Dassi continued. "Because Ari is going to kill me in the face."

"Ari, can you tell Dassi you're not going to kill her in the face?"

"What?" Ariel answered with a jolt, like he'd been startled out of some other train of thought. "No. No, I'm not gonna kill you in the face, Dassi."

The cabinet door swung cautiously open to reveal Kalman's wife clutching a bottle of pinot grigio, thoroughly embarrassed in that way that people are when they bring someone along to somewhere with human people, and then that someone shows their whole ass.

Like when you agree to meet your sister at a coffeeshop and she shows up drunk and loud and bitter about her ex-husband and knocks over the mug display. You know who you are.

"I am sooo sorry," she began immediately. "I had no idea she'd say anyth—and *Dovid*! I like, *just* talked to him, and, oh gosh, I'm just really sorry, Ariel."

"It's ok," he replied. "It's not y—"

"No! No, it's *not* okay! I couldn't even squeak out a, a thing! With people saying such *crazy* offensive things at my own tab—my *sister*? Ohmig'd this was so bad. I just..."

Dassi paused here, closed her eyes, and bit her lips together for a moment. When she spoke again, her voice was quivering.

"I just," she began, with glistening eyes. "I mean, Ariel, I know—I *know*—that this doesn't even affect me directly. But I don't see how you do it. I, like, I'm just having, I'm having a little bit of a hard time right now with just *hearing* what—" she broke off.

Dassi was really good people. And really good for Kalman. Ariel liked her. And he knew what she meant, and that she really sincerely meant it.

Which, honestly, meant a lot to him.

But when she began to cry—partially because of the newly (to her) unveiled prejudice of her kith and kin, partially because 3/4 of a bottle of pinot grigio, and partially because Day 23—he felt himself internally roll his eyes, cross his arms over his chest, and completely tune out anything else from that point on.

And somewhere from deep inside himself, an exasperated voice asked: *"Why do I have to deal with her right now?"*

It surprised him at first, and he was a little taken aback by it.

This wasn't the usual battle of heart v head v soul. This was a completely new and different voice. One that sounded like it was kinda annoyed with the bickering the other three usually did.

And, curious, Ariel leaned into it a little bit. Like he was dipping his foot into a pool for the first time.

Why, exactly, the voice continued, *do I need to focus my energy on making* other *people feel better about witnessing the assault that I actually endured? Like, can I maybe get* five *minutes to process that clusterfuck of a violation of my identity that happened just now? NO, I don't fucking want another shot...Okay fine, I'll have another shot...Founder's Reserve. Good stuff. But anyways, why exactly am I being made to feel obligated to soothe your tears and feelings right now?*

Because, I'm sorry, but I don't really feel like coddling and nurturing you at the moment. And I for damn sure don't feel like giving out absolutions to whatever guilt you're grappling with, alright? Go deal with your "I don't know what to do with my feelings about whiteness, because Jews aren't white, but we acted white just now with Jews who *definitely* aren't white, but I don't feel white around other white people, so what does this all mean" *feelings somewhere else.*

Also, really? "I can't believe this happened?" "I can't believe this happened at my table?"

Have you, like, just not been listening to shit I've been saying about anything, ever? THIS HAPPENS ALL THE FUCKING TIME. Hence, ALL THOSE STORIES I'VE TOLD YOU that apparently you thought were a dramatic retelling of a Gargoyles episode or something.

Like—and this is really a serious question—what exactly about your table made you think it was immune?

I mean, I know why I did, stupidly, but why did you? Did you think the horror stories I told were about that time when I was sitting around a Shabbat table with a bunch of people dressed in Klan hoods? Did you think I was showing up at tables where everyone was in blackface and then being inexplicably aghast when someone said something fucked up? Did you spray Racistz-Be-Gon^{TM} around the table before we sat down, and so you're shocked you didn't get the 8-12 hour coverage the can promised?

Like, seriously, what makes your table so special?

Because honestly, you being so out of your mind that something like this happened at "your table" is like knowing that car accidents are a thing but being astonished when you get into one because, "I can't believe this happened to me! In a Camry!"

Is there something inherent about Camrys, or you just owning car, that makes you think you're impervious to car accidents? Because otherwise I'm just not seeing it. And I hella drank that Kool-Aid.

"And then when Rivka came in with all that out of left field?" Kalman chimed in. "I was like 'Uh...so what do I do now?' I mean, talking over a Jew of Color to explain why Jews of Color are a thing feels like it's probably the worst possible thing to do, but, like, if I push back am I whitesplaining over her experience? Cuz then *that* isn't okay..."

"Omigosh, yes!" Dassi blurted out again. "Like, she's a Jew of Color speaking from firsthand experience that I'll never have, and her voice, y'know, *automatically* holds more weight on the topic—because it *should*—but, I don't agree with, like—what am I supposed to do with that?"

Manishtana

Wait, what? Why are we here? Why is this what we're talking about now? You can't even talk to your own sister and brothers-in-law but you're reaching across the aisle to worry about what to say to black Jewish folk saying crazy shit?

STAY IN YOUR LANE!

What your job is is to educate other white Jewish people. And yeah, that might be uncomfortable for maybe eighteen minutes, but when you don't, then we have to deal with their racist shit for THE REST OF OUR LIVES. If you're really about showing up, then you need to be showing up every day of your life, just like we have to deal with the bullshit every day of ours.

Because when you don't, that onus literally falls on us.

Also, why is Rivka some existential crisis for you that you're so paralyzed? Should the voice of Jewish Holocaust-deniers hold more weight than non-Jewish Holocaust scholars? What about female misogynists over male feminists? So how about you just worry about talking to your Dovids and your Nossons and your Chayas. Because over on this side, we're more than capable of coming for the Rivkys of the world.

And Kalman, dude, what the hell? What happened? You used to know better. You used to get that these moments aren't about you. What, you went and got married and so you're playing Clueless Well-Meaning White Guy now, because being woke is a single man's game or something? Like, I don't underst—

"Um, excuse me guys?"

Everyone looked up to see Tamar standing awkwardly in the doorway.

"Omig'd you're still here!" Dassi yelped. "I'm so sorry! I totally forgot—"

"No, it's okay. I kinda snuck away and've just been hanging out in the bathroom for the past twenty minutes. Just saying *Gut Shabbos* before I head out," she turned to Ariel, eyebrows set in that familiar apologetic arch. "It was really nice meeting you. Hope your dinner wasn't ruined *too* badly."

"It was great meeting you too," Ariel smiled back, enjoying her tactful non-acknowledgment. "Also, it's impossible for a dinner where you're talking about the origin of Snuffleupagus to be a total wash."

"Tamar, you're leaving *now*?" Dassi exclaimed. "But it's so late! And it's raining! Why don—"

"I'll be fine. Don't worry."

"Kalman, can you walk—"

"Dassi. I'm fine."

"I know you're fine but—"

"Guys," Ariel interjected. "I was about to head out soon anyway. I can just walk with her. We're headed in the same direction anyway."

It was an offer that calmed Dassi's hysteria, much to Kalman's relief, but was really just the escape Ariel needed from the exhausting environment the Meltzer's home had quickly become in the past few hours. He turned to Tamar. "Y'know, if you don't mind."

"Oh no, it's totally cool," Tamar shrugged, but instantly reading between Ariel's lines. They were rescuing each other from Dassi. "We can talk more Muppets trivia that way."

"Sounds like a plan," Ariel laughed, his eyes transmitting a silent *"OMG thank you"*. He waved to the Meltzers. *"Shabbat shalom*, guys."

"Gut Shabbos! I'm sorry!"

If you apologize again Dassi, I **will** *kill you in the face.*

✡ ✡ ✡

October had evaporated into November and snatched the last stubborn tendrils of summer's warmth with it, leaving Ariel and Tamar trudging through drenched streets against the cool night air, their shoulders hunched up to their ears and hands balled into tight fists deep in the pockets of not-warm-enough jackets.

Brooklyn didn't have the psychotically high property taxes of Rockland County to justify those leafy suburban carpets of gold and crimson, so here the usual grey of the concrete sidewalks were dappled with soggy gobs of brown and darker brown instead.

But at least here they *had* sidewalks.

Tamar lived about an hour away from the Meltzers, yet somehow Ariel and Tamar's three and a half mile journey seemed a lot less arduous than the hour and change it actually took.

But, y'know, time flies when you're pointing out that The Count is, in fact, *a vampire*, and then somewhere along the way you start kinda sorta flirting with each other.

Manishtana

It was gradual. The way their gazes lingered on each other, steady enough to hide behind the excuse of polite eye contact, but just a smidge too long. The voices that had started off brash and friendly, almost imperceptibly becoming softer. Lips that crept into unfamiliarly shy grins and barely repressed warm smiles.

Their conversation was innocent and casual enough, yet their bodies steadily drifted closer together the longer they walked, with body language relaxed and familiar, yet tentative and cautious.

Tamar, as it turned out, was a lot less the sullen quiet redhead Ariel'd initially pegged her for.

It's just that her emotions weren't easily hidden, and she'd never particularly been a fan of the additions Dassi'd brought into Kalman's life. Otherwise, just behind those slightly pursed lips there was apparently a smile just waiting to be coaxed out, and a laughing blush whenever Ariel returned a glance.

And those sneaking glances were plentiful.

Not at her perfectly slate-grey eyes or the overlapping constellations of light brown freckles sprinkled across her button nose. No, it was the imperfections that drew Ariel in. Her slightly snaggle-toothed incisors. The faintly peaked ears. Her left eyebrow that was bisected by a scar.

They were still drinking each other in with carefully measured sips when they reached Tamar's place, an attached house with a first-floor apartment she shared with three other girls.

Neither one of them remembered which one made the suggestion to just circle around the block a couple more times, to wind their conversation down before inevitably retiring for the night. Several loops later, the topic had turned to dating.

"Ohmig'd, dating is so crappy," Tamar laughed. "*Especially* once people find out you're divorced."

"Sorry. Any kids?"

"Thankfully, no. I got out of that trainwreck in time. But that's close enough for some guys, because I'm apparently 'damaged goods' now or something. Also, I'm turning 30, so clearly I'm already half dead."

"Ugh, c'mon guys."

"Seriously, if I have to hear *'It's not you, it's me'* just one more time I'm going to, I dunno. Kill. Like, *something*."

"Well. This conversation sure escalated quickly."

106

"I mean," she explained through more laughs. "I'm just so tired of telling people about myself, only for them to be like '*Nope, never mind.*' Seriously, how many times can you put yourself out there?"

"Man, preaching to the choir. Not even the choir, the *Pope*."

"Like," she continued, slightly blushing again. "I liked someone. But it was complicated. It's always complicated. And I really wanted it to be something but...*Why* are there so many games? I just don't get it. We're messy. Humans are messy messy creatures. That's *fine*. Just, like, be man enough to be a mess, y'know? Show me the real you, not the one you think you have to craft. The you who you were born to be, not what the world made you into."

"Easier said than done," Ariel confessed. "I feel like I just wish I was a better version of myself. Actually doing all the stuff I wish I was doing."

"I dunno," Tamar replied as the flushed crept up her cheeks again. "This version of you seems pretty good from where I'm standing."

They continued walking in bashful silence for a few steps.

"Um, can I ask you a question?" Tamar began. "I mean, given tonight's stunning display of cultural sensitivity, I totally get if you don't want to."

"Well, now that you've prefaced it..." Ariel laughed.

"Fair enough," she smiled back, then got very focused. "So, I can totally understand and respect the sense of invasiveness Jews of Color get when getting questioned about their background. But, if someone is genuinely curious, how *should* they go about asking? Like—and this isn't me—but I know people who don't mean it maliciously, but they find other people's Jewish stories really moving and uplifting. So how should people like that approach without being insensitive?"

"Well, my response to the first part is if they want to be inspired, then they should go to a **shiur**. I'm not a petting zoo, and it's *extremely* exoticizing and fishbowling to be on display for everyone to peer at. I don't like it to be assumed that I, one: have a story, two: feel like sharing that story, three: am interested in being some walking wellspring of inspiration, instead of just some Jew trying to enjoy his Jewish space just like you are. And there's, like, nothing more I hate than people I've never met, who may or may not even actually know my *name*, who think I owe them my story just because they asked. Here's your story: I was born. The end."

"I—I mean, I get that—but why do you say they think they're *owed* your story? Maybe they just really wanna hear it?"

"Because," Ariel sighed. "If they didn't think it was something owed, they would wait to find out whatever it is by getting to know me. There's a *lot* of things I'd really like to know about people, but I don't ask because it's none of my business—if they want me to know, they'll tell me. Like, imagine being at a full Shabbat table and someone you have never met before turns to you and is like, *'So I hear you're newly married now. What was that first night as man and wife like? Where did it take place? How did you feel? What positions did you try?'* and on and on and on, all while everyone in the room stops their own conversations to attentively listen to all the details. You wouldn't want to literally be swallowed up by the floor? You wouldn't feel angry or violated or mortified? Not everything in our lives are open to public forum to satisfy curiosity. And nosiness doesn't get justified just because you're looking for an 'inspiring story.'"

"I...Well when you put it that way, I guess I can't argue that."

They reached Tamar's place again, stopping in front this time.

"Thank you, Ariel," she smiled at him. "For all of that. And, uh, for all of this."

"Well, I, y'know. Yeah. You're welcome."

"I'm, well, I'm heading to Israel for the next couple weeks. But maybe, when I get back," Tamar began to redden for the millionth time that night. "We'll get to talk more at some point? Without all the terribleness and cold and walking?"

"Sure," Ariel grinned shyly. "Doesn't sound bad. I think I'd like that."

"I think I'd like that, too."

"*Shabbat shalom.*"

"*Gut Shabbos.*"

Ariel hadn't been back from his lunch break ten minutes—on his third day of work—when Chuck came to hover over his shoulder.

Chuck was a thirty-something Korean dude who blinked far too much for any human's good, yet somehow still imagined himself to be one of those "cool" bosses. On point. Or "on fleek."

Whatever.

Ariel had reached that conclusion two days earlier, while he inwardly cringed as Chuck proudly declared that the shipment of bedazzled rhinestone tees they'd just received was "the hot new thing in the hood." (Also, can we all just collectively agree to ignore whatever slang comes after "on fleek"? Kthanx.)

"Hey Ariel."

"What's up?"

"So, uh...what happened to those T-shirts in inventory?"

"Uh, I don't know, Chuck...What happened to those T-shirts in inventory?"

"Well, I know we scanned them in, and they were in the system Monday, but when I checked today, *poof,* they're gone."

"Wow, that's a crazy huge glitch. I mean, we—"

"Well, I think it's kinda obvious. We both know you've been stealing them."

"I've been—the petite belly shirts? I'm stealing them?"

"Look, I don't want to make this a big thing, but, um, I have to let you go."

"For *not* stealing bedazzled girls' T-shirts."

"I, y'know, I get it," Chuck said, punctuating each word with air-quotes. "With you being 'bout' that 'hood life' and 'being on the grind' just 'hustling' to 'eat.'"

"Those last quotes don't even make sen—"

"Hey, Ariel. Man. Like, you're a good guy. I like you. I just can't keep financing Robin Hood. Y'know what I'm saying? So you're done here...Also I've already called the cops. So you might want to leave. Like now."

Chuck turned to take a step away, then paused and turned back.

"Please don't drive-by shoot me."

Ariel slowly exhaled for about the millionth time, his hands in his pockets, head back and eyes closed, while he slumped against the wall.

He'd been riding the elevator up and down for the past twenty minutes, glued in the same position, listening to the doors ping open and closed, the shuffling of people in and out, feeling the glances in his direction while conversations awkwardly continued around his apparently comatose presence.

And, feeling as gutted as he did, he couldn't really care any less.

Another day back at Keaton & West, another fruitless meeting with Jumaane, another...Ariel just...just felt like he was drowning, honestly.

Like everything in the world was conspiring to crush and squeeze the life out of him.

Well "conspiring" might've been a tad egocentric, considering, as Ariel knew, that it didn't take much for him to fail at accomplishing something.

Because he knew he wasn't the type of person who could *succeed* at anything.

And every time he tried—and was inevitably trounced by the simplest of obstacles—those familiar waves of defeat, sadness, and worthlessness came crashing down around him, reminding him that he was only *pretending* that he was the successful, intelligent, hard-working person everyone thought he was.

How dare he forget that? How dare he act like his life wasn't a mural in a constant state of disarray just *barely* concealed from the rest of the world? How dare he forget that he *knew* that? That he *knew* it like he knew the sun rises in the east and sets in the west and that water was wet and that the sky was blue and that the Mets sucked?

It was a *fact*.

Not an opinion or a feeling. It was *a fact*.

The Mets *sucked*.

And so did he.

Ariel Shabbtai Dror Samson was a lazy, stupid, worthless inveterate loser, Ariel *knew*. And those people who didn't see it right away would find out sooner or later. And once they finally saw him for what he was, they would laugh in his fucking worthless loser face.

Like, just look at the past week alone. Pretty much *nothing* had gone down as expected. Not professionally, not personally, and definitely not romantically.

Between the orange-haired Jewish reincarnation of Stephen Fechit, and the very compatible creamy-vanilla derailment from Destination: Black Jewish Girl, it seemed like he was being made to choose between an organic honeycrisp apple full of glass splinters or a mouthwatering chocolate custard pie baked in all the coconut oil he was allergic to. (Huh. Didn't *that* allegory feel familiar...)

And if those were the choices, then Ariel would rather...*what* exactly? Find a way to live with himself for not having made the other choice?

He didn't really know.

So, what the hell, riding the elevator listening to tinny jazz music was as productive as anything *else* he'd tried his hand at recently.

...Ok fine.

Maybe he wasn't a worthless garbage person, he conceded.

Either way, it was pretty clear that he needed to sit down and have a conversation with himself about himself. About where he was. Where he was going. Where he wanted to be.

And who—not *"what,"* but *"who"*—he wanted to have at his side for the journey.

Because he was tired of living a cul-de-sac life.

Circling around in nice enough experiences and encounters, but always cycling back to the same spot. Something needed to really radically change. And Ariel needed to take those reins and make it happen.

Like, *now*.

Taking a deep breath, Ariel exhaled into the darkness behind his eyelids.

"Alright, G'd," Ariel said aloud. "I'm 27 years old and...and I think I'm done with all the preliminaries. And I'm *really* done with being a loser. I'm ready for my life to start now. Please and thank you. Amen."

Ariel could almost swear he heard a chuckle in response. Mostly because he was hearing a chuckle in response.

"Well. You aren't being weird at all," came an amused and clipped voice in a not-quite American, not-quite Yorkshire accent.

Ariel opened his eyes and lifted his head to see Ellis smirking at him.

"Uh...Um, *heyyy*," Ariel squirmed, instantly embarrassed and wishing that the floor would swallow him up whole. Or even piece by piece. Beggars couldn't be choosers. "I was just, that, I mean—"

"No, no I get it," Ellis held her hands up. "I just had my existential crisis a couple of hours ago. The fire escape on the 14th floor is *really* good for that. You can scream into the universe and the wind just, *whoosh*, carries the sound away. Hella convenient."

Ariel laughed his awkwardness away, while Ellis just shrugged matter-of-factly.

She was dressed to go home, he assumed, judging by the skull-embroidered scarf wrapped around her neck, the leather motorcycle jacket she was wearing, and her studded denim pocketbook which...

"Your, um, your condoms are showing."

"What?" she glanced down and saw the tail of party-colored prophylactics trailing from the corner of her pocketbook. "Oh! Thanks..." she said as she started stuffing the incriminating evidence out of sight. "These aren't for me, by the way. I just have this friend who's very irresponsible with her vagina."

"Irresponsible?" Ariel joked. "Like, letting it watch TV when its homework isn't done, or li—"

"She's a big big whore."

"Oh! Oh, okay."

"Yeah, well, those are her words, not mine. *I'd* be more inclined to say something like somewhere in her uterus is a chalk outline where her dignity used to be."

"What?!" he chortled in spite of himself. "You're horrible!"

"I know," Ellis shrugged again. "She says I'm not 'sex positive,' but I'm *pretty* positive she should *at least* start fingerprinting the guys she's having sex with."

"Wow," Ariel shook his head, still snickering. "I'm so done with you right now."

"Yeah, I should really harness my powers for...well, *less* evil, anyway. Anyhoo, what brings you back here? I thought you started a new gig."

"Yeah...about that."

Ariel related yesterday's events, just, just venting and letting everything pour out of him with all the stream of consciousness frustration and outrage and exasperation he'd been bottling up this whole time, and feeling strangely cathartic when he was done.

In a way he hadn't felt when he'd told Jumaane and Colin just the day before.

"Oh wow. That sucks," Ellis empathized in whatever a non-sequitur tone of voice would sound like.

"YUP. Anyway, that's that. At least it makes *your* day not seem so bad right?"

"Meh, doubtful. I'm—shit—" she answered, distracted and tugging at her left side where, this time, her neon blue carabiner of keys had indeed managed to get snagged on one of her skirt's chains. "I'm headed down to the parking garage. I'd offer you a ride, but my friend just got back from Maryland and she may or may not have accidentally left a copperhead snake in my car. So...yeah, *that's* a thing I have to deal with now."

"The same friend?"

"Yep. Shockingly incompetent around anything *remotely* phallic, apparently."

Ariel snorted again, and the doors pinged open on the first floor.

"Well," he said, stepping out. "Here's to you not finding a snake in your car."

"Oh, I actually *really* hope it's in my car. Because if it's not, then that means it's somewhere in my flat."

"*Oh*-kay. Well then here's hoping you *do* find a snake in your car."

"Pretty much," Ellis half-shrugged this time. "And hey, if they find me dead in the garage because I'm full of *snake venom*, have someone contact my sister," the doors began to close. "And then tell her that I said to punch Emily in the face."

I don't go to *shuls* anymore. Haven't in a *very* long while. Just got tired of all the *"Where are you from when did you convert what brings you here"* bullshit.

But near the end of when I still did, the one thing I hated even more than the pedophiles, was people telling me that I had a chip on my shoulder.

Like, that showed absolutely *no* grasp or appreciation for my experience of showing up in the first place *at all*.

It was pretty much the same for Ariel.

Take his morning, for example.

Ariel lived on the border between the neighborhoods of black (Flatbush) and Jewish (Midwood). It was almost a metaphor for his life. And this morning, like every Saturday morning, Ariel first had to walk through the stares of his Afro-Caribbean American neighbors as he walked through the black side of town.

Those judgmental gazes at the "confused" Black man they perceived Ariel to be. A sellout. Rejecter of the grace of the good lord Jesus. Lackey of the White Man.

True, there were scattered nods of approval. An appreciative "Good morning" from older black folks gratified to see a young buck who still knew how to dress respectably.

But for the most part, it was buses that lazily ambled by in clouds of brown-grey exhaust, full of shaking heads and disapproving frowns cast down from tinted windows.

Shouts of *"Hey! Hey you! Jewboy!"* from mischievous children up too early and with too much energy on a Saturday morning. Or the *"Hey! Hey, Sammy Davis!"* from the adults who should not only have known better, but should've had something more constructive to do with their day off.

Passengers leaning out of cars, jeering as they sat stopped at red lights, taking pictures or even videos with their cameraphones of this anomalous black dude dressed in a suit and skullcap, his flowing calf-length prayer shawl flapping in the breeze, as if he were the Jewish superhero of lost causes and identities.

And then Ariel would cross into the Jewish part of town.

And there he'd greet his fellow Jews with a *"Shabbat Shalom"* and be greeted with a blank stare of silence, a *"Gut Shabbos"* spat out so quickly it might've well been a sneeze, or—his favorite—a frozen smile and a *"Thank you."*

He'd get stared at by children and their parents from across streets, or have double-takes taken after he passed them by. (Without fail there was *always* someone Ariel caught staring when he turned around, and he secretly relished watching them turn the most magnificent shades of red as they quickly whipped their heads forward again.)

Not to mention the upturned noses from Jews old enough to have survived the Holocaust, yet somewhere along the way forgot what that look felt like.

And all that was *before* he'd even reached the synagogue threshold.

The fact that Ariel didn't walk into *shul* literally ticking like a time bomb and exploding was nothing short of a sheer miracle.

And I'm talking one of those *"OMG, the news just called a white 'lone wolf' shooter a terrorist!"* miracles. Not those *"OMG, a black person was killed by police and they* didn't *dig up that one time he got a 'Needs Improvement' in 2nd grade"* kinda miracles.

But that Shabbat morning Ariel was understandably just a *little* bit of a bundle of nerves. This, after all, was the week that he was being formally introduced to the Congregation Ahavath Yisroel community.

Which, given the rapid downward trajectory of the past few weeks, he wasn't entirely sure wouldn't blow up in his face.

Last night had been the "soft opening," he supposed. Even with Kalman spreading the word that the congregation would be vetting a new rabbi that week, they still only managed to muster five people for Friday night services.

Which apparently was two more than the usual attendance rate for the **Erev Shabbat** crowd.

But today's prayers saw practically the entire membership in tow, a total flock of a whopping nineteen or so, about a third of which being women.

Meanwhile, Ariel stationed himself in one of the pews near the back of the room while he mentally reviewed the sermon he had planned, playing Peek-A-Jew™ to keep himself too distracted to get too nervous.

Yes, "Peek-A-Jew™."

It was this game he used to play with himself when he was younger. He'd hold his prayerbook from underneath with both hands so they couldn't be seen, and he'd pull his *tallit* just enough over his head that his face wasn't visible.

And then he'd wait.

Sooner or later, someone would come over to greet him— wishing him a *"Gut Shabbos"* or a *"Shabbat Shalom"* like he was any other random Jew in *shul*—and then he'd get to see their real reaction to him when they actually saw his face, minus all the politically correct veils.

It was like a hidden camera prank show. But with racism.

And reactions ran the gamut from the fairly consistent shock or surprise, to the more frequent than it should've been recoil, to the wildly inappropriate disgust.

Ariel'd stopped playing Peek-A-Jew™ sometime in high school, getting depressed when he realized that more people would come over to greet him when they *couldn't* see what he looked like than when they could. Ever since then, he only pulled the game out of the mothballs when he was uneasy in a new synagogue and wanted to even the score by throwing everyone else off balance too.

So imagine Ariel's surprise at having his own tables turned on him, when the first CAY Peek-A-Jew™ victim was a face that was even darker than his.

"*Shabbat shalom,* brother," came the greeting and half-pound from a face with fierce beard game that made Ariel's naked chin seem, well, pretty naked. "You're Rabbi Samson, right?"

Ariel nodded wordlessly and with an unexpectedly pleased grin. He indicated that he was already in deep the "no talking" zone of prayers.

Theoretically, this zone is known as "***davening.***"

The other party nodded in acknowledgment, never breaking the grip between the two of them. It was a declaration of ethnic solidarity—like The Nod given between two black tourists chilling in Iceland, or the *"What's up, brotha"* to the only other black dude at the white Mecca that is Burning Man—part-pride at seeing another brother outchea who "made it" into those spaces black people weren't ever expected to reach, part-bittersweet at how far there still was to go.

"Yeah," Keith continued, visibly bursting with a barely contained energy. "Kalman sent out an email bulletin about you being the rabbinical candidate for the *shul*. My name's Keith. I'm not Jewish yet, but I'm finishing up my conversion soon. I'm really glad to see you here, and I really hope they choose you, bruh. Welcome."

And with that, Keith broke their handclasp of solidarity, nodded his head again, then made his way to his own seat a few pews ahead.

Well, Ariel thought. Maybe this place would be a better fit for him than he ever could've thought.

✡ ✡ ✡

Ariel's ***drasha*** was well received enough, he thought.

That week's portion was **Vayetze**, so he'd decided to focus on Genesis 28:16, when Jacob awakens from his dream of angels ascending and descending a heavenly stairway.

"Surely the L'rd is present in this place, and I did not know it," Jacob exclaims, shaken.

"Too often," Ariel expounded, pacing as he spoke from the ***bimah***, an old habit from his teaching days. "We think of G'd as some sort of genie. That He has to make some big entrance. Or maybe that he's, ***lehavdil***, Las Vegas. All bright flashy lights and bombastic sounds all the time. And so, too often, we forget the fact

119

is that He's everywhere and in everything and in everyone. He's in that babbling brook on I and 14th. He's in that homeless guy who's always outside of Bravo Pizza. He's even here, in this scrappy little underdog *shul* that, against the odds, continues to persevere and endure. The burden is on *us* to recognize G'd in the places we encounter, and in the people that we meet. And even in ourselves, too. In those times when we discover those resources and those wellsprings of strength we didn't know we had in us. Because surely the L'rd is present those places. You just didn't know it."

It seemed to be a hit, and Ariel followed up by leading the congregation in the **Mussaf** prayer. And as he soundlessly mouthed the words of the silent portion of the services in Hebrew, his mind whirred at a mile a minute in English.

Because that's what happens.

You're just standing there in place, rocking back and forth.

Everyone in the room is silent.

Words you've said a million times are either spilling rotely off your lips in phonetic chunks you've memorized, or like you're fluently speed-reading through a Dr. Seuss book.

And so your thoughts start pouring into your head while your body runs on auto-pilot. You start thinking about lunch. What time services are over. Where you last saw your *Lord of the Rings* boxed-set. Was that girl checking you out earlier? Was that boy?

Ariel would be the first to admit that it wasn't ideal, but the only times he had complete concentration on the prayers splayed out before him in austere black-and-white, was whenever something bad had happened to him.

Or if he was praying for forgiveness.

And even then, only if he was praying for forgiveness and it *wasn't* the High Holidays. Because *of course* all his brain wanted to think about in the middle of **Ne'ilah**, was the delicious little bad things he would like to do again in the new year.

It was like trying not to think about white elephants, and so obviously you start thinking about having sex with white elephants.

But today, Ariel's wayward Mussaf thoughts focused on Congregation Ahavath Yisroel.

He liked the place, he decided. And the people were that just right mix of quirky characters that synagogues only seemed to acquire as they neared the end of their lifespan.

The two or three ancient congregants who founded the *shul*. The cluster of less old people who grew up in it. The spindly barely-legal Lubavitcher with the crushed hat and half-goat beard that Chabad sent out like prospectors to struggling *shuls*, looking to establish new Rebbe veins to mine. The young enough and pretty enough single girl who was the apple of the congregation's eye, but was also just weird enough that she was, well, single and *there*. The shlumpy socially awkward guy you're always surprised to learn was married at some point and has grown children. The young 30-something couples that everyone swears will be the ones to turn this *shul* around and raise it up like a phoenix from the ashes. And just a dash of college kids looking for some no-strings-attached, no-pressure, no-obligation Judaism whenever they felt like it, without their attendance or non-attendance being seen as some commentary on their relationship with observance or belief. And—the role that Keith was quite ably filling—the convert-in-the-wings.

The only question was whether or not CAY had a use for a rabbi like Ariel.

The answer, obviously, was yes.

✡ ✡ ✡

The *kiddish* downstairs after services was surprisingly impressive for the small crowd, three folding tables stocked with all the "classic Jewish" foods that pretend that other classic Jewish foods don't exist.

Pickled herring. Hummus. Matboucha. Tuna fish. Egg salad. Potato kugel. Noodle kugel. Slimy quartered blobs of jarred gefilte fish in pale quivering jelly. Those Stella D'Oro Swiss Fudge cookies. Three different flavors of soda in varying states of emptiness and fizziness. Dry sponge cake. Drier marble sponge cake. Four different power-washed lettuce salads. Stale AF garlic-flavored Tam-Tams. And, of course, vodka and single-malt scotch.

Y'know, the good stuff.

Everyone huddled around Ariel as he made *kiddish*, and then, after the cups of ceremonial wine were passed out, the eating began, breaking the congregants up into the usual synagogue cafeteria tables.

The old couple sitting along together, earnestly bent over their meals because they likely didn't have one at home. The young thirty-something women giggling amongst themselves while a stern elder stateswoman looked on, unimpressed by these "modern" women and their lax standards. The young thirty-something men who never seemed to venture farther than a two-foot radius from the alcohol. The once-in-a-whilers trying to decipher what exactly those blobs of gefilte fish jelly were. And then everyone else, doing their best to navigate the food selections that looked like they were slapped together by a catering school degenerate one salmonella-laced dish away from being expelled.

For Ariel—who had converted his anxiety into hunger—the *kiddish* was like a band-aid on a severed limb. Which is the *only* reasonable explanation for why he was occupied with the tepid gefilte fish jelly, using the stale AF garlic Tam-Tams to shovel it into his mouth, when a congregant came over to greet him.

"Rabbi Samson?" came the voice, slightly timid. Its owner was maybe a very fresh nineteen, faintly radiating all the smoldering culture shock of a *yeshiva*-sheltered white girl suddenly thrust into the real world of the secular real world. And all the shattered preconceived notions thereby entailed. *"Gut Shabbos."*

"Hi, *Shabbat Shalom*," Ariel replied warmly, swallowing a chunky glob of that gefilte fish jelly, which—I *cannot* stress enough—is invidiously nauseating.

"Hi, I'm Chani Guildencrantz. I'm the features editor for *Hatikvah*? It's the student newspaper over at the Brooklyn College Hillel."

"Oh yeah! I went to Brooklyn College."

"Really? Whoa, cool! That is *so* funny! Because we're looking to do a Jewish reaction to things like Ferguson and Black Lives Matter, and I was wondering—as a rabbi, and someone black, and an alumnus too, I guess—would you like to write a short piece for us? Like, would you be interested?"

"Sure! I mean, what's the deadline, what are you looking for in tone, etc?"

"Well, Thanksgiving break starts on Thursday, so how about by Monday? And something progressive, Jewish, and thoughtful? Something only you can say that no one else can?"

"I don't see why not. Sounds like a plan!"

"Great! That sounds great! We've been trying to figure out a response for a while and your *drash* was *so* good that I figured, what the heck, I might as well feel you out about the topic."

"Well, consider me felt," Ariel beamed.

Wait, *no...*

"Hey," Kalman suddenly appeared at Ariel's side, rescuing him from himself while Chani turned bright scarlet. "Got a minute? Lemme introduce you to the board."

"Ohyespleasenow," Ariel quickly answered as Kalman led him away.

✡ ✡ ✡

Jerome Litwak was a mountain of a man packed and stuffed into a two-piece suit.

With a lightly wrinkled bald head, crinkly blue eyes, and a lightly-toasted tan, Kalman's vice-president was thickly built, reminding Ariel of one of those old vaudeville strongmen, or Major Alex Louis Armstrong from *Full Metal Alchemist*. Ariel could easily imagine a young Jerome wearing a dirty-blond handlebar mustache that eventually eased into the bone-white goatee that now rested on his face.

Jerome engulfed Ariel's hand in a beefy fist of a handshake and gave it two efficient tugs—one up, one down—instantly dislocating and resetting Ariel's shoulder in its socket with a gruff *"Shabbat shalom."*

There was something vaguely "Luca Brasi" about Jerome.

Which probably had something to do with his mother's maiden name: Bertolotti.

Rumor had it—because, Jews—that one fine Halloween weekend in the 1970's, as Rabbi Samuel Gellerman was being chased through the streets of Brooklyn by a gaggle of college-aged hooligans armed with frozen eggs, a twenty-something not-at-all college bound Jerome Litwak stepped out of the shadows to come to the older man's aid.

Some say Jerome was pissed that he'd been denied his cut from the stick-up crew he ran with, and was just looking for someone to take it out on.

Others say it was because the then middle-aged Rabbi Gellerman reminded the then-younger Jerome of his kindly little grandfather in his prime.

But *everyone* will tell you that Jerome proceeded to break every. Single. Bone. In the ringleader's arm.

Just because he could.

From that point on, CAY had gained its own enforcer—a half-Italian half-Lithuanian kid, neither Catholic nor Jewish. At least not until 1984, when the death of his grandfather spurred Jerome to make the formal leap into his paternally-inherited faith.

The *shul* unanimously appointed Jerome vice-president the following year, a post he held—uncontested—ever since.

Fiercely loyal to the congregation, Jerome was, according to Kalman, one of the major influences holding the Katz boys to their dad's deal with Ahavath Yisroel. What the other major influences were, Kalman neglected to say, but it seemed fairly obvious that at least one of them was Cate Finklestein.

She *was* the treasurer, after all. All 5'7" of her.

Well 5'3", really.

Four of those inches were the rhinestone-studded stilettos that made her long and shapely fifty-something year-old(!) legs put women half her age to shame.

With clear buttermilk skin that had yet to show any signs of sagging or stretching, she was more than aware that her body had kept up alluringly well in its battle against time—a likely result of having never borne children.

Possibly because she would've eaten them.

Her outwardly cheery veneer felt warm in all the wrong ways to Ariel, with a full smile that was somehow brittle and superficial, and a twinkling, sugary voice likely just as sweet as the nectar of a Venus flytrap. And through a lush flaxen canopy of feathered bangs, there glistened her brown doe-eyes stamped with crow's feet, dully lit with the same deceptive glow as a python's as it wrapped its coils around you.

She, like Kalman, was CAY royalty, daughter of one of its six founding families.

Or the daughter of *two* of them, depending on who you asked.

Rumor had it—because, see above—that Joel Englehart (CAY treasurer from 1950-1959), in a bid for more power, had gone about the task of seducing Ellen Finklestein, second wife of Gene Finklestein (CAY's president from the congregation's inception in 1946 until 1957). The result, allegedly, was Joel's proposals suddenly carrying more weight in board meetings, and—*allegedly* allegedly— a daughter born long after both Gene and Ellen knew that Gene suffered from ED. The biological disorder, not the music genre. (Although, same difference.)

They'd stayed, the Finklesteins, riding out the rumor mill of Joel and Ellen's affair, and becoming the only founding family to witness the ebbs and flows of Congregation Ahavath Yisroel as it expanded out of a storefront and into its own building, and moved along the Jewish religious spectrum from Conservative to Conservadox to finally Modern Orthodox.

These days, anyone who knew the whispered cloud hovering over her parentage was either dead or dying, and so Cate rode high on the less salacious legacies of her family name in the halls of CAY, using it to bludgeon anyone who fell out of her favor.

It's amazing how much no one ever really leaves high school.

And also how much synagogue politics resemble an episode of *Las Muñecas de la Mafia*.

✡ ✡ ✡

With one board member left to meet and greet, Kalman's introduction tour had to be temporarily halted, as Cate urgently needed his attention concerning the **seudah shlishit** meal logistics for later that afternoon, and the cream pie she insisted on having served.

And so Ariel found himself momentarily chaperone-less as he mingled with the CAY crowd, hopping from polite small talk to polite small talk, like when you only know the one person at a party, but that person's just bailed on you, and so now you're trying to act all cool and nonchalant as if you aren't screaming inside while you flounder in a sea of social anxiety.

Good times.

"Well look at you," suddenly came a rasp of a voice. A familiar older woman's pitch that sounded like she was dragging her vocal cords through gravel while chewing on broken glass. "*Rabbi* Ariel Samson."

Ariel turned in surprise, to see the thin-framed lady with wrinkled leathery skin the color of oatmeal, nursing a drink that in turn was nursing its own drink.

You figure out what that visual looks like. My job here is just to paint the picture.

"Professor Koegel?"

"Ehh," she waved the honorific away, punctuating the motion with a swig from her cup. "It's just Phyllis now. Or secretary. Whatever. So, *nu*, what's doing? How've you been? You were one of my favorite students, you know that?"

"Oh thanks!" Ariel said brightly, before realizing. "...But you, uh, you failed me."

"Yeah," she croaked. "But you were still one of my favorites. I don't just *give* F+'s away, honey. Where are you working these days?"

"I'm actually *very* funemployed right now," Ariel half-chuckled with a shrug.

"What?" Phyllis exclaimed, in gravelly shock. "A bright kid like you? What are you looking for?"

"I dunno, anything, really. Writing. Teaching. Editing—"

"You know this rabbi gig here doesn't pay right?" she stepped in closer to Ariel, almost conspiratorially. "Kalman *did* tell you that, right?"

Ariel laughed.

"Don't worry, I know," he assured. "This is more of a, I dunno, a favor, I guess."

"But how are you going to live?" Phyllis persisted. "I mean, I'll keep my ears open and—wait," she slapped her open palm into her forehead, nearly knocking herself backwards. "Liba Sheindel! Have you met her yet?"

"Liba who?"

"Come," she grabbed Ariel by the elbow with a grip like a bony claw, and began to lead him across the room to a group of younger women chatting by a table. "She *just* told me yesterday that something opened up by her job—Liba, honey!" Phyllis barked out to the group, which promptly melted away to reveal the object of Phyllis' bellow. "Liba. That opening you told me about Friday, can you put Rabbi Samson in there? You can do it, right? I can tell you he's an amazing—you heard him today, right? One of my old Medieval Lit students! And I'm telling you, he will just knock whatever it is right out of the water," she turned to Ariel. "You talk to her, okay? This is Liba Sheindel, she's the president of our sisterhood here. She'll take good care of you."

And that's when Ariel was introduced to Liba Sheindel Green.

Or "L.S." for short.

Pronounced "Ellis."

"Well," she smirked at his open-mouthed gape. "I guess we'll be working together after all, Kosher Meat."

The writer's room for *Late Late Night Night with Wes Valentine* was modestly sized and populated by about half a dozen writers. Nothing too crazy or hectic. After all, they were only a late-night talk show that streamed online to about 700k or so subscribers (or closer to 1.5m if you counted YouTube and Facebook followers), so no real pressure there, right?

WRONG.

Because L.S. "Ellis" Green was at the helm of this ship, and she ran it tighter than a vote for women's reproductive rights in a Republican-majority Senate.

Every loose wire, every cheesy prop, every low-production value was precisely as loose, cheesy, or shoddy as Ellis intended it to be, and not a fraction off.

Every off-the-cuff moment and spontaneous event, it was all part of the plan, all part of the show, and Ellis scripted it down to the millisecond.

Sure, she may have only had the title of "associate" producer in the credits, but there wasn't a soul among the crew who didn't believe in their heart of hearts that it was only because creating the position of "Grand Puppeteer" would be a paperwork nightmare for HR.

For Ariel, the whole thing—much like any other encounter with Ellis thus far—was both intimate and intimidating. There's probably some witty etymological hoodoo between those two words, but I just woke up, my raven hasn't brought me my coffee yet, and I don't really have the energy to wring that joke out right now.

Also, contrary to pop culture belief, Ariel was surprised to discover that the writers weren't a bunch of twenty-something bright-eyed hopefuls or forty-something disillusioned schlubs still looking for their big break.

No, these guys were actual, socially well-adjusted, productive members of society. One of them even paid for his *own* Netflix account.

Then again, there *was* Q. Who, somehow, Ariel immediately knew was the writer that Colin had sent Ellis' way.

"Q..." Ellis scanned a script with scrunched eyebrows. "Is this a joke about a vampire raping a horse?"

"Lemme see that?" Q looked over the stapled pages Ellis handed him, nodded, then handed them back.

"Yes."

"And that's funny to you. Horse-raping vampires."

"Well...yeah. I mean, just picture that: Some old vampire dude who hasn't gotten any in a hundred years or something, and he's just, y'know, giving it to this horse all like *'Yeah! Yeah! Take it, horse!'* and the horse is like whinnying, trying to get away and shit, but the vampire's riding the hell out of it and trying to bite its neck and everything, like *'Yeah! You like that? Who's your batty? Who's your batty? Yeah!'* Y'know?"

"...Q, I'm gonna need you to take some time off for the next couple days, alright?"

"Well actually, I—"

"Break. NOW."

Q slunk out of the room, and Ellis' incredulous exhale was met with a collective sigh of relief so deep that somewhere, in North Carolina, a Republican suddenly realized that they couldn't be both the "party of Lincoln" *and* upset that Democrats were tearing down their own Confederate statues, and instantly they exploded into a fine mist of First Amendment rights.

"So anyway," Ellis began, corralling some sanity back into the meeting. "Gather around, kids. First order of business: We have a new writer with us, Ariel Samson," Ariel waved lightly to his new co-workers. "He'll be working with some of you on skits and some of you on monologue, just to get the rhythm of the show, so—"

The door burst open, and a cocky figure with a swoop of perfectly coiffed hair, horn-rimmed glasses, and a smug attitude strutted into the room, preening like a mayonnaise-colored human peacock with a doughier midsection.

This, was Wes Valentine. The star and producer of *Late Late Night Night*.

Much like Ellis, Wes was "producer" in name only.

Except in his case, the title was a gross overembellishment.

His father was one of the big hoity-toity studio executive muckety mucks, and so Wes could afford to slack off because a fourth joke about Republicans.

If late night TV shows were starships, then Ellis would be cast as a sarcastically slanted Mr. Spock, while Wes played the role of a dumber Capt. Kirk, with more unearned swagger and vertically improbable hair.

"Hey Ellis," he asked, holding up a script. "Is this a joke about a vampire raping a horse?"

"Already taken care of Wes. I—"

"Oh no, no I like it. Can we work it into the opening monologue though? I just—"

At that moment Wes' eye caught sight of Ariel over Ellis' shoulder, and he erupted into a peal of obnoxious laughter.

"Who's *that* guy?"

"This is Ariel, one of our new writers," Ellis said while rubbing her fingers into her eyes, bracing for the imminent blundering about to transpire. "Ariel, this is Wes—"

"Wes Valentine," Wes sauntered over, extending his hand and shaking Ariel's. "Host of *Late Late Night Night with Wes Valentine*. I can definitely see you're gonna be a *huge* asset to the team here. Just the level of dedication alone."

"I'm...sorry?" Ariel asked, confused, as Wes pulled back and forth on his arm like he was trying to rev a lawnmower.

"I mean, wow," Wes released Ariel from the handshake and placed both hands on his hips, nodding in approval. "You've got the hat *and* the Jew-strings? You really go all in for the joke. What other costumes do you wear to get into the process?"

"Ah...Well, I'm not really in costume *now*, so, uh...no."

Wes' laughter roared like a crackling fire for a full five seconds, before Ariel's not-even-a-little-bit-joking expression drenched it into embers of uncertain half-chuckles. And it slowly dawned on the oblivious TV host that no one else was laughing with him either.

"Oh...Oh!" Wes composed himself, abruptly serious. "So, so you're really a..."

He spun his finger around the top of his head, indicating Ariel's *kippah*.

"Yeah. Hence the..." Ariel answered, mimicking Wes' finger movements.

"Oh. Oh, uh...*Shomer shabbos*, then."

"...Thanks."

An agonizing silence filled the room.

"Anyhoo, Ellis," Wes spun back around, rushing for the door. "I'll talk to you later about these vampires. Great stuff, guys."

He paused and solemnly turned to Ariel once more, just before closing the door behind himself.

"*Shomer shabbos.*"

And then he was gone.

Ellis exhaled into her hands and then clapped them once.

"Alright," she continued. "So, second order of business..."

✡ ✡ ✡

The studio was mischievously dim and brimming with a live audience that tittered with anticipation.

The house band was cooking with gas, serving up a brassy jam-session soup of trumpet, trombone, and saxophone, with sprigs of bass guitar and a drum kit garnish. Lights brightened on the stage, revealing a faux New York skyline and a thin middle-aged gentleman standing at a podium. The floor manager, his head framed between the two bulky cups of his headset, began counting the studio down. The band stirred a keyboard into the mix and turned up the heat.

"From Constitution Studios in New York," boomed the middle-aged gentleman. "It's *Late Late Night Night* with Wes Valentine!"

The audience erupted into thunderous applause that rumbled through the floor as they recognized the band segue into the TV show's familiar theme.

"Tonight!" the announcer bellowed. "Jessica Ducane! Eddie Ortiz! And musical guest Ninjas of the Dawn! Featuring the Late Late Night Night Band and me, Marcus Mann! And now, here he is: Wes! Valentine!"

The drums barreled to a crescendo and Wes exploded from behind the red velvet curtains to the welcoming cacophony of audience cheers, trumpet squeals, and trombone shrieks, as he strode to the stage with an infectious, nervous energy, wordlessly hamming it up for the people with kooky comedic body language and hammy finger jabs.

A shattering crash of cymbals echoed through the pandemonium, and the music evaporated from the air, leaving only the whoops and hollers of human voices.

And then began the show.

"Thanks everybody, welcome to the program," Wes greeted as the applause died down.

"*I LOVE YOU!*" came a cry from a random audience member.

"I love you too, sir," Wes shot back, adding a quip. "Always the men, never the ladies."

The audience guffawed.

"We've got a great show here for you tonight," Wes continued. "So, uh, anyone see the news today? No? Well, apparently, an Arkansas student is suing his university for placing copies of the Bible in the fiction section."

The audience *ooohed*.

"*Yeah*. Yeah, the college refuses to apologize, saying, 'This is Arkansas,'" Wes blurted out in laughter. "The Bible is in *every* section'."

The audience hooted and snickered at the low hanging fruit joke.

"In other news, the makers of Viagra are reportedly working on a birth control pill for men. They're gonna call it Niagra."

Scattered laughter peppered the room.

"I don't get it," the announcer offered with feigned confusion.

"Well Marcus," Wes began snickering before even reaching his punchline, clapping his hands and doubling over. "Because Niagra...falls."

The audience cheered and howled once more, delighted in the way that a newborn is after it discovers for the seventeenth time in a row that paper makes a crunching sound when you crinkle it.

Meanwhile, in the control room tucked into the corner of the studio, Ariel and a few of the other writers groaned.

"I think one of those jokes used to be mine," someone lamented.

"Well, them's the breaks kids," Ellis offered as she monitored the goings-on on several of the display screens. "We get paid to write it, not deliver it."

And so it went.

The core *Late Late Night Night* audience was clearly clinically depressed and/or suffering from early onset dementia.

At least that was the only plausible reason Ariel could conjure as to why they were so sycophantically mesmerized by Wes Valentine, his cocksure smugness, and his *"amateur night at the bar"* level of comedic competence. There was no other logical explanation except that his viewers led lives so utterly on fire, that it was all they could do to find comfort in consuming pointless, nonsensical, brain junk food.

Under Ellis' hawkish eye, the show *itself* had a decent handful of engaging and hilarious segments—and Ariel was sure that his fellow writers were grateful that whatever arcane magnetism Wes held over the audience, he at least kept eyes glued to the screen long enough for their work to not be in vain.

But *Moses on a matzah*, Wes' hosting skills were *atrocious*.

When he wasn't busy ruining his delivery—blurting out punchlines and laughing at his own jokes, while doubled over and slapping his hands together like a demented seal—he was conducting interviews with all the sophistication of an immature teenager, interrupting his guests with forced laughter whenever they said something barely remotely funny, while doubled over and slapping his hands together like a demented seal.

Wes Valentine was like that one guy at a college party who doesn't actually know how to have fun and is terrified of genuine interactions, so they're either randomly stripping off their shirt or screaming *"Who wants to do shots!"* the second there's any kind of naturally occurring social lull.

And just like that, Ellis' iron grip over production made sense. It was a defense mechanism to minimize as much as possible the naturally occurring damage of Wes barreling through the show.

Meanwhile, over on the back-end, writing for TV was a lot different than Ariel had imagined it to be.

Late Late's best and most veteran writer had been snagged by *Saturday Night Live*, leaving Ellis with a writer-shaped hole to fill. One that Ariel had tripped and fell into and fit quite nicely.

Counting Ellis and Ariel, it was a seven person writing staff—five men, two women—and mostly full of improv talent and YouTube bloggers, split into separate teams of monologue and sketch writers, with the occasional celebrity guest assignments.

For the monologue team, every day was a series of 30-minute deadlines for turning in batches of jokes, and hourly meetings with Ellis to winnow the joke-herd down before she told Wes what he was going to go with. The occasional hippophilic vampire aside. (Yes, I too was surprised to learn that a horse-lover is not, in fact, an equiphile.)

Over on Team Sketch, the process was practically the definition of procrastination, largely consisting of 10:00 am spitball sessions and praying that something miraculously cobbled itself together by 1:30 rehearsal for the show's filming at 4.

But for all its informality, the job was a lot less the imagined free-wheeling of sitting around in a room making characters and jokes out of thin air, and a lot more factory-like tedium of sending out emails, watching and pulling TV and movie clips and trailers, and watching tons and tons and TONS of news channels.

And then after that, the rest of the day was spent trying to find an angle for it.

After all, there were hundreds of shows doing the same thing, watching the same news, angling for the same jokes, all waiting to jump on something and parody it as its shelf-life diminished by the minute.

"Don't think of this as a late-night show," Ellis had advised Ariel. "It's a 24-hour show, because everything is online the next day. Think your jokes hard and fast. And don't get caught up in your successes or your failures. If it's awesome, great! Enjoy it for the hour or two. Then you've gotta get back on the grind for the next day. If it bombs, oh well. Sulk for an hour or two. Then prove yourself on tomorrow's show. Every day's a new day."

It was a crazy breakneck schedule, and Ellis had him alternating between the monologue and sketch crews to see where he was a better fit. So it was like constructing and executing a month's worth of lesson plans in a day, but with a gun to your head and covered with bees.

And he loved it.

Loved the feeling of working those long dormant creative muscles, the ones he'd abandoned long ago, reminding him that he was a writer at heart. A dreamer most at home imagining up noble swashbucklers on renegade ships, diaphanous elves fighting lava-kissed dragons, and steampunk heroines saving themselves *and* their princes *and* the day.

That *was* why he'd pursued a Master's in Creative *"Sure, this'll be insanely lucrative"* Writing, right?

So it felt good to be getting some use out of all that sweat and work of his college days. Or just being generally gainfully employed, to be honest. The 40k take-home wasn't too shabby, no sirree.

And neither was the company. Particularly when it came to lunch.

It was a routine Ariel and Ellis had taken only three days to immediately fall into.

Someone would decide which of the super overpriced kosher food spots would be feeding them for the day, they'd go lunch, then head back to the studio and get on the grind in time for rehearsals to start.

It was their thing. Today it was pizza.

"Feel like you're getting your sea legs yet, scallywag?" Ellis teased in her tea-and-crumpets voice.

Ariel laughed.

"Yeah, it's a little bit of baptism by fire, but I'm getting there."

"Great."

"You have any critiques? I mean, it's only been a couple of days, but somehow I figure you already have a detailed performance review written in your head."

"Heh. Well, yeah, you are very definitively a Creative Writing major."

"Really? How so?"

"It's...it's just how you operate in the space. You don't really seem to understand performative theatricality. Like, you're expecting audiences to be looking for subtext and nuance and motifs and whatnot. You're not getting yet that your characters only exist in the sketch they appear in. So no, there's no before or after. There's no character arc or anything. They are the entirety of who they are in that moment. I think that's why you do better at monologues. Because there's a sense of continuity with the audience that you're comfortable building on."

"I...huh. I guess I never really looked at it like that. That's actually really accurate."

"I know. You're welcome. Not my first rodeo, this."

"How *did* you break in? What was that like?"

"Me? I was doing IT and had a hilarious Twitter feed that got me discovered while I was an intern here my junior year. That was about two, three years ago. Started as a production assistant on *Janey's Funtime Place* when I was still in my senior year. Then about a year ago, the studio head needed his kid to kindly stop lying around the house, so they created *Late Late Night Night* to give Wes a toy to play with. For some reason I was the only one who could control him, so they moved me over and up to associate producer."

"Wait, this is Wes *under control*?"

Ellis gave Ariel a look.

"Wow. Well then. Kudos for being able to work with him."

"I *don't* work with Wes. I work *around* Wes."

"But why? You're, like, *really* good at what you do. Why stay here? Why not, I dunno, try to work for Conan or Colbert or something? On a real station?"

Ellis laughed uproariously.

"Oh my dear child, no. Do you know how hard it is to get a job in TV? TV does. And that's why TV routinely dangles these little carrots of working on some big-name show, with this tiny little catch of having to write 30-plus page submission packets. For free. Just preying on the desperation of TV writers looking for work and willing to do too much for no guarantee whatsoever that a studio won't ask for submissions, *not* hire them, use their free material, and then turn around and say *'Great minds think alike'* when you complain that they've stolen your shit. So yeah, no. Not doing that. Besides, no one's looking in this little black girl's direction. Not when there's droves of mediocre male Caucasity waiting in the wings."

"Oh. Well that sucks. But that's kinda, I dunno, a really jaded way of looking at it? Why not go for it anyway? If it's meant to be, it's meant to be."

"Ugh. See, that pie-in-the-sky stuff is exactly why you're a bad rabbi."

Ariel was taken aback.

"*What?*" he asked, shocked.

"Hm. Ok. Lemme rephrase that. I heard your *drasha*. Good stuff. You're an excellent scholar, and you talk good. But you're a terrible congregational leader."

"Um, that's better I guess? Also, how do you mean?"

"You're a little soft. And like, way too...I dunno. Shiny or something. Like, when life gives you lemons, what do you do?"

"Grab tequila and salt?"

"See, yeah? *That* right there? WRONG. When life gives you lemons, padawan, you *eat* those lemons. You eat those little yellow bitches whole. The skin, the pulp, the seeds, *everything*. And you stare life right the *fuck* in its eyes while you do it. Don't blink. And after life stops being such an asshole because you've shown it that you're done dicking around, *then* you grab tequila."

Ellis checked her watch while Ariel sat dumbfounded, absorbing this new life lesson.

"C'mon," she said as she rose from the table. "We're gonna be late."

When your number's up, your number's up, they say, and they usually say it when said number-calling is mired in a Rube Goldberg-esque series of convoluted coincidences. But isn't it weird how people only use that phrase to mean the *bad* things that happen to people?

Like Henry Ziegland, for example.

In 1893, Ziegland jilted a lover who then subsequently committed suicide.

The girl's brother then hunted Ziegland down, shot him, then turned the gun on himself, likewise committing suicide. Except the vengeful brother's bullet never actually struck Ziegland, instead only grazing his face and getting lodged in a nearby tree.

Decades later in 1913, happily thinking he'd dodged fate, Ziegland attempted to cut that same tree down. The task seemed so formidable that, genius that he was, Ziegland decided to blow the tree up with a few sticks of dynamite.

The subsequent explosion propelled the bullet—still lodged in the trunk—gently through Ziegland's skull, killing him 20 years after it was fired.

Or like Tsutomu Yamaguchi, for instance, who stepped off a train in Japan for a business trip.

On August 6th, 1945.

In Hiroshima.

Manishtana

Just in time for the detonation of the first atomic bomb less than two miles away.

Yamaguchi survived, spent the night in an air raid shelter—temporarily blinded—then returned home to a not radioactive Japanese city.

Three days later, Yamaguchi was at work relating his failed business trip in Hiroshima to his superiors—and presumably demanding some hella overtime pay because *ATOMIC-FUCKING-BOMB*—when he looked up at the calendar and realized it was August 9th, looked down at the map and realized that he lived in Nagasaki, looked out the window to see the *second* atomic bomb detonating, and then looked at the camera and shrugged as a laugh track played.

And he survived again, likely handing in his quite reasonable two weeks notice to HR not long after.

Hell, speaking of world wars, WWI only even *started* because some guy (Gavrilo Princip, who *really* wanted to kill Franz Ferdinand to death) was eating a sandwich in a café and happened to look up just in time to see Franz Ferdinand *literally* passing by that very second (having *just* barely dodged being killed to death just barely an *hour* earlier).

Crazy.

But, y'know guys, *sometimes* The Universe conspires in *good* ways too.

Sure, it might not seem that way at first, like when your most senior writer calls out with a yeast infection inflamed to the point of needing immediate hospital attention.

"My ladybits are ablaze with agony," Regina'd told Ellis. "Not to give too much away, but it looks like a platypus down there."

Or, when another writer is rushing both to the veterinarian *and* the hospital because, as Elmo said, "My cat ate all of my insulin. Also, I'm gonna need more insulin. Like, now."

And understandably, when the last member of your monologue team is MIA because they're still tripping balls from the shrooms they did the night before, and so they call to inform you in a terrified whisper, as Drake did, that "I can't come into work today, I'm an inch tall"—one *might* start to get a little concerned.

But it was all okay, Ellis thought.

She could pop out a good enough monologue with some back-up from Ariel, Buddy, and, ugh, even Q.

But Q, good ol' Q, had been kind enough to leave the voicemail: "Hey, this is Q, I'm down in Tewksbury. I just found out that, apparently, I have a warrant out for my arrest. I'm being booked. I'll call you back later."

And so, with no monologue team, one-third of her sketch team, and a week-old rookie, Ellis buckled down and set to work.

"Guys," Ellis sat Ariel and Buddy down in the writer's room at about noon. "There's only the three of us. We have half a monologue and four terrible rough drafts of sketches. We're having a working lunch, because we're at Defcon 4 right now. Rehearsals start in an hour and a half. And our guests tonight are City Councilman Jeffrey Grundman and Marli James."

Jeffrey Grundman was a popular local activist and twice-failed mayoral candidate, a progressive young Modern Orthodox firebrand recently appointed to replace a scandal-mired Brooklyn councilman in a special election the week before. (Something about Grundman's predecessor doing something inappropriate and sexual and abuse of power and, I dunno, pick literally anything from the news. *That*. He did *that* bad sex thing.)

The *Late Late* show would be Grundman's first media appearance since the hubbub surrounding his taking office, and his first chance to talk about his plans for the future.

Tonight's other big deal, Marli James, was the newest media darling/creepily young sex symbol, formerly hatched out of a Disney-channel show in her prepubescent years.

She was currently on one of those super binge-able non-descriptly edgy shows with an edgy non-descriptly gorgeous ensemble cast that sexily glowered at you from billboards in the subway.

Tonight on the *Late Late* show, she'd be performing songs from her soon-to-be released and highly-autotuned debut album, a staggering labor of love that produced ten songs composed by seventy-one writers who apparently all grew up on the exact same three Dr. Seuss books and beats by Timbaland.

"We *cannot* afford to flop this show," Ellis emphasized. "Let's get to work."

And worked they did, churning out rapid fire ideas, but producing ever-diminishing returns. The four terrible rough drafts were becoming four even worse fully fleshed-out bits. Frustrations mounted. Tensions rose. And everyone decided they needed to take a ten-minute break away from each other and then regroup.

The day was not looking good.

Would our heroes be able to save the show against these impossible odds? Would they emerge with their friendships, careers, and creative integrity intact? Will I ever shut up? Find out after the jump!

Ariel was trying—he was *really* trying—to rise to the occasion in this 11th hour crisis, to be the dark horse contender that pulled out a surprise victory for the team, but his mind kept choking up like a stalling engine.

Just turning over and over and over but not starting.

He, Ellis, and Buddy had been raiding the vending machines all day, so it wasn't a fuel problem.

But maybe—just maybe—it was a "spark" problem.

Which is why he'd taken the liberty of retreating to the 14th floor fire escape to partake in just a smidge of the devil's lettuce, his favorite muse. Ellis *had* mentioned the wind's tendency to whisk things out of range of detection, remember?

And desperate times called for desperate measures.

At first there were no thoughts.

Just the happy fog of chill nothingness. All formless and void. And then suddenly there was every thought. Flying at him. Randomly even, hurtling forward at a million miles an hour, then making an unexpected jerk to the left at the last second like a knight on a chessboard. Some ideas that floated by slowly enough to catch like fireflies. Some that zoomed down the trackways of his neurons like a runaway train, so fleeting that all he could do was watch their taillights receding into the distance. They came pouring in one after another, flooding his mind like an endless river.

And then, out of the blue, came a beam of inspiration hovering over the face of the waters.

"Ellis," Ariel strode back into that writer's room, grinning so wide that he could've split his own face in half. "I have an idea."

✡ ✡ ✡

Seven minutes of explanation later, Ellis was firmly shaking her head.

"Nope. Not doing it. No."

"Yeah, we are!" Ariel enthusiastically retorted, while Buddy neutrally shrugged. "C'mon, why not?"

"I mean, it's a good idea. I just don't trust Wes to not screw up in it."

"Can we *dan l'kaf zechut* him just this once? I'll put it on my tab."

"And now I'm even *less* inclined."

"But we *literally* don't have anything better."

Ellis waffled for a moment.

"Look," Ariel persisted. "I once pulled a lesson plan out of my ass with just half an Aesop fable and a Spice Girls song. We're *good*."

"Really. What song? 'Who Do You Think You Are'?"

"No. '2 Become 1'."

"Hmph...Well that's a good song, actually."

"I thought so, too."

Ellis paused, looking at Ariel.

"...You just talked to Miriam Jane, didn't you?"

"...Maybe."

"*Scheisse*," Ellis sighed, taking a small flask out of one of her skirt's many pockets, unscrewing the cap and downing a gulp.

"Alright," she said, grimacing against the taste as she screwed the cap back on. "Might as well give this a whirl. Write it up, get your props, meet me on the floor in twenty."

"Hey, if this sucks," Buddy offered as they rose from the table. "We'll just do it wrong and strong. Just like band camp."

"You mean loud and proud."

"Nope."

✡ ✡ ✡

"No, no stop," Marcus shook his head in disgust at his podium, interrupting Buddy—dressed in a garish pink-and-green polka-dotted chicken costume—from doing the macarena. "Just stop the bit. This is terrible."

"What?" said Wes in overdramatic shock. "What, no, this is great! This is comedy gold right here!"

"This is a dumpster fire, Wes. Buddy, did you even *show* this to the Late Late Rabbi?"

"No..." Buddy mumbled sheepishly, slumping into his shoulders.

"I thought so. Get outta here. And we're cutting your rations in half this week."

Buddy guiltily clomped offstage in comedically oversized chicken feet shoes, to the titters of the audience.

"Wait, what," Wes asked theatrically. "Who's the Late Late Rabbi? We have a rabbi?"

"Yeah, Wes," Marcus rolled his eyes like it was the most obvious thing in the world. "We have a rabbi in the back. He blesses all our scripts for us. And also Vinny's trumpet."

Vinny, one of the Late Late Night Night Band trumpeters, held up his instrument with a broad smile while a golden spotlight shone on it, the audience rollicked as a choir sound effect filled the studio.

"Why is this the first I'm hearing about this? Where is he? Come out here!"

The audience laughed and applauded as Ariel emerged from behind the curtains, looking exaggeratedly haggard, his arms full of manila folders overflowing with stacks of stapled paper.

"Hey, I know you! You're one of our writers! Ariel, right?"

"Yeah, Ariel Samson. Look, do you really need me out here right now? Because I've got some services to run after this."

"Wait, you're a *real* rabbi?"

"Um, *yeah*," Ariel delivered with practiced snippiness, channeling his earlier ire to Wes' genuine shock at rehearsal. "Congregation Ahavath Yisroel in Brooklyn," he ad-libbed, goaded on by the green applesauce still in his system. "*And?*"

"But, like, you're black."

"Yeah, it's amazing what they let us do nowadays. We sorta took that whole civil rights thing and ran with it."

The audience collectively chortled.

"And you bless our scripts every show?"

"Did you think you were naturally funny this whole time? Bro. You need as much help as you can *get*."

The crew, Ariel knew as he heard the chuckles, was loving that jab.

"Well, since we already have you out here, I've just—"

"There's no hole in the sheet."

"How did you know—"

"That's always the next question people have. So no, Jews don't do it through a hole in a sheet. That's ridiculous, and honestly, just a little bit insulting. Especially to black and Hispanic Jews."

"Insulting? Insulting like how?"

"Because how much sheet do you *really* think we'd have left after *we* cut a hole in it?"

Shrieks of hilarity leapt out of every mouth, and a rumble of applause spontaneously poured from their hands.

In a state of some kind of shock everyone turned to their neighbor, trying to keep the tears from their eyes and their lungs from closing up as they repeated Ariel's comeback, rocking back and forth with wheezing breaths choked up with laughter.

"Ariel Samson, ladies and gentleman," Wes shouted, doubled over and slapping his hands together like a demented seal. "Our freelance rabbi here at *Late Late Night Night.*"

And there was Wes' only mistake in the whole sketch.

The line had actually been: "Ariel Samson, our Late Late Rabbi, ladies and gentlemen."

But the audience went wild anyway.

✡ ✡ ✡

"Man," Buddy shook his head. "That really saved our asses, Ariel. Cheers."

A flurry of clinks and relieved "Cheers" and *"L'chaims"* followed, and then the serene hush as everyone took long drags from their beers, letting the ambient sounds of chatter, music, and the Knicks vs 76ers game command the air.

It had been a beyond stressful cliffhanger of a day after all, and Ariel, Ellis, and Buddy were enjoying a well-deserved drink at the bar directly across the street from work. It'd been an almost wordless consensus between the three of them the minute *Late Late* had finished taping.

And hey, they'd survived it. Came out on top, even.

There'd been four "Late Late Rabbi" bits—or "Freelance Rabbi," as Wes had continued to mislabel them—each one a clever smoke-and-mirror act distracting from the objectively horrendous sketches that'd been hacked up over the course of that tense afternoon. But, as Ariel had accurately predicted, who would really be paying attention to a polka-dotted chicken and a dated mid-90's dance fad, or a meth addict who only spoke in Percy Shelley quotes, against the novelty and hilarity of irreverently debunking anti-Semitic myths—

"Look, this whole *'Jews killed Christ'* thing is really stupid. That's like white people saying *'I hate the blacks because they killed Biggie.'*"

—or, say, the rules of kosher demystified—

"So if a shark chewed its cud and had split hooves you could eat it?"

"...Would *you* eat an effing *four-legged shark* with split hooves that chewed its cud, Wes?"

—by the unlikely source of a(n impeccably dressed) black Jewish guy? *Nobody,* that's who.

Nobody.

"It was a great idea, Kosher Meat," Ellis admitted. "And I've never seen Wes so on book before in the history of ever."

"See?" Ariel lightly gloated, teasingly. "So it *was* a good plan."

Ellis stuck her tongue out at him. "Whatever, shut up. I'm *still* not convinced."

"Are you serious? How are you not 100% convinced *after* we already pulled it off?"

"I'm 80/20," she wiggled her fingers. "But cautiously optimistic."

"Wow, whatever," Ariel laughed. "I guess I'll just take what I can get."

Colin and Jumaane suddenly appeared, plopping down at the table on either side of Ariel.

Ariel's work friends and life friends had collided in the elevator on the way out for the day, and—between the *Late Late* crew's 11th hour triumph and Colin's birthday—decided to combine parties and tackle the new bar across the street in a joint campaign.

"Hey, we're getting a round of Patron shots," Jumaane announced. "Everyone in?"

"Sure!" Buddy piped up, while Ellis shrugged obligingly.

"I mean, I guess. Wait," Ariel asked. "Do they have plastic cups here? Like disposable ones?"

"You can't just use their shotglasses?" Jumaane asked.

"Well it looks like all their glasses are ceramic and—"

146

"Is this another kosher thing?" Colin interjected. "Do you need a cow to drink it then spit it back into the cup for you?"

"Yes. That is *exactly*—"

"Oh my goodness, you guys are ridiculous," Ellis started laughing. "Dude, just have them put everyone's shots in plastic cups. Let's go, Mommy wants her tequila."

And have her tequila, Mommy did.

To be fair, she *did* warn them not to try and keep up. But boys will be boys, and egos will be egos, and it was a brutal bloodbath. Watching Ellis knock back shot after shot was like watching Legolas pick off orcs at Parth Galen at the end of *The Fellowhip of the Ring*.

Ariel bowed out after the first two shots.

Tequila wasn't his poison of choice, and he didn't particularly relish feeling the next morning like his liver had taken a shower in hydrochloric acid and washed its hair with barbed wire.

Besides, he figured it wasn't the greatest idea to try and go toe-to-toe with someone who brought a personalized flask to work.

Jumaane and Buddy, though, they went four for four. Colin had made it all the way to six.

But in the end, and in various states of queasiness, the boys looked on in awe and nausea as Ellis reigned supreme, downing Shot No. 8.

"You can take the girl out of Chabad," she crowed, chasing her victory drink with a gulp of Corona. "But you can't take Chabad out of the girl."

"You're Chabad?" Ariel blurted out, unsure of whether he was surprised or if suddenly everything made sense.

"I grew *up* Chabad," Ellis clarified pointedly, downing another gulp of beer. "Then I got better."

Ariel's follow-up question was promptly interrupted by Colin, violently expelling shots 4-6 into a trash bin at the end of the bar in a gargling roar of vomit.

Clearly, it was time to call it a night, and so—after gathering Colin up and guiding his lurching steps in the direction of the door—the five of them spilled out of the bar, into the chilly evening and the artificial glow of the streetlights, stumbling down 6th Ave with cheerful abandon.

Within minutes their group was down to four, with Buddy hitching a ride home in an Uber, and as Colin bent over the curb to make his second pit stop of the night, Ariel escorted Ellis to the corner and the glowing lime-green orb perched atop a streetpost, signaling the presence of a train station.

"Alright," Ariel cautioned as they reached the stairwell. "Watch the thing there—"

Ellis tripped, not seeing the crisscrossed metal of the first step jutting out further than it should've been, and Ariel caught her, helping her steady herself.

"*Gàn.* Well. Maybe the ninth shot was a mistake," she noted wryly, sounding like a tipsy Mary Poppins.

"Well, in dog shots, you've only had, like, one."

They both chuckled, exhaled, and grinned goofily at each other, because drunk. It was almost a moment.

"Look," Ariel started. "This has been bugging me since I've met you...but what *is* that accent?"

Ellis laughed.

"It's called my dad is Jamaican and my mom is a mix of a lot of things from Manchester."

"Like Manchester, England?"

"No, like Manchester, Narnia."

"Oh, so like from Spare Oom proper or just outside War Drobe?"

"*Funny,*" Ellis slapped Ariel in the arm.

"I try," he replied, performing a terrible curtsy in response.

"So, what are you and the idiot gallery doing after this?"

"Well," Ariel shrugged. "Colin's convinced that he's gonna rally, so we're probably gonna go make some memories worth repressing, then come in tomorrow hungover."

"Sounds like a fantastic plan that I'm going to pretend I didn't hear."

"Don't worry," Ariel laughed. "I'll be in on time."

"You'd better be, Freelance Rabbi. Anyhoo. Tomorrow."

"Tomorrow."

Ariel gave a sort of salute as Ellis descended into the stairwell, and he watched her until she reached the landing and disappeared around the corner.

He liked Ellis, he realized. As in *liked* her, liked her. There wasn't even a shadow in the valley of doubt about that. Which was just a bit of a complication. For several reasons.

Flushing the thoughts out of his head, Ariel turned and rejoined Jumaane and Colin at the curb to continue their night's adventure.

"What the *hell*," Colin sputtered, examining the contents of his stomach splashed across the pavement. "Are those *leaves*? You guys let me eat *leaves*?"

"Dude," Jumaane reminded. "We stopped at the salad bar, remember?"

"What the fu—"

Jumaane and Ariel leapt back as Colin busied himself once more with cleansing the lining of his stomach.

It was then that Ariel noticed Jumaane beaming at him.

"What?" he asked.

"Well lookit you," Jumaane replied. "I saw you over there tonight, and I stand corrected."

"About...?"

"You went and found yourself a two-headed cat after all," he clapped Ariel in the arm. "Get on that."

Ariel half-nodded and smiled an awkward half-smile in response, deciding on keeping his mouth shut. He couldn't help feeling that Jumaane was just one more person he'd be betraying by going on his date that coming Sunday.

With Tamar.

By Friday morning, *Late Late Night Night*'s tetrad of "Freelance Rabbi" skits had gained a cumulative 204k shares on Facebook, and 28 million views on YouTube.

Plus a piece from Mashable. And another from Jezebel. And The Root. Tablet Magazine. Very Smart Brothas. The Forward. The Grio.

All that in just under *two* days.

Maybe it was the increased viewership from all the hostage Gen X parents, being forced to witness Marli James' musical debut by their tween kids. For them, Ariel's jokes had been an oasis of maturity in a desert of screeching adolescence.

Maybe it was because a large chunk of college kids had tuned in to the show that Wednesday night—eager to hear Councilman Grundman's plans to push for tuition reform—and had incidentally been treated to Ariel interrupting the interview, as planned, with a tangentially-related rant about Jews believing in Hell (*"Of course we believe in Hell. We invented the concept of Hell. You think we live with the headache of all these commandments only to believe that nothing happens if you don't do them?"*).

Maybe it was because a *different* large chunk of students— mostly regulars at the Brooklyn College Hillel house—had been hotly debating Ariel's "Black Lives Matter" *Hatikvah* piece with their families over Thanksgiving break, and now, for better or for worse, they were able to put a face to the byline.

Whatever the reason, all that Ariel knew that Friday night, as he stood at the *bimah* ready to announce the page numbers for Erev Shabbat services, was that he was looking out at a motley crowd about 25 people strong. A rabble full of the curious, the hip, the alternative, the traditional, the weary, the searching, and the regulars who were just as astonished as he was.

From near the front of the room, Kalman took in the small flock, caught Ariel's eye, and replied to his friend's perplexed half-shrug with a wide smile, a passionate jab of a thumbs up, and a chest swelling with equal parts joy, pride, and relief.

And that's how it began.

That's how Congregation Ahavath Yisroel began crawling back on the face of the map, on its way to becoming a living, breathing, and vibrant place again.

✡ ✡ ✡

Ariel's coat wasn't heavy enough against the wintry air that swirled around him, and he'd underestimated the cold. It painted even *his* chestnut-brown cheeks a raw shade of rose-red, and whispered rimey nothings into bright-crimson ears.

An icy wind wolfishly howled through skeletons of trees and bit through his clothes just as savagely, leaving behind fang marks in the form of bumps that tingled up his arms and across his back. He shivered as he weaved through hedges of vacant cars feathered with frost, parked nose to bumper down both sides of the street.

It was cold as ass outside, is what I'm trying to say.

Which is what made tonight's turnout all the more surprising.

Chani Guildencrantz had come, bringing along a decent-sized crew of her fellow Hillel hangers-on, all of varying observance styles.

"Styles," not "levels." Because, as Ariel told one of Chani's entourage, "Judaism doesn't exist on a two-dimensional plane."

Then there was the brunette in about her 40's, with the two full sleeves of tattoos, who Ariel had ran into at the cornerstore late Thursday night. He may or may not have been on a munchies run at the time.

"Oh hey! You're that dude!" she'd said, likewise possibly or possibly not on a munchies run. "That freelance rabbi dude."

"Yep, that's me."

"That was so cool, man."

"Glad you liked it," he'd replied, eyeing her **Magen David**. "So, I'm gonna see you at services tomorrow night?"

"Yeah, okay," she'd laughed.

"No, I'm serious. Services start at 4:30."

"Wait for real? You're *really* a real rabbi?"

"And Congregation Ahavath Yisroel is really a real place. Come stop by. Bring some friends."

"Alright...alright maybe I will."

She'd followed through, it seemed. Ariel had spied her in the back of the sanctuary with a couple of fellow ink enthusiasts, one of which he assumed was either her boyfriend or a very serious situationship.

Ilan, surprisingly, had shown up too. Which was random, because he was very much *not* the *shul*-going type. Like, not even for the High Holidays.

"It just seems really *chutzpadik* to me," he'd explained to Ariel. "Like I'm saying G'd doesn't have so good a memory, so He needs me to show up and remind Him why I'm going to Hell."

Yet, there Ilan was tonight, and—miracles of miracles—*not* spontaneously bursting into flame. And also not pushing his illicit wares. Which, honestly, was the *real* miracle.

But of all the new faces, the most interesting, Ariel thought, were the young couple who came up to him at the end of services, excitedly introducing themselves as being "not Orthodox but firmly *shomer mitzvot*," Nahum the Husband had clarified, as if his lip ring and black fedora hadn't already broadcast both of those things.

"Most Shabbats I **layn** for an egal independent Traditional minyan," Chedva the Wife added. "But he doesn't really feel comfortable there, and none of the Orthodox places around us are the right fit either, so we don't really have a place to go when I have a week off."

"But this place is great!" Nahum the Husband gushed. "We're so excited we found it! Thanks *so* much for being here!"

"I'm pretty sure that's my line," Ariel joked. "But show up for services tomorrow at 9, and we'll call it even."

It was a funny response, and Ariel chuckled as he remembered it, pulling his coat tighter around himself and tucking his chin into his chest, inhaling air so chilled it almost hurt to breathe.

A pale, raven-haired woman appeared in Ariel's path, wrapped in a thick scarf and tucked underneath a cat-eared knit hat. She shuffled through the icebox of a night from the opposite end of the block, abruptly crossing the street as Ariel approached. He shook his head and kept moving forward.

It was too cold to engage the mental acrobatics of getting angry at her microaggression, feeling guilt at her fear of rape culture, and then circling back around to anger at the racialized stereotypes of predatory black male sexuality.

Yay, intersectionality.

Ariel jammed his balled-up fists deeper into his pockets and plowed forward on auto-pilot, walking through the clouds of his own breath, and thinking about how much he couldn't wait to see the look on Ellis' face at services the next day with all the newcomers.

Funnily enough, seeing as how the fresh faces were overwhelmingly women, Ellis might actually end up with a legit CAY Sisterhood, as opposed to—as she had called it one lunch break—the Mahjong League of Cat Ladies.

Ariel snickered, wondering how over or underprepared Ellis was for that to actually happen. It was a snicker cut short as he turned the corner to see two squad cars parked in the middle of his block, illuminated in silently strobing flashes of red and blue.

It wasn't a particularly alarming sight.

Ariel's block was constantly lively with either the antics of commuting college kids, or the medical crises of the elderly people who called the cops on their parties.

There were four of them perched in front of the glass double-doors, an Easter Island of stony-faced NYPD blue congesting the entrance to the apartment building Ariel called home.

"Is there something wrong, officers?" Ariel asked as he approached, just mildly a—

"*WHAT?*" one of the officers roared and took a step forward.

And then it happened. Too quickly.

Clap, the officer's hand was on his gun.

ClapClapClap, the other three followed suit.

Crash, Ariel's heart plummeted into his stomach.

Maηishtana

ThumpThump, it suddenly revved, because it was Shabbat and so

ThumpThump, no wallet and

ThumpThump, no cellphone and

ThumpThump, no ID, and*thumpthumpthumpthumpthump thumpthumpthumpthumpthumpthumpthump*—

Ariel's eyes darted to the silver badges on their chests until the letters of their names—Smith. Pirrone. Winitsky. Delgado—melted into the flashes of blood-red and cold-blue lights. Their hands were perched on their hilts. Ticking. An icy sweat broke out across Ariel's neck and trickled down his back.

Just breathe, Ariel. Slow...slow...Just breathe...Just—

Sandra Bland.

No, no don't—

Tamir Rice. Kenneth Harding.

No, we don't need to go th—

Tanisha Anderson, Derrick Jones, Rumain Brisbon, Yvette Smith.

Dammit, Ariel. Focus! Just, if—

AkaiGurleyDanroyHenryMiriamCareyKajiemePowellStevenEug eneWashingtonShellyFreyEzellFordVictorSteenDarnishaHarrisDant eParkerDeAuntaTerrelFarrowMalissaWilliamsMichaelBrownRonald MadisonAlesiaThomasTimothyStansburyJohnCrawfordIIIShantelD avisTyreeWoodsonOrlandoBarlowRekiaBoyd

We need to—

EricGarnerPrinceJonesShereeseFrancisEarlMurrayVictorWhiteII IAiyanaStanleyJonesAndyLopezMalcolmFergusonTarikaWilsonMcK enzieCochranKathrynJohnstonJordanBakerAlbertaSpruillOscarGrant KendraJamesJonathanFerrellNatashaMcKennaSgtManuelLogginsJrL aTanyaHaggertySeanBellMargaretLaVerneMitchellCarlosAlcisAuraR osserLarryEugeneJacksonJrMyaHallDeionFluddKyamLivingstonKim aniGrayKaylaMooreJohnnieKamahiWarrenMichelleCusseauxChavis Carter

The cold air wouldn't enter his lungs and the strange-fruit salad of names wouldn't stop surging through his head and his brain dissolved into a soup of conflicting instructions.

Stupid. Should've asked "Did something happen?"— SonjiTaylorRaymondAllenShemWalkerIrethaLillyRamarleyGraham KiwaneCarringtonVerneciaWoodardAaronCampbellKennethCham berlainPearlieGolden—*Or "Is there something I can help you*

with?"...MeganHockadayReynaldoCuevasAlexiaChristianSharmelEd
wardsPatrickDorismondYuvetteHendersonTamonRobinsonRonald
BeasleyShenequeProctor—*Maybe should've smiled? Smiled more?
Less? Said "sir"? Taken hands out of pockets? Take them out now?*—
ErvinJeffersonTimothyThomasFrankiePerkinsOusmaneZongoKendr
ecMcDadeDanetteDanielsJamesBrisetteWendellAllenJanishaFonvill
eDantePriceHenryGlover—*Freeze and ask again? Step back and ask
again? Step forward? Walk away and try to come back home later?*—
ReginaldDoucetNehemiahDillardNizahMorrisRaheimBrownAmado
uDiallo—*Take hands out of pockets?*

"I *asked* you what the *fuck* did you say?" the officer barked
again. Smith.

"I live here," Ariel tried again, with a dry mouth and scratchy
throat. Controlling the tremor in his voice from escaping. "Is
something wrong? Did something happen?"

They glared him down for an eternity. Or maybe not. Maybe
five minutes. Maybe five seconds. It seemed like it'd been hours
since he'd been cheerfully walking home. He stood motionlessly,
wearing a pasted-on smile as they scanned him.

There weren't enough YouTube shares in the world to matter
to the cops that they were looking at the Freelance Rabbi right now,
and the *kippah* he wore under his fleece beanie didn't make him
bulletproof, and his rabbinical ordination didn't matter, and the
drash he was supposed to be delivering to his congregants the next
day didn't matter, and the **cholent** he had stewing in his crockpot
didn't matter, and it didn't matter how excited he was for
Chanukah next week, and they didn't care that his favorite candy in
those oversized multicolored *dreidels* were the red gummy fish (but
they were *the worst* when they were stale), and it didn't matter that
he hated anything jelly-filled so he only ate the **sufganiyot** filled
with custard, and they didn't care that he was looking forward to
singing **Maoz Tzur** to the tune of Zelda like he did ever year,
because he was just another black guy out on a Friday night.

"Oh," Smith replied. His eyes bored through Ariel like an ice
pick. "Guess I misheard you."

Hands slowly descended from holsters.

But not Smith's. His stayed. Unapologetic.

The officers parted, but only just enough, and Ariel carefully
squeezed by the human blue wall, consciously willing his stilted
body movements out of their desire to seize up in panic. He

fumbled with his keys, feeling four sets of eyes on his back, as his numb fingers sharply jabbed at the metal of the lock for a few tense seconds, and dimly, somewhere in the back of his mind, he was very thankful that there was an *eruv*, and one that he held by, and that he'd been able to simply pull his keys out of his pocket.

Not fidget around at his waist to pull out an elastic key belt.

Or lean into the doorknob to remove a keyed tie-clip.

Or rummage suspiciously around his front door to retrieve a key from underneath a large enough rock.

Finally, Ariel's key caught the keyhole and he was inside, greeted by a rush of warm air and the scent of pine from the Christmas tree standing decorated and brightly-lit in the lobby. His heart continued beating madly in double-time until he made it safely inside his apartment, slamming the door shut behind him with enough force that he knocked a DVD case off the bookshelf near the door.

Ariel glanced at it and kicked it out of his path as he lumbered into his apartment in semi-shock.

The Walking Dead. Season Two.

Fittingly, he remembered the conversation at Kalman's table a month earlier about surviving a zombie apocalypse.

"Take me out in the first wave," he'd said. "Because nobody wants to survive the apocalypse."

It was a funny thing. He'd seen it on a T-shirt once.

But there was a thing that neither he or the T-shirt had said, because nobody at that table would've understood it. It came to him now, as he collapsed onto his couch, allowing the shudders to overtake him as his body processed its very near brush with death.

Why, he thought to himself, would he or any other black person *ever* want to live through a zombie apocalypse?

Surviving through the terror of the now was stressful enough.

Chanukah was in trouble!

Well no, not really. Just the Chanukah party. The Brooklyn College Hillel's Chanukah party, specifically. And, at the moment, as he sat in the executive director's office, Ariel was working through some exposure therapy.

See, the Hillel house at Brooklyn College—much like Hillel houses at other colleges—was the center for, and of, Jewish student life on campus.

Although, given that Brooklyn College had the 9th highest Jewish population of any college in the country, it seemed just a little bit like overkill for a campus already teeming with Jews to then have a separate exclusive clubhouse building on *top* of that, even to Ariel.

That sentiment seemed to resonant pretty uniformly among the non-Jewish student body as well, leading to certain half-joking whispers in decidedly more ethnic circles that perhaps the college should rename itself to The Hillel Institute of Higher Learning.

And, don't get me wrong, the Hillel wasn't *seeking* to be isolationist or exclusionary or anything. In fact, one of its core tenets was to increase understanding between Jews and non-Jews.

But, y'know...was it *really* though?

Glaringly, Ariel's own interaction with the building had been pretty spotty.

His first encounter was during his freshman year back in 2007—a Chanukah *menorah* lighting with some light refreshments.

He got the odd sideeye, but the overall experience was benign enough that he came to their **Tu b'Shvat** *seder* that January 2008.

Where he was promptly assumed by everyone in attendance to be the weed dealer everyone was told was gonna be there.

At the 2009 Purim event he thoroughly enjoyed mingling with his fellow students and being invited to join in the laser tag and karaoke battles. Until his Darth Vader helmet got too hot inside and he removed it, and suddenly no one was as keen to party with him anymore.

But his last adventure, after which he never returned, was when he came to the Hillel for their **Lag b'Omer** barbeque in 2010 and got stopped at the door. By the black security guard.

"Are you here to see someone?" the guard asked, blocking his way.

"Well excuse me, Uncle Ruckus," Ariel remembered wanting to say. "I was under the impression that the Brooklyn College Hillel was a Brooklyn College facility, and me, by dint of being a Brooklyn College student, am able to use said facility without having to need to be here to 'see someone' to be able to enter, *regardless* of what I look like."

A friend already inside the party called out to Ariel and waved him in, quickly dissolving whatever that confrontation would've ballooned into.

But now, sitting in the president's office with Cate—Cate Finklestein. The treasurer of CAY, remember? You're welcome— and the e-board members of all the different in-house Hillel clubs, he had the chance to *hugely* stick it to them.

It seemed, due to some kind of red tape and student government budget freezes, that the Hillel wasn't able to hold its annual Chanukah party.

Well, not its own premises anyway. And other venues on campus were already booked. And so, with heavy hearts, the Jews of Brooklyn College slowly began to accept that they weren't going to have a Chanukah that year.

It was like the plot of every Claymation holiday movie ever.

But then! One of the guest faces Chani Guildencrantz had brought to CAY that last Shabbat had the epiphany of proposing to

Ariel and his board if maybe they would allow the Hillel to host their party in the synagogue's basement. The Hillel would do some financial sleight-of-hand to cover the cost of food and music, they'd split the door charge revenue with the synagogue, and, *boom*, why not?

And so, here everyone was, looking to Ariel with large pleading eyes like puppies in the window of a pet shop, Chani leading the charge. And Ariel, being the high-road kinda guy he was, couldn't help but say yes.

Like, was he really gonna turn down an organization coming to him for help just because they had been shitty to him repeatedly over the course of his entire college career?

Hmph. I guess when you put it that way...

"Thank you so much Rabbi Samson, Ms. Finklestein," the Hillel director gushed. "We *really* appreciate you collaborating with us like this on such short notice."

...no, Ariel was *not* going to turn them down.

Because he was a much better person than you and I are.

Like, if it were me, sure I wouldn't've sicced a pack of rabid bears on them, because that's being extra, but I definitely would've Grinched the *hell* out of them.

Sorry, not sorry, that's just the kind of person I am.

If I ever tell you my heart grew three sizes in one day, that's not me becoming generous. That's me suffering an acute attack of idiopathic triple-dilated cardiomyopathy.

Seriously. Call for help. Because I'm possibly about to go into cardiac arrest.

Saturday, December 12, 2015
1 Tevet 5776

It was definitely a college scene party.

You'd know it just from the body language alone.

The nervous energy of the last hurrah before classes ended.

The way the guys moved with all the swagger of virility.

How the girls wafted by, finally proficient in the powers of their sex that they'd been practicing since high school.

And all of it emblematic of the dangerous intersection between having the most independence you will ever have, and knowing the least you will ever know.

The whole CAY board was on deck, with Cate at the door tallying receipts as people came in from the rain, Jerome lurking just around every corner in case the riot of color and sound got rowdier than it should, and Ariel, Kalman, and Ellis playing the face of the *shul*, welcoming the partygoers into the space and maybe culling some new service-attendees in the process.

Everyone was just a tad more hyped up than they needed to be, and for Ariel—still reeling and wary from last week's near disastrous run-in with the police—it was all pretty exhausting and overwhelming.

"It's ok, I understand," Tamar had said when Ariel called to raincheck their Sunday date. "We'll just reschedule for whenever. Like, when you're ready."

"Thanks. Really."

"Not even a question. Like, I can't even imagine what it would be like to go through that, but, I dunno, I can be an ear if you want."

So that had been nice. The chance to just regroup with himself and recalibrate. But tonight's party was maybe pushing his limits. Particularly since he was feeling like a social litmus test.

"Hi," said one girl, extending her hand. "I'm Lisa."

"I'm Rabbi Samson," he said, shaking it.

"This is your *shul*?"

"Yep."

"Cool! Well it was very nice meeting you!"

And off she went. She'd been the 6th or 7th one that night.

Punchcard tolerance, Ariel called it. Like they were trying to get enough hole punches on their humanity card so they could get a free soda with their next order of fries or something.

"See? I'm not racist! I talked to that black guy for a whole four seconds! *Click*."

It dawned on him that he couldn't remember the last time he'd actually enjoyed himself at one of these things. These Jewish event things. The young professionals parties, and the all-white Tu b'Av bashes, and the 20's and 30's singles events.

Hmph. Never really noticed that before.

Interesting.

A small circle of "cool" *frum* guys were bobbing their heads and mouthing all the words to an old school Tupac song that the DJ'd just started mixing.

Ariel snorted at the sight.

It was just so cute. At least until he soberly realized that they were probably exactly how he'd looked to the Caribbean Heritage Club, and at bashment parties back in college while he was grooving along to Spragga Benz and Mad Cobra.

Anyway, Ariel thought, maybe it was time to take a little break.

The rabbi's office upstairs had finally been excavated from its former storage room existence, so he'd probably retreat there for a quick recoup and—

"Ariel!" a distressed Dassi rushed over, shouting over the roar of the music. "A couple of people are complaining about this guy over here. Saying he's pushing the guys around and harassing the girls."

"What? Where is he?"

"Over by the bookcases. Big guy, brown hair, Greek letters T-shirt."

Ariel moved through the crowd like he was swimming through molasses, with the concerned Dassi on his tail, when he saw the offender—a huge oaf with a generous forehead and jaw who looked like he was just about to discover fire—trying to hit on Ellis. And like some kind of aural periscope, Ariel hyperfocused in on everything they said, even above the music.

"Hey, don't I know you from somewhere?" Bruteface smirked with a sleazy lip curl.

"Yeah," Ellis coolly said over the rim of her glass. "That's why I don't go there anymore."

"Damn. Are you a murderer? Cuz you're killing me."

"Are you a red light? Because stop, go the fuck away."

"Oh, c'mon," he said with a leer, and grabbed her arm.

"Yeah, no," Ellis shot back, jerking her arm from his. "I'm *shomer negiah*. Today."

Bruteface stopped and stared at her in shock.

"You're *Jewish*?"

"Seriously dude? It's a Chanukah party. You think some random non-Jewish black girl wandered into a synagogue?"

"What? Stop playing. There's no way *that* ass is Jewish."

Ariel had reached the scene by then, grabbing the guy by the shoulder and whirling him around, making the bigger guy face him.

"Hey, man. She said she's *shomer negiah*. So, shomer...*nigga*."

Not Ariel's finest street-moment, I know. We all know.

But Bruteface looked Ariel up and down and asked with a snort, "So what, are you Jewish too now? Or are all you guys just fucking around?"

"Wow, guy. You got me. This is my Purim costume."

Realization slowly crept across Bruteface's face as he actually took Ariel in and realized exactly who he was talking to.

"Mind if I ask you a question?" Ariel shot back.

"Yeah, what?"

"Like, where do you get the balls to ask shitty questions like that to complete strangers?"

The room stopped. The music had gradually been lowering as the encounter escalated, and now it was completely silent as everyone watched.

"Huh?" Bruteface was a bit taken aback at being challenged. "What are you talking about?"

"Where do you," Ariel asked more slowly. "Get the testicles. To ask complete strangers. Shitty questions like that."

"What, you mean the confidence? I'm a confident guy, I'll ask whatever the fuck I want."

"Oh really?"

"Yeah. What, you wanna do something about it?"

Ariel realized too late that he was being backed into a corner. Figuratively. Because if he were just a private citizen, at a private party, he would've taken Bruteface up on his obviously implied offer of physical retaliation.

And Ariel S. D. Samson had never been one to back down from a fight.

Not a physical one anyway. He didn't always win them all, but he put his money where his mouth was. It was something else he'd picked up watching those old movies from the 40's with his dad.

Don Diego de la Vega hadn't backed down from Captain Esteban Pasquale's duel challenge.

Robin Hood took Sir Guy of Gisbourne head on.

And Nick Charles hadn't even flinched while staring down the barrel of David Graham's pistol.

So Bruteface could definitely catch some hands.

But, for *this* particular scenario, there were two things wrong with that approach:

Firstly, he wasn't a private citizen. He was the rabbi. Having a buzz going around that the rabbi of Congregation Ahavath Yisroel was in the habit of fighting frat boys in the basement like an MMA cage match wasn't exactly a good look.

Secondly, Bruteface was *biiig*. And while that wouldn't have mattered either way to Ariel otherwise—there was no shame in losing a fight—it gave him pause this one time.

Because *this* fight wouldn't just be a fight.

This fight was a clash of *ideals*.

It was bigger than itself in the same ways that everyone tells skinny girls to never get in a fight with a plus-sized girl. Because that bigger girl isn't fighting *you*, Skinny Tasha, she's fighting every magazine cover, every mannequin, every pretty bra that doesn't come in her size, every nonsensical size chart in H&M.

She's fighting the *concept* of you, Skinny Tasha.

Bruteface was the arrogance of every Jewish space, and the entitlement of that space to demand that Jews of Color explain why they're there in the crudest of ways.

And Ariel was the embodiment of every Jew of Color tilting their chin up, throwing up both middle fingers, and retorting with a hearty "Fuck. You."

And that wasn't a fight he could chance losing.

Besides, there was also the third reason, the one Ariel was pretending he wasn't thinking about.

Which was that he was trying to impress Ellis.

And she didn't particularly strike Ariel as someone who swooned at the usual caveman primate mannerisms. Hell, she was probably already mildly annoyed that he'd stepped in at all.

"Do I wanna do something about it?" Ariel chuckled, stepping back and circling around Bruteface, buying time by repeating himself. "Do *I*, wanna do something about it?"

So.

He had to address the challenge, obviously.

But how to do it in a way that wasn't physical, was still potent, and didn't look like he was backpedaling out of being wiped across the floor in front of a hundred college kids?

Ariel continued his casual circuit around Bruteface, looking him up and down with a sardonic smirk, but really frantically scanning for anything that could be used to an advantage, like MacGuyver trying to build a bomb out of social skills, testosterone, and bruised egos.

AHA!

"Yeah. I *do* wanna do something about it," Ariel said finally, cutting his pacing short. "Firstly, I see your letters. You're a ZBT brother. So me and the Greek Council office are gonna have a little talk. And I happened to go to school with pretty much all of them, so it's gonna be a long talk."

"Yeah, okay," Bruteface snickered, unimpressed. It was a bluff he was willing to call. *Everybody* always said they knew a So-and-so from fraternity Such-and-such when it was convenient.

"Second—Secretary Koegel?"

"Present," Phyllis rasped, elbowing her way to the front of the crowd, drink in hand, obviously.

"Say hello," Ariel gestured in Phyllis' direction. "To the former head of the English department at Brooklyn College. Secretary

Koegel," he turned to her. "I'm sure you still have more than a few connections and colleagues you can tap on, correct?"

"Sure. English department, Classics departments, financial aid office—" she ticked off on her fingers.

"So, what," Bruteface mocked. "You're gonna tell all the teachers that I'm a bad bad boy? Please. I don't even *go* there."

"Oh? Did the Brooklyn College chapter of ZBT stop being Beta Xi? Like it says on your sleeve? Also, next time you try that lie you should probably hide your Brooklyn College Athletics wristband. Or at least remember that to enter this party, you had to show a Brooklyn College student ID at the door."

The sneer fell off of Bruteface's lips so fast you could almost hear it shatter as it hit the floor.

"And no, we're not gonna tattletale to your professors. We're just going to ask them for your home number and call your mother," Ariel said simply. "And by we, I mean the President of the Congregation Ahavath Yisroel Sisterhood. I believe you've met," he nodded in Ellis' direction.

Bruteface paled a bit as he understood exactly how much he'd chosen the wrong person to prey on, and Ellis curtsied while the crowed lowed and tittered.

"But—but—" he stammered.

"Thirdly, this party is done for you. Pack up your stuff, pack up your friends, and get out of this synagogue—*my* synagogue—right now. And, no, I'm not 'just fucking around' and no, do *not* test me. I *will* have the police arrest you for trespassing."

"What?! You can't do that. This is a synagogue and—"

"See, funny thing, contrary to popular belief, houses of worship aren't open to the public. They're actually privately-owned property upon which the landlord, caretaker, or spiritual leader," Ariel pointed at himself with both hands, "has the right to remove or bar entry to anyone they so choose. And seeing how, One—I'm the rabbi, Two—you insulted not only myself, but a member of my executive board, and Three—you were *repeatedly* getting physically aggressive towards *several* uninterested females in this space tonight, *period*. So yes, I very much *can* choose to do that. And I am."

Bruteface's mouth opened and closed wordlessly for a couple seconds.

"Not trying to hear it," Ariel held up a hand. "Now where are the friends you came with? I know you didn't come here alone."

Bruteface's cohorts were turned out by the crowd faster than it takes a vegan to tell you they're vegan. Again.

"Ah, one, two, and three? You're out too."

They began the grumblings and whinings of a protest that Ariel once again silenced with an upraised hand and dusted off his teacher voice.

"Don't care. If your boy here was comfortable enough to say and do all that in public, then you guys have obviously made it comfortable for him to make those kinds of comments in private. Vice President Litwak?"

Jerome materialized behind Bruteface's companions like he emerged from the wall.

"Please escort these gentlemen outside. Goodbye."

Bruteface and the Pussycats slunk up the stairs and out the door with Jerome looming behind them, exiting to the applause of the partygoers. Especially the girls, who now had four less roofies to worry about.

Of course, now all eyes were on Ariel, standing in the middle of the floor alone and surrounded by college kids.

Shit.

Okay...okay...how to keep the momentum of the moment, reignite the party vibe, but still gracefully extricate himself from the spotlight in a not-anticlimactic way?

C'mon now, Ariel. You've got this.

C'mon...

C'mon!

And in the last possible attosecond before the scene turned into awkward dead air, Ariel just decided to leap for legendary greatness.

Grabbing an open handle of Jack Daniels from one of the drink stations, he climbed up on the nearest table and began to shout.

"Happy Chanukah!"

A timid "Happy Chanukah" echoed back from the crowd.

"What the hell was *that*? I *said* 'HAPPY CHANUKAH'!"

"HAPPY CHANUKAH!" came a shout in return.

"*There* we go. Listen up guys. Welcome to Congregation Ahavath Yisroel—CAY, for short. My name is Rabbi Ariel Samson, and this is my house. Being subletted from the L'rd, of course."

They giggled like the grown-up schoolchildren that they were.

"I want everybody to enjoy themselves and have a good time and just let loose, on this," he shifted into faux solemnity, "our holy Festival of Lights. And I hope," he resumed his jovial tone, "that you'll come spend time with us not just for holidays, but every week here for our Shabbat services."

The crowd whooped and cheered.

"Buuuut," Ariel raised a hand to silence them. "But do *not* act like you have no home-training. Because if you do, then you'll have to answer to me. And if you have to answer to me, then you are not crossing my threshold again. We all got that?"

Assorted versions of shouted "Yes" filled the air.

"Alright!"

Okay...okay...now he needed a closer. What could he—oh, what the hell.

Ariel knocked his head back chugged the entire handle of Jack in his hand, much to the awed shock of the entire crowd.

He tossed it, empty, back to the bartender at the drink station.

"*L'chaim*, y'all. Now go party!"

A raucous cheer erupted like an auditory volcano from the crowd as it parted for Ariel, high-fiving him and clapping him on the back as he strode upstairs to his office. He could hear the music start up again as he closed the door behind him and the DJ shouting *"Let's give it up for the Freelance Rabbi!"* and the hoots that raised the roof so high—everyone pumping out every ounce of power in their lungs—that he could've sworn that the rain outside was streaming in.

And, as Ariel promptly showered the contents of his stomach all over the walls, floor (and somehow, ceiling) of his office, he vaguely remembered thinking about what Ellis thought of his performative theatricality *now*.

He might've slept in a pool of his own vomit that night, but that was the night when everyone learned that the Freelance Rabbi was every bit the force in person as he was on TV.

And he was *not* to be messed with.

You did not mess with him on the air.

You did not mess with him in his lair.

You did not mess with him in the pews.

You did not mess with him or his booze.

And when you come to *shul* to pray,

Manishtana

Act like you have sense when you walk into CAY.

shacharit
shacharis
shacharith

*O*ne *of my earliest memories shortly after receiving my smicha,*
Ariel continued laboring on his draft, *was the first time I was called
up to the Torah for an aliyah in a new synagogue. I was to receive the
honor of Shlishi, the third portion, when I was visiting a family friend.*

*I'm sure the sexton—the **gabbai**—probably thought he was
being quite welcoming and inclusive, handing the little laminated
placard to random Jewish Negro me without first administering a
fingerprint scan, requiring three professional references, and
providing a 613-question pop-quiz on my bar mitzvah portion.*

[Hold for uncomfortable laughter]

*Except, ironically, this is the one time that I should've been
asked a question. A very simple one that nearly everyone new to a
shul gets asked:*

*"Are you a Kohen, **Levi**, or **Yisrael**?"*

[Hold for silence while that sinks in]

*I assume that since I'm darker than what Jewish "looks" like,
clearly I couldn't possibly have paternal lineage from the two highest
castes in Jewish hierarchy. Obviously, I was a Yisrael. The common
folk of the Jewish people. The humans to the Kohen's elf and the
Levi's dwarf. And there it was: That delightful taste of the soft racism
of lowered expectation.*

To be fair, I am a Yisrael. But, y'know, the principle and all that.

But however micro that aggression was, it was nothing compared to when I handed my little placard to the gabbai, and began relaying the traditional patronymic formula of my Hebrew name for him to repeat.

"HaRav Ariel Shabbtai Dror ben Av—" I began.

"HaRav Ariel Shabbtai Dror ben Avraham," the gabbai finished for me, anticipating that my name would end in "ben Avraham," the typical rubric for those who claim our patriarch Abraham, the father of all Jews, as their spiritual father.

Converts, in other words. Or "Jews By Choice."

And so I paused, took a deep breath, then repeated myself, pronouncing my father's Hebrew name as pointedly and with as much sideeye as I could muster.

"HaRav Ariel Shabbtai Dror ben Avigdor Daniel."

The gabbai, to his credit, got summarily flustered, and hastily tried correcting himself while he turned beet-red.

And me? Well, I went ahead to silently make my point by dabbing the Torah scroll with my tzitzit and kissing it before the **baal koreh** *could point out the spot, grasped the scroll handles and stared straight ahead into space, making sure that there wouldn't even be the slightest inkling of a thought as to whether or not I was reciting the blessings by heart, or cheating by looking at the blessing sheet lying in front of me.*

But inside?

Inside, I felt like I was getting arrested for trespassing while walking around in my own home.

Ariel paused here, taking in his work, then nodded at the text on his phone, satisfied.

It was time for a little bit of a break, his foggy brain told him. But once again, he smiled triumphantly, the ol' Mexican cilantro had come through.

If you recall, when we last left our hapless hero he was sitting at a gala table—surrounded by his archenemies—and, having had consumed a respectable amount of combustible greenery, was just starting to feel it kick in.

That had only been six minutes ago, and so, at the current moment, the S.M.S. Samson was lazily sailing across a crystal-clear sea of euphoria at forty-five dreams per second, drifting towards a soft sunset glow on the horizon of awesome.

So sure, he could try and plow ahead some more on his speech, but he'd only end up forgetting that he'd already written that last sentence. So sure, he could try and plow ahead some more on his speech, but he'd only end up forgetting that he'd already written that last sentence. So sure, he could try and plow ahead some more on his speech, but he'd only end up forgetting that he'd already written that last sentence.

No, right now he was just...being. Entering that stage of contemplative zen that only the haze of Gandalf's cabbage could provide, that perspective of an objective eye removed from the immediacy of anything.

The speech would get finished when it got finished.

There was something to be said about watching yourself from the outside and gaining some sense of your place in the world. In your surroundings. The calm, detached sense of admittedly altered, but nonetheless analytical observation. Absorbing everything around you and suddenly noticing the rich details in the mundane.

Ariel took in the chatter of the room, the scraping of chairs as people rose to a standing ovation as the first speaker left the podium, the warm feeling of the creamy mushroom soup in his belly, the aroma of the fleshy pink strip of salmon, garnished with sprinkles of dill and chives on the green-and-white platter in front of him, and—oh right—Assemblyman Rosenstern and Rabbi Guildencrantz.

What made them the way they were, he wondered.

The cutthroatedness (was that even a word?). The near-schizophrenic duplicity (or wait, did he mean multiple personality disorder?). How could they just...wait, why wasn't he just asking them?

He should ask them, right?

Alright, let's ask them.

"So," Ariel began. "We're just *not* gonna talk about, y'know, *the thing*? From a couple months ago? Is that the plan? We're just gonna sit here and *not* say anything about it?"

The silly spinach had made him more confrontational. Or more blasé. He wasn't sure which. He wasn't sure he cared.

Assemblyman Rosenstern sat stock-still and tight-lipped in his chair, pretending as if he hadn't heard a word, being *profoundly* engrossed as he was in the second speaker's adenoidal drawls.

Manishtana

Not a terrible move for a controversial Trump-supporting Orthodox Jewish politician in a liberal Jewish public setting during the most venomous election year in modern American history.

Good call.

Rosenstern's aides followed suite. And Ariel wasn't terribly surprised at any of it. Rosenstern's place of power, after all, was in the gleaming spotlight of news cameras, or being insulated behind his near-libelous tirades of print, or cloaked in the faceless security found on the other side of a phone.

Ah, but Rabbi Guildencrantz.

Guildencrantz, Ariel knew, couldn't resist playing the sagacious elder bit.

Another chance to build on his mythos as the conciliatory diplomat, willing to reasonably hear out any opponent no matter how *clearly* and egregiously misguided they were.

Having become a congregational rabbi himself—and gaining firsthand experience wrestling with the multi-headed hydra of a public persona—Ariel reviled the deceit of Guildencrantz's methods, but had come to appreciate the man's craft.

"As tragic as what happened to your *shul* was, Rabbi Samson," Guildencrantz began, his fingers interlocked on the table in front of him. He tilted his head towards Ariel in a practiced gesture of body language implying concern, its falseness betrayed by the tone of mock gravity he applied to Ariel's title. "It would be dishonest of me to say that I'm mourning it. After all it is patently clear that your television appearances are still inappropriate, that you insist on sowing discontent in the community, and that you continue to provide kosher certification to questionable environments. Even *now* your flagrant disregard for Jewish authority is obvious, and it leaves me, and others committed to **ahavas Yisroel** and **da'as Torah**, with only one last appeal to make to you."

"Interesting. And that would be?"

"Cancel your 'Freelance Rabbi' segment and retract your rogue **hechsher**. Otherwise there will be no other alternative than to put you under **cherem**."

Ariel snorted, almost in spite of himself. Almost.

"Oh, *cherem*. That highest ecclesiastical censure a Jewish court can impose on a person," he said breezily. "I *think* I remember that from back in rabbinical school. The Jewish equivalent of Catholic excommunication, right? If I recall correctly," he tapped his finger to his lips in faux-thoughtfulness. "Depending on the specific terms, a *cherem* generally states that other Jews are forbidden from coming within a few feet of me, speaking to me, counting me in a *minyan*, or otherwise associating with me. Which only leaves *me* with the question: Your idea of retaliation is to threaten me with my average Tuesday?"

"Well, that's quite the flippant attitude in the face of potential excommunication."

"I'm sorry, rabbi. Let me try again: Yes boss, you're right. I's just an uppity negro. I swear's I don't means no harms. Is we good?"

"That wasn't an idle threat, Mr. Samson. End that show, and your activities, or you *will* be put in *cherem*."

"Oh, I don't doubt that you'll find two other religious thug mobsters masquerading as rabbis to pronounce *cherem* on me with. But I thought I'd already made it 'patently clear' that I don't just roll over for a beard and a black hat. Also, sorry, but what is it exactly that you think I stand to lose, again? That warm feeling of brotherhood and community? Oh! Perhaps the chance to marry one your daughters with no fear of bigotry? Yeah? No? See, rabbi, my rabbi, I know *exactly* where I stand. Besides, I'm in good company. I can hang out with the students of the Rambam now."

"Well, I guess you've chosen your course, Mr. Samson," Guildencrantz concluded, leaning back in his seat. "And that's all I have to say."

Ariel looked at Guildencrantz, silently.

Like, really took him in. His thin fingers and whiskered lips. His face looking far more gaunt than his 63 years should've. His salt-and-chocolate hair and beard. His shiny black satin **kapote** with its black-on-black paisley design. The black Stetson homburg he wore, a gray and beige speckled feather tucked into its wide black bowtie band.

Then Ariel spoke again.

"Wow. Are you really still *that* put out about your daughter marrying a black guy?"

A tick jumped in Guildencrantz's face. Ariel noticed Rosenstern trying to pretend that he still wasn't listening.

"A *schvartze*?" Ariel continued. "Or **kushi**, if you will? You shouldn't worry so much. *Ahavat Yisrael*, y'know? But you should know, I have it on *reasonably* good authority that your daughter is happier than she's ever been. Oh!" Ariel smiled broadly. "*Mazal tov,* by the way! Or is it *b'shaah tovah*? Sorry, it's so confusing. I never know which congratulation to give impending grandparents."

In a reflexive gesture of disgust, Guildencrantz's nose flared and wrinkled, and he recoiled away from Ariel, curling his lip into a sneer that revealed yellowing teeth. His skin paled into an oatmeal-grey and his face became rigid, with jaws clamped tight and teeth grinding.

Fixing Ariel with a glare that conveyed the deepest of hatred in his steel-grey eyes, Rabbi Dov Ber Guildencrantz—the **mensch**, the **gadol**—wore a grotesque rictus that at last truly reflected the rot of the man within, revealing everything else to be nothing more than a character he played.

This was the real Guildencrantz. And in that moment, he wasn't afraid to show it, nor was he capable of hiding it.

Meanwhile, Ariel chomped down on another lemon-artichoke chicken pocket and resumed typing on his phone.

Dayum, Ariel.

#coldblooded

According to the Codex Blackinus—as per the code set forth by Uhura, Shaft, and Calrissian (redacted by Tibbs and Winnfield)—it was Black People Law No. 3630 that, within the confines of overwhelmingly white spaces (OWS), the black people thereby contained are legally required to be either friends or foes, with no option for neutrality.

You were either Fred Sanford and Aunt Esther, or those two most annoying Wayans brothers, but in either case, there was no obligation to interact outside of the boundaries of the OWS.

Kind of like how you'd never invite your work friends home to eat at your table like they were people.

So, despite their friendly enough chats during *kiddishes*, Ariel was understandably surprised when Keith'd asked if he had time during the week to talk about some things.

✡ ✡ ✡

"Y'know," Keith opened, as they sat in a coffee shop not too far from Ariel's apartment. "I, uh...I don't think anyone else at the *shul* knows this, but I used to be a Hebrew-Israelite."

"Wait, forreal?" Ariel replied with genuine surprise. "Wow, I had no idea!"

Ahh, Hebrew-Israelites.

Manishtana

That question mark that always sat in Ariel's head whenever someone said that they knew a black Jew.

He'd nod tolerantly, wondering if they meant "black Jew"—as in *"a Jew hailing from a normative denominaton of Judaism who is of African-American and/or Caribbean descent, and is therefore a Jew who is phenotypically/ethnically black,"* or "Black Jew"—as in *"Hebrew-Israelite, but I don't really know or care enough about the difference between you guys."*

To be fair, it *was* a lil' bit confusing, because not everybody knew that the Hebrew-Israelite religion extended past the soapbox-standing, loudspeaker-using, Black Hebrew Israelites dressing like extras in a *Laurence of Arabia* music video.

But that image was so deeply associated with Hebrew-Israelites that most people had no clue there was also a quieter, more Messianic sect, practicing Jewish rituals pretty much exactly how white "Hebrew Roots" Christian congregations did.

And they for damn sure didn't know that probably 80% of the people they thought were "black Jews," were actually the Hebrew-Israelite branch that borrowed their practices almost verbatim from Conservative or even Orthodox congregations, but still refused to adhere to the normative standards of Judaism that would require their conversion.

True, it might've seemed petty from the outside looking in, but, like imagine if you showed up in your AKA letters to Howard homecoming, and here comes Sheena showing up wearing pink-and-green—when you *know* her Morehouse-looking ass is a Delta—talm some shit bout how her grandmama was an AKA.

You wouldn't be tight? Aight then.

"Yep, I was with *all* that nonsense," Keith chucked, somewhat abashedly. "That whole 'so-called black,' 'so-called Jews' nonsense. Had the chainmail suit, dressed in these crazy colorful-ass Power Rangers-looking outfits, talking about the end-times looking like a damn Viking from Compton. The whole shebang. Even had one of them wacky-ass names, too. Tazapanyah ben Yasharahla. Man. Running around swearing I was woke, but just dreaming in someone else's pajamas."

He shook his head in embarrassed nostalgia.

Ariel shrugged with a half-smile, empathetic, and wondering how very differently his brother would be navigating this conversation.

Because, forreal, Jake hated Israelites so much you'd've thought that they'd shot his parents in an alleyway after an *Uncle Moishe* concert, prompting him to travel the world sworn to revenge.

He *hated* the African Power Rangers.

He *hated* the Jesus freaks.

And he *absolutely* lost it when it came to the buttoned-down types that practiced so close to Judaism that they confused everyone.

Oh *boy*, did Jake hate them most of all.

"Their *entire* existence has only *completely* erased *actual* black Jewish history in America," he'd ranted to Ariel once. "Who was the first black Jewish rabbi? *Because it wasn't Matthews.* Who was the first black Jew to graduate from Yeshiva University? *Not Paris.* Have we even *had* a black Jewish *knesset*? No clue! But there's the Israelites everywhere in everybody's mouth, drawing their names all over our history like, like a fucking *two-year old in a coloring book!* Like, y'know what? What we *need* to do is start making a list of them."

"Whoa, *whoa*," Ariel had countered, trying to calm his brother down. "We're making *lists* now? What are we, the Negro Third Reich? Jake, just let them do their thing. Like, are they gonna *do* anything to us? We *know* who we are."

"It's not *about* 'us' knowing who we are! It's about *them* saying that *they're* us!"

"Dude, some of *them* don't even realize there's a difference between us. And, yeah there's definitely a few out there mining white Jewish guilt for money and deliberately misrepresenting themselves. Not even arguing that. But a lot of them are just tryna learn, too. Like, I don't even really see why we need to be caring about what Israelites are doing, anyway."

"Because they come strolling up in our spaces like *'I'm Jewish,'* and they get taken at their word, and then next thing we're at a Shabbat table and they're telling us *'Oh, my mother was inspired to only follow the Old Testament,'* on some Amare Stoudemire type shit—"

"So then just be more cautious about how we're engaging with people. I—"

"And when they start showing up to our *knessets*?"

"And what if they do? There's a *lot* of black Jews who can trace lineage back to being former Israelites. Maybe the ones that show

179

up are the first step to some new black Jewish family being born. *We* don't know. Like, a list tho—"

The look Jake had shot Ariel indicated that he was pretty much done debating the topic. And when your big brother is swole enough to look like he's been eating dumbbells at the gym ever since he was able to walk, perhaps it's not best to pursue the contrary kid brother deal.

But it wasn't like Ariel didn't get his brother's frustration.

How devaluing it felt that white Jewish media was teeming with neophyte reporters who would rather make their bones on exotifying brown communities practicing "unconventional Judaism," than amplifying the voices and issues of the brown Jews they actually shared a community with.

The resentment that bubbled up watching Jewish organizations bend over backwards to champion and fund quasi-Jews, yet never seeming to have any resources available for JOCs in the mainstream.

And of course, upon voicing these very real qualms, being told by other black people that you're some kind of "agent" only seeking to tear down black empowerment.

Ariel understood all of that. But still, people were people. And people have stories.

"Well," Ariel teased Keith, tongue-in-cheek. "I'm clearly not a great judge of character, but you don't *seem* crazy. So how'd you get tied up with Israelites?"

"*Heh.* I was just...searching, I guess...?" Keith considered, thoughtfully. "Growing up I always had a problem with how black people were always suffering all over the world. Living in—well not 'the ghetto,' but definitely not the *best* neighborhoods—it would really depress me at times. Like, all I really wanted to know was '*Why?*'"

Keith paused, gearing up to trudge through the tar pits of his memory.

"My dad's a reverend," he continued. "But Christianity wasn't really vibing with me, and Islam was too...cliché, I guess? No, not 'cliché,' but...vapid. As a choice, I mean. Like, '*Are you a black man unhappy with the establishment? Become a Muslim!*' I mean, not that that can't be a valid choice, but, know what I mean?"

"Yeah, I get you."

"It just felt like it would be the typical knee-jerk move. No critical thought or anything. But then I remember seeing these dudes standing out there, and yeah, they're looking crazy, but you got Jews walking around out here in knickerbockers and fur tires on their heads. But *these* guys, these Israelite dudes...they're over here preaching about black people being G'd's Chosen People, and how we messed up and rebelled, and so now we're suffering at the bottom of the totem pole. And, at the time, that really was the answer I needed. It *made sense.* It explained to me why black people suffered so much. It even gave me back my self-esteem, because they're out here talking about how we were a great people in history. How we were taking that back. So I just fell in with them, y'know?"

"I mean, I guess I can hear that," Ariel conceded. "But some of what they say is just so much nonsense. 'Jewish' means 'Jew-*ish.*' Kinda like a Jew, but not. So like, if I'm Irish, I'm from *next* to Ireland, but not really Ireland? Or the one that's like *'How can you be a Jew? The letter J doesn't exist in Hebrew.'* And it's like, really? We're really gonna act like Google Translate isn't a thing? We're gonna be out here acting like when you translate names into different languages they don't change? Aight, bet, here's one for you then: The letter 'J' doesn't exist in kanji. *So how is it called 'Japan'?* Fake country."

"Aight, aight," Keith admitted, laughing. "That *was* some of the dumber shit. That's actually why I left. Because the logic on some things just wasn't adding up. I was having questions the same way I was with Christianity, and I was getting the same kinda non-answers. Except the pushback wasn't *'Oh, you just need to have more faith'* anymore. It was more like *'You have questions? You must not really be black then.'* So then I bounced."

Keith stopped again, sipping from his coffee.

"So there I was," he started up again. "On my way out of what I'm starting to feel is a cult, but then I run into this *next* crop of Hebrew-Israelites that acted like they had some sense. Like, these were some dudes I could take to an office party somewhere or something. Wore normal clothes, even with the silly little graduation tassles on everything. No streetcorner bullshit, no Jesus mess. Just straight-up Torah. Or at least what I *thought* was straight-up Torah, anyway. Because they were still on that *'We're the original Jews and so we don't need to convert'* tip. And I was like

181

'*Cool. Bet.*' But then I started studying—like, *really* studying—for the first time."

"And so you had questions again," Ariel guessed.

"*Exactly.* I mean, how are y'all like '*We used to be Jews. We're just returning?*' Like, based on *what*? I know *my* parents are both Christian, and my grandparents too. If anyone was Jewish, they *been* since forgot it. Like, let's say you're right. Do y'all think being Jewish is like some carousel? You can just skip the line and hop back on whenever you feel like? Because you can't even do that on a *carousel*. You gotta go back on line, and start from the whole beginning again. And I'm sure *half* of y'all have never even *been* to an amusement park in the first place, namean?"

"Lemme guess, they weren't really tryna hear you on that."

Keith snorted.

"Nope. Almost had to throw some hands on that one. So obviously I left them, too. But I kept studying and studying and studying. And somewhere along the way it brought me here, where I found actual Judaism."

"Well, damn. You done journeyed to Mordor and back. Welcome."

"I know right," Keith laughed. "Thanks...I gotta admit, though, the one thing I'm really gonna miss is walking into a prayer space full of brothers and sisters. Like, back when I was an Israelite a lot of us didn't fully believe in that stuff. But we stuck around for the brotherhood, though. I mean, we said some *messed up* things about people who weren't us, but *damn* we had love and unity and a sense of purpose, and like...*belonging*, man. Y'know? And, don't get me wrong, being Jewish is my home, and I've finally found my true path, but—aside from with you and like Ellis—I do *not* feel that bond of brotherhood here. Like, maybe this is some leftover Israelite in me talking, but 'mainstream' Judaism has a space for Ashkenazim, and a space for Sephardim and Mizrachim and Russians and Lithuanians and everyone else, but not us. We don't factor into *any* of it. I feel like we need to develop, I dunno, the *African* flavor of Judaism. I mean, in accordance with **halacha**, obviously. But we need safe spaces, for one, and a community that celebrates our cultures and traditions, too. As misguided as Hebrew-Israelites are, the one thing I can say they get right hands down is that they have their own. They're not asking for a place at the table, they went ahead and built their own. So why don't black Jews have *our* own?"

"Well..." Ariel replied. "Firstly, what would be the 'African' flavor of Judaism, though? Africa isn't and never was a pan-continental culture, and none of us here in America all came from one single place. So—I mean, at least for me—trying to add or invent an 'African flavor' in Judaism is already a lost venture. But if we wanted to aim for an African-*American* flavor—or a *Caribbean*-American flavor for Caribbean-American Jews, etc, etc—then I think *that's* something plausible."

"Right...right...I can feel that..." Keith nodded. "But how would we do that?"

"Well first we'd have to acknowledge the reality of what exists now, and what we have at our disposal, and move and build from there. Pretty much the same way diasporic Africans created African-American culture and Caribbean-American culture. Because the fact is there are black Ashkenazim, Sephardim, and Mizrachim and others, both in **minhag** and some even ethnically. That is the fact. There are black Jews who are Orthodox, Conservative, Reform, Reconstructionst, all the way to secular. That is the fact. We can't move forward if we don't first accept that we are all these different things, and even if we were *white* it wouldn't be possible to come together as some kinda monolith. Reform and Orthodox believe differently. Conservative and Reconstrcutionist observe differently. Ashkenazim and Sephardim pronounce differently. What we would need to do, in whatever we construct, is to create something that can dovetail with those realities. Like, I dunno, some of my family says **Hallel** on 25 Sivan, because that was the first Juneteenth."

"Whoa! Really?"

"Yeah. And, y'know, I dunno how widespread that custom is, but it's ours. But my brother-in-law's family is from Mississippi, and when my sister told him about our family custom, he took it on but he also added not saying **tachanun** on 27 Shvat, because that's when Mississippi finally ratified the 13th amendment. February 7, 2013."

"*2013*?! Mississippi didn't agree that black people weren't slaves until *2013*?!" Keith's eyes widened. "That's *just* three years ago *last week*!"

"I know. Hence the no *tachanun*. But see, something like that is something we can build. Maybe having a Juneteenth *seder* every year like how Ethiopian Jews have **Sigd**. Jumping the broom at the **chuppah**. A special **kaddish** on **Tisha b'Av** for the victims of lynchings in this country. I'm just saying, we really don't need to reinvent the wheel from whole cloth."

"I am *so* onboard with everything you're saying right now. Because that would be a total dynamic changer. It's, like, the difference from being a guest staying indefinitely in the guest room, and being the one who has a home to call their own. One they can bring others into."

"Ugh. Preaching to the Pope."

"But how possible is it? Who would lead it? Where is the accountability? What are the potential threats to highjacking? I mean, I feel like there's enough black Jews so attached to assimilating into white Jewish spaces that we would inevitably have to fight sedition in our own ranks the whole time we were tryna get this off the ground."

"And that's why it can't be a grassroots thing. It'd have to start from the top and trickle down. We'd have to get a body of clergy together from across every denomination, sit down, hash things out from a common ground, then go back to our respective camps and implement it. Or hell, just forming an interdenominational board of mainstream black clergy, *period*."

"Well damn," Keith leaned back in his chair, appreciating Ariel with new eyes. "Yo, from where I'm sitting, it looks like *you're* the only one in a position to helm any of that. Like, maybe you should make CAY a hub or something."

"*Pfft*. Yeah, right. This isn't even my blueprint. It's my sister's. She's a lawyer, so attention to detail and all that. Also, another problem is that there's not an overabundance of rabbis that creating an African-American-centering Jewish culture is important to. And probably even less who are willing to join an interdenominational initiave."

"Ah, damn. That's a shame. Y'know, that's gotta be at least *half* the reason why everybody conflates mainstream black Jews with Hebrew Israelites. Because we don't have 'our own' and people expect us to. So they just guess the Hebrew Israelite institutions are ours, because we don't show up to establish black Jewish institutions to compare them to."

"Yeah, well...Jews. Making dysfunctional families great since always. Anyway, this can't be what you actually wanted to talk about."

"Oh right! Yeah..." Keith started, suddenly uncomfortable. "Yeah, I wanted to ask you, I mean, the thing is, um...Look, I'm just kinda nervous about this whole *bris* thing..."

"What's to worry about? It's just a pinprick."

No, Ariel didn't have preternatural knowledge of Keith's equipment, and no that wasn't a jab at Keith's size either.

It'd been one of their earlier conversations, when a nervous Keith had asked the newly-installed Ariel if there was a need for a second circumcision for an already circumcised convert.

That's when Ariel had quelled Keith's fears by informing him that instead of a full *brit*, he would would be undergoing what was called a **hatafat dam brit**, a symbolic drop of blood drawn from the area where his foreskin would've been. Much less traumatic.

"Yeah, I mean, I know *that*. It's just..." Keith struggled to find words. "I have a concern, of, um, a certain kind of concern that..."

Keith exhaled finally, leaned in closer to Ariel, and said quickly in a low voice.

"Look, I'm just nervous about something going wrong. And not completely by accident, know what I mean? I'm not clueless. I know that for some people their daughter bringing me home is their worst nightmare. And I'm not trying to get cut off at the pass, if you get me. Again, maybe that's still some of the Hebrew-Israelite white people paranoia left in me, I dunno. I was just hoping that...I mean, I'd like it for to be you to be the one doing it."

"Me? Wait, you want *me* to—"

"Yeah."

"I mean, I guess I *could*. But I've never—"

"It's just a pinprick, right? I mean, it *is* just a pinprick, right?"

"Nonono, yeah, don't worry, yeah," Ariel quickly pacified the rising hint of panic in Keith's voice. "It's totally not a big deal. I can totally do it for you. I'd be happy to do it for you."

Keith was beaming and relieved all at the same time, and Ariel scored himself a hot date that Sunday. With a dude's downstairs situation. Not that there's anything wrong with that. Happens to me all the time.

Keith and Ariel stayed at the table a little longer, maybe five minutes or so, trying to circle the conversation around to something less, um, *penisy*, I guess, before they both had to run off for other plans.

"Y'know rabbi, it's funny," Keith remarked as he pulled his jacket on, tucking a forest-green scarf embroidered with golden reindeer under his bearded chin. "This whole journey of mine started because it was, like, weighing on my soul how badly black people get treated. And then I found Judaism. And here we just spent most of this time talking about making our own Jewish way to get around how black people are treated *here*. Like...that's gotta be part of a plan, right? Like maybe **HaShem**'s plan is to use all this discomfort to push us into some kind of action? To get us to build what we need?"

"I mean," Ariel shrugged. "*Everything* is part of HaShem's plan. There's no such thing as coincidences. But what that plan *is*? Who knows. And us humans can either drive ourselves crazy trying to crack that code, or just live our lives trying to make the best choices we can. And I vote for Door No. 2. The only time *I* try to figure out what G'd's plan is, is when I'm guessing Lotto numbers."

✡ ✡ ✡

The Kent Theater was deliciously empty as usual for a Thursday night.

It's why Ariel liked it. It was Midwood's best kept secret: a cozy little building, really clean and pleasantly sleepy, with mostly sparse security and ticket prices that didn't feel like the movie was trying to cover their SFX budget in just under ten people.

The bustle of the concession stand, however, was a natural evil inherent to *any* theater lobby, and Ariel was surrounded by the excited buzz of anticipatatious conversation and the muffled staccato puffs of the popcorn machine, while he stood last in line, pondering whether to get the peanut M&M's or the Buncha Crunch (which, in my opinion, is the most overpriced way to sell a Crunch bar that somebody has clearly dropped and stepped on).

Usually, he'd just sneak in a soda and a burger or something.

But this was a date.

It was time for Classy Ariel. Not Frugal Ariel, the one who used to go to bars, check out their beer selection, leave, go to the cornerstore, buy a bottle from said beer selection at a fraction of the cost, then sneak it back into the bar and drink it.

Hey, don't you judge him. It was college. He was at the bar for the socialization, not because he could afford the highway robbery.

At any rate, what would be the harm in playing it by the book tonight? Being a student didn't give Tamar a whole lot of time to get out that much, so why skimp out the rare occassion that she did?

"I'm trying to wrap up an accelerated bachelor's of science in nursing," she'd told Ariel on their first date out. They'd taken a time-out from browsing the aisles at Barnes and Noble—where they'd passed the time mixing and matching their genre preferences like awkward stanzas in free verse—to sit in the café and snack, taking tiny pieces of their lives and telling stories about them.

"Whoa. So, like are you in like *school* school, or do you also do rounds, or...?"

"Both. We've been in clinical this whole time. I've been an intern since they matched me with a nurse in January. I'll be basically shadowing her through May."

"Are you specializing in anything?"

"Nope. Nurses don't specialize in bachelor's programs. That happens only in the master's."

"So just general nursery. Or nurse-ery."

"Awww, that's so cute."

"I try."

"Well hopefully all this'll lead me to take the boards in June to become an RN. Versus an NP. If I want to be an NP, I need to go back for more schooling, but I couldn't really pass RN. I mean I could, but not really."

"Wait, is this your first bachelor's?"

"Nope. I graduated with my undergrad bachelor's in 2007, then I went to grad school from 2009-2012 and got a couple of other things there. But in nursing you basically need a bachelor's first. In nursing."

"Well I should be uber grateful you were able to make it out then. Because you sound just hella busy."

"Yeah, it's just a high-pressure time. I'm not at clinical, like, *every* day. It's more like, the work and hoops they put us through. But yeah, they have us working on a lot of projects and writing a lot and doing a lot of things. But I'll hopefully be done in June. Except I'm not sure what happens after that and I need to start thinking about my future soon," she blushed a little here, wrapping her fingers tighter around her warm cup. "I mean, like where I want to look for jobs. Where I might move to next. If I move."

"Well, I'd like to think you'll be sticking around," was the natural thing to say next.

Or at least, that's what the line was in the script.

And maybe Old Ariel would've said it. Or I guess "Young Ariel" would be more accurate.

But our guy was finally starting to learn, just a little bit, that those spontaneous little synaptic bursts of romantic banter might sound lovely in the moment, but if you weren't sure what they meant or where you wanted them to lead, it was just like lifting someone into the air, then jumping off the seesaw and letting them crash to the ground when you decided you were done with the ride.

"That sounds stressful as hell," he said instead, tracing invisible lines across her nose with his eyes, connecting the freckles dot-by-dot.

"Yeah. It is..." a flicker of disappointment flashed across Tamar's face, so briefly that it didn't even register. "Like, sometimes when I'm out and about I think, *'Okay, nobody get hit by any cars, and no one die while I'm around you, because I'm going to have to do that CPR thing, and it was a total fluke when I did the Heimlich on that kid once.'* Like, knowing that I'd actually have to try is a *really* scary thought sometimes."

"Everything is really scary sometimes," he admitted.

Tamar hid a tiny smile, deciphering the subtext Ariel wasn't *not* saying.

Eventually they decided to ditch the café and head with their newly acquired literary booty to a real restaurant instead.

Except the sky decided to open up and empty out when they were only halfway there, so Ariel and Tamar found themselves sprinting across the frosted grass of a snow-slaked park, with plastic bags full of books jerking wildly on their wrists, and taking shelter under the domed roof an adorably snug gazebo.

nd there they stayed for hours, just talking, until the soggy lawn of snow shifted from a drab off-white under an overcast grey sky, to a bright orange-pink that reflected the luminescence of the streetlights back into the inky blue night.

No making out was had, despite how tempting and tingly the prospect, but they or may not have hooked pinkies while they huddled against each other against the icy sleet.

Swoon

Anyhoo, between getting swamped in clinical, and churning out projects on kidney issues in children, and studying about abortions, and freaking out to Ariel on Facebook because she was *convinced* she was failing out of school, Tamar and Ariel'd only seen each other about four times since they'd began, um...what did they begin actually?

Like, were they dating? Is that what this thing was? They *were* going on dates, so I guess by definition they were, right...?

Anyway, they were at Kent to see *The Revenant*.

Not Ariel's choice of movie, by the way.

If it were up to him he'd probably catch the send up of Golden-Age Hollywood that *Hail, Ceaser!* promised. Or indulging in the English-major equivalent of junk food with *Pride and Prejudice and Zombies*. Or *Kung Fu Panda 3*. Because, *Kung Fu Panda 3*.

Either way—rumors of Leonardo DiCaprio finally snagging his long elusive Oscar notwitshstanding—Ariel wasn't really enamored about watching yet another movie, where yet again black or brown or Native bodies were the lesson-providing sacrificial lambs, tasked with the sole mission in life of rescuing the white protagonist's humanity.

It was kinda like the converse of those romantic comedies, where the brown protagonist cycles through a revolving door of interchangeable brown potential-mates, who are all really just stepping stones to the protagonist achieving his blonde blue-eyed trophy goddess of societal acceptance and progress.

...Waitasecond, Ariel began to muse as he stepped forward in line. Which one was *he* in this thing between him and Tamar?

Was he the lesson-teaching plot device?

Or was he the black guy traipsing throught the forest singing "Some Day My Becky Will Come," waiting for his white princess to save him from suffocating in his masochistic world?

Huh.

Ariel hated the saying "**Shiksas** are for practice," and all its implicit and explicit dehumanization, but...had he ended up doing that anyway?

To Gabrielle and Christina and Dana?

Were they just incidental footnotes in the footer of his biography, the B-plot to the story of his life? He believed he'd seriously romanced them, but *had* he?

Or had he really just been fooling himself that "black" *or* "black and Jewish" were that important to him, and all he was *really* waiting for was the opportunity to be a Franz Fanon case study?

Y'know, "Franz Fanon" as in *Black Skin, White Masks*?

"Franz Fanon" as in *"one of the dynamics of colonialism is where the colonized male's response to experiencing racism is one of a fantasy and desire to reclaim self-esteem through a romantic relationship with a colonizer woman, imbuing her with symbolic cultural value in the contest between colonized and colonizer"*?

Uh oh.

Or—*OR*—maybe none of it was...anything.

Maybe Ariel and Tamar were just two people who were just two people, and Ariel just needed to, like, relax dude.

They were vibing, right?

So just vibe.

"Seriously," a properly smirking voice Ariel knew like the back of his hand came crashing into his reverie, with ironic timing and efficacy. "Don't we see enough of each other already? We *just* got off work two hours ago."

Ah, Ellis, of course. The baking soda *and* vinegar to the 7th-grade science fair volcano that was Ariel's life, romantic or otherwise.

Just the other day, Ariel—only slightly joking—had asked Kalman why he'd held out and never introduced the two of them.

"She was dating someone when I met her," Kalman shrugged in reply. "Besides...I figured you weren't her type," he added with a weird look.

Ariel wanted to ask what that meant, but Kalman had to dart off, late for a budget meeting.

After all, more congregants attending CAY meant more resources being expended, and the necessity of finding new streams of revenue. And Cate had been all over Kalman's back for the past week or so about him procrastinating on delivering the goods.

So, since she hadn't gotten anything in her inbox when she'd asked Kalman for it a week ago, she wanted it on her desk *that night.*

And so—after spending three or four hours banging out the stickier parts—Kalman and Cate had settled on the idea of creating a weekly CAY **Oneg Shabbat** dinner, open to anyone who had pre-paid a $25 fee to the *shul* earlier in the week.

So seeing Ellis at the theater was kind of funny, actually.

Tomorrow was going to be the first CAY Oneg—promising a robust turnout, thanks in no small part to Chani Guildencrantz using the Hillel newspaper to hype the event all over campus—and it just so happened to coincide with the *yahrtzeit* of Ellis' great-grandmother, Chana Gittel bat Moshe. It was decided the dinner would be declared in her honor and memory.

"So I'm gonna need you to stop stalking me," Ellis stepped back playfully, perennial smirk firmly in place and the lobby lights making the blue in her hair pop.

"Stalking *you*? You're in *my* neighborhood."

"Um, no. This theater is on *my* side of Coney Island Avenue. Go run back under your little Q-train back there."

"Look it's not my fault that you miss my face so much."

"You're right. It *isn't* your fault I have such terrible aim."

"Well. Walked right into that one."

"That's what she said. What're you catching?"

"*The Revenant.* You?"

"Ugh," Ellis made a face at Ariel's choice. "I'm catching *Force Awakens* before it's gone."

"Really?" Ariel arched an eyebrow. "Don't think I would've pegged you for a *Star Wars* fan."

"I'm not," Ellis lifted a finger and clarified. "I'm a *Darth Vader* fan."

"Ah. There it is."

"Yep. Plus, I wanna see what JJ does when he's *actually* doing a *Star Wars* film, or if he just used it all up in his *Trek* movies. R2-D2 in the first one was cute, but I did *not* appreciate Kirk yelling '*Punch it!*' at Sulu in *Into Darkness.*"

"Same. That was more than a little bit jarring."

"Grr. Anyway, you're here alone though?"

"No, I'm here with a," he paused. "A friend. They're already inside. Holding our seats."

"A, a friend?" Ellis teased.

Ariel opened his mouth to protest.

"Oh relax. Whatever. Anyway, just figured I'd harass you. My movie's about to start and my a, a friend is holding my seat too. Catch you tomorrow, yeah?"

"Sure," Ariel shrugged. "*The word is given.*"

"*He is intelligent, but not experienced. His pattern indicates two-dimensional thinking,*" Ellis replied over her shoulder as she walked away. "*Everyone* can randomly quote *Wrath of Khan*, Ariel. Calm down."

✡ ✡ ✡

Ariel knew the bear scene was coming.

They *both* knew the bear scene was coming.

It was impossible to have heard anything about *The Revenant* and *not* have heard about the bear attack that happened in the first half hour of the movie.

But what Ariel and Tamar did *not* know was how skillfully Alejandro Inarritu was going to craft that slow burn of tension in those weighty 109 seconds leading up to it.

They sat with their eyes riveted on the screen, barely noticing the candy failing to reach their open mouths.

Tamar's body became rigid as the slow crawl of the camera tracked Leonardo DiCaprio's Hugh Glass through the woods, watching the character unsuspectingly meander along. Her hand flailed for Ariel, while Hugh trudged across a mossy forest floor in eerie silence, save for the shuffling of fallen leaves and the snapping of dry branches underfoot.

Almost as if he could sense the audience watching him, Hugh paused to look over his shoulder, scrutinizing his surroundings as he chewed on an unidentified frontier foodstuff. The audience held its breath and the camera froze, as if they both were afraid that Hugh would catch sight of them.

But, detecting nothing, he hesitantly turned and continued on.

The audience exhaled at the close call, and the camera began to creep behind Hugh once more, now with increased caution, masking its movements with the rhythm of his steps.

But within just three paces, Hugh came to a stop again, feeling the roomful of apprehension at his back, and he removed his heavy fur hood to scan the light fog with vigilant eyes, in search of the movie's audience.

The camera narrowly evaded the sweep of Hugh's gaze, ducking and circling around him, staying careful to float just outside the edge of his vision. And Hugh, surely smelling a suspicious scent of popcorn on the air, gingerly edged forward, his shotgun now cocked and poised at eye level.

Two small cubs wandered into frame from the right of the screen.

Hugh heard the gasp of the theater first, and the rustling behind him second.

He snapped his head to his right, then spun the rest of his body around, just in time to be too late to stop a highly overprotective mama bear.

The next four minutes and thirty-three seconds were cranked up to maximum intensity: fast, terrifying, and, *ahem*, grisly.

It wasn't the initial attack that startled Ariel or Tamar.

There'd been enough of a visible advance before the beast collided with the man that it wasn't a particular shock.

But when a battered Hugh, having barely survived the first round of maulings, unloaded a shotgun volley directly into the bear's face that only seemed to enrage the animal more than injure it, the *second* charge—punctuated by a clawed rake across Hugh's throat that tore bloody gulches open across his neck—elicited more than a few yelps from the horrified onlookers.

It took Ariel completely off-guard.

The scene was so sudden and vivid that he impulsively jerked back in his seat and threw his arms up, as if he himself were trying to escape the furious bear onscreen. Tamar reacted too, but in her case she instinctively flung herself against Ariel's torso and grabbed on for dear life, burying her face into his chest for protection.

Obviously, Ariel would've preferred to be in *slightly* more manly of a position when that happened—perhaps something strong-jawed, stoic, and barrel-chested—but from that point on, she never let go.

They spent the rest of the movie with Tamar nestled in Ariel's chest, relatively relaxed, enjoying the incredible beauty of Calgary, Kananaskis Country, and Fortress Mountain that was lavishly splayed across the screen—the odd horrific frontiersmen vs natives scene aside.

Beautiful scenery, though.

And as Ariel sat there—inhaling the vanilla-scented fragrance of Tamar's shampoo, her hand on his chest, while his heart thumped in her ear—as they both watched Leonardo DiCaprio actually eat raw bison liver onscreen, Ariel was pleasantly surprised to find himself thinking that this was something he could used to.

The snuggling, not the eating raw bison liver thing.

Needless to say, after enduring that unappetizing trauma, Ariel and Tamar decided it was probably best to skip the dinner they had planned for after the movie.

The mostly plastic lancet felt oddly heavy in Ariel's hand, and a little slippery through the latex gloves he wore.

He'd be lying if he said he wasn't nervous, or that his mind wasn't whirring through almost *any* excuse to back out.

But a promise was a promise.

The last time he'd done anything close to this was on a frog back in Biology in high school. The frog had been dead, so the stakes were slightly less high.

Also, there hadn't been a phalanx of rabbis looking over his shoulder. Which is not something that isn't stressful in *any* scenario. It's not that Ariel was squeamish or anything, in fact, once upon a time, he strongly considered becoming a *mohel* himself.

It was back in 2004, when the city had been all abuzz with the news of a Rockland County *mohel* transmitting a fatal case of Type 1 herpes to an infant boy during a *brit*, and additionally infecting two others. The incident and its details had horrified Ariel, inspiring him—however briefly—to become a better caliber of *mohel*, and with a lot less icky practices.

Like mother, like son, apparently.

It was for similar reasons that the Samson boys almost ended up not having a *brit* at all. Or at least not without a fight.

Manishtana

See, remember Nadia? The old college friend of Ariel's mother, Shoshana? The one so ferociously against circumcision that she denounced the first and oldest Jewish tradition in existence as being inherently anti-Semitic?

Yeah, her.

Well, as the friendship between the two former collegemates was writhing in its death throes—just days before the planned *bris* of Jake, the first Boy Samson—Nadia had one final barb to hurl during that last brunch meeting.

"Well, if you're fine with a rabbi performing non-consensual oral sex *on your newborn son*," Nadia hissed. "Then you're not someone I want to associate with anyway."

"Oral *what*?! Non-consens—what the *hell* are y—"

"Hello? The 'suction' part?"

"Again, *what* the hell are you talking about?"

And so, with immeasurable bile and self-righteous pleasure, Nadia educated her soon to be ex-friend of the *metzitza*, the venerable tradition codified in the holiest of Jewish texts. How, after the swipe of his scalpel, the *mohel* leans over the wailing, red-faced, in shock and in pain eight-day old infant...and uses his mouth to suck the blood out of the fresh wound, to prevent clot and decay. How this was an indispensable practice enforced for millennia upon billions of Jewish children across the globe. How it was the fate in store for her own eight-day old baby. (And yes. That *is* how those three infants would come to contract herpes 23 years after Nadia and Shoshana's verbal melee. But at least it wasn't the sexytimes Type 2 kinda herpes. So there's that.)

Shoshana was aghast. And, this time, *legitimately* speechless.

"You don't even *know* what you're subjecting your son to?" Nadia laughed derisively, with no little glee.

And with that, Shoshana had left brunch shaken, and was *still* shaken by the time she got home to her husband that night.

"Don't come in the living room!" Avigdor held up both hands as soon as she walked through the door. "I dropped some food gravel and I'm looking for the sweep-stick."

It's okay if that sentence confused you.

Ariel's father, Avigdor, was frequently prone to forgetting the names of things and making up new names for them in the middle of a sentence without breaking stride.

After four years of dating and—at that point in time—one year of marriage, Shoshana was pretty fluent in Avigdor.

"Food gravel" was "crumbs," and the "sweep-stick" was the broom.

Sometimes it drove her crazy, like when he called the oven the "baker." Other times she wondered exactly why they *didn't* call a mailman a "post officer." It was endearing. That and his being able to name the cast and crew from any movie produced between 1931-1949.

"The broom is the pantry closet," she said simply, still off-center and dazed.

"Right!" Avigdor snapped his fingers. "I was making myself a meat-bread an—What's wrong?"

"What? Nothing."

Avigdor just looked at her.

"I dunno, I—I guess I'm just nervous about the *bris*."

"*Brit*. What about?"

Shoshana paused, unsure how to broach the topic.

She didn't want to start off being accusatory and putting Avigdor on the defensive. He was just as stubborn as she was, and would likely just dig his heels in even deeper. But in case Nadia was just making it up, she also didn't want to ask and look like an idiot for being tricked so easily about something in her own religion.

"...Well," she began. "I guess I'm still not really sure what's supposed to be happening. I was hoping we could walk through it together?"

"Oh! Sure!"

Avigdor grabbed a chair, while Shoshana crashed on the nearby couch, and he began detailing the ceremony.

How Shoshana would hand the baby to her mother-in-law Lahava, who would hand him to Avigdor's sister Zehava, to their sister Aliza, to Aunt Devora, who would hand the baby to her husband Uncle Yehoshua, and the congregation would rise and welcome the baby.

Uncle Yehoshua would hand the baby to Ariel's brother Raphael, who would hand him (probably *very* reluctantly) to their father Shmuel, who would hand him to Uncle Ariel, who would place the baby down on **Eliyahu's Chair**. The *mohel*—whom they had yet to find, by the way—would then ask the invisible prophet to protect the infant from any mishaps during the ceremony, and then Uncle Ariel would lift the baby up and give him to Avigdor, who would then place him on Rabbi I.I. "Cap'n'"s lap. From there, Avigdor would pick up the knife and hand it to the *mohel*, designating the clerical surgeon as his agent.

A blessing would be recited, snips would be made, Avigdor would be revived from where he passed out on the floor, he'd name the baby, and then everyone would eat.

"Easy peasy," Avigdor concluded.

"Can we go back to the *bris* part?" Shoshana began easing into her investigation. "What—"

"*Brit.*"

"Whatever. What happens with the actual circumcision? Like, how does it go?"

"K, so there's three parts. First there's the *chituch* where the mohel removes the foreskin, then the *priah*, when he uncovers the glans, then the *metzitza* when he suctions the blood out from around the cut, and then he bandages our guy up and diapers him."

"That middle part there. The *metzitza*? Do we, do we really *need* to do that part?"

"Well, yeah. It actually says somewhere in the Talmud that a *brit* is invalid without it, and that *mohels* who don't do it should be fired."

Shoshana swallowed a hard lump in her throat, unsure of what floored her more, the fact that Nadia was right, or that Avigdor had confirmed it so matter of factly, so cavalierly, like it didn't even matter. This couldn't be her husband. Not her Avigdor.

The man she loved was weird, and he called shoes "foot hats," and he knew that *The Black Shield of Falsworth* was even a *thing*, but he couldn't, the man she married couldn't possibly—

"Well, well maybe I don't think he should *have* a *brit*! Bris. Whatever!" she burst out, her voice shrill and panicked. "Maybe we should just wait until he's older to see if he wants one."

"*What?*"

"Well maybe he doesn't *want* one! And it's *his* body, right? Like, my mother pierced my ears when I was two and I *totally* didn't want that! So maybe he won't want this, *either*."

The words hung there in the air between them. Slowly, audibly, Avigdor inhaled, then exhaled.

"Shoshana..." Avigdor replied. Steadily. His voice cracked with restraint, as if his words were a dam creaking against a deluge of floodwaters. "Our son. Is having a *brit*."

He was using *that* voice.

His deceptively placid one, judiciously devoid of any emotion.

That measured tone Shoshana recognized whenever she said things that challenged his idea of Judaism, and it was taking his everything to subdue himself and not reflexively go nuclear in defense. She'd gotten very familiar with it during her year of conversion studies, when Avigdor would interpret the most innocent of her genuine questions as insidious heresy of the highest order, or like she was maliciously attacking his very existence.

"We're Jewish, Shoshana," her husband continued, wrestling with himself as both lion and lion-tamer. "The *brit mila* was the *very first* commandment given to us. It is the commandment that marked the birth of our peoplehood. It is the commandment that makes us Jews. And to deny the *brit* is to deny our people. And we aren't gonna be the ones who break that chain. My son—*our son*—is not gonna break that chain. He is having a *brit*."

Shoshana looked at her husband, matching his steady gaze with her own, not exactly sure where to go from here.

Because the thing is, she knew Avigdor was right.

Actually—and more accurately—it was *she* who believed in the same sentiments, regardless of what her husband was declaring.

She had adopted and embraced Judaism wholeheartedly because she *believed* in it. She might've been only a two-year old Jew at that point, but she *genuinely* believed with every fiber of her being that the *brit*—BRIS!—symbolized a profound covenant. A millennia old ritual that bonded man and G'd in body and spirit, and one she'd always believed that, if she had a son, was a time-honored tradition she would want him to take part in.

But this new information...Maybe it was just a little...

"...And you're just...You're *okay* with someone putting their mouth on our child's penis?"

"...What the hell are you talking about?" Avigdor's jaw dropped. "Why the hell would anyone put their mouth on an infant's penis?"

"*For the metzitza!* You *just said* the blood had to be sucked out for it to be a valid *bris!*"

"Yeah! With *gauze* and a *glass pipette*! Who told you the blood gets *literally* sucked out like that?"

Ah, that classic *Three's Company* kind of mix-up, amirite?

But, after some mutual research, it turned out that Avigdor and Nadia were *both* right.

The more full-contact suction that Nadia derided was called the *metzitza b'peh*, as in "suction with the mouth." Avigdor had been completely caught off-guard because his family had always practiced what was called *metiztza b'keli*, aka "suction with an instrument."

"Well," Avigdor commented, upon absorbing this new knowledge. "Now it makes *a lot* more sense why the kids in junior high would spread jokes about me getting blowjobs from the rabbi."

And so began the hunt for a mohel that, y'know, just to reiterate, *wasn't* going to put his mouth on a baby's penis.

Which is how they'd reconnected with Mikey Aroeste.

Sorry, *Rabbi* Aroeste.

Or, as Ariel had always known him, Uncle Mikey, who—as the convoluted ways of the L'rd would have it—also happened to be one of the triumvirate of rabbis overseeing Keith's conversion.

Uncapping the small disposable instrument under Uncle Mikey's watchful but approving eye, Ariel wiped at the target area with an alcohol pad, stretched out the loose skin with his free gloved hand, and made the quick jab.

A pinprick of blood quickly swelled to the surface, and Ariel dabbed at it with gauze.

"Thank you," Keith whispered under his breath, tears welling up in his eyes.

Ariel's nod was brisk, conveying something along the lines of *"Dude, thank me at* literally *any other time than the moment that I'm holding your junk."*

"Our G'd and G'd of our fathers," Rabbi Aroeste intoned twenty minutes later at the ceremony's conclusion—after Keith had taken his ritual dip in the *mikvah*—holding aloft a cup of wine. "Assure the continuing success of this convert, whose name is called in Israel: Tzefanya Yisrael ben Avraham...Tzefanya Yisrael, son of Abraham, our father...Spread over him Your lovingkindness. Guide him in the path of Your commandments and to actualize Your will in order to find favor in Your eyes. Amen, thus may it be Your will."

And just like that, Keith Taylor—formerly Tazapanyah ben Yasharahla the Hebrew-Israelite—was now Tzefanya Yisrael the Jew, his new Jewish name a conscious repudiation of the bastardized version he'd proudly touted once upon a time.

For his part, Keith was overwhelmed with the resonance that— after several stressful months of trying to secure an available date— the one day that the schedules of his rabbis miraculously converged in availability, for his final stage of declaring his religious love and commitment, happened to be February 14th.

The significance that on Frederick Douglass' self-claimed birthday, Keith found himself reborn in his new self-claimed religion, having endured a journey just as spiritually fraught with hardship as the great thinker's escape from slavery had been riddled with physical danger.

And even more, after five years of study, six years after he first began his odyssey, Keith Taylor entered the Jewish covenant on the fifth day of Adar, the sixth Jewish month.

Because, like I said to him later that week, echoing Ariel's earlier words, "There are no coincidences. "

And now, a plot kink!

It had been a good story meeting at the top of the week and they were working with a full crew: Ellis & Ariel, plus Regina, Elmo, Drake, Buddy, and even Q (or, as Ellis called them, the Frazzled Five).

There was a pretty funny Leap Day bit and a slightly edgy extended Black History Month sketch scheduled for the day, but otherwise the week ahead would be pretty softball.

"Alright, kiddies," Ellis began wrapping it up. "Let's—Oh! By the way, congrats to Ariel and Buddy. Apparently the Freelance Rabbi skits are pissing off non-freelance rabbis. Good job."

Ariel and Buddy looked puzzled.

"How so?" Ariel asked for the both of them, as Ellis rummaged through some papers to pull out one of the more popular right-leaning *frum* magazines. Y'know, the kind that replaced women's faces with challah rolls and whatnot.

"Yeah," she answered, flipping through its pages until she reached the article. "You got one of the Big Black Hats angry. What's his name, what's his name—ah! Right here. Dov Ber Guildencrantz."

"Wait, really?"

Ariel knew Rabbi Guildencrantz. Or knew of him, more accurately.

202

ARIEL SAMSON: FREELANCE RABBI

He was one of the bigger movers and shakers in Midwood.

Head of the Octagon-K kosher certification agency. Head rabbinical judge of the Beis Din Shaarei Tzedek religious court. Spiritual leader of Brooklyn's Congregation Orach Chayyim of Flatbush. And long distance Chief Rabbi of Eindhoven, the Netherlands.

Which, c'mon, man. You're doing too much.

Regardless, despite all the notches on his belt, Guildencrantz didn't have the most stellar reputation with the average man on the street. But he bumped shoulders with enough of the right people, knew enough texts to overwhelm enough of Midwood into the cult of his scholarship, and was positioned in all the right places to continuously drown those skeptical voices out.

But the grumbles of dissension still managed to leak through anyway.

"Yeah," Ellis continued. "Came out over this weekend. It's a whole ranty piece hacking at your background, your learning, your career, he's even dredged up some of your old Facebook posts where you talk about joining the Rubashkin boycott and being against releasing Jonathan Pollard."

Okay, first of all, look, maybe Sholom Rubashkin, former CEO of Agriprocessors—the once largest kosher meat-packing plant in the US—was acquitted of the charges of child labor law violations and conspiracy to harbor illegal immigrants that had sparked the boycott spearheaded by the Orthodox social justice organization Uri L'Tzedek.

But (aside from the fact that the acquittal doesn't mean he *wasn't* actually guilty. See: O.J.), he was *still* violating US *and* Torah law with the charges he *was* found guilty of, namely bank fraud, mail and wire fraud, and money laundering.

The man was *not* some martyred victim of virulent anti-Semitism.

Secondly, when it came to Israel, there was *already* a racialized dynamic in place, whether pro or anti-Zionist, used as a weapon against the "authenticity" of Jews of Color, whether racially or religiously.

Were you critical of the Jewish state? Then were you *really* Jewish, though?

Did you support the Jewish state? Then you were *clearly* a sellout complicit in genocide and colonialism.

And as far as the overwhelmingly pro-Israel American Jewish community was concerned, it was far more invested in amplifying the voices of non-Jewish pro-Zionist Christians than it was in examining why so many Jews of Color weren't as gung-ho onboard with the sancrosanctity of the State of Israel. Probably having to do with browner people sometimes not being able to even get off the *plane* once they landed at Ben Gurion. Not without a full body check and photographic recollection of everyone who'd attended their *bar mizvah*.

But when it came to Jonathan Pollard, it baffled Ariel that not only did uber-Zionists conveniently gloss over the fact that Pollard was *also* attempting to broker weapons deals and sell US intelligence to South Africa, China, Australia, Argentina, Taiwan, Pakistan, and fucking *Iran*, but even *if* Pollard was some selfless Diaspora Jew spying solely on Israel's behalf for the greater benefit of the Jewish people, *that was still the crime of spying and possibly treason against the US.*

Now, Ariel was pretty pro-Israel.

But if you're so pro-Israel that you're fine with someone violating the laws and security of the country you *actually* live in just because they were benefitting Israel with those criminal activities, then perhaps you should actually live in Israel.

"Oh, this is a really good line here," Ellis said, thoroughly amused. "*It is difficult to avoid the conclusion,*" she read. "*That Ariel Samson illustrates the warping of authentic Torah-true values to sanction the ills of 'liberalism' and 'social justice.' Samson sows the seeds of ultimate confusion in those lacking sufficient knowledge, and gives 'rabbinic' sanction to* **to'eivah** *lifestyles.*"

"What? *How?*"

"I think this is actually about your LGBTQ sketch from two weeks ago."

"Are you—*What*? Is he *kidding* me?"

Ariel sat fuming in his seat while flames of silent anger engulfed him.

Firstly, "*to'eivah*."

It was the favorite flashpoint catchphrase to throw around in right-wing Orthodox circles, justifying homophobia and homophobic violence.

The term technically meant "abomination," which was all that fire and brimstone-minded leaders needed to know to condemn

LGBTQ Jewish lives or to declare them as aberrations capable of being "cured."

But, funny thing, the word *to'eivah* appeared about 122 times in the Torah.

Eating non-kosher food was *to'eivah*.

A woman remarrying a first husband after divorcing a second husband was *to'eivah*.

Envy, lying, and gossip was *to'eivah*.

But somehow, none of those groups ever got demonized with the label of being a "*to'eivah* community," or subjected to the same level of ostracization.

Even according to the dubious logic of "Well *this to'eivah* has a death penalty attached," the argument was still pretty flimsy.

After all, Jews who didn't observe Shabbat were *also halachically* subject to the death penalty. But there was never a news story about someone getting beaten to death for not being Shabbat-observant.

I mean, outside of Beit Shemesh or something.

Furthermore, there was absolutely nothing about having same-sex attraction that was anathema in Judaism.

The prohibition was not only narrow concerning gender (there was no explicit prohibition against a '*woman lying with woman as one lies with a man*'), but even in its codified condemnation the Torah was concerned with a very specific act that, quite honestly— and statistically—heterosexual couples engaged in *far* more than male homosexual ones did.

In a similar vein (if undesirable comparison), being a kleptomaniac wasn't *inherently* a sin. It was the actual act of *stealing* that was prohibitied.

Secondly, "sanctioned."

Ariel hadn't "sanctioned" anything.

He was far too Orthodox for that, and he could admit to himself that, even though he was likely on the fringe when it came to acceptance and inclusion of LGBTQ Jews, he still likely hadn't evolved past a benevolent paternalism.

Because it was too uncomfortable of a space for him to think about.

As an Orthodox rabbi, he couldn't deny the biblical prohibition against guys inserting Slot A into Tab B as exposed in Leviticus.

But he also didn't believe that the LGBTQ community was doing anything worse than any other kind of Jew that they deserved to be vilified.

He wasn't really in the habit of judging people just because they sinned differently than he did. But even *that* sentence was problematic, he acknowledged.

Either way, Ariel had never been concerned with what people were doing, but more with what they *weren't*.

Okay, so you like sword fencing with other dudes.

Great.

What part of that meant you couldn't be Shabbat observant? Or keep kosher?

Ariel was aware that his take likely didn't answer any LGBTQ questions or struggles, but he was more invested in it being known that just because you admittedly weren't doing the *one* thing didn't mean you had to throw away all the *other* things.

There were 613 commandments after all. And there were people who proudly declared themselves "Orhtodox" who were topping off at observing maybe 300 at best.

At least LGBTQ folk were being honest.

But what part of being LGBTQ meant not keeping kosher? Or not *davening* three times day? Or not coming to *shul* on Shabbat? Or not wearing *tzitzit*?

Nothing, really.

The same way nothing stopped Jews from dealing in shady business interactions and fraud, but still being hailed as pillars of their *frum* ultra-Orthodox community.

But what had inspired Ariel's LGBTQ Freelance Rabbi sketch was one of Chani's Hillel crew members.

A young "they," born female but feeling male, they'd asked Ariel if they even *had* a place in Judaism, and what side of the *mechitza* that Judaism lie.

And, being kind of the rabbi that he was, Ariel sought out answers.

Because emotions were emotions. But *halachic* fact was *halachic* fact.

Contrary to popular belief, it's not like traditional Jewish thought didn't acknowledge gender dysmorphia.

After all, every *yeshiva* **bochur** worth his salt knew the **midrash** that Jacob and Leah's daughter Dina was originally destined to be born a girl and how—sensitive to her sister Rachel's feelings—Leah had prayed that the fetus she was carrying be born a boy, so that her sister contributed more than just the one son to the forming of the twelve tribes.

Less studied was the kabbalistic take that *both* Leah and Rachel were pregnant at the same time, and that Joseph was originally destined to be born a *girl*. So, as a result of Leah's prayer, originally female Joseph was born a boy, and originally male Dina was born a girl. And subsequently, gender stereotypes aside, their original gendered natures still manifested in their lives.

The whole episode of Dina and Shechem kicks off because Dina goes out "to look upon the daughters of Shechem."

Like a dude would.

Joseph gets into all his trouble because he's busying gossiping about his brothers and spends his time flouncing around in his pretty coat, "touching up his eyes" and "doing his hair."

Like a chick would.

In fact, contrary to the exclusively gender-binary system Judaism was believed to operate under, traditional Jewish thought acknowledged *six* different gender states:

1- Zachar: CIS male
2- N'keivah: CIS female
3- Androgonos: A person with both male and female physical attributes
4- Tumtum: A person whose sexual characteristics are indeterminate or obscured
5- Aylonit: A person who is identified female at birth but develops male characteristics
6- Saris: A person who is identified male at birth but develops female characteristics

That wasn't to say that there was a conscious science or sociology at play, or that it was super "progressive," or that it understood sex and gender as being separate things, or that it came anywhere *near* addressing gender reassignment surgery.

After all, Torah was more concerned with spirituality and legalistic religious obligation. But there it was nonetheless.

In the immortal words of NeNe Leakes: "I said what I said."

And that is what Ariel had objectively presented in his sketch.

He didn't get into that, *halachically* speaking, going from male to female was anathema under the prohibition of male castration that applied to human and animal alike, as per Leviticus 22:24.

He also didn't address that while not explicitly forbidden, female to male wasn't exactly "forbidden" but wasn't "sanctioned," either.

Kinda like when your parents go out of town on vacation and tell you not to throw any parties, so instead you decide to hold a symposium exploring the practical biochemical impact of *Cannabis indica* and ethanol on human pheromones and social interactions.

For science.

At any rate, he *did* bring forth the 1971 Orthodox *Tzitz Eliezer* ruling that, permissibility aside, the post-surgery gender is the one that is *halachically* binding.

And that's all Ariel's sketch had presented.

Good on him.

I mean, I'm not really sure where I stand on my gender these days *anyway*. And pretty sure the rabbis are torn, too.

At any rate, that's what traditional thought had to say on the matter. So that's what he'd said. Ariel was extremely committed to fighting Orthodoxy's steady drift to the ~~Christian~~ right, to bringing into light the stances and rulings that at times completely and uncomfortably contradicted the ideologies and practices that "Torah true" Judaism was purpoted to have.

On the other hand, he also didn't want to mislead people into thinking that either he or *halacha* was more progressive than either of them actually were.

But damned if you do, damned if you don't, apparently.

"Look, whatever," Ariel finally said. "Like, why is he even *on* the internet to see the show anyway?"

"Well how else is he supposed to know about the evils that peril his flock unless he's dabbling in them?" Ellis smirked.

Ariel rolled his eyes in exasperation of the hypocrisy.

"Um," Regina gingerly raised her hand on behalf of the bewildered looks of the rest of the Frazzled Five. "Is there anything *we* need to be filled in on? Because you two have been going back and forth nonstop, and, ironically, I failed Hebrew in Hebrew school."

Ariel squinted, looking from Ellis to Regina and back again.

Ellis shrugged.

"You started. I just responded," she answered Ariel's look.

Wait, what? When the—? How long had he and Ellis been Hebrewifying? Because he hadn't even *noticed* when or where he'd switched out of English. It'd just came so...naturally.

Weird.

"Anyhoo," Ellis answered Regina. "Nope, we're all good here. Let's get out there and hustle, guys. Oh, Regina?"

"Yep?"

"Can you put some time on my calendar before noon? I wanna tighten up some of the dialogue on the Black History Month skit."

"Gotcha. Eleven okay?"

"Perfect. Let's get it done."

Huzzah.

Bechdel test achievement marginally unlocked.

✡ ✡ ✡

"You must be really excited." Wes said to Elmo, who was dressed in the standard Black Panther uniform of leather jacket and gloves, dark sunglasses, and black beret. "It's a leap year, so that's, like, an *extra* day of Black History Month."

"Yep," Elmo confirmed, raising a gloved fist in the air. "One more day to fight the white devils trying to oppress my people."

"I, okay. But isn't it—"

"Yep, here we go," Regina wandered onstage, wearing a pair of overalls over a white tank-top and carrying a spittoon, affecting a Southern redneck drawl. "Them uppity negroes ungrateful for this country."

The audience laughed as Wes, Regina, and Elmo paused for a beat, taking each other in.

"Wait. Amanda Jo." Wes asked. "Do you have a problem with Black History Month?"

"Damn straight I do! All of them 'diversity' months," Regina's character griped, drawing 'diversity' out with a mocking whine. "There can be a BET channel, but heavens to Betsy that we have a White Entertainment Television channel. Them coloreds would *riot!*"

"Um, you mean 'television'?" Elmo shot back.

"Look," Wes jumped in, trying to mediate. "I think we can all agree that we have these months to highlight contributions that marginalized groups have made to this country that have been ignored."

"*Pfft*," Regina's character snorted. "'*Marginalized.*' Why, just last year there was an all-black cast for *The Wiz*. All black! But everybody would be up in arms if there was an all-white cast, right?"

"You mean like *The Wizard of Oz*?" Elmo countered. "Or like, *movies*?" Do you mean '*movies*'?"

"Where's *our* month?" "Amanda Jo" kept ranting. "When do we get to celebrate all the things that *white* people contributed to the history of this country? Huh?"

"I, well," Wes answered, feigning uncomfortability (but maybe not). "I really don't think that's for me to say. Travis 1619X," he bounced the question over to Elmo's character. "What do *you* think about that? Do you think there should be a White History Month?"

"Oh *absolutely* there should be a White History Month."

"Really?"

"Yeah! There should *totally* be a spotlight for things that white Americans have done for this country. We can talk about things like Jim Crow, the Ku Klux Klan, Madison Grant, the Indian Wars, Bacon's Rebellion, Black Codes—"

"Now wait a minute—" Regina's character interjected.

"Seneca Village," "Travis 1619X continued. "Japanese-American internment camps, the War on Drugs, Immigration Act of 1924, sundown towns, Chinese Exclusion Act—"

"I didn't mean—"

"Cointelpro, the MOVE bombing, Rosewood, Tulsa Riots, the Tuskegee experiments, redlining, Proposition 14, the Homestead Act—"

"Actually," "Amanda Jo recapitulated. "Never mind. Y'alls can have your month."

"Are you sure? We could give you *four* months even. One for every century my people have been oppressed in this country."

"Yo," Jumaane began, baiting Cervantes' "Fata Morgana" and punishing with Raphael's "Preparation Rampage" when Ariel fell for it. "Did you know that M. Bison from *Street Fighter*'s original name wasn't M. Bison?"

It was a Saturday night and the boys were chilling out at Ilan's place, playing *Soul Calibur V* on the Playstation 3 and visiting the Emerald City. (*Wink*). And everybody was about to get an education.

Because, unlike most people who pondered the mysteries of the universe or unleashed their shower thoughts upon the world, Jumaane spouted off random video game knowledge when he got blazed.

It always started off like he was going to reiterate the same retread overworn trivia people have heard a thousand times over—like the fact that in Japan, Mario's original name was Jumpman, or that his first appearance was in *Donkey Kong*—but then he swerved on you and pulled a surprise fact out of nowhere, like a quarter from behind your ear—like the fact that Mario and Donkey Kong were supposed to be Popeye and Bluto, but Nintendo couldn't get the licensing rights, and that Nintendo of America renamed Jumpman "Mario" after the company's warehouse landlord, Mario Segale.

Landlord. "Super Mario." Get it?

211

Manishtana

On rare occasion, Jumaane's tidbits weren't even about *videogames*, just about games in *general*, like the time he blew everyone's mind telling them that there were more total possible card combinations in a deck of cards than there are stars in the Milky Way. The Milky Way, by the way, has about 400 billion stars. But the number of permutations possible in a deck of cards is 52! (for those in the audience who failed algebra, that's "52 factorial," not a really enthusiastic 52). In real people numbers, that's 8.06 with 67 zeroes behind it.

"Like," Jumaane had explained as he quietly ruined Ariel's *Marvel v Capcom 3* Nova/Mango Sentinel/Spencer team with a solo X-Factor-activated Magneto (something Jumaane called the "Curleh Mustache"). "Say there's 10 billion people on every planet, 1 billion planets in every solar system, 200 billion solar systems in every galaxy, and 500 billion galaxies in the universe. If every single person on every single planet shuffled decks of cards a million times every second since the *beginning of time* and got a different result each time, they *still* would've only shuffled *less than fifty-quintilionths* of every possible deck combination!"

"Wow, man," Ariel had replied, slightly dazed by both the Kermit's hair and the explosion of sound and light utterly decimating his team. "That's, like, a lot of spades...Do you think those other planets call their black people spades, too?"

Jumaane was a font of random knowledge like that, and tonight, as his Raphael wiped the floor with Ariel's Cervantes, his topic was the storied history of M. Bison's name.

"Wait, the guy in the red suit and cape?" Ariel answered, watching Raphael block Cervantes' "Flash Geo Da Ray," grapple him with "Unending Stings," and juggle him into an 11-hit wall combo. "Did not know that. My parents weren't about videogames when we growing up. We didn't have a game system until my brother was in college and got a Playstation 2."

"What? So like, no *Sonic* or *Street Fighter* or *Super Mario*—"

"Or *Zelda*, any of that. Not until I was already a freshman in high school. And we ended up being more of a *Tekken* family, anyway."

"Ugh, *Tekken*," Colin groaned from Ilan's couch, beer in one hand, phone in the other. "It's like smashing keys and calling yourself playing the piano."

"Anyway, yeah," Jumaane continued. "M. Bison's original Japanese name was Vega, like the star."

"Wait, isn't Vega the—"

"The Spanish dude with the claws? Yes. But *that* dude's name was originally Balrog. And the American branch of Capcom didn't think 'Vega' was an intimidating enough name for the big boss, so they switched it. The Spanish dude became 'Vega,' and the boss became 'Balrog.'"

"So then why is he M. Bison now?"

"Ah, see, that's because Capcom was afraid that they would get sued by Mike Tyson for their big black boxer character named 'Mike Bison.'"

"Oh wooow, I didn't even *realize*—"

"—and so they switched his name with the boss, and the boxer became 'Balrog' and the boss became 'M. Bison.'"

"Yeah, that never really made any sense to me why he was named M. Bison. It was just so random. And I just thought they named the black guy 'Balrog' on purpose because of some low-key racism, like he was some kinda beast or something."

"I know right? For real, videogames be so racist, though. Like, *every* black dude in a fighting game is either a boxer—Balrog and Dee Jay in *Street Fighter*, Heavy D in *King of Fighters*—or a kickboxer—Zack in *Dead or Alive*—"

"Bruce in *Tekken*."

"—or does capoeira: Elena in *Street Figher*—"

"Eddie Gordo in *Tekken*."

"—or is a soldier: Jax in *Mortal Kombat*."

"Raven in *Tekken*."

"C'mon man, Potemkin in *Guilty Gear* is a soldier who was a *literal fucking slave* and has a *literal fucking slave collar* around his neck. Like," he added in an undertone lower than Colin could hear. "*Really* my nigga?"

"Nigga, please," Ariel answered in a mirrored volume.

Ariel and Jumaane burst into laughter, at the absurdity, at the crazy stereotyping, and at their ironic use of the n-word.

You'd never catch either of them saying it in real life, in real conversations, with anyone—friends or not, and regardless of race. (And yes, we're just gonna go ahead and forget that Ariel's "shomer nigga" episode ever happened.)

Manishtana

They didn't not use it because they imagined themselves as being particularly "woke" or anything, it just seemed to them that the word couldn't be "reclaimed" from a history of hate and oppression and racism, as if any of those existed in America's past and weren't still alive and well in its *present*.

Vandal? Sure, go ahead and reclaim it. No one's all up in arms about extinct East Germanic tribes sacking Rome anymore.

Hooligan? Have at it. The Irish have come a long way from days of being second-class citizens, and there's *tons* of respected Houlihans in the world. Like Major Margaret "Hot Lips." (*Sigh*...Oh, *M*A*S*H**, you had me at "Hello"...)

But "nigger"? Or "nigga"? (Because "brother" and "brotha" are two different words, y'know.) Not so much.

Ariel—who'd grown up only ever hearing it in the context of being screamed from archival footage of civil rights protests in old black-and-white newsreels—he remembered being thoroughly stunned during Field Day in 3rd grade when his classmate—also black—congratulated him for his 1st place relay-race performance, proudly declaring, "This nigga can run!"

He couldn't see then, and didn't see now, how the word he bristled against as the television shouted it at him—an experience urbane to the Samson's ritual Sunday evening viewing of *Eyes on the Prize*—could ever be adopted as a term of endearment.

Jumaane's father had felt the same way and instilled the same sentiment in his son, recounting tale after tale of travelling in groups six or seven strong through the white Queens neighborhoods of the 50's and 60's, a frightened pack of 10-13 year olds being brave for each other as they ran from adults hurling bricks and epithets.

So, between the two of them—and the two of them only—Ariel and Jumaane's n-word use was a wry joke. A meta-commentary on its legacy and "repurposing," and the toxic environments in which both of those surfaced. Which, naturally, meant they ended up using it satirically between each other more often than most hood niggas used it for real. Either way, they both agreed it was a word that white people didn't get to say.

"But if *we're* gonna say it," this kid once asked me, maybe 14 or 15. "Then how can we say that white people can't say it?"

"Well, can I call your mother 'Mommy'? No?" I replied to his offended expression. "Well, why not? Why do only *you* get to call her 'Mommy'? Either *everybody* gets to call her 'Mommy,' or *no one* gets to call her 'Mommy'. Sounds pretty stupid, right? Because the relationship between you and your mother *obviously* isn't the same as any relationship that *I* would have with your mother. Literally the entire world operates with an understanding that there is no scenario in life, in any place, anywhere, where people get to use words and names just because *other* people get to. But somehow, there's an entire crop of white people out there having this difficulty extending things that are basic laws of how human beings interact to black people. And you can tell *those* people: Welcome to being black. Welcome to walking through the world watching people doing things that you can't do."

I saw the sparks light up behind this kid's eyes and a balloon full of thoughts begin to expand in his brain.

And that kid? He grew up to be Ta-Nehisi Coates.

But enough about me.

"Videogames be *so* racist," Jumaane repeated, still laughing.

"Racist?" Ariel countered. "*Please*, videogames be so anti-Semitic though. There's not even *one* Jewish character in a fighting game! There are more undead zombies in fighting games than there are Jews. There's more *kangaroos* in fighting games than Jews!"

"Well, damn."

"I mean look at this," Ariel pointed to the screen, now showing the character select board and a score of 13-0. "We've been in the *middle* of the 16th century for *five* games in this series. *Six*, if you count *Soulblade*. How we haven't come across a *single* Jew yet?"

"Shit. You're right. You got Sophitia, Cassandra, and Pyrrha running around here being blessed by Olympus and shit, though. Greek gods from 3000 B.C. rolling up blessing people in 15-fucking-84? Sounds legit! But no Jews, though," Jumaane laughed again. "That's crazy!"

"I know right? Like, I can't even *start* to get mad that there's no black Jewish characters anywhere."

"Wait, Zasalamel from *Soul Calibur III* and *IV* is black, though. And he's got a Jewish name for his weapon. Kafziel. That counts right?"

"Having a Jewish influence does not something Jewish make. Otherwise you'd see *Neon Evangelion* playing every year for Rosh Hashana. Hell, *Bible movies* aren't even Jewish, and they're *our* stories."

"*NO!!*" came Ilan's furious scream from the bathroom, and everyone jumped.

Ilan wrenched the door open and stomped into the room, his nostrils flared, his face fearsomely red and absolutely livid.

It was so far of a picture from the chill laidback Ilan they knew and loved that it took everyone a shaken second to realize that he was actually responding to someone on his phone.

"*ME'ANYEN LI TA ZAYIN MA SHEHEM CHOSHVIM!*" he rattled off in a burst of Hebrew so rapid and rabid that even Ariel had a hard time keeping up. "*ZE HA MAKOM SHELANU! LO ASINU SHOOM DAVAR VE ANACHNU LO KOFTZIM KMO METUMTAMIM KI ZE MA SHEHEM ROTZIM! HA PTICHA YOM SHENI VE G'MARNU ZEEMEK!*"

The room was stone silent as Ilan stood in the middle of the floor, tapping his foot impatiently while he listened to the tinny high-pitched hints of a voice chirping on the other side of the line.

"What's going on?" Jumaane whispered out the corner of his mouth to Ariel, frozen in place. "What's the problem?"

"I dunno," Ariel whispered back, likewise not moving. "Something about opening something on Monday."

"Okay..." Ilan replied with a deflated sigh, after a few more seconds of listening. "Okay. We can talk about it tomorrow. Ok, I...Good night. Love you."

Ilan hung up the phone and tossed it on the cluttered counter nearby. He ran both hands into his long hair, frustrated, and just kept them there for a second. After a moment, he sighed again and looked up at his friends with a weary half-smile.

"Sorry I'm not so much fun tonight," he shrugged.

Ariel *did* notice Ilan seemed a little tense all night. Even earlier that day in *shul*. But he didn't anticipate something that would spark anything even *near* an outburst like that.

"Dude," Ariel started. "What *happened*? What's going on Monday?"

"Nothing!" Ilan spat out bitterly, then reigned himself back in. "The fucking, they're screwing me up. They're fucking up me opening my hookah bar."

"Wait. Stop. Pause," Jumaane interjected. "Who? What? What hookah bar? When did you get a hookah bar?"

"I *told* you guys about it."

"Yeah, no," Colin piped up. "I would've remembered you saying something about opening a hookah bar. Did you tell us in Hebrew?"

"No! I told *all* you guys! When I made the special lollipops, and we had them on the bench? I told you I was opening up a hookah place, then the dragon started with the hiccups, so we had to get off its back...Remember?"

Ariel, Jumaane, and Colin patiently waited.

"Oh..." Ilan realized. "There wasn't a dragon was there?"

"No," Ariel shook his head. "There very likely was not."

"Hm...That's probably why Colin was speaking in music. Okay. Cool."

Ilan shrugged and walked over to the coffee table Ariel and Jumaane were sitting on the floor in front of, grabbing himself the last beer.

"So, I have this hookah bar," he began, plopping on the couch next to Colin. "Well, it's more *we* have this hookah bar. Me and Michelle."

"Michelle?" Jumaane asked.

"*Michelle*. From Ari's *shul*."

"What?" Ariel scrunched his eyebrows. "Who—wait, 'Michelle Greenblatt' Michelle?"

"Yeah."

"That's so random," Ariel wondered. "Why would you start up a—"

Noticing the uncharacteristically bashful look on Ilan's face, it suddenly struck Ariel that his stoner friend and the "young enough and pretty enough single girl" Ariel had met during his trial run at CAY, was now the apple of more than just the congregation's eye.

Well. That solved the mystery of Ilan's continued synagogue attendance.

"Anyway," Ilan sped along, ignoring Ariel's widening eyes. "We decided we wanted to run a hookah spot, have a small bar in it, and make it kosher with some cheapy food. Like fries and nuggets and stuff," he took a gulp from his bottle. "But we're trying to get a *hechsher*, but they don't want to give it to us because of 'the environment,'" Ilan derisively put his fingers in air-quotes.

Ariel rolled his eyes in annoyance. Ilan replied with a look that screamed "*I know right?*" And Jumaane and Colin looked back and forth from Ariel to Ilan, and then at each other.

Manishtana

"So yeah," Colin piped up. "Can somebody explain things to those of us who don't speak Yahweh?"

Ariel was more than glad to so, because the politicization of the kosher industry was one of his least favorite things in the world to exist. Like, right under Beyonce's acting.

See—as Ariel interpreted for Jumaane and Colin—the business of letting Jews know what they could or couldn't eat was regulated by *hechshers*, rabbinical certification seals that came in all assorted manner of logos and letter combinations and influence. There were literally hundreds of them in the world, and they're probably crawling all over your food this very second.

That letter U in a circle on your Coke cap, or on the side of your Blue Moon.

The "K" hanging out in that funky backwards letter C on the bottom-left corner of your carton of Ben & Jerry's Half-Baked.

That star with the letter K just chilling above the "Government Warning" on your Sam Adams Boston Lager.

See? Told you, they're everywhere.

And aside from pre-packaged food products, kosher certification agencies also awarded certifications to restaurants and eateries and other sites that served food, provided that the establishment abided by the necessary standards of kosher.

And *that*, friends, is where things start to get a little mafia.

"I don't get it then," Jumaane was puzzled. "You're gonna serve kosher food, right?"

"Yep," Ilan answered.

"So why aren't they giving you this hacksaw?" Colin asked.

Great question, Colin. And the answer is: Because some certification agencies don't like staying in their lane, and decide that they're going to be the boss of everything.

If a restaurant served kosher food, but had artwork displayed that an agency didn't think was "appropriate"?

Sure your food's kosher, but no *hechsher* for you.

Didn't think the music was Jewish enough?

No *hechsher* for you.

The female wait-staff wasn't dressed head to toe in a burlap sack?

No *hechsher* for you.

The burlap sack wasn't the deepest shade of Puritan Black?

No *hechsher* for you.

And if you're trying to snag the fickle mistress that is a kosher-keeping clientele, then you *want* that *hechser*, you *need* that *hechsher*. It was literally your seal of approval, just as much as the Health Department's letter-rating in your window. Because *anyone* could say *"We swear we're kosher! Honest! You totally won't go to Hell if you eat here!"*

So through the hoops you jump.

In 2013, for example, a Manhattan restaurant named "Jezebel" was forced to change its name to "J-Soho," because certifying agencies didn't think it was right for a Jewish restaurant to have a name implying decadence and promiscuity. Or 9th century Baal-worshipping Ancient Israelite queens and their knack for wholesale slaughtering of true prophets of the L'rd.

And I can feel that. 1 Kings Chapter 19 was a rough time, so sure, *I* don't see how anyone could think it was a good name for a kosher restaurant *either*. But still, it's about the principle.

Like, I just need you to tell me whether this cake is kosher or not, not where you think I should eat it, *MOM*.

"So they don't like the *atmosphere*?" Jumaane gaped. "Which is what? What does that even mean?"

"Well, it's a hookah bar that doesn't close until 4am, so it's not a place that good Jewish boys and girl should hang out at," Ilan scoffed. "Someone might accidentally have fun with the opposite sex and find their husband or wife outside of a *shidduch* date."

"Or start mixed dancing," Ariel added sardonically. "**Chas veshalom.**"

"But why are they even commenting on anything besides the food?" Jumaane demanded.

"Exactly," Ariel nodded. "Welcome to La Kosher Nostra."

"Wow, that's some hostage bullshit," Colin shook his head. "See? This would all be a whole lot easier if you guys just had rabbis blessing your food. Then you could've just had Ariel stroll in, throw some holy water around and, **BAM**, done. Fuck you, hacksaw guys."

Colin sipped from his beer.

Ariel and Ilan looked at each other.

And a grin crawled across their faces.

The tiny café-esque storefront sat huddled amongst its fellow trendy brethren, boasting a tattoo and body-piercing shop, an organic deli, and a niche-jewelry boutique among its neighbors. Together they hunched their brick-and-glass shoulders against the drizzle as dusk became night.

People rushed underneath the swinging wooden sign that extended over the sidewalk, reading "Holy Smokes" in the same whimsical font as the gold-lettering on the large glass window.

Occassionally, the chalkboard screaming the daily specials in increasingly soaked and smudged pastels caught someone's eye, and, intrigued, they would enter, escaping the blustery damp chill for a warm mood, illuminated with tealights flickering in amber-and-red glass votives, where the volume was dozens of conversations loud, dueling with the live jazz-band electrifying the atmosphere.

It was a young crowd, mostly college kids and young Orthodox 20-something rebels, blurring the lines between hipsters and *hassids*.

Carbon monoxide, tar, arsenic, chromium, cobalt, and cadmium were in attendance, along with their dates nickel, formaldehyde, acetaldehyde, acrolein, lead, and polonium-210.

Together they hung in the air, seductive wisps of grey-white smoke that twisted in their own deadly and artistic way, forming ringlets of carcinogenic beauty that lazily floated adrift, stirred by the slowly rotating ceiling fans above.

Overpopulated square tables dotted the rustic tiled floor, with menus trapped under glass tops, and adorned with octopus-like apparatuses of grooved glass, burnished metal, and accordioned plastic.

And hanging above the bar, emblazoned with the lounge's logo, a framed posterboard as large as an oversized game-show check made a proud declaration:

"March 6, 2016
26 Adar I, 5776

This is to certify that all food cooked at Holy Smokes Hookah Lounge located at 1117 Pike St., Brooklyn, NY 11217, is under my strict supervision and is Kosher L'Mehadrin.
All food products are certified kosher by reliable hechsherim, and all beef products are strictly glatt. All poultry is strictly kosher under the most widely accepted hechsherim. No dairy is allowed on the premises. All beers and other beverages are hechshered. No outside beverages are allowed on the premises.
This certificate shall be effective for one year from the date shown above

Rabbi Ariel S. D. Samson
Rav of Congregation Ahavath Yisroel
508 Abrams St., Brooklyn, NY 11218"

Welcome to Ilan and Michelle's grand opening, launching—as planned—on the first Monday of March.

There wasn't any particular significance to the date, just something they'd randomly plucked out of the air. Literally.

They'd been high on MDMA and spent four hours trying to catch all the numbers floating around in Ilan's apartment before they flew out of the window. Because the refrigerator was hungry, and it would only open if you pet it and fed it odd prime integers, you see.

Obviously.

But regardless of how they came to choose it, today wouldn't have been possible if not for the brilliant solution that Colin, in spite of himself, had produced two nights ago, under several influences.

"I mean," Ilan mused after Colin's suggestion. "The people who are gonna want to come to this place won't give a shit about politics and beauracracy, anyway..."

"They see a *hechsher*," Ariel nodded with growing giddiness. "*Any* kind of *hechsher*, and they'll be good. And maybe there'll be some that'll look up the name. So what? They'll see I'm a real person with a legit *smicha* and I know what I'm talking about. So what if there isn't some big name organization certifying the place?"

"Besides," Ilan matched Ariel's grin. "Why would we need one if we're under the supervision of **HaRav HaGaon** the Freelance Rabbi, spiritual leader of the historic Congregation Ahavath Yisroel, assuring all our customers that we provide the highest standards of kosher? Hell, they might even tell their friends. Your *hechsher* might even become a thing!"

"Dunno about all that," Ariel shook his head. "But I *am* willing to cause just a little bit of trouble just this once."

They clinked bottles and laughed as Colin and Jumaane sat there feeling as lost as most Americans do in a World History class.

It was a deal.

That next day, when everyone was of sound and sober (enough) mind, Ilan, Ariel, and Michelle sat down to iron out all the basics.

Because Ilan was a friend, yeah, and Ariel was delighted to stick it to the Powers-That-Be, yeah, but before he signed on, there were some details Ariel needed to check first before he put his name on this kind of radical venture.

Was Holy Smokes gonna be closed on Shabbat? (Yes.)

What was the menu gonna be? (Six items—onion rings, chicken wings, chicken nuggets, pigs in blankets (beef, obviously), and regular and Cajun fries.)

Was the meat gonna be glatt kosher? (Yep.)

Any alcohol? (Only beers. And only *hechshered*.)

And was there...y'know...Like, I'm *not* saying there was some illegal drug-money paying the Park Slope rent...but *was* there illegal drug-money paying the Park Slope rent?

"Dude, no," Ilan laughed, assuring Ariel. "Green is legal in Cali and Colorado. I'm doing this only from my sales there."

"Oh, okay good," Ariel answered, relieved. "Cuz I wasn't sure if, like **halachically—**"

"*Halacha* is one thing. The IRS is something else."

"What," Michelle asked, a tinge offended. "Did you think he was laundering money or something?"

Ilan and Ariel exchanged a look that Michelle couldn't read.

"Nope," Ariel said simply.

Michelle let it go just as quickly as Karen Friedman did when Henry Hill handed her a bloodied gun in *Goodfellas*. *Lehavdil*.

Ilan was a little bit of a roughneck. An **ars**. Sure, he might not've been heavy into this or that, like gambling or prostitution, but he definitely knew people who knew people. But Ilan himself was pretty chill, as *arsim* go.

He was more like a half-*ars*.

If there were any truth to that old saying "the brighter the picture, the darker the negative," then Ilan would be the photographic equivalent of a black-and-white cookie. No real right or left or up or down, just depended on what angle you decided to look at him.

Anyway, after all the little ins and outs were squared away, it was all a go.

Ariel drew up the kosher certificate, Ilan found a printer that was open on a Sunday, and Michelle sent out the word that Holy Smokes would arrive at its destination on time.

Game. Set. Match.

So here they were, teeming with college kids looking for somewhere affordable to hang out without leaving Brooklyn, a slightly older non-denominational kosher-keeping crowd grateful for somewhere they could guiltlessly eat that was open past 11pm, the transgressive Orthodox and Orthodox-adjacent provocateurs eager to strike blows wherever they could at the establishment, and, well, *normal* people just looking for a good hookah place not in the city. The regulars from CAY made up the rest of the crowd, proudly supporting their rabbi and his understated but significant stand against the chokehold of *hechsher* politics.

And as for Ariel, he was enjoying watching the tube in front of him fill with the ghost-white tendrils of burning toxins, and, once it had filled up, he put his lips on the plastic cap and inhaled, feeling the sweet burning sensation of mango-flavored tobacco creep throught his lungs and throat. After a moment, he exhaled, watching the plumes of smoke dissipate.

This was a pretty cool place.

Ilan hadn't made the tobacco menu too big. It was only about three or four brands with a few flavors each. Mango. Mint. Coffee. Coconut. Strawberry. Cherry. Ariel watched the outside of the charcoal turn grey while it heated the tobacco brick sitting on top of the aluminum foil.

Even at the fairly economical prices Holy Smokes offered, there was no way this was a thing he'd be able to consistently indulge.

But Ilan had decided—*insisted,* really—that Ariel take the money that had already been budgeted to pay for a *hechsher.* Ariel relented in the end, consoling himself with the reality that half of it would end up back in Ilan's pockets anyway.

"Rabbi Samson!" a girl's voice shrieked from the crowd, and suddenly Ariel felt a pair of arms wrap around him in a hug.

As the arms released him, Ariel turned to see Chani's light-grey eyes beaming at him, possibly a bit buzzed.

They'd been talking more and more—ever since the Chanukah party, actually—and the Brooklyn College Hillel had developed a fairly strong, almost symbiotic, relationship with CAY.

Ariel had presented at several Hillel events, and the Hillel had co-sponsored and/or co-hosted more than a few CAY dinners and talks.

"Hey!" he greeted brightly. He wasn't that surprised to see her (a good number of Hillel regulars *had* become reliable clients of Ilan), but he *was* surprised to see what she was wearing.

A sequined mini-skirt over a pair of jeggings, a snug shirt with a loose enough collar that displayed all of the collarbone and just a *hint* of upper cleavage shadow. It wasn't terribly scandalous, but it was a far cry from the buttoned up, baggy shirt, ankle-length skirt wearing former-yeshiva girl he'd met four months ago.

Exposure to college life was taking its toll on her it seemed.

And suddenly Ariel was even *more* thankful that it was his name over the bar. Holy Smokes was a stop gap. A light in the dark for those kids who grew up perfectly *frum*...so long as they never had to interact with anyone that challenged their idea of how to be.

Without a Holy Smokes, who knows where a Chani would be?

ARIEL SAMSON: FREELANCE RABBI

Ariel saw it happen all the time, the kids who'd only ever known their cloistered existence, and the second they dipped their toe into the outside pool, they slipped, and fell all the way in.

Of course, there were those religious fear-mongers who capitalized on that. Touted it as an example why good *frum* **yidden** should stay away from interacting with the outside world, not waste their time with the **narishkeit** of higher education. And so more often than not, that left those more enterprising Jews, interested in interacting with a world larger than theirs, out in the cold.

There wasn't a rabbi to talk to about anything, because those rabbis pretended the kinds of crises that were being wrestling with didn't exist. After all, "good" Jewish boys and girls weren't in those kinds of places, and didn't do those kinds of things.

And so when they went off, they went all the way off. Even the ones who'd never intended to go that far.

There was no one there, no authority to sit them down and say, *"Okay look, here's what you can or can't drink at a non-kosher bar."* *"Here's what drugs you can or can't do over* Pesach.*" "Don't try to* daven *if you've taken such-and-such combinations of things." "I...well no, Judaism doesn't 'ban' premarital sex, per se, but it doesn't condone it, either. I...look, at least go to the* mikvah *first."*

And so those kids ended up not even looking for answers, because they knew that no one was even willing to entertain that there was a question.

Because they were *frum.*

And *frum* Jews didn't have questions or doubts.

No, questions and doubts were what **kiruv** organizations dealt with. To help those poor, misguided, theologically-helpless infants fighting against their circumstances of being born Conservative or Reform or secular.

But no, not for *our* precious *frum* kids.

The ones raised with the light in the way and the truth.

There's no reason to make space for questions for *them.* Because they already *have* all the answers. Because we *gave* them to them already. They *know.*

Riiiight.

And so that's why there was a Holy Smokes. And why Ariel was a part of it. For the Chanis. A kiddie pool they could get a little wet in, but not drown.

Manishtana

"This place is *so awesome!*" she gushed, taking the place in. "*Mazal tov!*"

And before Ariel could reply, Chani'd disappeared into the crowd, and he lost track of her for the rest of the night.

✡ ✡ ✡

A few hours later, the lounge was nearly empty and most of the crowd had left, which is when Ariel noticed a familiar flash of blue just few feet away.

It was Ellis, there as part of the CAY wall of solidarity.

Knocking back a beer, Ariel rose from the table and started heading over toward her with purpose.

Just, y'know, to say hey.

It was good to see her. He didn't even notice that he brushed past Ilan setting up some coals for a customer, who looked up, noticed Ariel's destination, then smirked.

Halfway to Ellis' table, though, Ariel suddenly stopped, before she had a chance to notice his approach.

What was he doing? He was in a thing with Tamar already.

And he honestly knew he wasn't just going over to say hi just to say hi.

He made an abrupt aboutface, only to find Ilan standing right behind him.

"Ilan, hey!" Ariel gushed. "*Mazal tov*, man! This was a really great turnout!"

"I know, man! This was so awesome that—*Yo!* Do you *see* that—?" Ilan's eyes widened at something over Ariel's shoulder.

"What—?"

Ariel instinctively turned around and, with a mischievous grin, Ilan shoved him forward...right into Ellis' path, knocking the cup full of partially-melted ice all over herself. She exhaled with a *"Really? Again?"* expression.

"Oh! Omigosh, I'm sorry! I—"

"I'm *really* starting to doubt that," Ellis replied with a non-plussed look, dabbing at her T-shirt.

"Sorry. Sorry," Ariel scooped up some napkins from a nearby table and shot a glare over his shoulder at Ilan, already behind the bar. Ilan shrugged and made the hand gestures for talking and pointed at Ellis.

"So," he began, handing her the napkins. "Crazy turnout, right?"

"Yep," Ellis replied, still occupied with blotting. "A fun establishment that just happens to be kosher tends to draw in a lot more people than kosher establishments trying to be fun," she looked up. "Anyhoo, I pretty much just stopped by to say hey and congrats to you and Ilan. So, uh," she gave a quick wave. "Hey. Congrats. And I'm gonna head out now. It's late, busy day tomorrow and all. Y'know."

"Yeah, definitely. Well, thanks for coming out and all that. Y'know, get home safe."

Ellis saluted and started to turn away. Just as Jumaane speedwalked past Ariel and slapped him in the back of his head.

"Hey!" Ariel blurted in response.

"Yeah?" Ellis turned, giving Ariel her attention again.

"Uh, do you...maybe wanna go out sometime maybe?" the question flew out of his mouth before he could stop it. "For...uh, coffee?"

Wait, what? Why the hell did he say that? What the *hell*, brain?

Ellis squinted at him. Ariel suddenly noticed that Colin was sitting at a table in his line of sight, purposely raising a beer bottle and gesturing at it.

"Or beer," he corrected. "Which is less lame than coffee. Y'know. To meet outside of work on purpose for a change?"

Ellis tilted her head, still squinting at Ariel, and the two of them stood in silence as Ellis fixed him with an increasingly uncomfortable stare.

"Oh, the answer's no," she burst out suddenly. "You're just a nice enough guy that I'm trying to find an excuse good enough that you feel bad that I shut you down."

"Ah. Well, that was, um, to the point."

"Yeah, I dunno. Usually, I'd go with the whole *'I don't date people I meet at work'* deal—"

"I didn't—I never said date."

"But you *meant* date, didn't you?"

"I...didn't *not* mean date."

"Yeah? See?" Ellis laughed. "That. That why I'd usually go with the whole *'I don't date people I meet at work'* deal, but..." she tasted the words out on her tongue as she felt her answer out. "I guess I...respect you enough to not lie to you like that...? Or something?"

"Oh, uh. Thanks, I appreciate that..?"

"Yeah..."

A silence that could either be described as awkward (by Ariel) or entertained (by Ellis) passed between the two of them, as they kinda just stared at each other like weirdos.

"But, hey," Ellis shrugged, smirking again. "If it makes you feel better, I'm *totally* up for having awkward sexual tension with you."

"Well that's great," Ariel smiled, rolling with the punch. "Lemme just...pencil that in," he pulled a pen from inside his tweed jacket, and started scribbling on his hand. "So that's Tuesdays and Thursdays in the elevator around lunch, right?"

"Sounds like a plan," Ellis laughed. "Well, I'm gonna go now. *You* should too," she paused, then continued in a suddenly sultry voice, her accent making it all the more sultry. "I mean, you've gotta get your rest, if you're going to be working *so hard* under me all day tomorrow..."

Ariel stammered, thoroughly flustered by the smoldering look Ellis gave him—and held—just before she burst into a peal of laughter.

"Oh, this is going to be fun!" she slapped his arm. "Tomorrow."

Chuckling to herself, Ellis turned and disappeared through the glass doors, leaving Ariel frozen in place, standing *cough* stiffly in the middle of the lounge floor.

"She *said* that?" Jumaane howled as the gang walked down the sparsely populated sidewalk that was bustling just a few short hours ago. "I love this girl!"

"Yeah?" Ariel retorted with more amusement than petulance. "Then maybe *you* should ask her out."

"No, I'm serious," Jumaane continued. "She's got balls. And she's not afraid to make sure you've got some too."

"Pretty sure there's an easier way to find that out."

"*Pfft*, you *wish!*" Colin laughed, engrossed in his phone nonetheless.

"Yeah, I—NO, I'm not talking to you. Actually, you either Jumaane. And Ilan too, if he were here. The hell was that tag-teaming nonsense about?"

"Hey, it worked," Jumaane shrugged. "Besides, I thought you could use a little push."

"Yeah, right off a *cliff.*"

"Oh, c'mon seriously?" Colin arched an eyebrow. "We did you a favor. Your little bitch-ass would've just hovered around the chick *forever*, never saying damn anything."

"Gee, thanks guys. Without you, I might've had to wait a whole two maybe three months to get that scathing no."

"You call that a no?" Jumaane snorted. "This one time I was talking to a girl and she gives a Hallmark card to her brother to give to his friend to give to my friend to give to me to say that she just wanted to be friends."

"HA!" Colin burst out. "Damn."

"Yeah, and this whole flirting thing she's doing now?" Jumaane continued. "That's that thrill of the chase, man. Playing hard to get, y'know? She wants to see what you're made of."

"Anger and shame," Colin muttered.

Ariel and Jumaane stopped in their tracks and looked at Colin.

"What the hell are *you* talking about?" Ariel asked.

"Hm? Sorry. I wasn't paying attention. One second?" Colin said, answering his phone just as it began to ring. "Colin here. Are you dead?...Because I said never call this number unless you were dead...Look, I don't care. I don't care! *I DON'T CARE!* With your fucking—"

Suddenly, Jumaane snatched the phone out of Colin's hand mid-rant, and hurled it across the street.

"Wha—?" came Colin's shocked reaction.

"Because," Jumaane hissed through clenched teeth, pointing a finger in Colin's face. "I wasn't listening to *that* shit again."

"Fine," Colin threw his hands up. "*You* explain to my boyfriend's father why he got hung up on, then."

Jumaane stared at Colin in flabbergasted silence, before exhaling with a sigh.

"Your stupid makes my brain so mad that I just wanna piss on you sometimes."

"What about my pho—"

"Shut up."

Tuesday night was Ariel's favorite night of the week.

It started, he supposed, back in fifth grade, when Tuesday nights were family *Buffy the Vampire Slayer* and *Angel* nights.

Everyone would be home by 7:45 sharp. From there it was the mad dash of making sure the antenna was in the right spot with no ugly static-y sound to roar over the dialogue, that the popcorn was popped, soda was filled, fries and onion rings were tossed in microwaves, and, sometimes, chicken fried and burgers grilled. And then everyone would retreat to their designated spots—Jake and Liora holing up in their respective rooms, AviandAri in the dining room with their mother, and their father in his favorite chair in the living room—only to emerge and converge en masse upon the kitchen during commercial breaks, replenishing their snacks while all abuzz with the latest cliffhanger or plot twist that had just left them in cruel suspense for the next 240 seconds.

It was a solid Samson family tradition, the last one they'd made in a while, and the last one they would ever make while all under one roof.

So, for a solid three years, in that Golden Age of television from 1997-2001, while blonde-haired waifs stood alone against the vampires and the demons and the forces of darkness, and brooding tortured souls helped the helpless, Team Samson was there for it.

And even years later, after *Angel* moved to Mondays, after *Buffy* ended after Season Five (because we do not speak of the UPN years), after Jake moved out and Liora next, after the Samsons evolved from apartment-dwellers to homeowners, Tuesdays still gave Ariel that warm and fuzzy feeling whenever they came around. Some days were warmer and fuzzier than others.

Or at least foggier and mossier.

Unfortunately, Ariel was ill-prepared this Tuesday night, so now he had to reluctantly venture out into the neighborhood to forage for snacks.

He'd just go to the Puerto-Rican bodega around the corner though, he decided. It was closer, plus the side streets were more deserted, and thus there was much less of a chance of him running into his neighbors.

He got along well enough with the people in his building.

That kind of hi-and-bye endemic to city life. When people are busy eking out a living, making their way through the hustle and bustle of the world, neighborly functions tended to be fairly perfunctory. And Ariel was extremely fine with that. It saved him the trouble of having to save prefabricated conversation branches in his head for when people ensnared him with small talk.

No, the people Ariel was hoping to dodge by heading to the bodega were the other denizens of the eight-block radius he called home. It always made him feel uneasy walking through his neighborhood, especially at night, or on the weekends when everyone was home for work or school.

It wasn't that it was unsafe, it's just that, in his heavily Caribbean-populated area, he always felt that he was under the suspicious gaze of hundreds of eyeballs watching "the Jew" walk through "their" neighborhood. Even better, Ariel was the worst kind of Jew, because you never knew what "side" he'd be on, apparently.

It was like high school all over again.

Like the time freshman year, when he was changing in the locker room and a "fellow" black student came up and asked if he was Jewish. When Ariel answered yes, the kid proceeded to hurl a handful of pennies at him and yell, "Then pick up the change, *Jew!*"

For years Ariel would replay that day over and over and over in his head, kicking himself every time that he hadn't thought of his comeback—*"Well damn, you don't have to* throw *your rent at me"*—until days too late.

Then there was the time when Ariel was shoved up against a locker with one of the darker, stockier football players yelling in his face for running around—with his correct enunciation and having geeky interests before a "blerd" was a cool thing to be—and trying to "be white," and that he was going to rip Ariel's "Jew gold" right off his neck.

Of course, Ariel's blue eyes didn't really help his "not trying to be white" case.

Especially when all the pretty black girls—like a certain football player's girlfriend, for instance—would call him over to talk just so they could look at them, wanting to know if he was "mixed," a crowd of thirsty high-schoolers who apparently hadn't yet been assigned *The Bluest Eye*, still chasing after good hair, light skin, and light eyes, hoping to unlock some hazel-eyed, wavy-haired destiny for their hypothetical offspring.

At any rate, it was only the happenstance appearance of a teacher rounding the corner that prevented the gold Magen David and light chain that Ariel wore—a *bar mitzvah* present from Savalava—from being demolished.

Ariel made it out that day unscathed, but being roughed up was fairly common of an occurrence.

And when it got too loud and rambunctious, the Italian gym teachers would come barging in, and everyone would say that "nothing" happened.

For the bullies, it was an admission that they really *did* believe that Ariel would get some kind of special privilege or treatment. For Ariel, it was him trying to establish that they were *all* just unruly black kids in everyone else's eyes.

A 17% minority in a student body sea of 44% white, 21% Asian, 17.5% Hispanic, and 0.5% "Other" that made up James Madison High School's Class of 2006.

But the locker room was just an entirely bad scene for Ariel. And he was still a couple semesters away from being confident enough to fix the face of people who thought playing keepaway with his *kippah*, while taunting things like *"Look at this Hanukwanzaa celebrating motherfucker over here,"* was funny.

So he took tennis for the next three years, and thusly avoided having to enter the locker room ever again.

But that didn't stop kids from putting orange peels on their heads, hanging spaghetti out of their pockets, and following him around in the lunchroom, though.

And unfortunately, it wasn't just the students either.

There was the English teacher who constantly took points off whenever Ariel—out of respect for the divine names—would write "G'd" and "L'rd" in his essays instead of their full spelling.

Then there was the math teacher who, while taking attendance the day after Purim, mockingly asked if Ariel had likewise been absent the previous day in celebration of the Jewish holiday—as his white Jewish classmates had—and was utterly flabbergasted when Ariel answered "Yes."

Oh! And the sociology teacher who asked if Ariel felt "trapped" by his culture.

Fun times had by all.

Ariel had spent a lot of those days confused and angry. Confused about things like why he got heat for not being into rap music at first (because apparently listening to Stevie Wonder, Earth, Wind, and Fire, Grover Washington, and Parliament Funkadelic wasn't considered black?). Angry about things like how when he *did* get into rap, he *still* hadn't proven his ethninticity, because while he liked OutKast, Luda, and Chingy, he was apparently disqualified because he also had Maroon 5, 3 Doors Down, and Evanescence in his playlists.

And also...betrayed.

He felt betrayed a lot, too.

Disappointed that he'd waited all of junior high school to be with people who looked like him, only to end his school days feeling just as dejectedly rejected.

In some ways deeper even, because some days in *yeshiva*, in 6th grade, and 7th grade, and 8th grade, as he struggled and trudged through each day alongside kids purported to believe like him, but sometimes acting anything but, he'd often associate the bad days with the fact that if only he had more peers around him who looked like him, then all would be well.

But, as the great Zora Neale Hurston would say, "Not all skinfolk is kinfolk." Hell, not even all *kinfolk* is kinfolk.

Of course, being ever hopeful and optimistic, "not all skinfolk is kinfolk" was a lesson Ariel needed a refresher course in from time to time. Like, for example, when he moved to his current apartment.

After a year of being a fly in buttermilk in Williamsburg, Ariel welcomed being in his great-aunt Devora's sublet in Midwood, finally amongst a sea of faces that looked like his.

For a good hour, his heart was singing as he strolled through his new neighborhood, only to be reminded within the hour, yet again, that "not all skinfolk is kinfolk."

"'Ey," a fresh neighbor nodded as he passed.

"Whassup?" Ariel beamed.

"You a Jew?" came the question, in a thick Guyanese accent.

"Yeah."

The new neighbor's face twisted up like he tasted something bad. Then he spit on the sidewalk in front of Ariel. And so any illusions of connecting with any fellow-hued locals flew straight out the window right then and there.

Although, funny thing, despite the more hellish than not stint Ariel endured in high school, he still *totally* got it.

Even as he was made to feel like he needed to creep by as unnoticed as possible past the barbershop, and the place selling roti, and the incense shop, he definitely understood where the sentiment was coming from.

He even felt it himself on occasion, whenever someone white and visibly Jewish found themselves wandering through his neighborhood.

That visceral reaction of *"What are you doing here?"*

See, Ariel was proud of his Judaism. He just wasn't sure how proud he was to be a *Jew*.

It wasn't "Judaism" that said a bullet came for Lincoln for setting "the blacks" free.

It was a "Jew." Rabbi Avigdor Miller.

It wasn't "Judaism" that pulled off the largest financial fraud in US history, decimating the life savings of thousands of people.

It was a "Jew." Bernie Madoff.

It wasn't "Judaism" that scoffed down its nose, wondering, how after slavery, Jim Crow, and the ongoing prison industrial complex, why black Americans didn't just pull themselves up by their bootstraps the way Jews did after the Holocaust.

It wasn't "Judaism" that didn't seem to get that comparing the black American and [white] Jewish experience was like comparing apples and nails. That didn't understand that there was a *very* large difference between escaping a terrible environment searching for new hope, versus being forcibly snatched away and deposited somewhere as farm equipment. That conveniently failed to factor in that when Jews pulled themselves up after the Holocaust?

It *wasn't* in Germany. Or Poland. Or the Ukraine.

That carelessly omitted that post-Holocaust Jews "got it together" *after* they *left* the countries that had rounded them up and slaughtered them.

It would be interesting to see how well Jews would've "pulled themselves up by their bootstraps" if they had to *stay* in Germany, continue living, day-in and day-out, next to those same neighbors that had sold them out the month or the year before, that had ransacked their belongings, that had sent countless scores of their relatives to their deaths in gas chambers and mass graves in icy forests.

In other words, pretty much the same way black Americans had owners, torturers, kidnappers, murderers, and rapists one day, and, y'know, "neighbors" and "landlords" the next.

It wasn't "Judaism" that belittled claims of black America's cultural state being the result of generational trauma, yet excused instances of [white] Jewish America's insularity, xenophobia, and other cultural norms...as being the result of generational trauma.

It was like that Baldwin quote:

"The Jew does not realize that the credential he offers, the fact that he has been despised and slaughtered, does not increase the Negro's understanding. It increases the Negro's rage. For it is not here and not now, that the Jew is being slaughtered, and he is never despised here as the Negro is, because he is an American. The Jewish travail occurred across the sea and America rescued him from the house of bondage. But America is the house of bondage for the Negro, and no country can rescue him. What happens to the Negro here happens to him because he is an American."

In short, Ariel was taking his Jewish ass to the Puerto-Rican bodega.

Ugh.

Of course, the bodega was out of chips, so to the corner store it was.

The actual experience of the store itself wasn't bad. The owner was a really chill older Jamaican dude, actually.

It was just the potential cast of characters to be encountered between Point A and Point B. Which is why, when Ariel's phone rang, he was uncharacteristically glad for it.

And I can totally feel that.

I *hate* the phone, personally. Just send me a text. Unless we're having a real-life conversation, don't interrupt my life with your voice.

"Kalman! What's up!"

"*Fucking Tamar!*" Kalman shouted in reply.

"Uh...What?" Ariel said, feeling a jolt of panic. Had someone said something? I mean, they *weren't*. But did so—

"I bought Dassi a Chinese dress in Chinatown for this Purim," Kalman explained, sighing into the phone. "And Tamar went off on me about 'cultural appropriation,' and I'm not really sure I buy that. Because, like, they're *dresses. I don't know!*"

"I'm...not sure where to weigh in on this."

"I mean, you can tell me I'm wrong. But my friend's mom, Mrs. Cho, owns a shop down there. She said it was cool. And she's like, old. So she knows everything. But now I dunno."

"Ha! Well, it's not a geisha costume, so that's definitely great. But I still feel like it's in some kinda grey area. But, I dunno. It's not my particular brand of offense, so I'm not completely confident jumping on that soapbox. I mean, personally I totally wouldn't want to see someone in a kinte cloth dress for Purim. Blackface or no."

Oh, the joys of Purim.

That magical holiday where offensive costumes were not only nary the exception, but you'd even be excused for thinking that they were, in fact, mandatory.

Go to any Jewish community on Purim and you were bound to see a reprehensible deluge of caricatured Indians (either curried or Columbused), Mexicans (in both their Schroedinger states of "Lazy Siesta Sombrero" Mexican and "Migrant Worker Taking All Our Jobs" Mexican), a pan-Asian pageant of the aforementioned geishas, in addition to a healthy sprinkling of Chun-Li/Bruce Lee wannabees, and about, oh let's lowball it and say, around 248 different versions of assholes in blackface.

But heaven forfend that a Shylock or Nazi costume make an appearance at a Halloween party, amirite?

It was a spectacle Ariel found himself subjected to every year, swallowing his upset at how gleefully his less-melanated faithmates relished in the stereotypes they got to play.

That is, until someone inevitably went too far and caught the media's attention. And then came the formulaic motions of the offending party, offering apologies more distressed about sullied reputations and not being seen as a "good person" than they were about how their actions were actively harmful to the culture that had to continue living in their skin, after having had it unwillingly borrowed for a five-hour drinking binge.

Last year, it'd been some fairly-visible Jewish politician in the pillory.

"Alright," Kalman answered glumly. "I guess I'll just return it and she can be, like, a clown or something."

Ariel rolled his eyes as he finally reached the store and pushed the door open.

Yes, I'm so sorry that this is such a terrible thing for you. I'm sure it's exactly how Anna May Wong must've felt when MGM put Luise Rainer in yellowface for the lead role in The Good Earth, *because having Wong as the lead and kissing the white male headliner would've broken the Hays Code prohibition of miscegenation. Seriously, man. What* happened *to you? You're, like, turning into a shitty garbage person, and I am way too blazed to deal with your bullshit at this particular point in the night.*

"Yeah, that's probably safer," is what Ariel actually said, entering the store. "I'll catch you later. Wha gwan dread?" Ariel greeted the owner at the cashier as he walked by, hanging up his phone and slipping it into his pocket.

If four years of dating a Jamaican had taught him anything, it was how to perfectly deliver that *one* phrase.

The old keeper nodded in response while he pored over his newspaper, sitting on his stool behind a ceiling-high plexiglass partition, lined with shelf upon shelf of batteries, Lotto scratch-offs, condoms, candy, medications, Spanish fly, packets of ground powders lettered with Asian kanji, and various herbal supplement pills of dubious nature and effects.

Manishtana

Ariel headed straight down the main aisle, looking for his standard munchies craving of Utz creamy ranch tortillas—all the ranch flavor of Cool Ranch Doritos, but with none of the non-kosher hellfire prison time of Cool Ranch Doritos—so singleminded in mission that he barely even noticed the trio of fellow customers, two girls and a guy, all amused by the patois-speaking Jew rifling through potato chip bags not two feet away.

Kinda like how videos of black people speaking Yiddish are guaranteed kneeslappers.

"Asalaam Alaykim," the guy called out to Ariel.

"*Aleichem shalom*," Ariel replied distractedly.

The two languages were similar enough that no one ever really noticed the difference whenever he answered the Arabic greeting with a Hebrew response. It was only ever other black folk who greeted him with the phrase, so he never bothered to comment on or correct their obvious assumption that he was Muslim.

Because why start off every interaction essentially saying *"No, you're wrong, I'm not like you."*

"Yo, you Muslim?"

Unless, of course, they asked.

"Nope, Jewish."

"You from *Israel*?" the questioner sauntered down the aisle to the crouching Ariel. "Cuz I know they got them Ethiopians over there."

"Nope, Brooklyn," Ariel shook his head, still scanning for chips, and slowly coming to terms that this store was sold out too. He rolled his eyes and sighed in disappointment.

"So, what, you pray with the white Jews, then?"

"Yeah," Ariel answered, rising to his feet, taking in his interrogator. Dressed in baggy jeans, a hoodie, and a bubble jacket, he was probably around Ariel's age and wearing an amused look, at least *partially* aimed at Ariel's slim-fit jeans, pinstriped blazer, t-shirt, and leather Chuck Taylors.

And, of course, his *kippah* and *tzitzit*.

He wasn't drunk, but he was definitely floating in that liminal state between soberdown and tipsytide, and the can of St. Ides he held, partially-concealed in a crumpled brown bag, would probably take him the rest of the way there before long.

He surveyed Ariel for a moment, blocking exit from the aisle like a bridgekeeper troll.

"You voted for Obama?"

"Hells yeah," Ariel snorted in a way that said *"I said I was Jewish, not Clarence Thomas."*

"Aight," the dude bumped Ariel's fist. "My dude."

"*Jamari*," one of the girls whined, standing on line while the second girl was getting two six-packs of Corona rung up at the register. "Come *on*. Just leave the Jew-man alone."

"What? I'm just asking questions," Jamari turned back to Ariel. "So what'd you wanna be a Jew for?"

"I didn't 'want' to be anything. I was born Jewish."

"Forreal? Huh. Like, your moms is white or—"

"Nah, she's black. An—"

"Moishe," the first girl snapped her fingers in Ariel's direction. "Can you tell our friend to stop with the questions so we can go home?"

"Oh *nooo*," the second girl turned around with eyes widened, half-laughing while she put her hand over her mouth. "You are *mad* disrespectful, Rashida. *What?*"

"What?" Rashida continued, dismissively. "That's alla them names. Chaim, Shmuely, whatever. Jamari, can we *go* now?"

Jamari's face darkened in a mixture of anger and embarrassment and he spun away from Ariel, the beer can in his hand crunching as his grip tightened.

"Damn, y'all *play* too fucking much," he shot at the two girls as he huffed past them. Angrily yanking the door open when he got to it, Jamari stormed out of the store.

"Jamari!" Rashida yelled after him, sprinting out the door behind him. The second girl looped her hands into the plastic bags for the beers to rush after her friends, when the cashier stopped her.

"'Ey," he said, pointing to the change and shaking the dollar bills in his hands. "It's twenty. You only give me nineteen."

"But all I—"

"Hold up," Ariel cut in, stepping up to the cashier, pulling a single from his jacket pocket, and handing it to the owner. "I got you."

Eh, why not?

It's not like the store had his chips.

Besides—on the rare occasion that he actually woke up in time to go to *shul* for weekday morning services—he ended up giving *tzedakah* to white Jewish people who probably didn't have that much higher an opinion of him than these girls did, anyway.

Like, there'd definitely been more than one occasion when the dusty *frum* panhandlers outside the kosher supermarket— hounding everyone who exited its doors with their jingling **pushkas**, regardless of how hectic, or overloaded with groceries, or exhausted—had turned their noses up at the sight of him, giving him a berth wide enough that his fistful of change couldn't even *accidentally* manage to make it inside their change boxes. (They weren't *that* poor, apparently.)

So, if he was gonna be a good Jewish boy and give charity anyway, why not get a **kiddush Hashem** out of it too? L'rd knows that Orthodox Jews could use the incidental good PR. Black ones, too.

"Thanks," the girl looked at Ariel in disbelief. Large bamboo-style gold hoops swung in each ear, with the name "Kayyriah" scrawled in cursive across the gap. Probably from the Arabic for "charitable."

Ariel shrugged with a half-smile, then turned and left the store.

✡ ✡ ✡

Actually, y'know what? No. No, dammit, he wanted his chips.

And that's why he was venturing out across the multi-laned game of vehicular cat's cradle that was the Flatbush/Nostrand junction, heading for the strip of Arab-owned mini-marts that kept the neighborhood greased and oiled 24 hours/day with junk food and booze around the clock.

Wait, it was okay to say they were "Arab-owned," right? Or was "Arab" derogatory?

Like, sure, it was really just a descriptor of geography or language. But, in the aggro-Zionist spaces Ariel often found himself in, "Arab" was definitely thrown around with a little more bile than it needed to be.

Kinda the same way that the relatively neutral "*goy*" had transformed from simply meaning "non-Jew," to bearing connotations of a sub-human lacking intelligence and morality.

I mean, seriously people, is there some famine of disparaging vernacular that we have to gorge on ruining the few nice words we have lying around? And this is why I set people on fire.

Anyway, Ariel's expedition had proved fruitful, and he stood on line in the narrow aisle, deliriously happy, with arms overflowing with chip bags. And two ice-cold Coronas for good measure.

He was only going to get the one at first, but then he remembered he'd only end up chugging it like water and be left wanting a second one to sip like a beer. So two beers it was.

The door jingled open while Ariel contemplated getting the two Coronas or switching one out for a Heineken, and he looked up to see two new customers walk in.

They looked liked they'd fit any description ever, much like Jamari from the Jamaican cornerstore. Stocky, imposing figures, NBA-inches tall, dressed in bubble jackets, hoodies, and baggy jeans—accompanied by the distinct scent of Vanilla Dutch/Black & Mild—and wearing resting gangsta faces that made most dudes look intimidating, but just came off looking like an angry hamster on Ice Cube.

The patrons on line ahead of Ariel leaned out of the duo's way, as they lumbered down the crowded path lined with magazines to one side and humans and candy on the other, when Ariel inadvertently locked eyes with one of them—the one with a broken nose—and a shocked recognition hit them both.

"Ariel?"

"Jermaine?"

"Yooo," Jermaine bumped his fist on Ariel's shoulder, seeing as how Ariel's hands were full. "Man, what's been good?"

Before Ariel could answer, Jermaine turned back to his companion, "Yo remember I was telling you that black rabbi cat everyone was talking about on YouTube and how I went to high school with him?"

"I remember. Black/Jewish conundrum of a dude."

"This is him! We used to game all the time!"

"Aw man," Ariel replied, laughingly cringing. "Don't remind me. I try to block out as much of that era as I can. One of my most un-smart periods of time ever."

"I know right?" Jermaine laughed with the same cringe. "Damn I was a piece of work back then. Yo, do you still game?"

"I wish!" Ariel exclaimed.

Truth be told, Ariel missed those days. Those Wizards of the Coast, TSR, White Wolf, Palladium, Marvel Superheroes role-playing days, slinging around d20s, attacking the darkness with magic missile.

"Well if you're free, me and Mo here are tryna run something soon. D&D."

"What edition? Because anything earlier than 3 is garbage and anything past 4th is trash."

"Damn. Why are you such a hater?" Jermaine laughed before turning back to Mo. "You needed to be in one of our games back in the day with Barnaby."

"Remember my Derek Powers character?" Ariel reminded. "For Barnaby's Marvel game?"

"What game was that? Was that the one with my Darkforce/Oblivion armor guy?"

"Yeah, that one!" Ariel turned to Mo, explaining. "I created a character that was a Daredevil/Gravitron mix. He was blind, but he could read gravity fields like a radar sense."

"Whoa, sounds tight!"

"Yeah and—Jermaine, remember when I almost killed Barnaby's brother with a gravity bomb?"

Ariel and Jermaine both started laughing, uproariously.

"He was like," Jermaine gasped. "He was like *'The only reason I haven't killed you...is because you haven't killed me first.'*"

"*What?*" Mo snorted.

"Yeah," Ariel added. "So obviously, I immediately gravity bombed him again and liquified his ass."

"Damn. We *gotta* get this game together."

"Yeah, we're a little bit hyped for Black Panther in the new Cap movie, so we're thinking of running this Afro-futuristic game. So just roll up a character and give him, like, rabbi-powers or something. I dunno"

"Sounds cool," Ariel nodded enthusiastically. "Well lemme know. I'm pretty free on Saturday nights and Sundays."

"Yeah, I see you getting your little internet fame on," Jermaine answered, approvingly. "Be careful now. You be putting some real shit out there. I'll Facebook you though, aight?"

"Definitely. Keep me posted."

✡ ✡ ✡

ARIEL SAMSON: FREELANCE RABBI

Five minutes later, Ariel was skipping home, chips in one hand, beer in the other, a glass pachyderm packed with Acapulco astroturf waiting for him at home, the potential of some tabletop role playing on the horizon, and not even caring that Rabbi Guildencrantz' latest screed had maligned him as a "pocket with very few coins in it, making a lot of noise, but empty of substance."

He loved his neighborhood sometimes.

Manishtana

Look, I don't even wanna hear you laughing, because you've probably done it once or twice yourself, at some point or another.

You get up early in the morning, hop on your commute, punch in on the clock, and just as you start fumbling around in your pockets with one hand (because the other one is holding your coffee), you realize that you've left your work keys at home.

Or, hey, you might've even done it in reverse, grumbling to yourself as you make your commute to work for the second time that day, trekking all the way back to the office because you left your home keys at work.

So how about a little empathy, alright?

Because Ariel was working with not one, not two, but *three* different sets of keys. I think we can give him a pass for forgetting his home keys at *shul* after Wednesday night's emergency board meeting.

Well not "emergency," per se. That's too dramatic. Maybe something more like "randomly urgent."

You see, they...well...the thing was, um...Actually, to be honest, Ariel couldn't really remember what the meeting had been about.

He vaguely remembered something about the upcoming *kiddish* that Keith was sponsoring that week (in honor of both his

244

birthday on Friday, and his conversion last month), and...something about a heating bill or something?

No idea.

He'd barely gotten any sleep the night before, so was too exhausted to do much more than sleep-nod his way through the entire thing.

But of course, as soon as the meeting ended he was wide awake. Or at least awake *enough*, seeing as how he absentmindedly left his house keys behind when he headed out with Kalman.

Phyllis had already left, Cate was in her office, and Ariel had lost track of why Jerome said he was staying for a little bit after the meeting.

"So what did you do about the whole Chinese dress deal?" Ariel asked once he and Kalman were outside and walking.

"Eh, I decided it wasn't worth the hassle."

"Sounds cool."

"Yeah besides now that I returned it I can probably splurge and get an extra bouqet or something for tomorrow."

"Oh right! You guys have an anniversary tomorrow!"

"Yup. Two years."

"Wow, *mazal tov*! That's insane. It feels like it just happened!"

"It did," Kalman joked. "Two years ago."

March 10, 2014.

It was a cute story how they'd picked out the date.

Kalman's birthday was January 3rd. Dassi's was February 7th.

1/3+2/7=3/10.

It'd been Ariel's last time attending a Jewish lifecycle event as a civilian. He'd earn his *smicha* three weeks later, at a **chag hasmicha** ceremony where his family attended, beaming with pride.

Well, most of them attended anyway. But the void of the absentee Samson was more than filled by the radiant, crinkle-eyed glow of Savalava's face.

"I'm *so* proud of you," she grinned later that night, after the ceremony, after dinner at some upscale Midtown kosher restaurant where everyone's heads had exploded at seeing so many black Jews in one place, after they'd headed back home and everyone had gone to bed for the night. Once the coast was clear, Ariel and Savalava had snuck out under the cloak of night to go smoke at their favorite spot by the park.

"Stay humble," she'd warned. "That's where all your success has come from. Don't go and get cocky now. You've got your *smicha*, you've got your own apartment now, you stopped dating that girl. You're off on the right track. Now don't screw it up."

"I promise," Ariel promised, grinning. He loved how Savalava always tried to overcompensate for engaging with her grandson in illegal drug use, by inundating him with wholesome life advice. Though, as amused as he always was, he never took her jade pearls of wisdom for granted. She wasn't in the best of health, and she was getting up there in years, so he didn't waste a moment.

He never knew when it would be the last time.

He didn't know that this *would* be the last time.

She died a week later, on a Sunday night, peacefully in her sleep.

The next day, after coming back from an early morning funeral and burial, the Samson family rolled up its sleeves and buried its grief in dinner preparations for that evening, the first *Seder* night without its matriarch in attendance.

Out of respect for her memory, for the first and only time, the endives weren't the only green vegetable consumed that night, and leaning to one side during the meal was significantly easier.

"Alright, this is me," Kalman announced, stopping at the usual corner of Clark and Terrell and pulling Ariel in for a pound. This is where he'd make the right on Terrell, heading down to the B/Q station at Newkirk to catch the train home.

"Later," Ariel said, breaking the embrace and continuing down Clark. "And I probably won't see you before, so *Shabbat shalom*, and tell Dassi *mazal tov* for me."

"Will do," Kalman shot back, tucking his green scarf closer around his neck, and they headed off in their separate directions.

The weather was pretty mild, and it was a visually pleasant enough walk from CAY to Ariel's apartment. Which were two things in the situation's favor once he reached his lobby door twenty-five minutes later, and realized that his keys were sitting pretty on the desk back in his office at the *shul*.

Thoroughly annoyed, he turned around and dragged himself back in the direction of Congregation Ahavath Yisroel.

At times like this, Ariel wished he had a car.

Or maybe a scooter. Or at least knew how to ride a bike.

He didn't really dress for bikes, though. He cringed at the thought of getting the gritty black sludge of axle grease ground into his pant legs, and had an irrational fear of getting wayward shoelaces tangled up in the gears.

Besides, he enjoyed walking. Even if his shoes didn't.

Not that it was their fault. Forty-dollar Italian snakeskin shoes weren't really meant to be walked in, and anything more expensive than that was even less so.

Alas, the price we pay for beauty.

Cate's familiar silver Acura was still parked across the street from the synagogue when Ariel finally made it back—an hour after he'd first left—which at least meant that the synagogue door would be unlocked.

It slightly irritated Ariel, as he pulled the doors open and climbed the stairs, that the keys he *did* bring, he didn't even get to use.

Wait, why was Cate even still *here*?

It was nearly 9:30, the meeting had ended over an hour ago at this point, and—actually, Ariel decided, never mind. The less he knew about Cate's goings on, the better.

They'd been working together for four months, and Ariel still couldn't shake that uneasy vibe he had when he was around her.

There was something unsettlingly predatory about her that raised his hackles, ever since first meeting her.

Far from the warm interaction he'd had when introducing Ariel to Jerome, Kalman had sort of introduced Cate then stepped back, kind of like when a trainer safely deposits you in front of a bear and then retreats to a corner to cautiously watch, ready to jump in once you signal the safe word.

Anyway, Ariel entered his office to find his keys patiently waiting for him, smugly gleaming on his desk in a pool of pale orange beams streaming through the window from the street lights outside.

Shaking his head, he snatched them up and turned to leave when he heard the crash of glass shattering like a million marbles onto the pavement and the chittering electronic pulses of a car alarm.

Maneuvering around his desk and chair, Ariel quickly shuffled over to the massive window taking up most of the office wall directly opposite the entrance to his office. It overlooked the front of the synagogue, one of the two arched windows bookending either side of the large stained-glass Magen David decorating the façade of CAY's building (the second window belonged to the office where the Sisterhood generally met), and it gave a view of the street both in front of and across from CAY's entrance.

That's where he saw the spray of grey-green glass glittering on the asphalt around Cate's car and the gaping black hole where the passenger's side window had been. A quick glance down the block revealed snatches of a group of teens sprinting around the corner.

Damn, Ariel shook his head.

He'd rather avoid being the messenger, but it was only right he found Cate and told her so she could gather any valuables before they went missing.

Checking that this time he had *all* of his keys, Ariel locked his office behind him and took the flight of stairs leading down to the lower level, inhabited by the kitchen, the multipurpose/dining hall, the bathrooms, and the executive board offices.

Cate's office was right off the stairs, but to Ariel's surprise, even though it was open and the lights were on, it was empty.

She was probably in the bathroom then.

Following the turn of the hallway, Ariel came to bathrooms.

He knocked and tried calling, but there was no response.

Hm. Not there either.

He remembered that Jerome said he was staying later after the meeting to take care of something that still escaped Ariel's mind, so maybe they were both in *his* office, down at the other end of the corridor.

Venturing down the dim hallway to Jerome's office, Ariel felt something soft underfoot as he passed the closed double doors of the dining hall. Bending down, he recognized the distinctive dark-green color and the golden glints of embroidered reindeer.

Keith's scarf.

Weird, Ariel thought as he picked it up and continued walking. He must've left it...when? Keith hadn't been at the *shul* since last Shabbat, and he'd been wearing it then. So maybe—

Ariel froze, unsure of what he just heard.

He waited, silently, slowly tilting his head as if it would help him better locate the sound.

Then he heard voices. A woman's. Then a man's.

Coming from...the dining hall it sounded like? He turned around and walked closer following the sound of conversation.

Yep, Ariel realized, picking up his pace. It was definitely coming from the dining hall. Cate and Jerome must b—

Ariel paused as the sound he heard earlier echoed again. He scrunched his brow.

No...There's *no* way he heard what he thought he heard.

Reaching the double doors, Ariel realized that they weren't entirely closed, but just slightly ajar. Opening it the rest of the way, Ariel entered to deliver the bad news to Cate.

"C—" he began, and her name got stuck in his throat.

Because apparently, he *had* heard what he'd thought he'd heard. And what he'd heard, were moans.

There Cate was, eyes closed, laying on her back on one of the tables, her hands tightly clinging to the edge, still fully dressed in her business suit but with the skirt bunched up around her waist. Her legs spread as wide as possible, a man stood between her thighs, bent over her while the palms of his hands rested on the table on either side of her head. They were moving in rhythym, not romantically enough to be making love exactly, but definitely showing a strong grasp of the underlying fundamentals.

Another unmistakable groan escaped Cate's lips and she threw her head to one side, her eyes flying open.

Noticing Ariel, watching the proceedings in open-mouthed shock from the doorway, she smirked at him.

Cate's shift in focus alerting him that someone else was in the room, Kalman's head snapped to the door, shock evident in his eyes.

And now, a word from our sponsors.

Manishtana

The hurt crashed around Ariel in cold waves, then withdrew to make way for a frothing blanket of anger to roll in, an endlessly alternating ebb and flow of emotions, neither of which would leave him alone long enough to get any productive work done.

"No, you're *not* fine," Ellis insisted, after she pulled him aside at work the next day. "I'm sending you to the 14th floor, then I want you to go to lunch after that. Go smoke it out, then eat it out, then come back, and work it out."

"No, I—"

"I know, sending you off to smoke weed and eat munchies on the clock. I'm such a *bad*, naughty boss. Maybe someone should *spank* me."

"...I'll shut up now."

After a few puffs, the jade dragon started helping him peel back the skin and sort out all the different kinds of messed up Ariel was feeling on several levels about all this.

Which was really just various degrees of the familiar angry, hurt, and betrayed.

The anger he felt as a rabbi that his *shul* was being used for sexytime hookups. The betrayal of friendship, and apparent disdain for Ariel's office, that Kalman had displayed in being one of the culprits. (How long had this been going on? From before Ariel was the rabbi? Did it start after? Did Kalman think he was able to do it just because he was friends with Ariel?) And also not to mention how furious he was about Kalman's infidelity, which, he couldn't even figure out why he was so upset about that one.

I mean, it was stupid, like, it wasn't like *Ariel* was the one who was married to Kalman.

So why did he feel like he'd been wooed and then deceived?

Or maybe Ariel was more angry with himself, really.

Mad that he'd let himself look like a fool for befriending Kalman in the first place. That he wasn't prepared for a shoe to drop because he'd spent the whole friendship pretending that he hadn't been waiting for a shoe to drop.

But, truthfully, there's always a shoe, and we're always carrying around these invisible shoes in our heads about other people, waiting for them to drop, and *especially* about the people who aren't like us.

But then we go ahead and pretend that we don't, and that we're better than we actually are—better than how our parents raised us, better than the culture or community or religion that we're a part of—and we make friends with those "different" people, and pretend that we see them as being just like us, and that we never think the different things about them, and that we're never just waiting for them to show the "true" colors that we know we're not supposed to think that they have, because we're Good People™, you see, and so we spend years of friendships tapdancing around the elephants in our own heads.

But then we get into a fistfight with our black friend, and yep, there it is, that shoe that black people are angry and violent.

Or we find out that when we sent our Jewish friend to buy the Really Cool Thing for us, they told us it was slightly more than it actually cost and they kept the change, and *of course* they did, because there's that Jewish shoe dropping.

Our best guy friend leans in for a kiss because we look so good in that dress, because, *duh*, guys can't *really* be just friends with girls. Shoe drop.

And then we get mad at ourselves for lying to ourselves that we weren't waiting for that shoe to drop the entire time, anyway.

Mad that we've been outed to ourselves that the whole time we really just saw our "Asian friend" as our friendly Asian.

And mostly mad at our deep dark shameful voice chortling *"I told you so. I told you what they were really like"* in gleeful vindication.

So Ariel was kinda mad that he'd been whacked in the head with the *"white guy who doesn't respect the black guy the same way he would another white guy"* shoe.

Because would Kalman have used CAY like the backseat of a '57 Chevy at a drive-in if Ariel had been a white rabbi?

Likely not.

So yeah, Ariel felt a little...actually, Ariel realized as he took a long drag, he *always* seemed to be feeling betrayed or hurt, right?

Like, when it came to experiencing the full rainbow of emotions, Ariel was pretty sure that for him it literally meant just the seven colors.

Let's see, there was feeling betrayed. Hurt. Gutted. Angry. Embarrassed. He was often amused, but he couldn't remember ever feeling "happy," though. Or like, "joyful."

Geez, his emotional palette was *starving* for variety.

Oh!

"Surprise"!

He felt surprised a lot. Although he supposed that was more of a state than an emotion, right? Like awkward.

Although "awkward" was more of an emotion than a state.

But it sure *felt* like a constant state of being to Ariel.

Then again, what *is* a state of being, anyway? Isn't that all in someone's mind? Like, what's being in a state of "normalcy," really? A large enough group of independent minds declaring that how they view things is the way everyone else should too? I mean, when you think about it, the brain is basically a machine built to release a standard measure of chemicals to process information, and keep most humans at some arbitrary semi-standard view of "reality." So "normalcy" wasn't really anything more than a group hallucination.

...Shit. This was some good weed.

ARIEL SAMSON: FREELANCE RABBI

For all his pontifications, by the time it was Keith's sponsored *kiddish* that Shabbat afternoon, Ariel still had no answer as to what to do next.

His stomach was so tied in knots that he wished he could skip the celebration, but he was the rabbi, so everyone expected him to be there, with a smile on his face and a *l'chaim* in his hand.

And so there he was, wishing all the while that he could just crawl under a rock.

Whether it was a mutual dodging of each other or just a one-sided one, Ariel and Kalman had yet to cross paths since Friday night services, despite both being in attendance. And today, with the *knesset* bustling with people, it was even *less* likely that they'd have to interact with each other.

Ariel was mingling in the crowd, welcoming new faces and shooting the breeze with old ones, when he felt a hand clamp down on his shoulder.

"*Shabbat shalom!*" a voice boomed, and Ariel turned to see a middle-aged man he found very reminiscent of a 1950's game show host. Bright white teeth and smile, skin like almond milk, classically-parted brown hair that greyed at the temples, and a lacework web of crinkles around his eyes.

"Rabbi Samson, I presume?" the man extended his other hand, with fingers well-manicured. "Howie Gottleib."

"Great meeting you, Mr. Gottleib," Ariel smiled and shook the older man's hand. "*Shabbat shalom.* What brings you to our humble *shul,*"

"Oh, I just wanted to see what all the fuss about," Howie scanned the room, nodding his head in approval. "You've done an amazing job here with the place. I used to come here. *Years* ago. Good to see there's some life back in the old place."

"Well, I'm glad to hear that. Why don't you come back, too? The doors are always open."

"Oh no," Howie shook his head, his curiously prominent lips quivering in mock horror. "This place is way too Orthodox now. It's not like the old days. These days, when I *do* show up to services, I go to the Conservative ones over in Park Slope. But the wife still comes here with the Orthodox. We like to say we have a mixed marriage," he laughed and Ariel laughed with him.

"Well I'm honored to hear that I have your stamp of approval. It means a lot that the original congregants think I'm doing a good job here."

"Well I should hope you are," Howie grinned. "The way you call board meetings all the time. But clearly," he gestured around the room. "It's worth it!"

Ariel squinted, puzzled.

"Oh, *there* you are honey," a female voice said, and arms appeared from behind Howie and wrapped around him in a hug that seemed more like a spider capturing prey.

Cate's head appeared next to Howie's shoulder, and she placed a peck on his cheek.

"Speak of the devil," Howie winked, as Cate fixed Ariel was a look of coy innocence. "I trust you recognize my wife, rabbi? I barely even *see* her, you put her to work so often."

"Oh, I don't think I put her to work at all," Ariel replied, doing a masterful job of keeping his surprise under wraps. "I actually didn't realize you were married, Cate."

After all, he never remembered ever seeing Cate wearing a ring, and she didn't cover her hair. She wasn't even one of the *shul* coverers who wore a hat or scarf or doily in the sanctuary, but roamed bareheaded during the week.

"Yeah," Howie clarified. "She's didn't want to change her name—because of work—and it didn't really bother me, so she never became Mrs. Cate Gottleib. I guess technically, she's still a free woman," he winked without the slightest hint of irony, and Ariel weakly chuckled back, feeling his stomach turn.

"Ariel!" Dassi called from across the room, dragging Kalman in tow, doing his best to seem as not-reluctant as possible. "Omigoodness this *kiddish* is amazing!" she turned to Howie. "Hi Howie!"

"Hey sweetheart," he smiled broadly, in a very father-daughter kind of way. "Looks like your man and my woman are at it again. Amazing job here guys. All three of you."

"Seriously," Dassi beamed. "I've never seen this place as alive as I've seen it these past few weeks."

"Oh, I'm sure it's a combination of things," Cate piped up. "No offense to the rabbi, but I'd have to say that, working under Kalman, I've seen an impressive sustainable growth."

Her eyes slyly dared Ariel to comment. Kalman remained silent, replying with a half-grin/half-shrug. His eyes flicked back and forth between Cate and Ariel, trying to gauge what the other's next reaction would be, nervous as a black Yankees fan in Boston.

"Well," Howie added. "I was just saying to the rabbi that he defnitely keeps our spouses chained to the grindstone!"

"I know right?" Dassi agreed. "What synagogue board meets three times a week?"

"Sorry, guys," Ariel chuckled insincerely, "Can't say that it's not my call."

He answered technically truthfully, but in a way he knew they'd take the opposite way. That was the cancer of lies. They took on a life of their own and spread, reproducing more of their kind spontaneously in unwilling victims.

"Keith!" Kalman shouted, waving the man of the hour over. Likely in a bid to diffuse the mounting tension.

The guest of honor waved and came striding over, wrapping Kalman in a huge hug and then Ariel after him.

"Happy birthday," Ariel clapped Keith on the back, with genuine sincerity.

"Aw man, this is great," Keith smiled, glistening with the sweaty sheen of a *lot* of Johnny Walker Red. He turned to Kalman. "By the way, thanks! I've been looking *everywhere* for that scarf."

"Sorry," Kalman laughed uneasily. "It was just really cold one night and I saw it and just wore it home to borrow it. Had no idea it was yours, but glad I got it back to you."

Ariel wore an engaging smile as the banter between all the parties involved bounced from person to person, but inside he was fuming.

How dare they, he screamed internally, watching them hem and haw.

How dare they make a mockery of the *shul* and its offices? How dare they flaunt it in front of their spouses, in front of Ariel—in front of *G'D*—as if they'd done nothing wrong? How dare they—no.

No, he was going to end this right now.

"I'm sorry guys," he apologized, interrupting the conversation flow. "I hate to do this to you even right now, but I need to borrow my president and treasurer for a quick second."

Howie and Dassi both groaned.

"Don't worry, you'll have them back soon enough."

Everything about being the rabbi of Congregation Ahavath Yisrael up until this moment had been fun and exciting, and yes, even uncertain at times.

But playtime, Ariel resolved grimly, was over now.

Kalman and Cate had committed all the adulteries.

Literally.

Adultery in common (aka Christian) parlance was defined as extramarital sex by a married man *or* woman.

But Judaism was a religion that sanctioned polygamy. So the biblical Old Testament definition of adultery was only when a married *woman* stepped outside of her marriage.

Exodus 20:13 doesn't say "Thou shalt not covet thy neighbor's *husband*," does it? Because if a single lady wanted a married man so much, she could just as easily marry him.

But this situation right here, Ariel thought—sitting at his desk, with Kalman and Cate sitting across from him like two defiant teens in the principal's office—this was both of the wrongs on all of the levels.

And yet, Cate was laughing.

"I don't believe this," she managed to compose herself enough to say. "You're seriously asking us to step down from the board?"

"No," Ariel replied, quietly but firmly. "I'm not. I'm seriously *telling* you."

Cate's laughter cut itself short in her throat. Kalman sat with a smug half-smirk, but his eyes were hooded, scanning Ariel's face. Narrowing her eyes, Cate leaned forward in her chair, using Ariel's desk to slowly raise herself out of her seat.

"You. Pompous. Little. Shit," she hissed, walking her hands across the desk as she leaned into Ariel's personal space, her shoulders hunching up around her ears, resembling the flare of a cobra's hood. "You think you can just walk in here and—"

Ariel rose from his chair in response, with none of the uncertainty or doubt Cate was used to seeing in him, and she instinctually shrank back.

Because this wasn't Ariel the Person speaking right now. Or Ariel the Teacher. Or Ariel the Speaker. Or Ariel the Writer. Or Ariel the Diplomat.

This was Ariel the Rabbi.

There was no second-guessing here. The grey area of social interactions didn't exist here, in his place of power, in the certainty of black and white, right or wrong, and the confidence of religious absolutes. This was not an Ariel that Cate was used to, and one Kalman had only witnessed brief glimpses of. And every word this Ariel spoke was written in fire, delivered by a man with an unyielding backbone built vertebrae by vertebrae from book after book, text after text.

"You seem to be under the misconception, Ms. Finklestein— *Mrs.* Finklestein," he began. "That I care about who you are, or how you're related to whoever founded whatever about this synagogue. I don't. I was appointed here to be the spiritual leader of Congregation Ahavath Yisroel, and if you thought that I took this position to play the part of convenient figurehead, then I'm sorry to have misled you. So let me clear the air right now. This is my *shul*, under my auspices, and I've been entrusted to safeguard the state of its spirit. And I will not have it subject to a festering rot flourishing in its midst. Say what you will to your friends. Give whatever excuses to your spouses. None of that is my concern. But your days of using this place of worship as a cover for your illicit affairs. Are! *Over!* The *both* of you are now done here. *Today.* You have the coming week to gracefully exit yourselves, or I *will* do it for you. AM. I. *CLEAR*," Ariel smashed a fist down on his desk, punctuating his point, making his lampshade dance around on its base for a long moment.

His declaration had been uncharacteristically thunderous, and the room had seemed to darken and bend around him.

It was the "BILBO BAGGINS! *Do* NOT *mistake me for some conjurer of cheap tricks!"* moment from *Fellowship of the Rings.*

Only this time, there'd be no moment where Bilbo comes running contritely into Gandalf's arms.

No, in the silence that reverberated in his office, after his words had boomed away like decaying thunder, in Cate's deafening muteness, and in the glint behind her eyes, Ariel knew that this was only the deep breath before the Nazgul screeched, the calm before Smaug arose from the floor to decimate Watertown.

And, walking past both Cate and Kalman as he headed for the door, Ariel decided that he'd jump off that bridge when he got to it.

"Isn't it forbidden to terminate a contract on Shabbat, rabbi?" Kalman said mockingly, just as Ariel's hand touched the doorknob.

"Isn't adultery forbidden *always*, Kalman?" Ariel replied over his shoulder, to Kalman's silence. "Just consider this **pikuach hanefesh** on behalf of the *shul's* soul," Ariel opened the door, then paused. "Now if you'll both excuse me, I have a *kiddish* to return to, where I have to continue lying to the newest member of our faith about how upright and moral the people that he's joined are."

✡ ✡ ✡

Pasting a smile on his face, Ariel descended the stairwell that had led to his shocking discovery just three days prior, and eventually re-entered the *kiddish*, crashing into Ellis, yet again, and spilling the contents of her own cup all over herself, yet again.

"Oh come—are you *serious*? Are you really—" she began, stopping short as she saw Ariel's face, immediately seeing through his façade. "Hey, are you okay?"

"Why are you always asking me that?"

"Why are you always not okay?"

"I'm *fine*. I just—"

"*There* he is," Keith voice came booming through the room. He made a beeline towards the rabbi, pulling a slightly concerned/slightly confused middle-aged black woman after him, while Ellis grumblingly wandered off in search of napkins.

"Mom," Keith announced when they'd both reached Ariel. "This is Rabbi Samson. This man has helped me, *so much*, on this journey and I've, just," he placed his hand on Ariel's shoulder and began tearing up, partially overcome with emotion, and partially overcome with the alcohol overcoming him with emotion. "I've learned *so* much from him, and—"

"Whoa, hey, it's alright man," Ariel pulled Keith in for a hug, and getting crushed in reward. "The honor is all mine," he wheezed through constricted ribs, gasping for air once Keith released him.

"Rabbi Samson," Keith wiped his eyes and puffed out his chest, presenting the woman at his side with a small flourish. "This is my Mom."

"Rabbi," she extended her hand, a twinkle of amusement in her eye.

She was a short, stocky woman with the same dark, earthy skin as her son, and rivulets of silver-grey played hide-and-seek in her glistening black hair. Her neck seemed oddly bare and vulnerable, as if it were self-conscious of the cross she'd decided against wearing that day. But the rest of her outfit—particularly how flawlessly her rhinestone-studded hat matched her sequin-lapeled suit—made it readily apparent that, even if she *hadn't* been a preacher's wife, she was still undoubtedly a woman who knew what to wear to a place of worship.

And, obviously. Because, black.

That was one of the many things—right up there with how they let their kids talk to them, and why they don't understand *that salt and pepper are not seasonings*—that black people would never understand about white people: how they come dressed for church. (Or synagogue, for that matter.)

The same white dude who shows up impeccably dressed to The Olive Garden, will slide up into services in a pair of wrinkled Dockers and a polo shirt with the collar half-in and half-out, wearing some Buster Browns that haven't been invited out with polite company since 1987.

Meanwhile, if you walk into a black worship space wearing anything less than a five-piece suit, chile, you might as well be clapping on the one and three, you soulless heathen.

Hell, church suits were such a serious situation that it made black people not even see *color*. Because when it came to talking to G'd, there was no such *thing* as colors. If your suit didn't come in a *flavor*, then you were doing it wrong.

"Nice to meet you, Mrs. Taylor," Ariel shook her extended hand. "You must be so proud of your son. I know I'd be."

"Nice to finally meet *you*, rabbi. I've heard so much about you. How do you do it? How do you deal with all this?"

The look in her eye made it patently clear what she meant by "this." The black person in a white Jewish world thing. The Jewish person in a black world thing. The devoutly religious in an increasingly secular world thing. A person of color occupying a space of authority in a largely white ecosystem thing. And a sly grin made it clear she was including handling her elated but highly inebriated son in the "this" as well.

"I..." he began, trailing off as he noticed Kalman and Cate re-enter the room, and rejoin their spouses.

How did he do it? Great question. One that he should probably find an answer for. Because as it stood—

"The rabbi has this great saying that he's told me," Keith leapt in, impassioned. "Because I was struggling sometimes. Like, *really* struggling, over the disconnect between the way of life I just fell in love with, and, well, pretty much the real world everything else. And—" he turned to Ariel. "Do you remember what you told me?"

"I say a—"

"So he told me," Keith barreled on, turning back to his mom. "That to stay engaged, to keep your feet planted in this ground, you've gotta remember that Judaism comes with three rules."

A sniggle escaped from Ariel, as Keith's declaration jogged his memory.

"The first one," Keith listed. "Is don't let Jews ruin Judaism for you. Number Two: Don't judge Judaism by its Jews. And the last one is to remember that they can be a great people. They wish to be. They only lack the light to show the way. So sometimes your job is to be that light."

Ariel chuckled, self-deprecatingly, as his own timely advice echoed back at him.

It was like that moment when you tear your house apart looking for your keys, and then you find them in the most logical spot ever.

Because you're smarter than you think you are, and if only you'd give yourself some credit you'd get so much farther so much faster.

"That last message is *so* profound," Mrs. Taylor gaped. She turned to Ariel. "*'They* wish *to be, they only lack the light.'* What *is* that? Psalms? Proverbs 31?"

Ariel half-shrugged, sheepishly.

"Superman 47:18."

✡ ✡ ✡

Shabbat had ended, and Ariel trudged upstairs after making sure that the leftover food and drink from the both the *kiddish* and *seudah shlishit* had been properly stored away in the kitchen.

Usually it was Kalman and Cate who volunteered to clean up the *knesset* after Shabbat.

Now Ariel knew why.

Speaking of, Ariel'd been planning on bringing up the idea of a committee of rotating congregants to help with **moztei Shabbat** clean-up at the next board meeting, anyway.

Maybe now it was time to fasttrack the idea.

Of course, Ariel realized, gathering his coat and keys from his office, the next couple of weeks would likely be packed with the busywork of considering candidates for the soon-to-be publicly vacant posts of president and treasurer.

Although maybe Kalman and Cate having to vacate their positions was a blessing in disguise. A way to get some of the newcomers involved in CAY's infrastructure and invested in the *shul's* growth.

And then there was the other elephant in the room, resting specifically on Ariel's shoulders: the issue of whether or not he had a *halachic* obligation to inform Howie Gottleib about his wife's infidelity.

Did he tell Howie and potentially ruin the family's reputation? If he didn't, was he responsible for Howie continually living in sin with a woman who, according to traditional law, was now forbidden to him and he was mandated to divorce?

He didn't know.

And in the couple of hours since Shabbat had ended, Ariel had been alone in the *shul* wrestling with the question, an argument raging in his head with the scholars of the past, like a council of Jedi force ghosts.

"Look man," said the Nodah b'Yehuda. "I don't even know. You should probably just ask Rambam or Rosh. Cuz this could go either way."

"Yo, just blow up her spot!" Rambam shouted. "Bros before hoes. Sorry, not sorry, and not my problem. I'm not trying to hear about people getting all in their feelings."

"Dude," the Rosh shot back. "You can't just go around ripping people up like that. Like, let the man have his dignity. He doesn't need to know all that."

"Yeah," Rema agreed. "I'm gonna just go with Rosh on this one."

"*Pffft*," Shulchan Aruch scoffed. "Snowflake."

"Really though?" Divrei Chaim interjected. "Do we really *need* to let him know, though?"

"I mean, exactly," Maharish agreed. "*We* don't *know* if anything actually happened. Were we all up in their business like that? Were we all up in there making *sure* they were full-on getting it in?"

"He might not even believe us anyways," Ran added.

"Actually, y'know what?" Shulchan Aruch piped up again. "Let's get Dassi up in this convo, too. If she's running around thinking her husband is being so faithful then we *definitely* need to put her on, on some *lashon hara l'toelet* tip, know what I'm saying? Get her that good good *ketubah* money. Make it rain *zuzim!*"

"I mean, I see what you're saying, but..."

And on the debate raged.

At any rate, Ariel nodded to himself as he locked his office door behind him, he knew he'd done the right thing ordering Cate and Kalman to step down. There were very few moments in life when Ariel felt that he knew exactly what he was doing. This was one of them.

Heading across the foyer to shut out the lights in the sanctuary, he realized someone was still inside, sitting hunched over in one of the pews.

"Hey," Ariel knocked on one of the doors to get their attention. "I'm locking up now."

"Oh!" the person's head popped up. It was Keith. "Sorry! I'd just lost track of time. Lemme just grab up my stuff here..."

"Oh, no prob," Ariel answered, surprised. "I didn't even realize you were still here. I thought you'd already gone home to continue the party."

"Yeah. That..." Keith said with a false smile spreading across his face. "I mean, I *did*. And, y'know..."

"Is everything alright?" Ariel frowned.

"Yeah. Yeah..." Keith waved his hand dismissively, then paused and rubbed his fingers into his eyes. "No...Not really."

"Why?" Ariel came down the aisle and sat next to Keith, who plopped back down into his seat. "What's up? I thought today went fine. Did something happen?"

"It's...well..." Keith started. "I actually invited *both* of my parents to come today. Y'know?"

"But your dad isn't crazy about your conversion," Ariel deduced.

"*NOPE*. He's a reverend, remember? So I guess I'm not really sure why I thought that would be a thing," Keith rolled his eyes and smirked mirthlessly. "I thought, I dunno, maybe I thought he'd be glad that I found a spiritual path instead of just still floating around like I've been."

"But your mom seems to be okay with it, right? Maybe she can run interference for you between you and your dad? Mediate?"

Keith snorted.

"My mom and my dad are two *very* different people. And once my dad's head is set on something..." Keith shook his head with a huffed chuckle and bowed it, letting it hang.

He sat silently for a moment, and Ariel sat with him, a patiently waiting sounding board.

"Like," Keith started, raising his head to stare at the ceiling. "Telling my parents that I was converting to Judaism was one of the hardest, most frightening things I've ever done in my life. I mean, it kinda sounds backwards, but I wanted them to know that it was *because* of the values they instilled in me, and how a good a job they did raising me, that I was able to make this step. And my mom, yeah it was easier telling her. I can't say she was always onboard, but she's always been really supportive of me, so she would check up on my progress, ask me how my classes were going, and she was always really fascinated about what I was learning, and she even said a couple of times how certain things just 'made sense' to her, y'know?"

"Well that's big."

"It *was*. But when I started scheduling potential conversion dates, though...things got a little prickly between us. Like, it wasn't *'I'm studying to be Jewish'* anymore, it was *'This time next month I'll be a Jew.'* And I guess it scared her a little bit. I remember her finally breaking down and crying and saying that she understood that I had to do what was best for me, but she was afraid that when I had kids—not 'if' by the way, but 'when', because apparently she'd *already* converted to being a Jewish mother."

Keith laughed, and Ariel empathetically chuckled along.

"But anyway. She was worried that she wouldn't be able to relate to her grandchildren because she didn't understand Judaism. And we talked for a long, *long* time about how she was still gonna be my mom, and how I would never alienate her for that...But we were both afraid of what my dad's reaction was gonna be, I guess. Like, duh, he's a reverend. He's *always* been so much more zealous about religion than any of our family. Like, he has cousins that are deacons at megachurches down in Atlanta. It's in his *blood*. It's funny though, because I always felt closer to my dad religiously than I did to my mom. Like, everything about how I practice Judaism, I get from him...And when I told him that I was converting, he just, sorta, just looked right through me. And all he said was *'Do you still believe that Jesus is the savior?'* And I guess, I guess I really should've expected that question, y'know? Had some, theological, I don't even know, or something. But I just blanked out and was just like *'No.'* And the conversation kinda ended right there."

Keith sighed heavily, and took another pause.

"And so last month, it's the big day. And I'm standing there, at the edge of the *mikvah*, and...and it felt like I was standing at the tip of forever. And I couldn't help thinking, in that split second, about my dad and how disappointed he'd be. Like, I could *hear* him in my head. *'This isn't my religion. This isn't the religion I gave you. This isn't the faith I worked to nurture you in. This isn't...this isn't...'"* he swallowed deeply. And Ariel realized that Keith was staring at the ceiling to keep the tears welling up in his eyes from spilling over. *"'This isn't my G'd...I didn't give you this punishing G'd with all these rules...What I gave you wasn't good enough? Why did you throw it away? Why did...Why did you throw me away?'*...And what do I say to that? Hm?" he laughed, anxiously. "What *can* I say to that?"

"Keith, look, I'm sure your dad doesn't think that. He probably just nee—"

"Rabbi," Keith looked at Ariel finally, dabbing at the tears in his eyes with one hand and pulling his phone out of his jacket with the other. "I appreciate what you're trying to do. I do. But I'm not sitting here because I *think* he might say that. I'm sitting here because I'm right. He emailed me. Today. Saw it when I turned my phone on after Shabbat. Here," Keith scrolled across the screen then handed the phone to Ariel. "It's pretty to the point."

Reluctantly, Ariel took the phone and began to read the few quick sentences onscreen:

"Keith. This is a difficult email for me to write, but I am finding strength in Christ to get through it. I received your voicemail and am emailing you to inform you that no, I will not be attending your Sabbath celebration of your birthday, nor giving my blessing to the detour you have decided to take off the road of true faith. Furthermore, I will not be visiting you now or anytime in the future, nor will you be welcome to step foot in my Christian home. The Jews you want to join don't want you. You will never really be one of them, and they know it. But you'll have to find that out the hard way. You've turned your back on your family, on our Lord Savior, and on His grace, so now you'll have no one. Have a good birthday and a good life. Goodbye, Dad.

'He who rejects Me, and does not receive My words, has that which judges him—the word that I have spoken will judge him in the last day.' John 12:48"

"So yeah," Keith smiled an empty smile, as a speechless and a shocked Ariel returned his phone. "I really hope this 'Jew' thing pans out, then."

"Keith...I'm sorry. I—"

Keith waved Ariel's sympathy away.

"Don't worry about it. I knew the choice I was making. And...Y'know, what? I'd do it again, too. It just sucks that I had to lose my dad over it, y'know?...Anyway, you're closing up, lemme just get out of your hair. Thanks for listening though, rabbi."

Keith rose up from the pew, and began heading towards the exit.

Manishtana

"*Shavua tov*, rabbi."

"*Shavua tov*, Keith."

Staying behind in his seat, Ariel heard Keith's retreating footsteps as they descended the stairwell, the creak of the front door opening, then the heavy thud of it slamming closed again. And then Ariel was alone in the silence of the deserted building.

He sighed heavily—his emotions tied up with Keith's distress, the contemplation of the Cate and Kalman fallout, the burden of whether or not to have a very difficult conversation with Howie—and collapsed back into his seat in the pew, looking up at the ark.

"*Da Lifnei Mi Atah Omed*," the letters etched into the arch above the curtain read.

"Know Before Whom You Stand."

It wasn't a direct quote from any scripture, but the idea came from Moses' first encounter with G'd at the Burning Bush, that classic scene where—having been tapped to lead a ragtag group of holy misfits, troublemakers, and ne'er do wells out of the house of bondage—Moses argues with G'd for seven days—*seven days*—that the Almighty has got the wrong guy.

Ariel couldn't fathom anything like that.

Sure, he'd've felt the same way (hell, he felt that way leading a congregation just barely approaching *sixty*, let alone a people six hundred *thousand* men strong), but to argue with G'd to try and get out of it?

Nope. Nope nope nope.

The only thing he'd've been able to muster then, would likely be the same thing he said aloud now, alone in the silence of the sanctuary.

"So, G'd. I'm *really* honored that You think I'm up for these tests and challenges. I appreciate it. But, Y'know...You *do* grade on a curve, right?"

ARIEL SAMSON: FREELANCE RABBI

The house standing in front of Ariel was quaint and homey, a long, American Gothic-style building, milky-white, with pine-green shutters framing the windows that lined either side in double rows, its saltbox roof covered with granite-hued asphalt shingles.

It was something much more at home in the deer-infested suburbs of New Jersey or the suburb-esque outlands of Queens, but not so much inhabiting three-eighths the length of a skinny triangular wedge of a city block in Brooklyn.

A large cross sat posted atop its chimney-cum-belltower, and in golden letters the words "New Zion Baptist Church" arched over the doorway. A small, manicured lawn stretched out beyond the short flight of steps, and the entire property was enclosed with a tall fence of rounded brushed-steel bars, set in a severe perpendicular pattern of horizontal and vertical lines that reminded Ariel of a jail cell from *Law & Order: SVU*.

It was almost as if it were constructed to be a cage for G'd.

Wasn't that really church in a nutshell, though?

Not intentionally, of course. But practically?

A place to "go to" whenever you wanted to talk to Him?

A sort of divine kiddie pool you dropped Him off at, went off to play with your friends all week long, then came back on Sunday, apologizing that you forgot about Him because you were having so much fun and you lost track of the time?

Ariel wondered how much of that ideology had leached into Reform Judaism when it broke ranks from the traditionalists to mimic its enlightened Christian neighbors, moving the cornerstone of Jewish life from the home to the temple, like a disgruntled wife making her husband sleep on the couch.

The Conservative movement followed suit when it eventually came along, ruling that driving a car to celebrate the Sabbath in synagogue was more important of a priority over the Torah literally saying in Leviticus 23:2, that the point of the Shabbat was to dedicate the day "unto the L'rd *in all your dwellings.*"

Like, dude, synagogue *whatnow*? Where you "dwell" at is at home.

Of course, Ariel admitted, maybe that was just a tad of his Orthodox bias showing.

I mean, let's be real, Reform and Conservative Judaism might've created a cage for G'd in Space, but the Orthodox had done a pretty good job of imprisoning G'd in Time, in some amorphous mythical period of revisionist history and fabricated homogeneity, where Europe was the only Jewish "Old Country," and Moses wore a brown fur **shtriemel** and a black polyester **bekishe** over black silk knickerbockers and white knee-highs and colonial buckled shoes as he led the Jews—piously separated by a **mechitzah** into the only two genders that exist—through the Red Sea, while the married women with fully-covered hair played the tambourines to drown out the sinfully sultry sounds of their voices.

Ah, the messiness of faith.

He remembered when his sister had lost hers.

More than his sister.

Aviva was his *twin.*

They were supposed to navigate this crazy thing called Life together, side-by-side, the caboose-end of the Samson train, them and their kooky twin-powers against the world.

And for a while they did.

And everything was fine until suddenly it wasn't.

Until suddenly Aviva was done, and she set her faith on fire, pushed it out to sea, and waved goodbye as the tide pulled it further and further out into oblivion.

Ariel...hadn't handled it well, to say the least.

Less than kind words were exchanged, bonds were broken, and, in the aftermath, it'd been almost three years since a set of twins had last talked to each other.

She'd been the one Samson who hadn't shown up to Ariel's *chag hasmicha* ceremony.

Ah, the messiness of family.

And so here Ariel was, trying to help Keith and his dad succeed where he and Aviva had miserably failed.

Even from outside, Ariel could hear the booming impassioned voice of Reverend Taylor, raging about the brimstones of Hell and the salvations of Jesus' embrace.

Or at least that's what he imagined the good reverend was sermonizing about.

He'd never personally been inside a church ever.

As per Orthodox doctrine, it was anathema, a forbidden implicit theological stamp of approval, as sacrilegious as serving Coca-Cola at a Pepsi office party.

So all Ariel had to go on was the impressions he'd gleaned from black family movies.

"Black family" meaning "Christian family," obviously.

Before long, Sunday services ended (meaning by around 5:30 in the evening) and the doors exploded open into a sea of Steve Harvey suits and Stacy Adams shoes, plump church mothers wearing their signature white gloves, judgmentally scowling at the younger ladies looking for their Boaz while outfitted in dresses that made more than Jesus rise, followed by old men in lime-green pinstriped suits with matching hats, canes, shoes and pocket squares, and, of course, a parade of black women church hattiquette—a flamboyant, multicolored, veil-draped, pearl-encrusted panoply of mushroom caps, conch shells, paper cranes, *Chicoreus florifer*, Georgia O'Keefe, Edible Arrangements, Vegas tailfathers, Frank Lloyd Wright, and Sydney Opera House.

(But seriously, can we talk about that 5:30 thing?

Like, what are you guys doing for *six hours* in church?

We Jews can barely make it through six-hour days three times a *year* for Rosh Hashana and Yom Kippur.

Y'all do that *every week*?

Like, what the hell are y'all doing in the space of a *week* that you need to pray it off *that much* every single Sunday?

I mean, dammit, *pace* yourselves.

I really can't with you.

Why the testimony gotta be longer than the sermon, though?

And tell your mans on the organ to chill.

You don't need him to be running up and down the keyboard like a mouse on Ritalin at the end of the sermon just to help emphasize the reverend's point.

Also, c'mon now, stop interrupting the man, screaming out "Yes L'rd!" all loud like you're not just tryna hide the sound of the peppermint wrapper you're trying to sneak in your mouth.

"I...I...I knoooooow I've been changed?"

Well I know *I've* been here all day, Ethel.

Wrap it up.)

The emptying churchgoers quickly filed into the cars parked up and down the curb, eventually driving off into the waning rays of sunlight, the air heavy with the scent of foil-covered plates of soul food.

Ariel began to cross the street, approaching the church just as the last congregant exited the now quiet building, pulling the door shut behind him and locking it.

Descending the short flight of stairs, the man wore a pair of frameless glasses and was dressed in a natty Blueberry Blast suit with a crisp white shirt, and a cherry-red tie with a matching pocket square. A golden crucifix pin encrusted in crushed diamonds glinted on his left lapel, and a tie chain linked the points of his shirt collar with a light gold chain, nestling yet another cross in the soft folds of his tie, just underneath the knot.

Round, gold cufflinks with a ruby center bedecked both cuffs, matching the gold chain around his wrist, and a class ring sat proudly on his right hand, while a wedding band and onyx pinky ring graced his left.

"Reverend Taylor?"

The man looked up. He had to be in at least his sixties—Keith, after all was nearly forty—but he didn't look a day over 45.

"Black don't crack" was *real.*

"Yes, son?" he answered pleasantly, with the perfect balance of friendly clergyman and wary stranger.

"I'm Rabbi Ariel Samson," Ariel removed the fleece beanie from his head, revealing his kippah. "I'm the rabbi of a synagogue about twenty minutes away from here?"

"Ah. I'm familiar with your name, rabbi," he replied with a sudden stiffness as he reached Ariel, standing at the open entranceway of the fence, but staying on the church side. "If you're here to lure away more believers, you should've come earlier. Services start at 11. Or do you only scavenge on those having a crisis of faith?"

"I'm not here to prey on anyone, reverend," Ariel replied, holding his hands open at his sides, as if to show that he wasn't carrying any weapons. "I'm just a rabbi of a small synagogue, and I have a distressed congregant. An upstanding, upright, moral person, who's hurting right now, devastated about his relationship with his father. And I was hoping that I could prove him wrong. Do you think you could help me with that, reverend?"

"I don't see how I could, rabbi," Reverend Taylor replied coldly. "Seeing that I don't have a son."

"I don't think you really mean that."

"I think it's pretty straightforward logic. I'm a Christian. My wife is a Christian. My parents are Christians. I run a Christian church. And I have a Christian family. So any child raised in any home of *mine* being a congregant of *yours* isn't any more possible than a rock becoming a tree."

"I think we both know scripture well enough to know that rocks can do a lot of things when they're touched by G'd."

"Things against their nature, perhaps. But they never stop being a rock."

"Then I'd like to say Keith never stopped being your son."

Reverend Taylor stopped, stumped.

A rueful smile grew across his face and he lifted his head and his hands to the sky.

"Oh, I see you've called me, L'rd," he declared to the clouds, his voice shfting into a preacher's tenor. "To take this test. You bring me the adversary at my own doorstep! Dressed in my own skin to tempt me!" he lowered his gaze to meet Ariel, fixing him with a searing look. "But in Jesus' name, I *will not* falter. I will put on the full armor of G'd and take my stand against the devil's schemes."

The reverend's look was a familiar one to Ariel.

It was the same look he'd get back in high school and in college, when he'd tell his classmates that Nell Carter or Rashida Jones or Walter Moseley were Jewish.

271

That look of revulsion as if he were stealing one of "their" people from them. Like he was renaming the syndicated reruns of *Gimme A Break* with *Nu, Can I Get A Deal?*, or retitling *Devil In A Blue Dress* as *Dybbuk In A Blue Shmata*, or relaunching *Parks and Recreation* as *Shtetls and Shuls*. Overstepping his bounds by not being satisfied with Lenny Kravitz taking up the anomalous quota torch passed down from Sammy Davis, Jr.

Of course, here, the sentiment behind the look was far more personal.

"You can make your own choices, rabbi," the reverend said steadily. "It is what you were raised in, and I can't fault you for abiding by it. In fact, I can even respect that. But Keith grew up in a household of salvation, and instead of seeing that his interest in Judaism is G'd's way of calling him back to Christ, he's spitting in His face."

"Maybe its not about Keith *rejecting* anything, reverend. Maybe he saw the same tenets that you raised him with, that he *values*, and found those same values in Judaism in a way that makes him feel fulfilled in—"

"A life without Jesus is *not* a fulfilled life! It is *not* a godly life! *'Do not follow after the crowd to do evil.'* Isn't that in your book?"

"'If this endeavor is of human origin, it will come to nothing. But if it is of G'd, you will not be able to overthrow it, and you would be found even to be fighting against G'd.' Isn't that in yours?"

"The Word already countered your argument centuries ago, rabbi. *'Do not believe every spirit, but test the spirits to see if they are of G'd, because many falsehoods are gone out into the world.'* 1 John. *'Now I say this that no one may delude you with persuasiveness of speech.'* Colossians. *'Take heed that no one deceive you through philosophy and empty deceit based on human thinking and not based on Christ.'* Colossians."

"'You have been deceived by your own pride because you live in a rock fortress and make your home high in the mountains.' Obadiah 1:3."

"'Therefore, thus says the L'rd, "Behold, I am laying stumbling blocks before this people And they will stumble against them, Fathers and sons together; Neighbor and friend will perish."' Jeremiah. *'And with every unrighteous deception among those who are perishing, they perish because they did not accept the love of the truth in order to be saved.'* 2 Thessalonians."

"'*He will restore the hearts of the fathers to their children and the hearts of the children to their fathers.*' That's my book, reverend. Malachi 4:6. '*For I came to set a man against his father, and a daughter against her mother, and a daughter-in-law against her mother-in-law.*' That's yours. Matthew 10:35."

"But my book is the book of salvation and grace, rabbi. It transcends the old sacrificial covenant of your scriptures. '*And the grace of our Lord overflowed for me with the faith and love that are in Christ Jesus.*' 1 Timothy."

"Forgive me reverend, but it seems awfully hypocritical to use a book of 'grace and love' to justify denying extending the same to your son. Doesn't 1 Corinthians 13:13 say '*Faith, hope, and love abide, these three; but the greatest of these is love?*' Doesn't 1 John 4:8 say that '*One who does not love does not know G'd, because G'd is love?*' Doesn't 1 Corinthians 13:4-7 declare love as being patient and kind? That it doesn't insist on its own way? That it bears all things, believes all things, hopes all things, and endures all things? You stand behind your devotion to the gospels, but what about Romans 13:8? '*Owe no one anything, except to love each other, for the one who loves another has fulfilled the law?*'"

The rabbi and the reverend continued tossing scripture back and forth at one another as they paced back and forth on either side of the fence, a duel of theology like Gandalf the Grey and Saruman the White battling in the bowels of Orthanc, deflecting blow after blow with chapter and verse, each one borrowing the other's weapons to disarm them with their own ordnances.

"You're well-learned, Rabbi Samson," Reverend Taylor admitted, impressed. "But you are what you are. You were born a Jew and you'll stay a Jew. And there's nothing wrong with that. But Keith was born a Christian, and where he belongs is being Christian. A rock can't become a tree."

"Reverend Taylor, you keep saying that. And you know what? You're right. A rock *can't* become a tree. But maybe it was never a rock. Maybe it was an acorn covered in grime and dirt and it just *looked* like a rock, and now it's growing into the tree it's always been. You can either accept that or not, but it's going to keep growing either way. And if you throw it away now, it'll *never* be a tree that you can call yours."

Manishtana

A pained expression flashed across the reverend's face, and he deflated slightly. And for a split-second Ariel second-guessed himself, wondering if he'd gone too far.

After all, sure the reverend's email had been extremely harsh, but...I mean...Young Reverend Taylor, when he was bouncing his little Keith on his knee—his little newborn who didn't know his right from his left, or how to lift his head on his own, or what his reflection even was—that proud Christian father was dreaming an entire future in those little moments.

One where his grandchildren surrounded him in church, celebrating Christmas mass together. One where the girls were decked out in their spring dresses and the boys in their fresh suits, lining the pews on either side of their grandfather at Easter.

And now?

Sure, there might be grandchildren. But they'd be Jewish grandchildren.

And likely Orthodox ones, too. Keith becoming Jewish had snatched a lifetime's worth of daydreams away. And that *had* to feel to the reverend like he was burying generations of offspring he'd never even met, before they'd even had a chance to live.

But none of that was Keith's fault.

He deserved to be loved for himself, his *actual* self, not the *idea* of himself that his father had spent decades building in his head.

One which, quite honestly, was constructed on a scaffolding of Reverend Taylor's own self-image, and how he expected his children were a reflection on himself. Not only to society, but also to his idea of a vengeful god who punished parents for failing to raise "good children" of whatever their own religion was.

"Rabbi Samson," the reverend answered steadily. "I have a maillady who gives me my mail. And she is the nicest, the sweetest person in the world. Would you know that when she knew my wife was sick once, she not only delivered our mail, but also brought us a thermos full of steaming hot homemade chicken soup? But she's a lesbian. I have the nice young man who comes and mows my lawn in the summer and shovels my snow in the winter. He checks in on us when it's too cold, and makes sure our air conditioner is working when it's going to be too hot. And he's an atheist. And then there's the delightful young kindergarten teacher who helps me, every Thanksgiving, and together we volunteer at soup kitchen feeding the homeless. And then again for Christmas. Even though he's a

Muslim and doesn't celebrate either one. And I have...my son. My son who is now a Jew...I'm a reverend, rabbi. A Christian Baptist reverend. *'I am the way, the truth, and the life. No one comes to the Father except through Me.'* Jesus said that. *'For if ye believe not that I am he, ye shall die in your sins.'* And that's not something I can just go around. I have these wonderful people in my life, but not a one of them knows Jesus. And if, when I die, I were to see them, I were to see them enjoying heaven with me, then it would be a truly *truly* joyful sight...But that's not how grace works. And what I want isn't the same as what I believe."

Ariel stood and considered the older man's words for a second.

There were so many things he wanted to say in response.

Like how weird it'd be for the reverend if Jesus ever did end up coming back, because he'd likely go to Ariel's synagogue before he ever went to Reverend Taylor's church.

Or how backwards it was to disown a child for following the same laws as the very founder of your religion, in the name of a G'd you're convinced has meted out the identical eternal punishment to both Hitler and Anne Frank.

And if he really believed in a G'd that would do that, then, as a reverend, wasn't he really in the business of saving people *from* G'd, not *to* Him?

But, in the end, Reverend Taylor was just a man who didn't want to see his son in Hell.

He didn't want to see a *lot* of people going to Hell. And he didn't want to change any of them, either. He wanted them, as they were, as he knew them, to be with him up in Heaven.

That deserved some kind of credit, right?

"Keith may not be the Christian you raised him to be," Ariel said finally. "But he's still the *person* you raised him to be. And I'm glad and privileged to know him."

"And if it were your child, rabbi, how would that sentence comfort *you*? If the shoe were on the other foot, how would *you* walk in it?"

This time it was Ariel who was stumped.

Ariel thought about Aviva.

And it would be a monstrous lie for Ariel to pretend that he didn't know what Reverend Taylor was feeling.

That he didn't know the panic of wondering whether you'd be leaving a loved one to an afterlife of torment.

Manishtana

It was a lot of why Ariel couldn't bear maintaining contact with Aviva after she'd gone OTD.

It was a fear he thought of constantly about his own theoretical future children. What he'd do if they ever decided that being black in a white Jewish world was just too much to be worth it, and to just leave it all behind.

There was a reason why black Jewish kids had a difficult time becoming black Jewish adults.

But that was religion and faith for you, wasn't it?

It had to be uncomfortable. And messy. It had to put you in places you'd rather not be, and make you think about things you'd rather not think about. It had to draw its lines, unyieldingly, and stick to them.

That's what gave it value.

Reverend Taylor and Rabbi Samson looked at one another, each one tugging on either side of a bond of mirrored ecclesiastical principles.

"I don't know," Ariel admitted, truthfully. "It probably wouldn't. I'd probably be disappointed with myself. I'd feel like I made a mistake somewhere in teaching or being a role model. I might put on a good show about things being his choice and his path, but I'd still secretly hope and, yes, pray, that he came back to my faith, just as much as he'd probably hope that I came over to his side, and that's the new way we'd love each other. But we *would* still love each other. *That* I *do* know. Because he'd still be my son. I'd still call him for his birthday. I'd still expect him to come visit me on mine. And yeah, I'd probably stew in my internal hypocrisy of preaching 'live and let live' for other people, but wanting him to live like me. I don't know if I would come to his wedding. Or if I'd like his wife. But I'd love his kids. I don't come from a family that celebrates Thanksgiving, but I would, just so we'd have a neutral ground to come together and celebrate life. Because he'd still be my son. Because love covers all offenses. Proverbs 10:12."

Reverend Taylor was silent for a long while, taking in the young, passionate, Jewish spiritual shepherd at his threshold.

He drew himself up, inhaling deeply, then exhaled just as intensely.

"What I believe and what I want are not the same thing, rabbi...They can't be. I wish to G'd that they were, but..."

Ariel nodded, a slow, sad nod.

ARIEL SAMSON: FREELANCE RABBI

And an unspokenness passed between the two clergymen.

Manishtana

The audience tittered as Ariel stood on stage, dressed in the 1989 Batman costume.

"Freelance Rabbi," Wes pondered aloud. "You seem a little different today. A little overdressed. What gives?"

"Nothing much, Wes. Oh! You mean the costume! Yeah, I'm just *really* excited for next week. I can't wait!"

"Next week? What happens next week?"

"What happens next week?! Oh, it's only *one of the most fun holidays on the Jewish calendar!* We've got alcohol, we've got costumes, we've got noisemakers, we've got noisemakers in costumes drinking alcohol—it's like Jewish carnival!"

"Oh *right*! I heard about this! Jewloween, right?"

"*Purim*, Wes."

"Yeah. Purimoween. So what is it, anyway?"

"Well, next Wednesday night marks the beginning of Purim, which is a minor Jewish holiday that's a little bit Halloween, a little bit Easter, and a little bit Mardi Gras all rolled into one. It celebrates the time when the Jewish people—who were living under Persian rule in conquered provinces from India to Ethiopia—escaped mass extermination 2,500 years ago."

278

"Yeek. Sounds pretty morbid."

"Yeah, well, you know how Jewish holidays go: They tried to kill us, G'd saved us, let's eat. You can catch the whole story in the Book of Esther. Which, by the way, we'll be reading as part of the holiday. In fact, you're supposed to get *so drunk* that you can't tell the name of the story's hero from the name of the story's villain!"

"That's amazing! That's also how I made it through *The Old Man and the Sea.* Any other traditions?"

"Well, we eat these funky three-sided, fruit-filled cookies called *hamantaschen,*"—"*or* oznei Haman," Ariel mentally amended—"hand out *shalach manot*, these little Easter-basket looking thingys full of food and booze,"—"*correctly called* mishloach manot," Ariel thought—"and we perform general comedic sketches or pranks called 'Purim *spiels.*' And, of course, there's the costumes."

"Well costumes sound fun! I always love a good costume party!"

"Oh, costumes *can* be fun, Wes. And they can also very *not* be. Actually, do you mind if I talk to the audience for a second?"

"Sure, by all means, go ahead."

Ariel stepped to the edge of the stage and a spotlight irised in on him. The audience giggled uneasily, not sure where this was going.

"Hi, my name is Rabbi Ariel Samson. You might know me on the show here as the Freelance Rabbi. Some of you might know me in real life as the spiritual leader of Congregation Ahavath Yisroel. But I would like to take just a moment and talk to you about costumes. The custom of dressing up for Purim probably derives from carnivals in medieval Europe, but since then it's taken on a deeper significance. Esther's name, for example, is related to the Hebrew word for 'hidden.' Esther conceals the fact that she's Jewish from King Ahaseurus. The name of G'd doesn't appear once in the Book of Esther, and Divine Providence is instead 'disguised' throughout the story as coincidence and fortutitous twists and turns. Almost nothing in the story is how it seems. And in commemoration of this, millions of Jews across the globe will dress up and 'hide' themselves, some drawing inspiration from biblical figures, and others from historical contexts, current events, and even pop culture characters. But one thing Jews should *not* do, is dress up like this—"

Manishtana

On the screen behind Ariel a Jewish elementary-school aged girl—with her eyes blurred out—stood beaming in a geisha costume.

"—or this—"

The girl was replaced with a shot of a *frum* family of seven with their faces obscured, crossing a busy Boro Park street, while dressed presumably as Native Americans.

"—and especially not *this*."

The family was replaced with the unblurred photo of a middle-aged man at a party, dressed in a shiny three-piece suit and tie, wearing a gold chain and slicked-back hair, holding a mic while slathered in brown facepaint.

The audience gasped.

"Hey!" Wes piped up. "Isn't that Republican Assemblyman Aryeh Rosenstern?"

"Yep," Ariel confirmed.

"Isn't he the one who took Mel Gibson to task about his anti-Semitic rant?"

"Indeed."

"And went after Tiger Wireless for slowing down its network in Jewish neighborhoods?"

"Mm-hm."

"And led the protests against Brooklyn College for hosting anti-Zionist writer Dalton Glass?"

"That's the one. And this is a picture from the Purim party he threw at his home last year."

"Wow. You think he'd know better."

"Well, in his defense, he's an adult man in New York City who didn't realize blackface was offensive."

The audience snickered and applauded at Ariel's deadpan delivery.

"Now look," Ariel continued, after the noise had died down. "I understand that some people might genuinely be unaware of how their costume might offend or impact people. But just because a depiction of a culture is so commonplace that you can't see how it would be offensive, doesn't mean that it actually isn't. And even *if* you fail to see the racist nature of these types of costumes, I'd like you to imagine for a moment a world in which there are black Jews, Asian Jews, Hispanic Jews, Jews from every country and culture...Oh wait, you *don't* need to imagine it, because that's the world we *live* in. And what better time to remember that than Purim? After all, the Book of Esther talks about the salvation of the Jewish communities that lived from 'India to Ethiopia,' not from 'Germany to Poland,' or from 'France to Portugal.' What message are you sending to Jews of Color when you show up in these costumes or in blackface? You're sending the message that our skins and our cultures are valuable only as 'a disguise' for your entertainment. We owe our fellow Jews, and fellow humans, better. We owe *ourselves* better. So next week, when you dress yourself, or your children, remind yourself that if it's a culture, then it's not a costume. Find an alternative that doesn't tread on someone else's identity. This Purim, let's celebrate with *hamantaschen*, not hate."

Manishtana

Wednesday, March 16, 2016
6/7 Adar II 5776

It had been Kalman's dilemma over the Chinese dress that had inspired Ariel to take a stand against the unnecessary inevitability of seeing a parody of himself sitting in the pews in *shul* for Purim.

The hashtags #HamantaschenNotHate and #HNH were trending topics on both Twitter and Instagram for two days straight, getting an unexpected viral boost from the strangest of places, and having the unintended side effect of rehashing old history.

Although, it wasn't *completely* unexpected that Assemblyman Rosenstern's racially insensitive gaffe from the year before was being dragged back into the spotlight.

That was half of why Ariel had chosen to include Rosenstern, as an example of how *not* to celebrate.

It had been an event that everyone vividly remembered, and Rosenstern was a high-profile enough figure that naysayers couldn't fix their mouths to say that Ariel was being "oversensitive" about blackface on Purim being something that happens, couldn't say that it was something they'd *never* seen, and couldn't say it was something only done by children in "good faith."

After all, this was *the* Assemblyman Aryeh Rosenstern, the Orthodox Jewish politician particularly well-known for demanding apologies for even the slightest zyklon-scented whiff of anti-Semitism.

In fact, not the month before Purim 2015, the good assemblyman had lambasted a controversial fashion designer for being seen out and about town in a black bowler and a black-and-white striped scarf, claiming that the choice of dress was a delibrate mockery of ultra-Orthodox Jews.

So surely, just a month later, when confronted with the charges that *his* choice of attire had been found to be offensive towards an oppressed minority, historically discriminated against with offensive imagery and stereotypes, undoubtedly the vociferous demander of apologies would offer a penance just as robust as those he himself demanded from those who slighted him and his.

Right?

"Hey, look, it's Purim and we wear costumes," Rosenstern had shrugged into the camera. "We've got people out here dressed like blacks, people dressed like Arabs, it's a costume! This year I was, I just wanted to dress up like one of those, y'know, those black preachers. Next year, I might even dress up like a gay! Is that okay? Can I do that? It's just fun for a holiday. If people are offended, I'm sorry they're offended, it's all in good fun, and that's all I can say."

That's a winner right there, folks.

The apology was ludicrously lackluster, and found itself followed by many impassioned cries from black New York community leaders for Rosenstern's resignation, which were summarily ignored.

Of course, this time around it was an election year, and the zombie resurrection of his terrible apology was likely the last thing the embattled Rosenstern needed, particularly having not too long ago engaged in a very public political brawl with fellow Orthodox Jewish politician—and former *Late Late* guest—City Councilman Jeffrey Grundman (whose office, incidentally, was doing its best to make sure that *Late Late's* "Hamantaschen not Hate" clip was circulating as widely as possible).

So it made perfect sense when, the Wednesday after the video dropped, a voicemail was left with Constitution Studios, concerning a certain late night TV show and its infamous "celebrity" rabbi.

"This is Assemblyman Aryeh Rosenstern," the gruff voice rumbled over speakerphone. "I'm trying to see if this is a Purim *spiel* or an actual campaign. Please call my office tomorrow, have a pleasant day."

"Wow," Ariel shook his head with eyebrows raised, leaning back in his chair.

He and Ellis were sitting hunched over her phone, listening to the voicemail in her office.

"It's probably not a good sign that he thinks this is some huge joke."

"That's really the least of my worries," Ellis frowned, concerned.

"What? What's the big deal? I'l make the call, we'll talk. Look, I'm a rabbi, he's trying to get re-elected, I'm sure we can iron whatever it is out."

Ellis gave Ariel a look.

"...What exactly do you know about Aryeh Rosenstern?"

Ariel shrugged.

"Orthodox Jewish politician. Total douche. Irritatingly conservative and right-wing. Ferociously anti-LGBTQI."

"That's it?"

"What else is there?"

Lots, Ariel.

Lots.

Aryeh Rosenstern was far more than the Google snippet of his Wikipedia page touting him as being an Orthodox Jewish assemblyman with a well-documented tenure of vocally opposing anti-Semitism, representing Brooklyn's 44th district since 1980.

True enough.

Rosenstern *had* undoubtedly established himself as one of the most influential Jewish politicians in New York—earning himself the nickname of "Chessmaster"—and finding himself with no end of political upstarts seeking to curry his favor, delivering pivotal support and the Orthodox Jewish voting bloc to candidates best suited to "send a message to President Obama."

But hidden in plain sight was the fact that the Machiavellian Rosenstern had come of age in New York politics in the mid-1970s, as a member of the League of Macabbees (LOM), an extremist network of Jewish vigilantes that considered themselves proud acolytes of Meir Kahane, the genocidally fanatical rabbi-turned-Israeli politician, who called for the ethnic cleansing of Palestinians and the establishment of a theocratic state of "Judea" in the West Bank.

Having spent some time personally mentored under Kahane's wing, Rosenstern's long and storied career included being heavily active in LOM and their activities of "protecting" [white] Jews living in black and Hispanic neighborhoods, being arraigned in federal court for tossing smoke bombs into several Jersey-area mosques, going on record as being in support of forming a group of intelligence professionals to assassinate Nazis and supporters of the Palestine Liberation Organization, and being an FBI person of interest in a string of eight bombings against Arab-American targets in New York, New Jersey, and Massachusetts—in which two men were killed and twelve were injured.

"So if you're on his radar," Ellis explained, her brows unfamiliarly knitted with worry. "I actually kinda hope he really *does* think this is some big joke. Guildencrantz is one thing, but... just...just be careful with this, okay?"

Ariel wordlessly nodded, never having seen Ellis so apprehensive before.

Manishtana

Thursday, March 17 2016
7/8 Adar II 5776

Ariel made the call the next day, just before his lunch break.

"Assemblyman Rosenstern? This is Rabbi Ariel Samson."

"The Freelance Rabbi guy, right?"

"Yes, that's right."

"Yes, well," the gruff voice on the other end of the phone jumped right in. "I'd just like to know why you didn't ask Aryeh Rosenstern to make a statement first? Maybe he had something he'd like to say?"

Ariel was confused for a moment.

He was sure the voice sounded the same as from the voicemail, and he was sure the person he was speaking with had already identified themselves as Rosenstern.

But perhaps he'd misheard, and he was just speaking to an office aide.

"Well," Ariel answered. "Last year Assemblyman Rosenstern already issued the statements he was going to make, and he said it was all he had to say. Why would anyone go back and ask him again now? Also, if he had something to say then why wouldn't he have said it yet? That would be *his* job to offer any new apologies, not anyone else's job to run after him for it."

"So your response this year is to try and bury him?"

"Well, #HamantaschennotHate isn't about 'Aryeh Rosenstern.' He isn't the problem. He's just a symptom, a teachable moment. This campaign is about *Purim*. It's about sensitivity not only concerning offending 'other' cultures, but also that those 'other' cultures can, and sometimes *do*, share the same religion being used as an excuse to offend them."

"I really don't see how my costume was offensive. That's just identity politics."

"I, what—Who am I speaking with?"

"Aryeh Rosenstern."

"Oh...kay, so, that's just really confusing when you switch back and forth like that to—"

"When does it become blackface?"

"What?"

"If I use brown paint is it still blackface?"

"What? *Yes*. It's still—"

"Isn't blackface when you use black shoe polish and white lips?"

"...No, that's not the only—What does—"

"It's only blackface if there are white parts and black parts," Rosenstern decided. "Covering your whole face in paint isn't blackface."

And then things got weirdly Talmudic, as if it happened once that David Duke, Richard Spencer, David Lane, Willie Lynch, and D.W. Griffith were reclining on a plantation in Mississippi, discussing racism all night:

"Blackface only includes covering from the forehead to the bottom of the chin, not the backs of the hands."

"If Mayor DeBlasio decided to dress up as his son, how is that offensive? He married a black. He has a black child. How is that offensive?"

"It can't be blackface unless a consensus of the blacks agrees."

It was such a dizzying array of arrogance, stupidity, and racism that Ariel wasn't even sure what life on Earth even was.

He was reeling like a white feminist discovering that Susan B. Anthony said she'd rather cut off her right arm before "I will ever work or demand the ballot for the Negro and not the woman."

(Yeah, she said that. To Frederick Douglass. Her black friend.)

"I see Grundman's been promoting this," Rosenstern continued his rambling. "Have any news outlets picked this up?"

"I—what? No," Ariel replied, still feeling as bewildered as if he brought a gun to a gunfight, but the other guy showed up throwing 5-lb gummi bears.

"See? You're just some angry nobody, and your little campaign is clearly just a smear job with no actual merit—wait, are you recording this? Is someone *else* recording this?"

"Ohh, how I wish."

"Well next time you try to come after me, try doing a better job. Because I'll chew you up and spit you out like a baby angel."

"What the hell does that even *me*—"

"Your campaign is a stupid waste of time. Goodbye."

Ariel took his phone down from his ear and stared at it, bemused and incredulous, just...just trying to figure out what the hell just happened there.

✡ ✡ ✡

"Ariel, did you hear me?"

"Hm? Sorry, what?"

"Can you watch my books? I'm going to the bathroom."

"Oh, sure."

It'd only been about a month since Ariel and Tamar's last date, but their Barnes and Nobles romantic excursions already seemed to have lost their luster. Things on the whole weren't really progressing or regressing, actually. In either direction. It sort of felt like they were on a treadmill that wasn't really going anywhere, but they had to keep at it otherwise they'd slip backwards.

Hell, things between Ariel and *Chani* were actually developing more, and they weren't even *in* a relationship.

Well, not a romantic one anyways.

But they'd definitely gotten closer as they worked on more and more collaborations together between Hillel and CAY.

They'd just finished meeting about an hour ago actually, working out the logistics for next week's Hillel/CAY Purim extravaganza, when Ariel realized he was running late for his date with Tamar.

"It's ok!" Chani had replied with suspiciously false brightness, almost as if she were hiding disappointment. "I can just write up the rest and email it to you later. Or—actually, just take my number and call me whenever your date's over. I'll be up all night anyway."

We see what you did there Chani. We see what you did there. Game recognize game.

But honestly, what was really taking a toll on Ariel and Tamar's whatever-it-was, was the Kalman situation.

Kalman and Tamar had been friends since childhood, and she'd never really taken to Dassi. So how much had she known about Kalman and Cate? Were there more *besides* Cate? Had Tamar ever been one of them?

Show me your friends and I'll tell you who you are, the saying went, so while Ariel intellectually knew those questions were crazy people talk, it didn't keep his imagination from running amok and giving Tamar the serious sideeye.

That, combined with his earlier, mind-numbing conversation with Rosenstern, and Ariel was just suddenly very conscious about about being out and about with Tamar.

And how it looked.

Especially as he was getting recognized more and more often.

He heard loud laughter and looked up to see a group of black girls descend on the empty table two rows away.

Ariel recognized Rashida and Kayyriah from that night at the cornerstore, and he froze.

Shit. What where they doing *here*?

This is *exactly* what he needed. To be caught out with Tamar by *these* guys. Hanging out on a date with a white girl.

Wait, "caught"?

Well. That was certainly interesting, Ariel's internal monologue.

But Ariel was too preoccupied—tilting his face away and hiding it behind his hand, hoping the girls wouldn't notice him—to catch the interesting wording of his thoughts.

At that moment, Tamar returned from the restroom, smiling as she sat down across from Ariel, and oblivious to the pack behind her.

Wait, "pack"?

Well. That was certainly interesting, Ariel's internal monologue.

"So hey," Tamar began, stretching her hand out to touch Ariel's, only for him to snatch it back. She quickly drew her back too, startled.

"Sorry!" Ariel blurted out. "Just caught me off guard. Um. Can we, um, you wanna go somewhere else right now? It's nice out, let's go walking or something."

"Oh..okay," Tamar replied, still a touch frazzled. "Sure."

"Great!" he exclaimed, gathering up the books they'd collected, and Tamar reached to help. "No, it's cool, I've got them. I'll, actually, I'll just put these back for the both of us and meet you downstairs by the exit."

"I—alright..."

"Awesome."

✡ ✡ ✡

"Ariel, are you...Are you embarrassed to be with me?"

"What? *Embarrassed?* No, why would you, why would you say that?"

It was pretty obvious why Tamar would say that, Ariel.

She'd been feeling the disconnect between them, too.

The uneasy energy radiating off of Ariel that had been steadily magnifying since they'd first met, with a sudden swell in the past week that she could even read through his terse texts and G-chat messages.

And, of course, if their trip to the bookstore just now hadn't tipped Tamar off, the walk to the park definitely had, with Ariel hovering in that weird grey area of walking just too close to be strangers, but with just enough distance to plausibly deny that they were together. Executing a cough or sneeze always just a millisecond before each attempt Tamar made to hook her fingers into his, with such consistent precision that she was convinced he had to be watching her in his periphery.

They were sitting on a park bench under a leafy canopy of trees now, out of sight of passers-by, and only the occasional biker zooming past. And so now, finally, they were sitting acceptably close enough for people who may or may not have been dating.

But no, he wasn't "embarrassed" to be seen with her.

Just...y'know...Just...

"Well, *are* you?"

"I already said no, Tamar," Ariel shot back, more irritated than he meant to be. "Why are you still on this?"

"I just...it feels like I'm sitting on your doorstep, Ariel. It feels like I'm sitting on your doorstep, and I can hear you on the other side saying you'll be there in a minute. But the minute never comes, and I'm still outside. And you never actually say that you'll let me in. Like you could plausibly deny you'd ever invited me if you wanted to. If you needed to."

"What do you mean *'If I needed to?'*"

"You tell me, Ariel."

"Maybe I'm trying to be more careful in my relationships?" he snapped back defensively. "I *was* engaged once. So that could be a thing, too. Me being careful."

"I was *married* once, Ariel," she reminded him.

Ariel didn't have a response to that.

"So...are you?"

"Am I what?'

"Just 'being careful.'"

"I could be."

"But *are* you?"

"I-I-I don't know! Are you—are *you* just experimenting?" Ariel lashed out, frantic, his voice rising.

"Am I *experimenting*? Where did that—Is *that* what you think this is?"

"*Pfft*, I dunno. *Is* it?" he flared, irrationally, helpless against his mind armoring itself unbidden against reason and patience, barreling forward like a freight train with no breaks. "Like, do you even *have* any other black friends? Maybe I'm just a, a field trip for you, or, or a clinical case study or something!"

"You're not the only black guy I've dated, Ariel."

"I, well, I, I'm—" Ariel stammered.

"...You don't want this fight...do you?"

It was phrased like a question. A quiet, melancholy question.

But Tamar pronounced it with the certainty of knowing its answer. That it was a matter of definite fact

She didn't mean the fight they were having now. She meant the future fight, the every day fight of being an interracial couple, of the two of you against the world and society, and sometimes each other, clinging tenuously to a love that might not be enough to keep you together.

Manishtana

Ariel turned to look at her. Or seemed to look at her. He was really just focusing on the space between her eyes, suddenly finding it just as awkward and uneasy and inappropriately intimate to make eye contact with her, the same way he generally hated making eye contact with everyone else.

Did he want this fight?

Was this, was him and Tamar, something he wanted to fight for?

And was it something he wanted to fight for on top of all the other things he *already* had to fight for?

Did he want to fight his black community for being a "sellout" as a Jew *and* for dating, and maybe eventually marrying, a white girl? Did he want to fight his Jewish community invalidating his every accomplishment as being mere means to gain proximity to whiteness? Did he want to spend his life as an other in Tamar's world? Being a perpetual ambassador for every black person to have ever existed? Did he want to deal with a bigoted uncle's comments every other Shabbat meal? Did he want to play *"Guess Who's Coming To Seder?"* with *his* family?

Did he want this fight?

Did he want to deal with even more ignorance than he already had a heaping serving of on his plate?

American history was not the kindest sun to shine on interracial relationships, and while among the Jewish community he wasn't exactly going to end up an Emmet Till, for too many Jews that kind of racist ideology was *emet* still.

Or maybe he *would* end up an Emmet Till.

Wasn't that Elliot Rodger's gripe?

Why he'd terrorized Isla Vista, killing six people and then himself? Hadn't his rambling manifesto screamed *"How could an inferior, ugly black boy be able to get a white girl and not me?"*

"I have to do it. You rape our women and you're taking over."

Weren't those Dylan Roof's words before he'd massacred nine African Americans at the Emanuel African Methodist Episcopal Church?

It wasn't like unhinged characters were solely the purview of non-Jews (Levi Aron), or that shooting up places of worship was solely a Christian phenomenon (Baruch Goldstein).

What was stopping a jealous wacko from shooting up CAY?

Or what if, one fine day, he and Tamar got into a heated argument in public?

There'd be a fair enough chance of the cops being called, and in the eyes of the police, being an unarmed black man was apparently reason enough to shoot, let alone in the name of protecting the virtue and safety of white women.

Yes, "white women."

Because Tamar read as white.

When people called the cops, they weren't going to first consult a sociologist to ask Tamar if she "identified" as white or with the cultural narrative of colonialism. When the cops came, they weren't going to engage in a thought exercise of whether or not she was "really" white in light of the views of white supremacists, or take into account white Jews being "newly" or "provisionally" white or not.

And for damn sure, no one would ponder if Ariel was "black" or "black-passing" since he was really Jewish.

Nope, it'd be a Black Guy getting aggressive towards a White Woman. And how would that really end?

Did he want this fight?

The one with himself? The one where he wondered if he was copping out or abandoning a piece of himself? Wondered if he'd be making some implicit admission that white women were more attractive than black women? Wondered if he was going to lose his blackness somehow, have it drip away until he was left a shell completely neutered of it? Would he become a human blackface? Did he want to wrestle with his love for women who walked in their power like his mother and sister and grandmother, to jeopardize their rejection by yearning after their white and possibly fetishizing opposite numbers?

He looked at Tamar, just briefly took in the trepidation of the inevitable on her face, her look not exactly pleading, but...no.

No.

He didn't need to have this fight. He didn't need to have any fight except the one he wanted. And the fight he wanted was to find a black Jewish Orthodox partner.

Look, whatever, it wasn't prejudiced to want to pass on your cultural heritage to your children, and it wasn't biased to want a romantic partner who understood what it's like to experience the same kind of oppression that you do, and it wasn't racist to want the religiously observant household that you believed to be your truth.

Part and parcel of being black or being Jewish in America—or anywhere—was to constantly serve as the portal into some arcane, vilified world that "normal society" often saw as dangerous, primitive, or both.

It was a burden of education and "teachable moments" that lurked at school, at work, on the train, and—for a Jew of Color—in the synagogues and sacred places that the "right" looking Jews could access unmolested, and in the ethnic communal spaces that their fellow skinfolk could enter with nary a second glance.

And it'd be nice to, y'know, not have to be "on call" in the intimacy of his marriage, too.

He faced enough micro-aggressions throughout his day to not want to—or *have* to—deal with them in his own relationship while navigating the disconnect trying to explain why it was necessary for the children to partake in certain religious practices, or why it was important for his wife to share certain cultural experiences with his, or why it wasn't cool for his wife to smear fetishizing stereotypes all over him in the bedroom, regardless of how good that scented oil smelled.

Catholics could only want to marry Catholics, Baptists could only want to marry Baptists, and Mormons could only want to marry Mormons all day and night.

But a Jew only wanting to marry a Jew?

Now *that* was an elitist racist.

Did Tyler Perry movies ever ask *"Why does he have to be a good Christian man, though?"*

And then there was the Jewish camp. The bastion of white Ashkenormativity. The one that charged him with looking for reasons to be marginalized so he could feel like a special snowflake.

"What does it matter? A Jew is a Jew is a Jew! Judaism doesn't care what color you are!"

Which is all well and good and theoretically true. In a vacuum.

But Ariel didn't live in Theoretica off the coast of Idealia en la Vacuum. He lived in America, the land of Race I Am—America's anagram, if you were wondering—where your race *absolutely* dictates your experience, regardless of your religion. The land where white Jews only seemed to remember that they weren't "really" white when other *whiter* white people were around.

294

"Well maybe you shouldn't let the racist actions of other people dictate who you decide to be with."

Just...no.

Because, stop.

This wasn't a high-school required reading novel about star-crossed lovers. This wasn't *Romeo and Juliet* or *Titanic* or *Gatsby*. This was his *life*. Also, spoiler alert: Leonardo DiCaprio died in all three of those movies, so that should probably tell you something.

Ariel knew what he wanted. He wanted black. He wanted Jewish. He wanted Orthodox. He wanted to come home to the wholeness of his experience as he saw it.

Did he want this fight?

"No," he said, finally, softly, his eyes still locked with her eyes. "I don't. I'm sorry."

The sigh was resigned and heartbroken, signaling the end.

It escaped quietly, its sound unnoticed, the slumping of Tamar's shoulders being the only indication of its coming or going.

And that was the moment she gave up.

Whether on Ariel's gender or race was a larger question, but in that moment, definitely on the man himself, at least. Her milky features buckled just slightly, and she lowered her head, biting her lips and nodding wordlessly.

Then a mirthless snort burst out, almost a sob, and she chuckled, still shaking her head.

"Serves me right, I guess," she said with a rueful smirk.

And here it was, Ariel thought. The shoe dropping. The *"I'm better than you and this is the thanks I get"* shoe.

"The other black guy I dated? He was Jewish, too," Tamar continued, staring at her hands in her lap. "But it was...complicated. No. No *I* made things complicated. Like, I literally looked both ways before kissing him in public, like, what the hell? *Why?* Was I was crossing the street or something?" she shook her head at herself, with an embarrassed laugh. Ariel stayed silent. She was clearly more just talking out loud, and this wasn't nearly the shoe he was expecting.

"And I didn't even realize how hurtful I was being when I did that. I was just in my own head and not wanting people to stare or judge, or for it to get back to my father before I was ready to tell him myself. Before I figured out *how* I was going to tell him myself. Bottom line, I was just thinking about protecting myself. I wasn't a particularly good partner. I guess I was trying to prove how much I didn't care about other people watching, or like I wasn't subconsciously aware of how dark he was and how fair I was everytime with touched. But I wasn't really getting him. Or hearing him. He wanted me to get angry with him about the same things and I just...wasn't."

She looked up at Ariel, her eyes starting to water.

"He told me once 'You might love me, Tamar. But you don't love my race.' And that hurt. A lot. I think mostly because back then, it was true. I didn't want that fight. And so we just sorta broke up. And I guess I know what that feels like now. When someone doesn't want to fight for you..." she sniffled and wiped away a tear rolling down her cheek with the back of her hand. "Fucking suuuucks," she laughed, self-consciously.

Ariel gave a cringing shrug, letting Tamar's awkward laughter break the tension.

"Maybe you should, I dunno, talk to him?" he advised, gingerly.

"Yeah. Maybe I should," she mulled over. "Yeah. And apologize. For everything," she looked to Ariel again. "I guess...I guess this time around, with you, I wanted to be that better partner. But apparently I've got some **teshuva** to do first. Because if I hurt him anywhere near as bad as this feels right now, then I owe him a huge apology."

"I'm sorry."

"Me too."

"No, *really*. I'm—"

Tamar put her hand to Ariel's lips.

"It's ok. I have to go anyway. I have a test to study for anyway," Tamar said, rising up from the bench with a sad half-smile. "Take care of yourself, Ariel."

"I...You too, Tamar."

And then she was gone.

And they were done.

The stars began to shimmer into existence, and a long, slow, somber sigh escaped Ariel's lips, his eyes remaining fixed on the empty grassy path Tamar had fled down, growing darker and darker as night descended like molasses.

ARIEL SAMSON: FREELANCE RABBI

There are just some key phrases that black people use when they are about to hit their limit. Cultural little red flags—usually telegraphed with silent rocking and soft laughter—that the knowledgeable can spot from miles away.

For guys, it might be along the lines of *"Ay look, y'know what?"* or *"I just find it funny how..."* or *"First of all..."*

The ladies have their pick of *"So what you're not gonna do is..."* or *"Let me not say nothing"* or *"I *clap* Am *clap* Not *clap* The *clap* One *clap*."*

And black parents of either gender have the classics of *"Oh, so you grown now?"* and *"You better fix your face"* with the odd *"Oh, you must think I'm Bobo the Fool"* or *"Keep talking like that, you won't wake up tomorrow. You'll come to."*

These were the lines whose subsequent actions always caught white people off-guard.

Because they never really seemed to grasp the fact that every black person has the innate power to reach through the Veil and summon their gangsta thuglife doppelganger.

No matter how Ivy League, how Uncle Tom, how CEO, or how Barack Obama, all black people have the power to reach down into the primordial well of blackity blackness and go *from "Salutations and good day to you, sir"* to *"I wish a motherfucker* would*"* at nary the drop of a maroon Kangol.

Like, just try to imagine some Upper West Side old-money trust fund baby trying to tap into some inner redneck or frontiersman or something, talking about "over yonder" and "tanning hides."

Nope, not gonna happen.

That's why they always end up having to hire goons to take care of things for them when they're in the shit.

Of course, when white people on occasion *do* try to pull off the "white-collar badass" bit, they end up going too far and channeling, like, Beowulf or something. All kinds of Hannibal Lecter eating people's livers and putting their heads on spikes nonsense.

It's like, be easy, white people. You're doing too much.

You don't see us going all the way back to blowdarting you in the face and going all Anyoto Aniota on you, right?

Just chill.

At any rate, between the Kalman/Cate situation, learning Tractate Blackface with Rosenstern, and the not-breakup of his not-relationship with Tamar, recent events had brought Ariel to the *"I see niggas wanna* try *me today"* stage in his relationship with his Jews. (Although it was probably reciprocal in Tamar's case.)

Either way, it was time for some browner company, so Jumaane'd decided—given the particularly racial inflections of Ariel's current anxiety—that what could be more cathartic than bowling, a game where the entire point was to take a huge black ball and hurl it at a dozen or so white pins with red necks?

"Yo man," Ariel sighed in relief. "Thanks for coming to hang out with me tonight. I mean, with all the stuff at work and—"

"It's not even a thing, man," Jumaane waved it away. "Besides, it's been a minute since just the two of us hung out."

"Well," Ariel needled. "It can't go any worse than it went last time."

Jumaane winced, and Ariel laughed.

The last time they'd hung, it'd been a disaster. Jumaane'd invited Ariel out to a Black Student Union alumni get together.

Although, since graduating, one of the more vocal members had become quite the "conscious" brother.

And by "conscious," I don't mean the *"Garret A Morgan was the African-American inventor who created the traffic light and the gas mask"* kinda conscious.

I mean the *"We wuz kangz"* and spewing inane ludicrosity like "overstand" and "innerstand" and spelling the possessive pronoun "I" as "e-y-e" kinda conscious.

He was one of those leadership adjacent hanger-ons in the background who was using the currency of seniority to substitute for leadership. Kinda like Jesse Jackson and Al Sharpton.

"My nigga," Brotha Hotep insisted. "You can *not* be gay and conscious. Homosexuality isn't even an African *concept*. *Europeans* imported it in. The Greeks? The Romans? Just look at their mythology...! Zeus running around with Ganymede, Hercules and Iolaus and Philoctetes and doing other gay shit. You won't find none of that faggotry in Kemetism, because that's the *real* shit."

"Yo," Jumaane had spoken up. "You're not making any kind of sense right now."

"Like, forget about offensive, that's not even *factual*," Ariel added. He never liked this guy back in college anyway. "Egyptian mythology is *literally* dripping with homosexuality. You've got Atum who creates gods by finishing in his own mouth and spitting it out. You've got Set trying to sleep with Horus in a power play, but then Horus outsmarts Set and feeds him lettuce with his secret sauce salad dressing. Hell, the whole story behind the 'Eye of Horus' symbol is about Horus regaining the strength of his eye that Set shot off in, so I don't even know what you *think* you're talking about."

"Of *course*, the fake-ass Jew had to chime in," Brotha Hotep rolled his eyes. "You know what your problem is? You need to stop running after them white Jews who are never gonna accept you and get back to your African heritage. Quit messing with that garbage European plagiarism, cuz that's why y'all ain't got no myths or legends except that golem bullshit made up some white German man, because your whole shit is *already* fake."

"Wow, that's not even a *little* bit true. Yeah, we got the golem. And we have the Leviathan, king of the sea, the Ziz, king of the birds, and the Behemoth, king of the beasts. There's the immortal city of Luz, the Unfinished Corner of Creation, inhabited by earthquakes, winds, and demons. The Great Lion and Great Deer of the Forest of Bei Ilai. The River Sambatyon, where the sons and daughters of Moses live. There's Ornasis, King Solomon's vampire. Asmodeus, king of the demons. Hell, we even have a shoutout back to the Bible and hundreds of stories of Elijah the Prophet coming back to Earth to help people in disguise all the time. So no, I don't need to 'get back' to my African heritage, I—"

"Jumaane, come get your pet Jew-boy over here. This is black mens talk happening right here."

"Woooooow, *forreal*? His pet Jew? Ay look, y'know what? I've been holding my peace all night. Hell, I've been holding my piece all through college, cuz you're Patrick's peoples and I wasn't tryna mess up his friendships. But look, I dunno what beef you had with me back *then*, but we all grown-ass *now*, and obviously somewhere in your life—your boss, your landlord, whatever—somewhere in your life there's some white Jew who rapes you on a frequent basis, but you're not saying anything to 'massa,' but then you see *my* black Jewish ass and all of a sudden you got balls to pop off and tell this Jew about himself? I'm not impressed by your bitch-assery. Aight?"

Needless to say, things took a sharply physical downturn from there.

"Yeah," Jumaane shook his head, remembering as he tied his rental shoes. "That was a hot mess. But hey, you don't get to say nothing. You *willingly* go be part of a community where not everyone isn't convinced that you're not cursed, so..."

"Well that's different. That's because *G'd* said I have to be there."

"Said every slave owner ever."

"Ugh, really? Are we really doing this?"

"Nope. Just saying you've clearly got lowered expectations. I'm just not sure for which group."

"Y'know, I never really noticed until just now how much you and Colin are just different *types* of smug."

"I'm almost offended. That's like saying an empty jar and a jar of pickles are different kinds of the same thing."

"That's almost fair enough."

"Just get ready to get your ass kicked, Gutterball King."

"Yeah, keep dreaming, son."

✡ ✡ ✡

"I'm really starting to think I'm just objectively bad at anything physical," Ariel grimaced, beholding a whopping score of a whole 83 points.

"Hi, welcome to the past eight years of me knowing you and probably all twenty of the years before that."

"So, the entirety of my life, essentially."

"Sounds legit," Jumaane shrugged, sitting pretty on a respectable 187.

"In more ways than one," Ariel snorted.

"Speaking of, what's the deal with you and Ellis? Haven't heard much out of you on the loverly front."

Hah. Funny.

Well, Tamar and Ariel hadn't talked since Thursday, and they were both kinda content to let their friendship just fade away and die its natural heat death.

And as for the elusive, alluring Ellis? Well...

"Nothing."

"*Nothing?*"

"Nothing."

Jumaane sighed deeply, put his beer down, then turned to Ariel.

"Ariel. I've known you a long time. And I love you like a little brother. And I mean this with all the constructivity in the world: You are a force to be reckoned with. With a literary talent that comes far and few between. You have an insane drive against legitimately intimidating odds, the likes of which movies about white men on the frontier get written about. Your intelligence is eclectic and very nearly all encompassing, except maybe when it comes to yourself. You're clearly an amazing and inspiring clergyman. But when it comes to women, *figure your shit the* fuck *out*. With everything I just listed, there is *absolutely no reason* why I should be having the *same* conversations about the *same* dilemmas with '2016 post-college, post-grad school, post-rabbinical school, leads a congregation, currently generally viral semi-famous figure' Ariel as I did with '2008 sophomore in college ass, gets purple splotches on his body because he's allergic to coconut but drinks coconut rum, anyway' Ariel."

Ariel was stunned into silence by Jumaane's intensity.

Bursts like that were so far and few in-between, and usually directed at people who were not Ariel.

"I..." he started. "I..."

"Like, I really don't see how you've just been letting Ellis get away," Jumaane continued fuming in well-meaning rage. "You work together at the station. Then you go to lunch together. Then you work together some more. And then when you're *off* work, you're doing *more* work together for your synagogue. Do you literally not see that you guys spend so much time with just each other that you're practically a married couple? Like, I've *never* seen you so happy as when you're answering Ellis' bullshit texts about work talking about nothing."

"Ok, well, maybe I'm, just—I mean, I like that she texts, because I hate the—"

"Because you hate the phone. I *know*. We *all* know. But if you're expecting me to believe that you get that goofy-ass smile on your face just because she doesn't do what you think is insipid small talk, then—"

"I don't *think* it's insipid, it *is* insipid. You're not calling me to ask about everything about my life, you're calling me to borrow my, my starship or whatever. So just get right to asking me about that then. I *promise* you I won't be offended by you *not* wasting my time."

"Your starship. That's the first thing that jumped into your mind for that example. An entire Federation starship."

"Look, it just, it just popped in there, okay?"

"It just popped in there? You sure it didn't *beam* in?"

"*'I do not believe this was a fair test of my command abilities.'*"

"*'A no-win scenario is a possibility every commander may face,'*" Jumaane shot back. "*Everyone* can quote *Wrath of Khan*, Ariel. Calm down."

"So it see—"

"What did you like about Gabrielle?"

"What?"

"What did you like about Gabrielle?" Jumaane repeated. "And Christina. And Dana."

"What'd I—I dunno...I liked how Gabrielle made me feel like a kid again, without any grown-up hangups. I...I liked how driven and focused Christina was, and how I got more of my shit together just being in her orbit. And Dana, I just...I liked how she was smart. And funny. And had goals and...and she just made you want to become the man you want to be, y'know? Just—"

"Alright. So what do you like about Ellis?"

"What do I like about Ellis? She...I dunno. I just do. She's just cool. I just...Y'know—Anyway what's your point?"

"*'Love that is dependent on a specific cause, when that cause is gone, the love is gone. But if it does not depend on a specific cause, it will never cease.'* Isn't that one of your guys?"

"Ethics of the Fathers. Chapter 5, verse 19," Ariel squinted at Jumaane. "Did you just outJew me?"

"Or maybe you Jew so well that it's rubbed off," Jumaane shrugged blithely. "Perhaps I'm just your kindly magical gentile."

"Well, where are you for the rest of my life then?"

"What do you mean?"

"What do I mean," Ariel chuckled mirthlessly. "It's just...I see so many people who seem to just get everything right from the very beginning. Any given second they're two steps ahead, y'know? And I just feel like I'm treading water the whole time, and I just wanna, wanna run to one of those people and just shake them, like, *'How the* fuck *do you do that?!'* Y'know?"

"Well, firstly, they probably don't. You're just seeing the outside. I'm pretty sure if there were *so* many people with their lives *that* together, then we'd be living in a very different world. Secondly, hate to be blunt, but they're also probably not autistic."

"They're probably not—wait, what? What does that have to do with anything?"

Ariel looked at Jumaane, confused as a kale and cheddar salad on a black Thanksgiving table.

Jumaane's eyes began to narrow, screeched to a halt mid-squint, then widened just as quickly. Because it dawned on Jumaane that Ariel had absolutely no clue.

"...Wait, you seriously don't know?" Jumaane asked, incredulous, reluctantly and inadvisedly using his bachelor's in psychology and impending MSW to diagnose his friend.

"Know, *what?*"

"Nigga. You have Asperger's."

"I...what?"

"Well, they don't call it that anymore, so I guess technically you have high-functioning autism spectrum disorder."

"The fuck are you talking about? People with Aspberger's are, like, *weird*, man. I definitely don't have Aspberger's."

"Yeah, dude. You seriously do."

Manishtana

"How?"

"Well, firstly, you're pedantic."

"I'm not pedantic. I just happen to value specificity," Ariel defended himself, being pedantic.

"My bad. I guess that part of the autistic diagnosis isn't my forte," Jumaane baited, deliberately pronouncing the word as "fortay."

"Fort! If you are describing something you have proficiency in then it is pronounced as your *'fort'*. It is *not* pronounced 'fortay,'" Ariel barreled on, unable to stop himself. "'Fortay' is a *musical* term that means to play the piece louder than the rest. It's *simple* grammar. Like, 'irregardless' is not a word. Neither is 'conversate.' Stop using 'literally' to mean 'figuratively' and 'I ain't' is actually grammatically correct. *'She* ain't?' *'They* ain't?' *That's* wrong. But *'I ain't'* is the first person negative conjugation of the verb 'to be' and is the contraction of 'I am not.' She *isn't.* They *aren't...I* ain't."

"Secondly," Jumaane continued coolly. "You rely heavily on rules and following them to the letter."

"What does *that* prove? I'm an English major! It's *literally* what I went to school for!"

"And how about the rest of your life? Like, I remember you pretty much flipping out during that one road trip we made that you were gonna miss afternoon services."

"Gee, sorry I'm Orthodox and actually follow all the rules," Ariel shot back defensively.

"Well that's probably how you've gone so long undiagnosed, because you've just blended in. You're an English major, so having grammatical pet peeves and a pre-occupation with the precise meanings of words is understandable. You're an Orthodox Jew, so being beholden to ritualized schedules is something that all religious people get poked at for. And becoming a rabbi likely disguised your narrow Aspberger's concern for book learning and formal rules. But then there's also your obsessive knowledge bases and consuming interests in specific subjects. Which, also, you've managed to constructively mask."

"What are you talking about?"

"What does...I dunno, Psalms 176:2 say?"

"There's only 150 chapters in Psalms."

"Fine. Psalms 79:1, then."

"'A psalm of Asaph. O G'd, the heathen are come into Thine inheritance, they have defiled Thy holy temple, they have made Jerusalem into heaps.'"

'When is the second appearance of Superman's electric costume?"

"*JLA*, issue 5 in the Morrision/Porter run that also introduces Tomorrow Woman, who dies in the same issue until her brief return in *Hourman* issue 2. Congratulations, you've just proved I'm a biblical scholar with a penchant for comic books."

"Yeah, you're a little bit more than that, Rain Man."

"Wow, that's really—look, I'm not even on that level. It's not my fault I have a photographic memory."

"Ariel, *no one* has a photographic memory. *Nobody*. What they're thinking of is an *eidetic* memory—"

"Fine. I have that then."

"—which only occurs in between 2-15% of children and generally not at *all* in adults. And when it *does* happen it creates a mental image that only lasts for a few *minutes*. Not days. Or years...But sorry, I didn't mean to rile you up. What's the line? *'If we shadows have offended/Think but this, and all is mended...*something something *'If we be friends/Let us make amends ...'*"

"'If we shadows have offended/Think but this, and all is mended/That you have but slumber'd here/While these visions did appear/And this weak and idle theme/No more yielding but a dream/Gentles, do not reprehend/if you pardon, we will mend/And, as I am an honest Puck/If we have unearned luck/Now to 'scape the serpent's tongue/We will make amends ere long/Else the Puck a liar call/So, good night unto you all/Give me your hands, if we be friends/And Robin shall restore amends,'* Ariel finished in a mixture of exasperation and resignation. "...shit."

"Yeah, see? Usually that kind of memory can hinder social skills. You just happened to luck out and be born an English major geek in a religious learning culture where all of your Aspberger's skills came in extremely handy."

"...Alright," Ariel said forlornly. "I'll bite. I don't agree, but I'll bite. What's the rest?"

The list got longer.

Lack of eye contact. Being late causing extreme stress. Tendency to be overly naïve, gullible, and extremely trusting.

Dogmatic.

Manishtana

An unusual hypersensitivity to textures. Being terrified of talking on the phone. Feeling drained in social situations and needing to retreat.

A very select collection of very few friends, and struggling with social reciprocity.

"And," Jumaane finished. "Don't even insult my intelligence by denying the depression. I've known you too long for that. You seriously didn't notice *any* of this?"

"I...thought it was normal and that life was just weird," Ariel mumbled.

"Well both of those are true," Jumaane conceded. "But now that I know you had no clue about your autism, your romantic life makes *so* much more sense to me now."

"Well please, doctor, enlighten me."

"Change resistance and boredom. The second you detect an approaching change in the relationship, you shut down and you turn off. You fall for people and they become this idealistic fixation in your mind, and when they begin to change—simply as the result of being in a relationship—you don't know how to handle it, and you try to pressure them back into being the person you first met. But *you*, you sly creature, you pick people who necessarily *have* to change for there to be the happy ending you want in your head. And so you self-sabotage. You pick the girls who aren't the thing you're looking for, and then when they start to take steps towards *becoming* that thing, you try to change them back into who you met *and* simultaneously start immediately judging them on your impossibly high standards of what you want the end result of that change to look like. Gabrielle was stupid, she was never going to be smart enough for you. Christina was super-Christian, and Dana just wasn't that interested in being Jewish, so neither were ever gonna be Jewish enough for you. But there you were in those relationships, slowly feeling more and more miserable because— with your autisitic inability to genuinely empathize—you felt that they wanted too much. Too much contact, too much communication, too much emotion. And it felt really draining and boring. And now here's Ellis, kicking all of your asses in all of the ways and you don't know what to do. Because *this* time you might actually succeed, because she's *exactly* what you've been saying you wanted in a partner this entire time, and that scares you...So what's your move gonna be?"

ARIEL SAMSON: FREELANCE RABBI

Ariel sat staring at his empty bottle as Jumaane dressed him down. Almost like he was watching his life flash in front of his eyes, seeing all his mistakes simultaneously amplified and absolved all at once. Sitting there in silence of Jumaane was done, Ariel felt his stomach tying in alternating knots of regret and relief that, if nothing else, was making him feel extremely gassy.

"This...," he said finally. "Is a lot to take in all at once...I'm, I'm gonna go get something from the bar..."

✡ ✡ ✡

Ariel ordered a Jack and coke at the bar, because whoa.

So far tonight's outing had proven to be a lot less decompression and a lot more introspection than he'd been anticipating.

Like, having his entire cognitive perception of himself kicked out from under him and shattered like a glass Lego castle wasn't quite what he'd been asking for when he'd texted Jumaane if he was free to hang tonight.

Ariel absentmindedly swirled the sweetened whiskey in his glass, listening to the clinking of the ice cubes, and allowing himself to escape into the hypnotic refuge of the vortex gently spinning in his drink. It was a lot more relaxing to him than drinking it would've been.

In fact, now that he thought about it, it'd always been the motions and rituals around the act of drinking that Ariel had found more appealing than the actual alcohol involved.

He let the drink settle, pondering how much of that epiphany was owed to his newly-realized autism, as carbonated bubbles wriggled beneath the weight of unyielding chunks of ice before escaping and shooting to freedom at the top of the glass.

It probably wasn't a metaphor for his life, but it totally could've been, right?

Ariel brought the drink to his lips—after all, part of the motions of drinking was actually drinking—and sipped, letting it sit in his mouth, savoring it for a moment, closing his eyes and dwelling on the flavor, before swallowing. It wasn't really the alcohol content that brought the tiny smile to his face—although it *was* a strongly made drink—but the completion of the action tree that gave him the satisfaction.

Maแishtana

Almost on autopilot, he started swirling his glass again, because life was weird and strange.

"Heey, whassup!" the bartender strolled on over, greeting Ariel with a broad smile like he recognized him. "Jay's friend, right?"

"Who?"

"Jay's friend," the bartender repeated. "You know Jay, right?"

"...Maybe by face...? What's his last name?"

"Her."

"Welp," Ariel laughed. "I guess that's a no."

"Oh wow, sorry. You just look so familiar though. Name's Clemente," he introduced himself, also laughing, and extended a hand.

"Ariel," said Ariel, shaking the other man's hand.

"Oh wait! You're that dude with the show! The rabbi dude!"

"Yep that's me."

"*That's* where I know you from! I *knew* you looked familiar. Me and my wife watch it all the time. That's gotta be a hard deal, bruh. Like, it never ends, right?"

"Yeah, pretty much," Ariel admitted, taking another gulp of his drink. "If it's not one side, it's the other."

"I hear you. So what brings you in here?"

"Just...Things in life have just been really crazy lately. Needed a little change of pace."

"I got you, I got you. Ah, man, don't worry about any of it. Everything blows over."

"So I keep hearing."

"Yeah man, you'll see," Clemente shrugged. "Don't even stress yourself out about it. See me, I don't bother about nobody. Blacks, Whites, Jews, Christians, whatever, we're all people. Like, me right? I'm Puerto Rican, but my Mom looks white and my dad looks Black, y'know? I was raised Catholic, but I'm a practicing Protestant. And my best friend is a Jew."

"Really."

"Yeah," the bartender proudly pointed to the gold crucifix hanging around his neck. "Jesus!"

Ariel snorted.

"See?" Clemente grinned. "None of that stuff really even matters. And I tell you, my wife is the same way. Hold on. Vee! *Vee!*" he yelled at another bartender at the far end of the bar, a chestnut-brown-skinned woman with short-cropped hair, standing with her back to them and stretching out kinks in her neck. "That's my wife," he explained to Ariel.

At hearing her name, Vee turned in response, wearing a smile that froze just as instantly as the expression on Ariel's face, the both of them looking as if they were staring through time, shocked to see a ghost at the other end staring back.

"Aviva," Ariel said, emotionlessly, addressing his estranged twin sister for the first time in almost three years.

"Well," A"Vee"va sauntered over, smirking. "*Here's* a reunion I was hoping to postpone until never."

She held her arms open.

"What," she added wryly. "No hug for your expatriate apostate big sister?"

Ariel just stared at her silently in response.

"Ah," she lowered her arms, with a smirk that poorly hid the rawness of having her embrace expectedly rejected. "Of course not."

"So, uh..." Clemente awkwardly excused himself from the crosshairs of what he quickly recognized was some bitter family drama. "I guess I'll just let you two catch up?"

The twins—Aviva standing, Ariel sitting—continued in silence in the moments after Clemente made himself scarce, until Ariel broke the quiet with a sigh, reaching into his wallet and laying some bills down on the counter.

"What?" Aviva demanded.

"I really don't need this right now," Ariel answered wearily, rising up from the bar and turning away to leave.

"*Seriously*, Ariel?" Aviva shot daggered words at her brother's back. "*You* don't need this. Of course. Never change, little brother. Never change."

Ariel stopped and spun around, feeling the burning of ~~hurt~~ anger rising in his chest.

"What, Aviva. Were you expecting something happy? A jaunty tune? Balloons and confetti to shoot from my ass, maybe?"

"Right. Here we go."

"Well, what *were* you expecting? Huh?"

"I thought maybe, oh I dunno, that maybe this time around, after all this time, that maybe you'd be able to actually *hear* me."

"*Hear* you? About *what*? You *left* Aviva. Everything we were raised on, everything we believed in, everything Ima and Aba taught us. You. *Left*. At least you had the *decency* to wait until Savalava was dead before you did it in public."

"Don't. You. Fucking. *Dare*." Aviva whispered so fiercely that it stopped Ariel's next sentence in his throat, but the pain in her eyes made his anger flare up again, and now he was angry at the both of them, him and her.

"What were you really expecting from me '*Vee?*' To say everything was all sunshine and roses between us?"

"No, *funny thing*, I expected my brother—my fucking *twin*—to *listen* to me. Or at least *consider* what I had to say," tears started to form in the corners of her eyes. "But no. Apparently you're still the same dogmatic ass."

Just as Ariel felt the anger rise up again, the word "dogmatic," spoken about him twice now tonight, stabbed a hole in his fury, deflating him along with it.

This was it. This was the proof.

This was the less glamorous and advantageous debris left in the wake of Autistic Ariel, he realized. The gap of empathy he couldn't leap over. Or at least that he hadn't leapt over before. Or couldn't. Because he hadn't realized before that just maybe, and just maybe in *this* case, the problem might actually be with *him*.

Crap, Ariel.

Now what?

"Look," he began, falteringly. "I was just...I thought I was doing what I supposed to do. Alright? Standing up for truth and Torah and Judaism and the American Way. Or something. Standing up for what I believe. And what *we* used to. We're *twins*. We were supposed to be partners."

"Oh yes, the *great* Ariel," Aviva raged on, too angry now to register Ariel's change in voice and the apologetic lilt of his tone. "Youngest of all of us, and having experienced the least, here to show us all the error of our ways, because apparently we were all sitting around with our thumbs up our asses until you arrived fully formed from the womb to show us the light."

"*You just left me out here, Aviva!*" Ariel screamed, beginning to feel his own eyes burn. "You left me out here? To do this on my own? *Fuck! You!*"

It was Aviva's turn to have her words freeze in her throat, with Ariel's words, in all their raw vulnerable honesty, splashing her in the face like a bucket of ice-water. And maybe now Aviva was finally able to hear her brother, *too*.

"And I'm sorry that, but I thought—I just—" Ariel visibly struggled, wringing the air with his hands, his deluge of emotions rapidly outpacing his vocabularly to describe them.

"I'm sorry, okay, Ariel?" Aviva replied, reviving their long dormant bond of being able to understand each other even without words. "*I'm sorry!* But I couldn't do it anymore. I just *couldn't do it*. Especially not without Savalava here. I couldn't keep willingly going into that—that...Every *week*? Praying with people who don't see you in the street? Whose children just stare at you all the time? To have to always have your guard up *all the time*?...I'm *so sorry* I left you, Ari. I really, *truly*, am. And I'm sorry that I left you holding the bag all alone. And that you felt—that you still feel abandoned. But that's *all* I'm sorry about..."

Ari absorbed his sister's words—and really *heard* them, too— but he stood his ground, a foot away from the bar, unsure of what to do next.

He didn't have a script for this. And Avi didn't either.

So, wordlessly, she turned, reached into the fridge behind the bar, and retrieved two Heinekens. Popping them both open, she placed one next to Ariel's mostly finished Jack and coke and held the other one herself.

"*Baruch ata Adoshem Elokeinu, Mekech ha'olam,*" she looked directly at her brother, reciting the blessing for beer. The first time she'd said it in a long time. "*Shehakol n'heyeh bidvaro.*"

"*Amen,*" Ari mumbled in response as his sister took her first sip.

She gestured at his untouched bottle with her own, and he trudged back to the bar in response, taking his seat again. He took up his bottle, clinked with hers, then took his own swig.

Obvious across his face was so many things, three years worth of things, that he wanted to say.

And after two more gulps apiece, he finally got it out.

"I miss you Avi. I miss my sister. I miss the us we used to be."

"Ari...Me too."

A silence passed between them for a good while.

"Well not your farts, because you are a rancid beast," Avi amended. "I don't miss those."

Ari snorted, and they both broke into laughter. A wonderful, tension-breaking laughter. Ari looked up at his sister, wearing a sideways pensive smile.

"Also," she continued. "Even though you were a huge dick to me, I've *always* been proud that my little brother became a rabbi."

"I'm sorry. I didn't mean to be."

Avi let it sit. She knew what he meant. Not every joke needed to be gone for.

"The hell," Ari shook his head after a minute. "How the hell did our parents get through all this shit in one piece?"

"They didn't," Avi chuckled. "Also, *Aba* went through it. Ima showed up when she was already a grown ass woman."

"*True.*"

"I mean, I love Ima, but that would annoy the *shit* out of me *all the time*. She was like '*Why is it so hard for you to wake up, daven, go to school, get your homework done, study for your* bat mitzvah, *learn* **Chumash**, *live a social life, have friends, do all your chores and keep your room clean? It's all so easy, I do it all the time!*' Like, woman, I'm *eleven*! You were *not* doing this when you were eleven. It's *hard* okay? Also, yup, just got my period, so now *that's* a terrifying thing I have to figure out now."

Ari laughed.

"Stop laughing! Like, no joke, I felt so alone growing up."

Ariel stopped.

"Really? For real?"

"Um, yeah? Who was there for me to learn from? Ima didn't grow up black *and* Jewish. Aba did, but he didn't grow up a black Jewish *girl*. There was only Savalava really..."

She got quiet.

"The only one of us who's really got any of it together is Liora," Ari noted.

"*Pffft*, yeah, because she went and became a lawyer then married a doctor. She gone and went full Jew on us."

They laughed, and another lull settled in.

"Y'know, I, uh," Avi offered. "I saw your show the other day. That Freelance Rabbi bit. It's pretty funny."

"Thanks."

"I mean, I'm not...I'll still always support you, y'know? But I..Remember that summer when we were eight? When Ima was

312

working at Gan Miriam? And they had that trip to the indoor water park for all the girls and Ima took me along too?"

Ari nodded.

"Well I remember being in the park, floating by myself in that lazy river they had? Ima was, I dunno, I guess she was off supervising some other kids further downstream or something. But anyway, up ahead of me, I see this little bitty white blonde girl, probably one of the pre-schoolers, couldn't've been older than four. And she's doing this thing where I can tell she's getting ready to jump into the river too. And I knew—I could see she was gonna overshoot that jump and smack her head on the other side. And I look over at her mom and the white lifeguard, and they're busy just, chatting up a storm behind this girl, paying her no mind at *all*. And, like, I could've *easily* reached up and caught this girl mid-jump...But then I was like, oh wait, I'm the only black Jewish kid on this whole school trip, teeming with innocent little white Jewish girls, I don't even go to this school, Ima is off supervising another group somewhere, and I was just...I was just so scared at having to explain why my eight-year old *schvartze* ass is wrestling on this little white girl for apparently no reason, and, and wondering what kind of outrage I'd have to deal with from her mother, and maybe the lifeguard, and maybe the park—like, would I get kicked out the park? Would Ima get fired for bringing me? Like...So I just decided to float on by and made sure not to look...And...Damn, I'll never forget the scream that little girl made. And then when I turned around, there was the mother and the lifeguard pulling her out of the water, because, sure, *now* they're paying attention. And there was this, just, *blood* just, just *pouring* from her mouth, all over her little pink swimsuit, spatter all over her water-wings, and, like, there was no fucking way her jaw wasn't broken. And all because Jews that look like us, hell, *people* that look like us, are criminalized just by *showing up* to places. That family's day could've gone *so* differently if an eight-year old could've felt like she was safe and welcomed in a Jewish space the same way all those other little girls were. Not like she was just *tolerated*. Or that people were just watching her and waiting for her to prove to be some wild animal or something..."

Avi took a gulp of her beer, and stared at the bottle while she continued.

"I don't want to have to spend my life killing a part of myself, smothering what makes me a human, just so I can survive. Just so I can keep myself safe," she looked at her brother. "I just want to be happy in my life. I want to be able to care about people. I want to be somewhere where I'm *accepted*, not tolerated. And I am now. And Judaism isn't a part of that life."

"I...I understand," Ari swallowed sadly, staring at his own bottle. "I'm not happy about it, and I don't agree," he looked up at her. "But I can understand."

Avi looked at him, with a quivering smile and glistening eyes.

"Thank you," she half-whispered.

He gave a half shrug, took a swig of his beer, and smiled back at her. Sincerely.

"But you're tripping if you think I'm tipping you."

Avi smirked then smacked Ari in the head.

"Whatever. My kids'll be Jewish regardless, so relax, you won't have any little heathen nieces and nephews, alright?"

Ari made a face at her, then nodded his head in Clemente's direction at the end of the bar.

"He seems nice."

"He *is* nice."

"Good."

"What about you?"

"There's a girl. Kinda reminds me of you a little bit, now that I think about it."

"I hate her already."

"Ha."

"So...what's the deal then?"

"It's...complicated."

"What does 'complicated' mean?"

"It means I like her and she doesn't like me back I don't think. Not in that way."

"That's not complicated. That's just called 'no.'"

"I know, but...like we work together all the time and she's kinda flirty sometimes...?"

"Oh! Why didn't you say that? That's just called 'no,' but with a sense of humor.'"

"Well aren't you just a font of advice."

"I dunno, maybe somebody should have a grown-up conversation with somebody else, instead of this weird pining from a distance thing like you're a Victorian novel."

"Well...we kinda did...and she kinda said no, she didn't want to date."

"Well then congratulations, you have a friend. Get over it."

"True, I guess."

"You guess? I'm not sure why I even had to *say* any of that. Is this the kind of bullshit you've been pulling with girls without me around to kick your ass?"

"Uh...no?"

"Well *that* sounds convincing. What'd you do Ariel Shabbtai Dror?"

"Wow, my *whole* government?"

She glared at him.

"Well I, uh..." he cleared his throat and blurted out the rest under his breath as he took another swig. "Ikindasortadidntdateawhitegirl."

"*NO.* You did *not*," Avi's jaw dropped, a combination shocked and bemused.

"It was a...situationship, I guess?"

Avi started cackling, covering her mouth with her hand.

"Don't tell anybody, okay?"

"You don't tell anyone I'm married to a *goy*, and I won't tell anyone about your tapioca pudding fling."

"Ugh, I can just see the looks on their faces. Ima'd be pissed at me for mine being white, and pissed at you for yours not being Jewish—"

"And Aba'd be happy yours was at least Jewish and that mine is at least black, like, *adjacent*."

"Well apparently we're still getting into trouble, I see."

"Still."

Ariel and Aviva smiled at each other. AviandAri. Not quite together again. Or ever again, really.

That was a lifetime ago.

But this something new was a good start, they thought.

"Well," Ariel pushed himself up off the bar. "I'm gonna head back over to my friend. Probably call it a night."

"You do that." Aviva smirked.

Ariel saluted and turned from the bar.

Manishtana

"Ariel!"

He turned at his sister calling his name.

"Im ey pa'am tiztarech masheu," she said, earnestly. *"Rak tagid li. Ani eheyeh sham bishvilcha."*

Ariel looked at his sister, and a small smile grew on his lips as he nodded.

"Ani yode'a."

Thursday, May 5, 2016
27/28 Nisan 5776

"Look out," Buddy warned as he bumped into Ariel on the way to the writing room. "Ellis is on the warpath today."

"What? Why?"

"No idea! But she's been sniping at people all morning. Like, even for *her*."

"Wow," Ariel's eyes widened as they turned a corner. "That's saying a—"

And there Ellis was, in the middle of the hallway, heartily tearing the inexplicably still-hired Q a new orifice.

"Well, you sir," Ellis continued, a dangerously sarcastic enthusiasm in her voice. "Are in luck. Because today my responses come in three—count them: *three*—delicious flavors. You have your choice of Strawberry Sarcasm Surprise, Rum Raisin Ridiculously Pissed-Off Pistachio, or Vanilla. Would you like to try a free sample?"

"Um...vanilla?"

Ellis' eyes narrowed into thin slits.

"Right. Going."

Q sped down the hall and out of sight just as Ellis noticed Ariel and Buddy standing nearby.

"You're late," she said, shooting daggers at them.

"Sorry!" Ariel and Buddy nearly yelped in tandem.

317

"Don't be sorry. Be productive. We're already behind for today, so get your asses in gear."

"Yes!"

Ellis spun around in headed off in some indiscriminate direction.

"Yikes."

"See? *That.*"

It was an all-around tense day, but everyone hit their marks more or less and filming went off as usual and without a hitch. And once it was done, everybody—including Wes—peeled out as fast as their legs could carry them to avoid getting caught under whatever cloud Ellis was still under, a cloud that even *sponsors* couldn't escape from unscathed.

"*How* are you mad that we don't have a fax line?" Ariel had overheard just as he reached her office to ask where she wanted to get lunch. "It's *2016*. I don't have an on-staff carrier pigeon either, and we just shot our last delivery pony behind the shed. *Email* me, you dingaling."

So, seeing as how he'd dipped out on their lunch routine, Ariel was particularly keen on abandoning ship with the same alacrity as the rest of the crew. Which is when he remembered that he'd left his phone charging in the writer's room, and had to double back.

Creeping down the empty halls as quickly and gingerly as possible, Ariel slipped into the room, yanked his charger out of the wall, scooped up his phone, and headed back out to the elevator just as it was starting to close.

"Wait! Wait! Hold it!" he shouted.

If he missed it now, he'd have to wait for it to come all the way back up, increasing the chances of running into a Mad Ellis.

The doors reopened in reply to Ariel's request, revealing Ellis—*obviously*—standing in the bay and hold a large bag of assorted candy.

Gingerly, Ariel slipped inside like he was climbing into a shark tank while bleeding profusely from a gaping chest wound.

"Thanks," he squeaked.

Wordlessly, Ellis reached into the bag and handed Ariel a lollipop.

"This has not been a good day. I've been in a mood."

"So I noticed. I mean, "we." We all did. All of us."

"Yeah, well. Also, it's Yom Hashoah today, so I guess it makes sense."

"It's—Oh, wow, you're right! I totally forgot about going to the event at Hillel last night."

"...*Holocaust Remembrance Day* slipped your mind?"

"Well, in my defense, I was too busy getting lynched over here in America during the Holocaust. And for the next thirty years after that, know what I mean?"

"...Ah."

The elevator jerked suddenly, and Ariel and Ellis struggled to keep their balance as the car shuddered to a stop.

"The hell—?" Ariel started.

Ellis began pressing buttons that became increasingly clear were being unresponsive.

"Aw, no you've gotta be kidding me," she groaned before jabbing at the emergency intercom button. "Louis! Louis, are you there? We're stuck in the north, uh, elevator!"

✡ ✡ ✡

"—we're trying to get someone down here now," Louis' voice crackled through the intercom. "But it's after hours so you guys'll have to sit tight for a while."

"Great," Ariel groaned, slumping into a cross-legged sitting position on the elevator floor.

"And is this a while like 'twenty-five minutes?'" Ellis asked. "Or a while like 'a couple hours?'"

"A while like 'how long my wife has been sleeping with my boss.'"

Ariel and Ellis exchanged uncomfortable glances.

"Um. Yikes...?" Ellis offered.

"I know right?" Louis' voice crackled. "Awkwaaaard," he started laughing then abruptly stopped. "But seriously, she's a bitch."

"*Oh*-kay, um, just, just keep us posted okay?"

"That's what she said."

"I, I really don't see how that makes sense, but okay."

Ariel rubbed his fingers into his eyes, feeling just, some kind of cross between elated and irritated.

319

Manishtana

Of course he'd get stuck in an elevator with the person he'd most want to be stuck with in the world, and *of course* she didn't feel the same way.

Or did she?

Was she the work-wife soulmate Jumaane seemed to think she was and all he had to do was stick it out, or was he just building things in his head and he should just listen to Aviva telling him to stop being a creeper in an obvious just-friendship?

Ugh.

"Ellis—" he began, opening his eyes, stopping short when he saw her sitting across from him, also sitting cross-legged in her corner, her bag of sweets splayed open beside her as she shuffled a deck of cards. "What the—What are you—?"

"What? Cuz we weren't gonna sit around playing Truth or Dare like fourteen year-olds."

Ariel just laughed and shook his head. Whatever. This was ridiculous. Ellis was ridiculous. Life was ridiculous.

"Okay, what are we playing then?"

"Kosher strip poker," she answered, just slightly pulling at the wrist of her longsleeved Fallout Boy cardigan. "See? Wrist! Ooooh!"

"You are ridiculous. Or a psychopath."

"Eh. I go both ways."

"That's what *she* said."

"Yes. That is literally what just happened."

✡ ✡ ✡

As it turned out, Ariel was just objectively bad at playing *any* kind of game. Nine rounds in, and nearly all the candy Ellis had given him to use as chips was back in her pile.

"So..." Ellis began, amused at Ariel's terrible luck.

"Yeah?"

"We've worked with each other long enough, and we're friends—"

"We're friends?!"

"Fine, lukewarm adversaries. You twisted my arm."

"Aw..."

"Anyway, I think we've known each other long enough for me to ask you what your deal is... So what's your deal?"

"My deal?"

"Y'know. You're a rabbi. And black. That couldn't have been easy. So how'd that happen?"

"Well, I killed a rabbi and ate him. Then I absorbed his powers," he flipped his hand of cards over. "High card seven."

"Royal flush," Ellis laughed, showing hers.

"Dammit."

"Your turn to shuffle," she chortled as she slid a mound of candy towards him. "Here, take it. You're out of candy and I feel bad. By the way, I was serious about the question. Dick."

"Ah. So. Well, there was this girl."

"Ah. Say no more."

Ariel finished shuffling and dealt himself and Ellis new hands. Studying his hand for a few seconds, he looked over them at Ellis studying hers, and felt the sudden need to just...vent.

She'd asked him what his deal was, right?

He rested his head back against the cool elevator wall and looked up at the ceiling.

"I have a confession to make," he blurted out, resting his cards in his lap.

Ellis stopped configuring her hand and looked over at her friend, patiently.

"I am unapologetically Orthodox," he announced, then looked at Ellis. "Like, is it weird to say that?"

"I dunno," she shrugged. "Depends. Why do you say that?"

"Like, it's just the result of a realization that sort of hit me when I found myself in the kinds of multidenominational spaces that I sometimes find myself in. I mean, I remember this one time when I was at a **Shabbaton** for, I dunno what, probably something all social justicey, but I remember inwardly cringing as I asked if there was kosher wine at the meal. And then I heard this voice in my head like *'Why the* fuck *are you cowering about asking for kosher wine, for kiddish, AT A SHABBATON? Why is this a thing that is happening?'*"

"That does seem a tad backwards."

"*I know!* And then the thing is, I ask the guy in charge of the event about the wine, and I don't even understand, because he *totally* gave me a blank look when I asked him if the wine there was **mevushal** or not. But then not ten minutes later, there he is up at the podium giving the opening remarks and rattling off, like, eleventeen different Jewish words like he's playing Scrabble with Moses."

"Seriously! What *is* that about? Like, I'm *so* glad I'm not the rabbi, dude. Because non-Orthodox Jews are confusing as *fuck*. It's like, use standard English terms like 'repairing the world' and everybody gets all offended like *'I* know *what* **tikkun olam** *is, asshole.'* But then go the other route and use just Hebrew words like **'ma'arit ayin'** and everyone gets all in their feelings like they're being talked down to. Can we just make it a thing for everyone to carry around Jewish vocabulary flash cards so everyone's on the same page?"

"Ellis, you're insane," Ariel laughed. *"Anyways,* at that *Shabbaton* is when I decided that the shrinking Orthodox violet deal wasn't really going to work. I mean, I'd like to think I'm somebody who tries and intends to respect other people's Judaisms and identities and definitions and religious practices and ideologies and all that. Shouldn't I get to expect to have that same safe space in turn? And, y'know, I don't mean it in some obnoxious *'You guys are doing everything wrong so can I have space to do it the right way?'* kinda way. Like, I don't think being 'unapologetically Orthodox' means dominating the conversation in a pluralist space, it just means not whispering your part in that conversation. Because if you *do* whisper through your monologue when it's your line, all that does is perpetuate the notion that Orthodoxy deserves to be an aside because it's this archaic thing that needs to be tucked into some corner and apologized for. Like somebody's racist grandmother from 'a different time.'"

"Well...except for when it is, though..."

"Ohhhhhmiigoossshhhhhh you're right and I can't even. Like, how are you *consistently* either on the wrong side of history or absent from the field entirely? Like, take slavery, right? Team Reform has David Einhorn. Bernhard Felsenthal. Kaufmann Kohler. Meanwhile, history textbooks are like *'Among Jewish clergy, save for Rabbi Sabato Morais, there were no Orthodox Jews in the anti-slavery movement. Only Reform Rabbis and Reform Jews declared themselves avowed abolitionists.'* That is fucking *embarrassing,* man."

"Yuuup."

"Then the Civil Rights movement rolls around and—being *extremely* generous, mind you—Team Ortho has Berman,

Drachman, Greenberg, Jung, Landes, Soloveichik, and Teitz. But then Team Reform & Conservative just *swamps* us with Borowitz, Braude, Brickner, Dresner, Fogel, Goldstein, Goodman, Goor, Herzog, Hirsh, Jick, Leeman, Levy, Lipman, Mantinband, Nussbaum, Robinson, Rosen, Rubenstein, Saltzman, Sanders, Secher, Sills, Vorspan, Wax—"

"And, of course, the big-daddy Colonel Sanders-looking patron saint of bleeding-heart Jews everywhere: Abraham Joshua Heschel."

"I know right? The closest we get to a Heschel is who? Emanuel Rackman? Now jump forward about fifty years and, gee, does the disproportionate loss of black lives at the hands of law enforcement matter? Hart, Rothstein, and Yanklowitz say they do. And also Held, Talve, Barash-Hagans, Leider, Rothbaum, Falick, Brous, Steinlauf, Rosen, Creditor, Kolin, Bachman, Kahn-Troster, Limmer, Jacobs, Zevit, Feldman, Cohen...Quick, guess who plays for which team! I mean, talk about gay marriage and at the drop of a hat you'll have 100 Orthodox rabbis signing off on a protest letter quoting Leviticus 18:22, but then talk about police killing minorities and you can't even find a *minyan* of those same rabbis who remember that Leviticus also has a Chapter 19, and it says something in there about *'Don't stand idly by the blood of your neighbor'* or something?"

"Yep. That's pretty shitty, guys."

Ariel paused in his rant to just exhale. And breathe. He looked up at Ellis and her calmly expectant half-smile, then looked down at his fingers while he nervously fidgeted with them, feeling weirdly exposed.

"...And then there's me...You know how back in school, even if you didn't have assigned seats, you kind of sat in the same seat all the time anyway? And how everyone knew it was 'your' seat? And then you had those days when you walked in and someone else was sitting in it, and everyone was kinda like, *'I guess you can technically sit there...but you know you don't belong there, right?'* ...I'm that kid. The one sitting in the 'wrong' seat. The one showing up Orthodox to social justice spaces, or young to rabbinical conclaves, or any other round whole that it's been squarely decided that I'm not 'supposed' to be, and with all the requisite stupid things said that I was supposed to 'take the high road' on and just brush off my shoulders. And y'know...I was really starting to get sick of it. I...it felt like all my shoulder brushing was wearing my fabric thin, and that the stitches were starting to fray, and that I might need a new 'Ariel' suit soon."

Ellis put her cards down and hunched forward, lacing her fingers together.

"Ariel...Why do you stay?"

"What do you mean?"

"Why do you stay? Why do you try to fit in? I've known you maybe six months, and this is like the eleventh time I've heard you say some variation of you not fitting in. Every other time we talk, it's about you feeling troubled, confused, and trying to find yourself. It's like you're John Mayer's entire discography come to life."

"Ouch."

"Sorry, not sorry. So...Why are you still here? Why do you stick it out? You *do* know religion isn't an endurance sport, right?"

"Funny. An ex-fiancee of mine said that to me once. About our relationship."

"Well then maybe you and Judaism are in an abusive relationship."

Ariel looked at Ellis, his uncomfortable smile to her non-plussed arched eyebrow. That last bit had unexpectedly cut deeper than he was ready to probe.

"So," Ariel cleared his throat, picking up his hand of cards and busying himself with them. "What's *your* deal, Ellis?"

"He asked, changing the subject," Ellis wryly noted, picking up her own cards. "But sure. I wanted to be a dinosaur when I grew up. Apparently, one cannot grow up to be a dinosaur, so here I am."

"Seriously? That's seriously the answer you're gonna go with?"

"Fine. Killjoy. I—" she began, just as her cell began to ring. "Oop! One second," she glanced at the number , sighed, then picked up. "Whu yuh wan now?...Mi nuh bizniz wid dat. Do whu yuh wan...Yuh nuh undastan mi? Mi seh mi nuh fix dis fuh yuh. Yuh nuh mi pickney. Go ax yuh mudduh fi do dat...Mi seh yuh fi do whu ya wan...," she sucked her teeth, annoyed. "Mi done talk now. Bye."

She looked up at Ariel's amused expression.

"So obviously I'm Jamaican."

"I remember now. I keep forgetting because of the British accent. Just a likkle bit."

"Oh? *'Likkle bit?'* Well looky here."

"My ex was Jamaican. The ex-fiancee I was telling you about."

"Really? What part?"

"Kingston."

"Pfft," Ellis snorted. "You should've *known* she was shady then. Jamaicans don't live in Kingston. Jamaicans *die* in Kingston."

"Wow, okay."

"Just saying," she shrugged.

"What part are *you* from then?"

"Sav-La-Mar. But not me. My dad. My dad's dad, actually. I guess that technically only makes a quarter, not—Ok, lemme start from the beginning."

Ariel put his cards down again while Ellis gathered her thoughts.

"Ever heard of the Harlem Hellfighters?" she began. "First World War. 369th infantry in the Army. Mostly from Harlem, obviously. Saved tons of white asses. Got French medals of honor. Anyway, after the war they all head back to America except for James Henry Tandy III, my great-granddad. He's like *'Fuck America. France treats me like a person,'* and so he stays behind and becomes part of the French occupation. So there he is, chilling in the Rhineland, and that's where he meets a little German-Polish girl, Chana Gittel Pacht, my great-grandmom."

"Wow, ok cool."

"Yep. So they get married—Chana's family sits *shiva* for her, of course—

"Of course. Based on the *nothing* that says to do that."

"—And they have two kids: my grandmother Samantha 'Zelda' and her little brother Edward 'Anshel.' Then the Nazis happen, as they do. Nuremberg Laws. Kristallnacht. And one night great-granddad James—African-American, former Ally soldier James—doesn't come home, because he's been snapped up by the Gestapo, and so his family never sees him again. And that's when great-grandmom Chana decides it's time to get out of Germany. Luckily, there's a ship leaving. A little boat called the St. Louis."

"Oh no."

"*Oh yeah.* So Chana, Zelda, and Anshel go down to the docks to board the St. Louis. But they end up getting separated in the bustle, and only native-German Chana and able-to-pass Anshel make it onboard, and suddenly there's this little brown girl on the docks. Get out of here little brown girl!"

"Omigosh."

"So Zelda spends the next couple of months honing her scavenging skills that'll come in handy for when she gets captured and taken into Auschwitz, and then Buchenwald after that."

"*Whoa.*"

"I know right? It gets better. She gets liberated by the 76ith battalion, and that's how she meets my Jamaican grandfather, William. He also doesn't return back to the States, and together they move to England, get married, and have my mother and uncles. My mom ends up going to NYU for college, meets my Jamaican-American dad, and *they* get married. They have my older brother and sister and then me—by the way, my mom and uncles grew up completely secular."

"Really."

"Yeah, she didn't get interested in her Jewish identity until college, and because of Chabad. But she still married my agnostic dad anyway. But then the more she got into Judaism, the more interested my dad got, and he ending up converting and becoming Chabad. Which is how I grew up Chabad, and the only one out of my siblings born to *two* Jewish parents. Which, by the way," she added sarcastically. "Is just a *great* sibling dynamic. Anyway, on days like, say, Yom Hashoah, I tend to get a bit sensitive and angry at everything and everyone."

"I'm sorry."

"It's ok."

"I meant specifically about what I said before. With the lynching thing."

"I know. Sorry that the Ashkenormative Jewish narrative is probably used like a muzzle to silence and erase yours. But it's still my narrative. And it's still a valid one."

"I...yeah, you're right. That was shitty of me. I'm sorry."

"Apology accepted. Actually, no. Gimme half that stash back. *Then* apology accepted."

"*Fine*," Ariel feigned a mope as he slid half his candy pile back to Ellis. "Why do you even *have* this much candy with you today?"

"Because there are only two things I love in this world, Ariel: booze and candy. And I don't drink on Yom Hashoah."

"Really?"

"Nope, not a drop. That only happens for two days: I don't drink on Yom Hashoah and I don't drink on St. Patty's day."

"Why not St. Patty's?"

"Because it's *Saint* Patty's Day. Duh. I'm a lush, not an **apikores**. Not even when I *was* OTD."

"*You* went OTD?" Ariel's jaw dropped. Like, what the hell, who *was* this woman? "*Wow*, that's so weird."

"With all your bellyaching *you* never did?"

"Nope."

"Now *that's* weird."

"Well, how did you, like, what made you go OTD? What was that like?"

"I remember *exactly* when it happened. It was the last Sunday before I was moving to the States for college, so me and the family went out for brunch. I'm standing there at the sink, washing my hands, I'm saying the **beracha**, and there's this little six-year old standing next to her mother and little brother right beside me, both staring at me, and their little eyes are so large that their skulls are structurally unsound at this point. And the girl's like *'What is she doing Ima? Why did she was her hands for* **motzi***?'* And I'm like, alright fine. She's six, she's never a black Jewish person, fine. But then her mother, definitely loud enough for me to hear, says *'I'm not sure children, I don't know what's going on here.'*...Really bitch? You have *no* idea what's going on here? That, I dunno...I mean, I was *already* spending my life downplaying my Jewishness so that non-Jews would leave me alone and so I wouldn't get bothered by the regular Jews who were 'properly Jewish' either."

"*'Properly?'* Are you being British right now, or...?"

"I mean 'properly' like, had parents who were always Jewish, and siblings who were fully Jewish, and yeah, I know my siblings are technically 'fully Jewish' because Jews round up, but when my dad gets an *aliyah* and he blesses his kids, my brother and sister are *'ben and bat Avraham.'* And I'm *'bat Yehudah.'* It's...awkward."

"Yeah, I could totally see that."

"*Yeah*. So after I moved here for college from Manchester and was finally out from under a convert dad and a BT mom—*exactly!*" she replied to the cringe face Ariel made. "That's like *the worst* combination of religious parents any sane person can have, and I just wanted to figure out how I felt about being Jewish on my own. Like, I dropped pretty much everything by the end of freshman year. But somehow in college I managed to gain a ton of Jewish friends anyway, and a couple of years ago I decided to come back."

"Was that hard? Coming back?"

"Yes. No. I dunno. Like, it always seemed to me like everyone else was way more into it than I was, even when I was religious. And now people are all like *'When did you become Jewish?'* and *'You're not, like,* really *Jewish though, right?'* So I pretty much feel, I dunno, too Jewish to be a *goy,* but not Jewish enough to tell people I'm a Jew," she squinted. "Does that make sense?"

"It's...I mean, I can see that."

"Meh. But what I really can't stand though, is the assumption that I 'rejected the fun party life' when I became a BT. Like, maybe those of us who are *frum* by choice weren't that kind of person in the first place. I mean, I think it's pretty insulting to assume that someone's former life was all fun and gratuitous debauchery. Not all of us decide to change our relationship with observance because we woke up on the floor of an opium den again or just finished hopping off our fiftieth dick, know what I mean?"

"It's like complimenting someone's makeover, but backhandedly saying they used to be an eyesore."

"*Exactly!*"

"I got you. It's kinda like when people tell me they're so impressed that I'm religious despite everything I go through. It's like, oh, so you *realize* that the religious community has too much of a tendency to be a racist, disgraceful cesspool that makes a mockery of G'd and Torah and should probably be abandoned. Cool. So..."

"I know right? Like, stop being so shocked and go fix your shit."

"Amen, sister."

✡ ✡ ✡

"NO! You did *not* try to grill a cheese sandwich in your DVD player at *fourteen!*"

"Hey," Ellis shrugged. "I was very hungry, and very lazy, and technically only thirteen and a half."

"Ellis. Unless you're talking about *months,* that's not really an excuse."

"Oh, yes, I forgot you didn't do silly bullshit when you were younger, Mr. I Was In A Fraternity Called Phi Busta Kappa."

328

"I was! I was Kosher Pork, Colin was Snowflake, and Jumaane was Chocolate Thunder!"

"You are such a—I'm gonna punch you. In the ear."

"Not with *those* skinny wrists you're not. They'll shatter upon impact with my ruggedly handsome jaw of granite."

"I'll have you know these 'skinny wrists' made division champions out of *whatever* softball team I was on. *Everyone* in the Manchester Girls Softball League started to sweat when *this* switch-hitter stepped up to the plate."

"I don't really see you as the athletic type."

"Don't sleep on me just because I've mellowed into a life of wine and spirits in my old age," she said, slapping at a stomach with a layer of fat only *technically* squishy enough to classify as pudge. "Pick the sport you want to lose to me the least in, and I'll try not to demolish you too badly."

"I'll believe that when I see it," Ariel teased.

"Then keep your eyes open, bitch," Ellis smiled back just as teasingly.

"Ooh! Spicy!"

"Whatevs," she laughed. "I'm used to people thinking there's no such thing as me. I'm a British-Jamaican-German, I'm a female gamer *and* kickass athlete, I'm a black Jew, I'm b—"

"You guys still there?" Louis' voice crackled through the intercom.

Ariel and Ellis jumped, startled by the intrusion. Ellis climbed from the floor to push the intercom button.

"Yeah, we're still here."

"Alright, sorry for the huge wait, but the technician's here now. We should have you guys out any minute."

"Oh. Uh...Thanks."

Ellis released the button, and she and Ariel looked at each other in a mixture of awkwardness and...was that...disappointment?

"What," Ariel said jokingly. "You wanted to stay here all night?"

"*Pfft.* With *you*? Hell no. I have a limit to how sucky my birthdays can get."

"Wait, today's your *birthday*? Why didn't you—"

"Because I didn't want all the—" she waved her hands around like sparklers. "Y'know?"

"No, I'm sorry, birthdays are a *huge* thing," Ariel grabbed Ellis' bag of sweets and started rummaging through it. "We're taking care of this *right* now."

"How—"

"Aha!" Ariel pulled a saltwater taffy from the bag triumphantly and placed it in Ellis' hand. "Here, hold this."

"Dude, seriously, what are you—"

"Shh!" he shushed her, snapping off the stick from a lollipop and rummaging through his pocket. In two quick moves, Ariel impaled the taffy with the lollipop stick with one hand, then lit it with the lighter he pulled from his pocket with the other.

"Ariel!" Ellis exclaimed in alarm. "*Holy shi—*"

"Happybirthdayhappybirthdaymakeawish!"

"DUDE!"

"Blow it out! Just blow it out before the alarm goes off!"

Flustered, Ellis frantically blew at the melting plastic stick in her hand until it finally went out. Still agitated, she gave Ariel a look.

"So...What'd you wish for...?"

"I wished you hadn't burnt up part of our oxygen setting a plastic stick on fire."

The elevator jerked, nearly knocking them both over.

✡ ✡ ✡

Ellis' dingy white 1999 Camry slowly pulled up in front of Ariel's building.

She'd graciously offered the ride. And Ariel had graciously accepted.

And now here they were. In front of his place. Graciously.

"So..." he began.

"Yeah..."

"Well, thanks for the ride."

"No prob. I figure you were stuck with me for an hour and change, another twenty couldn't hurt. Besides it just didn't make sense for you to have to wait around for a train, especially not when we're so close to each other."

"Good points, good points...Well, y'know, see you tomorrow."

"Yep. Pretty much."

Ariel reached for the door handle, fumbling around for it for a little bit, then sat back in his seat.

C'mon you idiot, he was thinking. Do *something!*

"I have Asperger's," he blurted out.

"Well. That sentence proved its own point. Very efficient."

"I," he laughed uneasily. "Yeah, I guess it did. I'm just," he looked at her. "I just, y'know. *Like* you like you."

Ellis stared at him for a moment.

"Ok."

"...Yes."

"Well...I've already said the 'no' thing...So what do you expect me to do with that?"

What *did* he expect her to do with that? Did he even know? What was his plan exactly?

"I, uh, I dunno. I guess I...I guess I just wanted you to know that."

"Dude, I've already known that. I've known that this entire time. And, look, I think you're cool. But that's not what I'm looking for. Not with you. And not right now."

"Okay. Okay that's fine, I just, I mean I hope I didn't retroactively ruin earlier tonight now and make it all sucky."

"Generally? Yeah. Yeah, that would've retroactively made earlier tonight sucky and ruined the good friendship time we were having by making it seem empty and superficial and just a means to an end."

Ariel cringed inside himself.

"But," Ellis continued. "Luckily for you, I work with writers all day. Some of them are even good. So I'm used to people where the inside of their brain is a terrible place, and things come out and come off the wrong way. And I'd also like to think that I know *you* well enough to know that you, personally, are clueless as fuck sometimes."

"Most times."

"I didn't say that. But now that it's out there, I'm not gonna walk it back."

"Fair enough...Can I ask why though? I mean, you don't have to answer or anything. Just figured it couldn't hurt to ask."

"You're right," Ellis smiled, amused. "It *didn't* hurt to ask. And I *don't* have to answer."

Ariel grinned tightly, looked down, and shook his head at his own ridiculousness.

"Night, Ariel."

"Night, Ellis. And happy birthday...Um, buddy."

"Thanks...pal."

✡ ✡ ✡

Ariel was at the usual Brooklyn bar with the boys later that night, still enjoying or reeling or whatevering from his and Ellis' conversation. It'd been nice. Weirdly awkwardly raw, but still...somehow comfortable?

Weird. Just, weird.

"Ariel, you're up," Jumaane informed him, taking a swig of beer and backing away from the pool table.

"So what'd you guys get up to last night?" Ariel asked as he lined up his shot.

"Not much. We did the bar-hopping thing. Ilan and I tried to score some chicks."

"Any luck?"

"Well," Colin offered, while texting, obviously. "What started out as cougar-hunting turned into whaling, so I'd go with a no."

"Thank you, Colin. Thanks for that. *Anyway*, I hear you and Ellis had quite the magical evening today. An hour and a half, was it?"

"Dammit. See, I was trying to preemptively deflect this conversation."

"She didn't take your virjewnity did she?" Colin asked.

"My—Did you just say 'virjewnity?'"

"She'd just better make an honest man out of you," Jumaane added with mock seriousness.

"Look," Colin continued. "You've valiantly held on to your V-card despite our numerous *numerous* attempts to get you laid. Including, but not limited to, the infamous escort/fake job interview incident."

"And again, thank you for that, Colin," Ariel echoed Jumaane. "Thanks ever so."

"Hey, I'm just saying Little Ms. Ellis better know not to expect to get the milk without paying for the cow."

"Thanks...Mom."

ARIEL SAMSON: FREELANCE RABBI

"Although if you get stuck in the elevator again," Ilan piped up. "It totally doesn't count if you do stuff between floors."

Manishtana

Thursday, May 26, 2016
18/19 Iyar 5776

"Whoa! Careful now," Ariel goodnaturedly chided the bride, to the jittery laughter of the attendees, the bridesmaids, the groomsmen, the groom, and the bride herself.

She'd nervously taken a slightly bigger gulp of wine than she'd intended from the silver goblet her soon-to-be husband had handed her.

Which normally wouldn't have been a problem, if the bride and groom—as per Ashkenazic wedding tradition—hadn't both been fasting since dawn.

"Most brides wait until at least the ring is on their finger before changing their last name to Chardonnay," Ariel kept joking as the bride's cheeks filled with a rosy flush, the wine making quick work of ten hours of no solid food. "You okay?"

She nodded vigorously, her cheeks full of nerves and suppressed laughter.

"Alright, then. Let's get to that ring."

The sanctuary—decorated with modestly-sized bouquets adorning the room like small bombs of fiery-colored fragrance, the *bimah* draped with gauzy bands of sheer-white voile—vibrated with excited tittering, a restlessness that bubbled just under the surface, as Congregation Ahavath Yisroel hosted its first wedding in over 25 years.

ARIEL SAMSON: FREELANCE RABBI

Since 1988, to be exact. Thursday night, July 28th.

It also happened to be the first ever wedding that Ariel had ever conducted, because, just in case we haven't learned by now, there are no coincidences.

Standing with the bride and groom under the wooden latticework *chuppah,* draped overhead with the groom's rainbow-striped *tallit* of his former bachelor days, Ariel examined the simple yellow-gold band handed to him by the groom before summoning the groom's two witnesses—also doubling as his groomsmen—to verify its being of value.

It was a small wedding party. Two bridesmaids. Two groomsmen. No flower girls or ringbearers. Efficient. Possibly a little rushed, but that part was understandable.

The groom was only in his third year into his surgery residency, and the bride was still interning at her hospital.

They weren't exactly gifted with a wealth of free time, or, for that matter, money. Which is one of the reasons they'd reached out to Ariel. The other was that they also weren't gifted with a ton of family who approved of their union.

Well, the bride wasn't, anyway.

The guest list on the groom's side included parents, *yeshiva* study partners, some work friends, but the bride—beaming at her groom from underneath her veil—looked like she couldn't've cared any less that her side was a tad sparse, populated mostly by school friends.

And, honestly, maybe Ariel *had* felt a little iffy about their union when they'd first approached him.

But there was something about the chance to officiate a wedding—where a black dude in white tux-and-tails and a *kippah* would be walked down the aisle to the instrumental of Young Buck's "Get Buck"—that you could not have *paid* Ariel to turn it down.

(The bride had walked to Paramore's "The Only Exception." It was a very Salt and Pepper romance.)

Either way, Ariel wasn't about to let them get away with scraping together the bare necessity of two witnesses to validate their union as Jewishly legal and binding, or even the bare minimum of ten men required to be able to perform the full gamut of canopy blessings. It didn't matter that they weren't members or had never once attended services at CAY.

Manishtana

If they wanted to be the first couple ever married by Rabbi Ariel Samson, then the wedding wasn't allowed to be some clinical pro forma ceremony. For all their sakes.

Getting married—with family approval or not—wasn't some shameful, quick and dirty thing to get over with, and Ariel wasn't about to build a reputation of being a rabbi who popped out assembly line weddings in basements like some speakeasy bootlegger.

The wedding became a *shul* event.

The couple had been reluctant at first. Like when someone offers you a $20, and you *really* need it, and you *really* want to say yes. But you don't. And you stick to that 'no' two, maybe three times. And then you end up relieved when they don't ask you a fourth time, but kicking yourself that they didn't give you the chance to give in.

If it had been any other couple, perhaps Ariel wouldn't have pushed so much.

But—when Young Buck's dirty bass and gospel chorals had died down, and the saccharinely melancholy chimes and twangs of Paramore filled the air, when the congregation turned their heads, standing and gazing at the glowing bride entering the room, flanked by her bridesmaids, when the groom took his beloved's hand and guided her up the steps of the *bimah,* to her place at his side in their private **Gan Eden** under the *chuppah,* when the electrified stillness descended upon the sanctuary as the bride circled her beloved seven times, building a wall of love, wholeness, and completeness impossible to attain separately, stepping in time with the ***chazzan***'s melodious chanting of "*Baruch Haba'ah*" to the instrumental of Sara Bareilles' "I Choose You"—Ariel knew he'd made the right call.

"Alright now," Ariel said to the groom, handing him back the ring after the witnessed vouched for it. "Take the ring with your right hand."

His hand shaking slightly, the groom obliged, holding it poised to be slipped on his bride's finger.

"You raise your left hand," Ariel instructed the bride.

With an anxious giggle, she complied.

"Now repeat," Ariel addressed the groom. "'*Harei at...*'"

"*Harei at,*" the groom repeated.

"Hey, hey, hey, don't look at *me*, look at *her*," Ariel teased, and the room laughed again.

"*Harei at*," the groom tried again, grinning, this time looking into his almost-wife's eyes.

"Okay, now '*m'kudeshet li...*'" Ariel continued, interrupting the ritual formula just enough so that the bride wasn't accidentally ending up married to the wrong person.

"*M'kudeshet li.*"

"Good. '*B'taba'at zu...*'"

"*B'taba'at zu.*"

"Great. '*K'dat Moshe v'Yis...*'" here Ariel trailed off, just to hedge his bets against unexpectedly gaining a wife.

"*K'dat Moshe v'Yisrael*," the groom finished with a faint tremble in his voice as tears began collecting in his bride's.

"You may place the ring on her finger."

Tears starting to collect in his own eyes as well, the groom slid the ring onto his bride's waiting index finger, where it gleamed in the light.

It was a plain yellow-gold band. No stones or designs, as per tradition.

The reasons why came in many flowery romantic varieties.

That it symbolized how the marriage should be one of simple beauty. That the circle of the ring represented the hope for the eternal nature of the couple's marriage.

But, like most things in Judaism, the actual reason was fairly utilitarian: to prevent the groom from misrepresenting the ring's worth, possibly tricking the bride into accepting the marriage proposal under false premises.

Us Jews. Surpisingly practical.

But also mystical as well.

After all, the circle—and, by extension, the ring—was the most perfect form in all of nature.

Yet in it's dimensional relationship to itself, it paradoxically produces an irrational number. A transcendental number, even.

And that was marriage.

The *perfect* marriage, really.

The perfection of the circle of the ring, containing the imperfection of the humans bound in it. Two souls, two streams of light, tied up in one another in a never-repeating, neverending series of adventures, burning brighter from their being united.

Manishtana

The dirge-like melody of *"Im Eshkachech Yerushalayim"*—a reminder that despite the great joy of the day, the destruction of the Temple in Jerusalem is still mourned—wafted solemnly on the air, eventually supplanted by the first stanza of "Lift Ev'ry Voice and Sing"—an equally sobering testament to the African-American struggle, past, present, and future—and the ceremony's conclusion was signaled by the groom stamping on the napkin-wrapped glass underfoot, following by rising cheers of *"Mazal Tov!"* rattling the sanctuary.

The newly married couple stepped out from under the *chuppah* to the cheers of the wedding attendees, paused, then leapt down the short flight of stairs, over the twig broom festively decorated with sparkling bows of gold and silver and shimmering ribbons of navy-blue.

Watching the bride and groom dash from the room, followed with a procession of clapping, laughter, and song, seeing the look of pure joy on the bride's glowing face, Ariel contentedly decided that, whatever his misgivings, being Mrs. Tamar Watkins looked really good on Tamar Denebeim.

✡ ✡ ✡

The room buzzed with happy vibes, all fired up by the music being laid down by the band, playing tunes that fell somewhere between hip-hopified klezmer and klezmered hip-hop.

"Ladies and gentlemen," a voice boomed over a loudspeaker, echoing through CAY's dining hall. "Introducing—for the first time—Mr. and Mrs. Benjamin and Tamar Watkins!"

Benjamin and Tamar entered the room, beaming, and to thunderous applause. The standing ovation continued—with some extra whoops thrown in for good measure—as the happy couple made their way to the head table, grinning from ear to ear and tightly clasping each other's hands, waving to their guests, friends, and the CAY community that had come out in full force to make their special day so special.

Hopefully, the newlyweds would remember Ariel's advice and stay put in their seats on the raised dais at the front of the hall, where a table adorned with the room's sole centerpiece sat in front of two tongue-in-cheek wicker peacock chairs—one bone-white, the other ebony-black—and draped in gold, silver, and blue tulle.

"Unless it's to dance," Ariel had insisted. "Do *not* leave your seats. Do *not* go and mingle with your guests. Everyone is *literally* there to see *you*. They will find *you*. Eat your food. Do. *Not*. Go. *Anywhere*."

But, watching the couple already drift towards a squealing crowd of Tamar's nursing classmates, Ariel shook his head and chuckled at the lost cause.

Then again, the entire process of counseling Tamar and Benjamin had been so weird that if there was any piece of advice he was the least invested in them following, it'd be this one.

The text had come out of the blue on a Monday afternoon, while Ariel and Ellis were debating what to try out at Mexikosher for lunch. Or, more accurately, while Ariel was waiting in exasperation for Ellis to decide what she was more in the mood for (although she was leaning "80/20" towards a chimichanga over the tacos.)

"Hey."

That was all the text had said, with elegant awkwardness.

After all, Tamar and Ariel hadn't talked in months. Not since that night in the park.

"Hey. What's up," Ariel sent back.

"This is really awkward but, small talk, small talk, small talk, I'm engaged..."

"Um. Mazal tov?"

"...And I was wondering if we could all meet up to talk about you doing the wedding."

"Um. Well. You were *not* kidding about the awkward. Lol. But why me?"

"It'd be easier to explain in person."

And so the three of them had agreed to meet the next night at Holy Smokes.

It was all very *Casablanca*. A smoky lounge with a live piano lushly tinkling away in the background. The slightly furtive atmosphere hovering around the rendezvous. And, of course, our players, with Ariel and Tamar as the former lovers Rick and Isla, and introducing Dr. Benjamin "Baruch" Watkins as Victor Laszlo, Ilsa's once and future king.

And the second Benjamin walked through the door behind Tamar—a tall, broad-shouldered mound of dark sepia who looked more suited for the physical rigors of nursing than the delicate tedium of cardiothoracic surgery—Ariel knew exactly why they'd called him there.

Apparently, as the couple had subsequently filled him in, Tamar had made good on her resolution to make amends.

She and Benjamin had ended up talking and meandering towards some kind of closure for the both of them. And it'd gone really well, actually.

Well, *eventually*.

At first it was an emotional trainwreck that jumped the tracks, plowed into a forty-car pileup on the highway, rolled in a fiery ball of destruction off a nearby dock, and crashed into a sinking cruise ship.

And then a plane fell on it.

See, at first, Tamar had broken the seal on an entire Negronomicon's worth of pent-upness Benjamin had been holding onto the entire time they'd been dating, and it all came howling out in that first conversation.

About how he felt she'd never really listened to him when he said it felt like everyone was watching his every little interaction to see if he did something "black." Or how her friends judged him when he was being "too black" and questioned him when he wasn't being "black enough." Or how she talked to him at times like he was a child, in some condescending tone like she was trying to "civilize" him to make him suitable for eventually meeting her family.

Or, in his words, *"Like you were trying to make a house nigger out of a field slave!"*

The resentment he'd felt every time she told him to *"Be careful out there. I need you back here,"* whenever he went out.

How—maybe not in and of itself, but in the context of everything else?—how Benjamin felt she dismissed the everyday danger of ~~Driving Shopping Walking~~ Living While Black, making it all incidental to *her* fear of *her* potential loss.

Not that disproportionate police brutality towards minorities was an objective problem, not that racial profiling or random stop-and-frisks were dehumanizing, not that these were terrible clouds for someone to have to live under, but the concern that Benjamin might not make it back to (for?) *her.*

But *after* all of that—the yelling, the crying, the venting, the storming away, the storming back, the defensiveness, the shouting, the apologizing, the trying unsuccessfully twice more to dam the floodgates—after all of it had burnt off and away, they both realized that a lot of the *good* feelings between hadn't ever exactly been buried, *either.*

And so, finally, they talked.

To each other, not *at* each other. And they listened. To the actual words, not just so they could respond to them.

They talked about how they were *both* guilty of forgetting that *people* were in their interracial relationship, not racial demographics. And how neither one of them had really taken that into account.

Like Benjamin's struggle with internalized anti-Blackness and anti-Semitism, separately and together. Or how many moments of casual racism he buried or micro-aggressions he'd spent years desensitizing himself to, just to get through an evening out with co-workers or a Jewish event with friends. And then how it felt to realize that he was hearing it in his relationship too. How on the good days, it felt like they were just two people who really loved each other and were doing life together. And on the bad days, it was like their racial histories were in so much conflict that there was no hope for it ever working.

And Tamar admitted her own past missteps and less than pretty actions. Her internalized racism, how she was actively trying to dismantle it, how she'd come a long way—a *long* way—from when they'd first started dating, but that she was still able to recognize that sometimes her best wasn't enough. And maybe it always wouldn't be enough. But she was willing to do the work. To change. To have those hard, ugly conversations.

It was a good start.

So they kept talking.

Over the next few weeks. The next few days. The next few hours.

Until it was pretty obvious to the both of them what was happening, and what was going to happen next.

And they decided that *this* time, they were going to go for it.

All the way.

They were gonna figure out how to live with their beauty and their beasts. They didn't want the fight. But they *did* want each other.

Manishtana

So it was time to pull back that hair, take off them earrings, Vaseline up that face, tuck some razors in their cheeks, and square up. Who wants a buck fifty?

First up? The parents.

Tamar's, not Benjamin's.

No, Benjamin's parents—an interracial Orthodox lesbian couple in their fifties who scandalously referred to themselves as "Orthodykes"—had already met Tamar during her and Benjamin's first go around at a relationship. They liked her well enough.

And at any rate, they were much more concerned about Tamar being able to bring their son back to keeping **cholov Yisroel** than anything else.

But Tamar's family?

Well, let's put it this way: when driving through Washington Heights a week earlier, Tamar's little brother noticed a group of Dominican 3rd-grade girls and pointed out the window at the "baby maids" as they passed by.

He was 24.

Shockingly enough, once they'd reached their intended destination—the 97th birthday party of their grandmother, formerly of the South African Jewish Board of Deputies—the level of racial sensitivity did not seem to significantly increase.

So their reaction to Tamar's news had been fairly easy to anticipate.

"They've stopped speaking to me," Tamar confirmed, nodding matter-of-factly. "*Pretty* sure I'm disowned. But, y'know what? I don't care. I never really wanted to be Tamar Denebeim, anyway," she looked up at Benjamin, with a soft glow in her eyes that Ariel had never even seen a *shadow* of before. "But I'm ready to be Tamar Watkins. I'm *ready* now."

It was a movingly delivered statement.

A declaration full of all the vulnerable determination worthy of a Meryl Streep-starring role, in a cinematic ode to colorblind love and admiration for the simple bravery of an intrepid white woman daring to love, risking it all most some the condemnation of her white family and white friends. A tale of timeless dignity, honoring the struggle of giving up fifteen, maybe twenty percent, of the privilege of her everyday life. (Unless she, like, left her other half in the car or something. Then it was back up to 100%.)

It would probably have Dennis Haysbert in the co-starring role, with his subplot about navigating backlash from his black family and friends likely featuring in the trailer, but being cut from the movie. All the scenes of him being congratulated for "marrying up" would make it in, though.

But *"I'm ready to be Tamar Watkins?" That* would be the clip they'd play at the Oscars.

Luckily for Tamar and Benjamin, Ariel wasn't nearly as cynical as I am.

Did he wonder, when Tamar and Benjamin eventually had kids, if she would instruct her black children that the key to staying out of trouble with authorities was to be respectful and polite? As if being respectful and polite didn't still end up with black Americans killed by police or any other community watchman loon with a gun?

Maybe.

Was it concerning to him that Tamar might advise her children—or even Benjamin, if his financial fortunes experienced a downturn—about the "opportunites" that were just lying about, available to some amorphous Everyone, as if laws and biases hadn't been weaving a centuries-old net that made even present-day access to much of those resources untenable, improbable, or illegal for black Americans in ways just as de facto as modern segregation?

Possibly.

But they seemed genuinely happy together, so that was good enough for him.

And honestly, if they hadn't figured their relationship out yet, then they definitely wouldn't have it figured out in the sixteen days they had left until the Lag b'Omer wedding date they were *adamant* on making happen.

Besides, wasn't that the point of the wedding day? Wasn't that why it was considered a personal **Yom Kippur** for the bride and groom? A personalized day of atonement where all their past mistake were forgiven, and they emerged with a clean slate, merged into a new singular soul?

So yeah, Ariel thought as he watched Benjamin and Tamar waltz through their first official dance together, maybe there were rocky times ahead on the horizon. Then again, maybe there weren't.

But today was today.

Manishtana

And today, they were happy. And they worked.

Watching Benjamin and Tamar together—cheesy smiles ablaze, giggling into each other's necks, melting into each others' eyes like there was no one else in the world but the two of them—it reminded Ariel of Jake and Liora's respective weddings.

His sister had gotten married first in the family.

Dr. Yoel Hendricks. A strapping young resident at the time, not unlike Benjamin.

The night that Liora had discovered that she'd passed the bar—on the first try!—celebratory drinks were *clearly* in order. All of them. All of the drinks. Because seven years of school.

But Liora's vice of choice was cigarettes, never alcohol really.

Next stop: the ER. Because alcohol poisoning. All of it. All of the alcohol poisoning.

And that's where she'd met her future husband, their marriage inevitable from the moment she'd drunkenly shout-whispered at the young doctor (so the nurse wouldn't hear, obviously) with the laughably cringeworthy, uncharacteristically tawdry attempt at a pick-up line: "Hey...*Hey!*...Are you K for P, Dr. Hot Chocolate? Because let's get married and I'll be OU-D."

Immortal words that, eight years later, her siblings were *still* forbidden under pain of death to reveal to their parents.

(For those of you struggling to unravel this deliciously naughty masterpiece, the "P" in "K for P" doesn't stand for "Passover," and the "D" in "OU-D" doesn't mean dairy.)

Yoel had admirably struggled to keep a straight face in response, and when he came back around later on that night to check in on her, she was sober enough to be so mortified that she was pretending to be dead.

Which, naturally, left him no recourse but to ask her "comatose" body out on a date. Because he'd just moved to New York from Cali and was feeling a little bit lonely and overwhelmed by the culture shock of it all.

Besides, what was a cup of coffee between two black Jews?

And from there on out they were inseparable.

Or as inseparable as second-year resident and equally busy fresh new lawyer got to be.

But when they *did* get to have the time for each other?

They spent every second being the center of each other's universe. It was that corny kind of love that just radiated out from

344

between them and touched everyone else in their lives with its heat, eliciting simultaneous eye-rolls and genuine happiness for them.

Within months they were engaged, to the surprise of absolutely no one, and before anyone had a chance to blink really, they were Dr. Yoel and Mrs. Liora Hendricks, Esq.

And they'd been together ever since, walking through life arm in arm, never letting fun become unimportant, and knowing that sometimes it was alright to go to bed angry, from the highs of Yoel becoming an attending physician and Liora starting her own firm, to the lows of their miscarriage, adding yet another Samson clan tragedy to a year that had already taken Savalava, seen Aviva leave her religion behind, and hosted the complete disintegration of Jake's marriage and family.

Speaking of, Jake had gotten married the year after Liora did.

Probably because Liora's wedding had put some fire under his ass. Or maybe it was Anita.

Anita "Ayelet" Mercado. A fiercely Puerto-Rican Latina Jew.

Jake's mother had felt some kind of way about Anita not being black when they'd first started dating. Which lasted until AviandAri had pointed out to their mother how *she'd* felt for so many years about Savalava feeling some kinda of way that she was a convert.

Their mom had quickly backed down after that. Although her mother's intutition was right.

Anita and Jake were just *not* good for each other.

They both suffered that romantic mistruth that your soulmate was your other half that completed you, and so they went about searching for someone who'd make them whole instead of realizing that they needed to feel whole themselves first.

But no, against everyone's advice they went and got married, then quickly popped out a kid to fix it.

And then when that didn't work, they popped out *another* kid to throw at the problem. Which, c'mon guys, babies aren't duct tape. They're not duct tape for relationships. That's not...that's not how they work.

And you can't just stuff in a baby into things and use them to plug up holes like they're steel wool, either.

See, they were great at loving each other, Jake and Ayelet, but when it came down to washing the dishes, and putting gas in the car, flushing the toilet, and taking out the garbage—when it came to the tedium of every day life, they were more than incompetent.

Manishtana

They were downright *poisonous.*

It had been a whirlwind romance, hot and heavy, and the divorce was just as ugly and messy, with every vindictive thought and breath posted and plastered across social media almost the second it formed in their cerebral cortex, until they both of them were standing in the ashes of the bridge they'd burned while still standing on it.

Because marriage was hard work.

Or so I've heard anyway.

Never been married myself, and not ever gonna. I spend way too much time on the road for that to ever work out. Hell, I don't even have a *pet.* Which is kinda torture because dogs *love* me.

But nope. Sorry.

Marriage was a difficult thing that deserves the kind of work that I can't put into it.

But when you *do,* when you put that work into it, you have a precious thing. A beautiful thing. Something more than a ring worn or a paper signed or 45k of debt, but a private, hidden, sacred space. A cleft in the rock where one soul can whisper to another in the darkness, speaking devotions in the secret language that only its other half can hear.

Why would anyone throw that away, I do not know.

And, as he watched Benjamin and Tamar being hoisted into the air, nervously clutching onto the edges of their chairs for dear life, precariously bobbing in the air in the hands of their friends, Ariel didn't know either.

"Hey," came a voice, and Ariel looked up to see Kalman's uneasy smile.

Kalman had been fairly sparse at the *shul* these days.

And when he did come, he and Ariel rarely interacted more than passing niceties.

As far as the congregation knew—as far as he'd told them in his farewell speech from the *bimah*—Kalman had stepped down from president to accommodate for the extra responsibilities he was taking on at work, and Ariel had publicly wished Kalman well at the *kiddish* afterwards, saving Kalman more face than he deserved, for Dassi's sake.

A few days later, Ariel heard through the grapevine that Cate was circulating the story that she'd relinquished being treasurer to follow an entrepreneurial venture with her husband.

Otherwise, however, she'd simply vanished, not returning to CAY since the Shabbat afternoon that Ariel had ordered her and Kalman to step down. Which, *totally* not a thing Ariel should've felt concerned about at all.

In any way.

At all.

Anyhoo, CAY had a new president now. Sruli. A scarily typical bleeding heart knee-jerk liberal in his 30's.

The kind of person who, well, isn't "asleep" really, but definitely not "woke."

More like that half-groggy feeling-around-for-your-phone-to-turn-off-the-alarm state. But they're mostly woke. Like 5/8th's woke.

And 9/8th's tone-deaf.

They'd also scored a new treasurer, too.

Blair.

A Jew of Color who introduced herself as being "half-Jewish and half-Japanese. And for either side, that's half too much."

There was probably also something to be said about Blair being the new treasurer, Asians, Jews, math, and money, but we're not going to say that something.

The point being, Congregation Ahavath Yisroel was thriving still, even in Kalman and Cate's absence, finding itself a new groove in its Rabbi Samson era.

And it seemed like Kalman realized that, Samuel Gellerman's grandson or not, he didn't really have a place there anymore.

But Tamar was a close friend. And she *was* getting married today. So there he and Dassi were for the wedding.

"Can, uh, can we talk?" Kalman asked. "Like, alone? In your office?"

Ariel fought off his initial reflex to say no.

But, he remembered, he was the congregation's spiritual leader. Even for the wayward of its flock.

He didn't get to talk to just the people he liked.

In fact, maybe the ones he *didn't* like needed it even more.

"Sure."

✡ ✡ ✡

Ariel stood, leaning against his desk with his arms crossed in front of him. Kalman sat in a chair across from him.

Manishtana

They sat there for a moment, only two feet apart, but they might as well have been on opposite sides of the Grand Canyon, trying to recognize each other across the distance. Too far away to make out what used to be their friendship anymore.

"So?" Ariel asked curtly.

"I...I want to ask you about adultery. Like, explain it to me like I'm a four-year old," Kalman said with a weak smile, haltingly answering with the signature line of Denzel Washington's Joe Miller character in *Philadelphia*. It was the movie that Ariel, Kalman, and Ilan had watched on that first night after getting kicked out from Mayanot.

"Look, Kalman," Ariel rose up from the desk and started to head for the door, annoyed by the cheap appeal to nostalgia. "I've got a wedding happening right now. I don't have time to fo—"

"NO!" Kalman leapt up from his chair, taking Ariel aback. Kalman stood between Ariel and the door. "Just...*please*..."

There was a rawness, a desperation to his voice that struck Ariel. He didn't recognize it.

"I, just...can you tell me?" Kalman composed himself, using a gentler, almost pleading tone. "Yeah, I *know* it's one of those things we studied back in Israel, but...Please?"

Puzzled, and now a bit guarded, Ariel settled back down against the desk.

"Okay...Well, technically 'adultery' refers specifically to relations with a married woman. A married man and a single woman is still impermissible, but it doesn't fit the *halachic* definition of being an adulterous relationship. Now, when it comes to consequences, a woman who has had an adulterous relationship is forbidden both to her husband and her lover. She can't divorce one and then go marry the other. And when it comes to punishment, adulterers are subject to penalties in both the human and Heavenly courts of law. In the human courts, adultery is punishable by death for both parties, either stoning in the case of a betrothed woman, or strangulation in the case of a married woman. Divinely, the punishment of **karet** is decreed against the adulterers."

"And, um, *karet*," Kalman said softly. "Can you, uh...can you just go over that with me?"

"...*Karet* is the divine punishment of excision from the Jewish people. It can manifest physically—as dying before the age of 60,

348

dying without children, or experiencing the death of one's already living children—or it is inflicted spiritually, by the total annihilation of one's soul after death. According to the Ramban, if a sinner's good deeds outweigh their bad ones, they're punished with dying before their time in *this* world, but retain their portion in **Olam Haba**. But if their bad deeds outweigh the good, then any good they've done is rewarded in this world with a lengthy life, and after death they have no portion in *Olam Haba.*"

"And uh, what if...what if it was an accident?" Kalman asked, looking down at the floor.

Ariel scrunched up his face.

Really? Ariel thought. *Youre gonna go with that? What, did you trip and land repeatedly into Cate's—*

Kalman raised his head, looking up at Ariel with wide, scared eyes.

"What if someone didn't want to do it?" he asked pleadingly. "What if they didn't want to do *any* of it?"

"In, uh...in *unintentional* or inadvertent cases," Ariel said cautiously, now concerned. "One doesn't get punished with *karet,* but then they have to offer a **chatat** offering. Nowadays, *teshuva, tefilla* and *tzedeka* would serve the same purpose...But—Kalman...*what* are you saying exactly?"

"That I hadn't, that I didn't have a choice, and...it just...Dassi's pregnant, Ariel," Kalman's voice was quivering as he looked up at his friend, imploringly, nervously wringing his hands.

"Rabbi, is our baby gonna die because of me?"

✡ ✡ ✡

As it turns out, no one spends years in real estate without learning how to wiggle out of even the most iron-clad of contracts. And especially handshake agreements made a generation ago between two deceased parties.

The Katz brothers weren't still invested in Congregation Ahavath Yisroel out of the goodness of their hearts or because of some wistful nostalgia. They never had been.

C'mon now.

Did you *really* think, that when Kalman became president of CAY, that a couple of real estate movers and shakers—in negotiations for a *federal* contract—not only gave a twenty-something the time of day for some reason, but had *actually* managed to be convinced to grant some arbitrary grace period to "turn things around" like a teen movie plot point?

Yeah, no.

Kalman might've been the first Gellerman to cross CAY's threshold since its shift from Conservative to Orthodox, but the Katzes were very much the Denethor to Kalman's Aragorn.

And they were not interested in bowing to this ranger from Boro Park.

So, despite Kalman's rallying in his first few days of being president, and the numerous ignored voicemails being left with the Katzes, CAY was still only months away from being sold.

And that's when Cate Finklestein had come into the picture.

"She said that she believed in me, in my passion to revitalize the shul," Kalman recounted, staring into the small cup of water Ariel had gotten him from his new water cooler. "She said that together we could get the Katzes ear. And I believed her. I was so determined to save this place that...I mean, I believed everything she said. Anything. And I guess she delivered, because all of a sudden, *boom*, there we were in the Katzes' office signing a 90-day agreement...I was so stupid. It probably had nothing to do with me or CAY at all. We were probably just some tradeoff or leverage or something so Cate could pull off whatever else shady machinations she had going on or something. She'd driven us over to the meeting, so when it was over she drove us back to her place to celebrate. Her husband was out of town on business, I guess. She opened up a bottle of something expensive, I don't even know what, and I hadn't eaten all day and I was all excited because I thought we'd really pulled something off, so I was really knocking it back and...The next thing I remember is waking up in the middle of...it...Of her...she was...Anyway, when she was finished, she just gave me this look, like the way a cat looks at a mouse, y'know? And she said something about how we probably shouldn't say anything about it, and how it was just a mistake...And...And I thought that was it. That it was some large huge mistake and, I mean it was **Rosh Hashana** the next week, and...But from then on she'd call these 'budget meetings' and if I didn't show up, she'd threaten to tell Dassi, or tell other people that I'd forced myself on her, or head back to the Katzes to terminate the agreement...and I didn't, I just didn't know what to do. So I kept showing up. I was so stupid. So fucking stupid. I should've never..."

"Hey..." Ariel put his hand on Kalman's shoulder, ignoring his flinch, comforting him. "Kalman, you didn't...I mean...How long did this go on?"

"Six months. From about a month before when I ran into you again at the bar until the week you caught us. Was driving Dassi crazy."

"You told her?"

"And tell her *what*? That, that I was being—no. I just...No. But we'd stopped, y'know, I mean, I couldn't be sneaking around at Cate's beck and call and then climb into bed with her like I wasn't out there. That wouldn't be right. But then that made Dassi start feeling like I wasn't attracted to her anymore and just...I was just, *so* happy when you caught us," Kalman exhaled in relief, the quiver returning to his voice. "Because she couldn't do anything to me anymore. She couldn't trap me. And you'd made the *shul* alive again, and everybody knew about it, so the Katzes couldn't strongarm *you* either. And...I'm sorry Ariel. I am *really* sorry that, just, about everything, and—I mean I *know* how it must've sounded when I asked about terminating our contracts on Shabbat when you were throwing us off the board. But I was just, just so low and covered in *so* much grime and sludge that I was hoping that I wasn't getting some on you, too. And—"

"Kalman."

Kalman stopped, and looked up. Finally meeting Ariel's eyes. And seeing a friend in them again.

"It's not your fault. None of this. It wasn't your fault. You understand that?"

Kalman nodded wordlessly.

"Now I want you to get out of here. I want you to go downstairs and celebrate with your friend who just got *married* today. I want you to dance. Then take your wife, your pregnant wife, and go home. Go home and be a good husband. And wake up tomorrow and start preparing to be a great father. *B'sha'ah tovah*, Kalman," Ariel ended with a grin, selfishly grateful to know that his friend was still somewhere in there after all.

Although, honestly, he probably should've been more concerned with what Machiavellian machinations a scorned Cate

Finklestein was cooking up in retaliation for being ejected from her place of power.

But, again, Ariel wasn't nearly as cynical as I am.

And I, personally, was too busy being confused by people being confused by Benjamin's lesbian parents being practicing Orthodox Jews.

Like, I watch the news, and apparently there's this entire genre of Orthodox Jews that's able to touch little boys and still call themselves *frum*.

Is there something about the lack of pedophilia or the presence of consent that blows people's minds when two consenting adults in a same-sex relationship identify as Orthodox?

I dunno, man.

But hey, that's none of *my* business.

ARIEL SAMSON: FREELANCE RABBI

Friday, May 27, 2016-Friday, June 3, 2016
19/20 Iyar 5776-26/27 Iyar 5776

"*What?*"

"I *said*, aren't *you* a little motherfucking *short* to be a motherfucking *stormtrooper*?"

Satan L. Jackson hollered while Ariel struggled to keep his balance on the deck. But Ariel's heavy white helmet was making it was hard to hear the devil over the screeching of metal as an iceberg dragged across the side of the RMS Titanic.

"*What?*"

"*Say what again!*" Satan's eyes began to glow bright-orange in a face that looked identical to Samuel L. Jackson's, except for the pointy little red horns. "Say! What! Again! I *dare* you! I *double* dare you!"

Ariel was raising his E-11 blaster rifle to fire another volley of badly-aimed shots at his immortal foe, when the familiar chirping of an off-brand Overworld Theme prickled in his ears, nudging him awake from the bizarrely recurrent dream you probably thought was a one-off joke thirty chapters ago.

Groggily fumbling around for his phone, he saw it was Ellis calling. And that it was 6:17 in the morning.

"*Shalom?* I'll be in in a couple hours, why—"

"We're in trouble Ariel. From Rosenstern."

"...What?"

353

Manishtana
✡ ✡ ✡

In the great tradition of Paris Hilton, Lindsay Lohan, and other spoiled white kids with so much money that it hurt, 24 year-old Pinchas "Pinny" Rosenstern, oldest son of blackface afficionado Assemblyman Aryeh Rosenstern, had decided that drinking and driving was a thing he was going to do, and ended up arrested and cited for driving under the influence in the wee hours of Friday morning.

According to the police, there were also traces of a substance that could tentatively be identified as a "usable amount of cocaine."

Which is funny to me. Like, what's an "unusable" amount of cocaine? Like are there crackheads running around like *"Man, I'm not even going to bother with that. Might as well just sprinkle it in my tea."*

Anyway, Junior Rosenstern crashed his 2005 Mercedes-Benz SL65 into a sidewalk somewhere in Prospect Heights, with surveillance video showing his white convertible jumping a curb and getting wedged between the last two trees in Brooklyn, with its front left headlight smashed into a parking meter.

Being slightly injured in the 4:30 AM wreck, Junior was cited and released because he'd been admitted to a local hospital.

And the problem for our gang?

An event photographer saying that he'd seen Pinny Rosenstern climbing into his car, looking "completely wasted," after leaving a night of heavy drinking and smoking...at Holy Smokes.

Accompanied by a blonde older woman. A cougar in her fifties with particularly long and shapely legs.

That's right.

That one.

✡ ✡ ✡

The swift hand of the jury of public opinion descended quickly across Facebook, Twitter, and the lowest circle of Hell otherwise known as the comments section of every article ever.

And nothing was to be spared, from the fact that Holy Smokes should apparently never have existed in the first place:

"Why does a place like this exist??? Where our young people can be exposed to *shtus* and unsavory environments??? By Achashverosh's party there was also kosher food! If you want to be out so late drinking then go to some non-kosher bar and leave Judaism for the MODEST and the RIGHTEOUS!!!!"

To those criticizing Ariel for giving the *hechsher*:
"Who does this 'rabbi' think he is? He knows better than the OU or Star-K or Kof-K? Such ego!"

To those attacking CAY:
"What do we expect from someone who's the 'Rav' of the CONSERVATIVE temple CAY. They've *always* been against the Orthodox. Women coming to services in tank tops and pants and guys with tattoos? Orthodox? Yeah, right. Lemme know when the Yom Kippur social justice clam-bake fundraiser is."

To those criticizing his "Freelance Rabbi" persona:

"The *Late Late Night Night* show is not a place for a *frum yid*. I take offense by all those that are celebrating an Orthodox Jew being a television and internet fixture as some huge achievement and *kiddish Hashem*. These are our goals now? 'Making it' on a TV show? Being a rock star in a *yarmulke*? Since when is late night TV kosher? This is just another example of how far we have strayed and how our values have deteriorated. No thank you 'Rabbi.'"

To those bringing his blackness into the conversation for some reason:
"Who gave this *schvarzte* monkey a *smicha*??? Defrock this fake rabbi and good riddance!! The Jewish community doesn't want black Jews anyway!!"

To those laughing at him getting burned by white Jews:
"LOLOL. That's what he get. Negropeans tryna be with the Jew-ISH Ashke-NAZIS and running behind the Synagogue of Satan and surprised that he's getting treated like a nigger?? White supremacy is a helluva drug. LOLOLOL."

On the bright side, there were also some supporters:

"To everybody up in arms about 'Freelance Rabbi' being a role model for our kids, you should all ask yourselves if you are a role model when you walk down the street on Shabbos and don't say '*Good Shabbos,*' or when a commmunity is so divided by its 'leaders' that they resort to secular courts to settle disputes. And let's not talk about all the molestation cover-ups and corruption. Oh wait, we already don't. We have much bigger problems to address than worrying about a rabbi being on late-nite TV."

"What a shame this place and rabbi are getting such a bad rap. My 22 year-old daughter runs with a mixed crowd of girlfriends and they found Holy Smokes last month. I can say firsthand it's a great place where they can be a little daring, drink/party in a 'with it' NY nightspot, and it satisfies her *kashrut* needs while being welcoming enough for her non-Jewish friends, and as a parent I love the fact that my daughter can eat while she drinks and temper the effects of the alcohol. If this lounge ends up closing because of all this uproar, her mixed group will still end up at places that are hip, but she'll end up only being able to drink but not eat, and my worry will increase every time she goes out."

But by and large those next few days were a firestorm of terrible, and Ariel—between the news crews showing up outside the studios and synagogue, to the *frum* protesters picketing outside Holy Smokes—was being swamped by it.

Assemblyman Rosenstern led the charge, obviously, his bellowing red face dominating the local news cycle either from the other side of a bullhorn at a protest, or as a talking head on the morning news.

And this time he found himself a perfect tag-team partner in none other than Rabbi Dov Ber Guildencrantz.

"Ariel Samson's craving for recognition by the outside culture has led him to trample, with impunity, on our prized traditions of **hashkafa** and *da'as Torah*," Guildencrantz decried on an early morning radio show. "He kept on pushing the envelope as far as he could and waited to see if anyone pushed back. And this unfortunate incident is the inevitable outcome of our silence in the face of his un-Orthodox recklessness. We can no longer just stand on the sidelines and watch. Yes, it is late. Yes, we should have dealt with this earlier. But it is not *too* late. He must be dealt with swiftly and seriously, before his influence can continue to poison the younger generation."

Calling in the clergyman was a canny move by Rosenstern, removing City Councilman Jeffrey Grundman from the board as an ally on Ariel's side, and an expertly crafted strategy in a two-pronged attack, with Rosenstern mauling Ariel in the public sphere, and Guildencrantz raking him over the kosher coals.

Ellis, ever Ariel's rock, had ordered him not to come in on Monday, and to just work from home the next week while things died down. And so he'd spent the whole week holed up in his apartment, gorging on Netflix and supervising the hookah lounge via Skype.

"Are you alright?" Liora had asked when she called to check in on him, three days into his stir-craziness.

"I'm ok. I'm fine. I can handle this."

"You sure? You know that if you just say the word, we'll be there. All of us. You *do* know that, right?"

"Yeah, I know that Lee."

"Good."

"And, seriously, it really means a lot to hear that right now."

"No worries, baby bro. Also, if you end up needing representation, I've got you covered."

"Thanks, I—wait, 'also?' So what did you mean before when you said you'd be here if I needed?"

"I don't know what you're talking about," she said coolly. Like a pocketknife dressed in business suit. "We never had that conversation. And most certainly not over the phone."

Manishtana

It was a dark and stormy night.

Which, until I said it aloud just now, I suppose I've always been too dazzled by that line's literary pedigree to notice how redundant it actually is. Of *course*, it was dark. It was night.

And yet, here we are, on a dark and stormy night, with Ariel standing in his bathroom—looking not-too shabby in a 3-piece black pinstripe suit and tie—trying to convince his reflection that he wasn't about to barrel into a raging dumpster fire.

I mean, he probably was.

But he didn't need to *feel* that way.

After all, it's not like he had a choice either way.

Nope, that much was made clear yesterday, when the Constitution Studios CEO had decided to stop playing Clockmaker and start playing Deus Ex Machina, sending in Leslie "Les" Valentine III—Chairman of Constitution Studios Television and Online Content, and father of Wesley "Wes" Valentine—to right the cart, cancelling the day's *Late Late Night Night* taping to call an emergency meeting with the core staff.

"Our balls are on the line here," Les started, in a clipped tone that burst the bubble of antagonistic silence he'd filled the room with. The elder Valentine—with grey-and-silver hair just as vertically improbable (yet not as lush) as his offspring, a swagger

358

well-earned, and shades of an equally doughy frame now winnowed by age—swept the room with a glare that seemed to be a face-saving pretense for the askance frown he rested on Wes. "The 'Freelance Rabbi' character has become so intertwined into the identity of *Late Late Night Night* that the two are almost inseparable. And that popularity has translated into *Late Late* becoming synonomous with the face of Constitution Studios. So if this show goes up in flames, the studio stands a very good chance of going with it, which means that none of us have jobs."

And, surprisingly, no thanks to you, Les' glance said to Wes.

"So I'm guessing you've been sent down here with a plan. Or an ultimatum," Wes deduced, with rolled eyes that said *Really, dad? Are we really going to do this right now?*

"Well it's no secret that our former flagship show, *The O'Halloran Outlook,* has been swamped with accusations of alleged sexual harassment in the past few weeks," Les continued, his cleared throat practically bellowing *Why* not? *Why* not *do this right now? Because you don't want to be embarrassed in front of your little friends? Because it's my fault you've flunked out of every private school I've ever put you in and squandered every opportunity you've been handed? Honestly,* Wesley, *you've been a constant disappointment to me since the day you were born, and if I could, I would let* Late Late Night Night *crash and burn and be done with you.*

"And months. And years," Wes muttered, bitterly shooting back with an unspoken *I truly, madly, deeply apologize on behalf of the nurse who misheard you and wrote 'Wesley' instead of 'Leslie,' and oh so unjustly robbed you of a namesake. Although you really could've ju—*

"So it's in the studio's best interest," Les said over Wes. "To help shift the focus away from *Outlook* and onto our biggest asset, *Late Late.* But we can't jump on a different burning ship either. So tomorrow, *you,*" he pointed at Ariel. "Rosenstern, and Guildencrantz, are all gonna show up on *Outlook* tomorrow night for a special town hall meeting. Get all your drama out in the open, dealt with, and *over.* I don't care *what* you do. Talk about flat-ironing your sidecurls for all I care. But get this resolved."

"Well, we don't really have any say on whether *they* think it's resolved or not, do we?" Wes answered with challenging smirk. *Not all Orthodox Jews wear long sidecurls, Dad. Some just don't cut their sideburns, or they tuck the hair behing their ears. Orthodoxy isn't some Hasidic monolith.*

"Get. This. Resolved. Yesterday." *Oh, so you hire a rabbi for six months and now you're some expert on Jews now?*

"Aye, aye captain," Wes saluted, sardonically. *It's called investigative journalism. I was a journalism major in college. You do remember that, right? Or did you forget while you were busy trying to shove me into the family business? But, oh, I'm sorry, you were saying something about me squandering all the choices you decided I got to have while you were trampling the ones I actually wanted?*

"Tomorrow night. Make it happen," Les reiterated evenly, this time addressing the room and ignoring the very specific subtextual argument he was passive-aggressively having with his son.

Thus came the mandate from on corporate high. So let it be written so shall it be done.

But, as the equally as urgent emergency CAY board meeting later that day had proved, this did not at all seem like a good idea.

"This does not at all seem like a good idea," Jerome intoned.

"I know," Ariel sighed with resignation. "I was more than happy just trying to steer clear of Rosenstern. And now he's got back up this time around."

"Couldn't we," Sruli spoke up, this only being his third board meeting as *shul* president. "I dunno, couldn't you just write a letter or publicly apologize or something?"

"Sruli. They've got people out there *protesting*. The apology ship sailed so long ago that Spain is still waiting for it to bring back gold and slaves," Ellis remarked wryly. "Rosenstern has been a pain in our ass once, and now he's got his chance to really sink his teeth into us. And now that he's got Guildencrantz on his team, we need to drag this hydra kicking and screaming into the light and slay the beast."

"I dunno, Ellis, I..." Sruli sniffed the air, made a disgusted face, then turned on Phyllis, sitting across the table and enjoying a beverage of no less than 300-proof alcohol while she jotted down increasingly illegible notes. "What's that *smell*? Is that scotch? *Why* do you always smell like scotch?"

"What I smell like, is *bourbon*, you philistine," Phyllis retorted from behind her indoor sunglasses, taking another full-mouthed gulp mostly out of spite.

"What's the *difference*?"

"*Damare konoyarou*," Blair groaned, groggily lifting her head from the table, still fairly hungover from it doesn't matter because college student and alcohol. She was rallying, but just unwell enough that her angry Japanese was still coming out. "Scotch is malted barley from Scotland. Bourbon is from Kentucky and is 51% corn. *Baka*."

"See? I knew I liked you," Phyllis beamed at Blair, then rolled her eyes and gestured at Sruli. "*Kuchikitanai*."

"*Uzaeeeeeeeeeee*," Blair bleated in agreement, returning her forehead to the soothingly cool tabletop.

"Whatever," Sruli muttered under his breath. "Glad you weren't ever any teacher of *mine*."

"Honey. If I'd've ever been your teacher, you would've turned out a lot better than you did."

"Guys," Ellis corralled the meeting. "I don't like any of this, either. But we *can* do this. In fact, there really isn't anything to lose, so we might as *well* do this," she looked at Ariel. "But you're the rabbi. This board will have your back either way, but this is your call."

Everyone nodded in silent acquiescence, holding their breath, waiting for what the word would be like the Israelites waiting for Moses to descend from the mountain for a second time.

Ariel looked to Ellis. *Do you really think we can? That this is a good idea?*, he wordlessly asked.

Ellis gave him a smirk, with an eyebrow arched.

It would read as confidence to anyone else. But, at this point, after almost half a year spending nearly every waking moment with each other, he could read Ellis' eyes screaming *Honestly? Do you want me to say that I'm fucking terrified? Fine. I'm fucking terrified. I am terrified that, together, Rosenstern and Guildenstern will drag you through every mud imaginable and play you like a Bob Marley album in a white college kid's dorm room. You do not have to do this...But since you're probably going to anyway, I'm rallying the troops. You're welcome.*

"Alright then. We're going in," Ariel decreed, steeling himself. "Game faces everyone. Debate's tomorrow night."

And so we return to the dark and stormy night of the debate, with Ariel staring at himself in the mirror, trying to mentally hype himself up.

Manishtana

It was easy enough to rally the masses behind your persona. But not so much in the quiet time of just the you you know yourself to really be. And it was hard enough to do without a pair of pale blue eyes staring back at you.

Sure, they belonged to Ariel, but in a way, they really didn't. And to be completely honest, he never really felt they did.

He kinda hated them most days, actually.

They were as much the physical manifestation of his barred entry into blackness as his skin cast him as an outsider in Jewishness.

And together they worked to create the begrudging category he always found himself a member of from either point of attack.

The exotic club of *"Oh, I've heard of black people like that. Do you..."*

No.

No he didn't have ocular albinism, or a white parent, or heterochromia, or Ashkenazi ancestry, or Waardenburg syndrome, or Ethiopian ancestry, or bilateral isohypochromia. There was no eye surgery or conversion, genetic mutation or racial cocktail.

There wasn't anything "wrong" to explain his eyes away, or some box of "not *all* black" to dent his blackness with his Jewishness. This was him, the wholeness of him, not something deficient or extra to make him more palatable.

Just the manifestation of his story and the unlocking of his genes.

Sorry if that made people scratch their heads.

Actually, y'know what?

No. No he wasn't. He wasn't sorry that people were myopic. He wasn't sorry that the all of him made people lose their minds.

And he for damn sure wasn't sorry that Rosenstern and Guildencrantz apparently had hurt feelings about him taking up his rightful space.

Fuck. That.

He looked back at the pale blue eyes—at *his* pale blue eyes—twinkling back at him.

"Yeah," he repeated to himself, nodding at his reflection as he backed out of the bathroom.

"It's showtime," his reflection answered back.

Plucking his phone up from the dining room table while heading for the door, it began to ring, and he answered it.

"*Shalom?*"

"Answer. Your phone. The hell. In English."

"Colin? Look man, I'm about to head ou—"

"I know. I'm outside waiting. Let's go."

✡ ✡ ✡

Much to Ariel's surprise, not only was Colin *actually* waiting outside the apartment, Colin was waiting *while sitting inside his car*, a crisp, shiny beast of a black pearl 2011 Acura RL that didn't look a day over 2015.

Colin reached over the passenger seat and threw the door open, while Ariel stood on the curb, mouth still gaping.

"Get in," Colin said. "You didn't think me and Jumaane would let you do this alone, did you?"

"Wow," Ariel exclaimed. "In your *car*? Are you *sure*?"

"Just get in," Colin sighed. "Before I change my mind."

Ariel peered into the backseat.

"Where's Jumaane?"

"Taking the train. He'll meet us there."

Ariel looked at Colin.

"What?" Colin rolled his eyes in exasperation. "When half the Jewish army is on *his* ass then he can get a ride in my car, too. *Get in.*"

Shaking his head, Ariel climbed into the car, pulled the door closed behind him, and off they went.

Manishtana

Wednessday, June 8, 2016
2/3 Sivan 5776

No matter how old you get, there's always a part of you that will never feel quite safe in the adult world. And that part will always find a way to stubbornly cling onto some vestige of your childhood, reluctantly dragging its feet into maturity like an insecure boyfriend to the feminine hygiene aisle at 11:00 on a Thursday night.

It's a terror us adults like to pretend doesn't exist by calling it "nostalgia" or "being young at heart."

For some people it's a sweet spot for Lisa Frank binders or Hello Kitty merch. For others it's the weekly Wednesday excursion to the local comic shop, catching up on the familiar vigilant vigilante's newest adventures.

For Jake Samson, it was Frosted Flakes. (Yes, the cereal. I hear it's great. I wouldn't know, I'm more of a cake for breakfast kinda guy. Homemeade.)

At any rate, Jake lumbered into his apartment around 9:00 that night, loped into his kitchen, poured himself a bowl of his favorite comfort food, and plopped down in his kitchen to munch, absentmindedly eyeing his place over like a bored panther reclining on a tree branch.

It wasn't large. Just a studio apartment in Philly.

But every bit the mess his ex-wife had sworn his living condition would be if she weren't around to clean up after him.

Although, in his defense, he'd only moved in a couple of months ago.

A little bit of chaos and still-packed boxes was to be expected.

And also, by the way, it was perfectly fine to wash all your clothes in cold water.

Separating someone's laundry into lights and darks and warms and colds didn't make you some kind of selfless martyr. Particularly when said someone never asked you to.

So he was fine with the piles of dirty laundry.

He was fine wirh a lot of things now.

Before?

OMG he'd've been offended at the mere hint of an insinuation that he was inherenrly untidy or unorganized. But these days, he was simply surprised to find he didn't really care.

Not "didn't care" in the "fuck you" kinda way, but more like he was okay with it.

The peace that was now part of his day-to-day was far more worth it.

It wasn't that his ex-wife, Ayelet, hadn't loved him. Or that he hadn't loved her.

Please.

He was her king, she was his queen, and together they believed they were richer than all the money ever created.

But it was a hollow kingdom, predicated on Jake hiding his broken insides.

Anita—Ayelet—had wanted the happy version of him. The rock. The teddy bear. The—in Jake's opinion—safe Ken doll.

An accessory, sexless and without those baser desires and needs. Something to cuddle with and vent to, and then turn over, and go to sleep, and not expect any hopeful poking—the value judgement of expectation or just biological reaction aside.

That was Jake's assumed role.

The instant smile and ear. The warm, comforting things to say. But not expected to want something given back. As if the practical reality of expectation across any realm of social, emotional, or sexual reciprocation were ludicrous or unwarranted.

And so, in those four years, Jake grew to feel more alone with Ayelet, in his marriage, than he had ever felt as a single man. And it was a loneliness that slowly and steadily grew, creeping into every crevice of Jake's soul.

Manishtana

After all, Ayelet could be broken and expect Jake's love and patience, but Jake couldn't be sad or upset for more than a few hours before Ayelet's impatience grew at her emotional golem's failure to live up to her expectations and demands.

And, gleaning those inadvertent scraps from his father and his notions of manhood and chivalry that his little brother wholly embraced, Jake would stop himself, swallow down whatever pill was bitterest to him in the moment, and continue on.

It was just "tough love" that he'd convinced himself was justified.

He was the husband, after all. The guy. The man. He was expected to soothe Ayelet's scars even as she cut newer, deeper ones into him.

But then came that day when Jake was unable to mask all his hurt. Unable to just switch on some "happy side." Unable to just ignore all the prickles into his soul that he'd ignored in the name of "empathy" and "patience" and "compromise" and "family," and the realization that none of those had been applied to him from her.

Realizing that that had been his entire life. That he—by dint of being the firstborn, and enjoying two non-abusive parents—had always been expected to be "the Rock."

And that's when the beginning of the end had begun. Or at least that was Jake's take, anyway.

Looking on from the outside in, some people would've said, at best, that Jake and Ayelet's theological, social, and moral ideologies were fundamentally incompatible in the first place, and the Jake never should've proposed marriage. At worst, Jake'd be demonized and derided for having unrealistic expectations. That he was all tied up in seeing what "could" or "should" be, but ignoring what actually *was.* And then punishing people for not living up to his ideals.

"Dogmatic," they might call him.

Which would be a worse mistake than the person who created jarred gefilte fish.

Because Jake was *not* dogmatic. His *father* was dogmatic. His *brother* was dogmatic.

He was *stubborn.* There was a difference.

And every time Jake talked to Ariel he was acutely reminded of that.

"You can't just *make up* Jewish holidays for black people," he'd snapped at Ariel. It was freshly after the divorce had been finalized, so his fuse was shorter than usual with his brother.

"I'm not," Ariel had insisted, resistantly. "If a bunch of Jews experienced something and wished to celebrate it, why *can't* they? How is it different from Ethiopian Jews having Sigd, or the million mini-holidays that Chabad has?"

"Ariel. Juneteenth happened for a *blanket* amount of black people, and maybe a *small* amount of those were also Jews. It's not the same. Sigd happened specifically to Ethiopian *Jews*. Chabad holidays happened specifically to Russian *Jews*. There's no **chag** for the fall of the Iron Curtain. Because that wasn't specifically a thing that affected *Jews* but Russians *in general*. There are no non-Jewish Ethiopians celebrating Sigd. There's no non-Jewish Russians celebrating Chabad holidays. This whole having a 'Juneteenth *seder*' thing is ridiculous."

"So you're saying that unless something solely affected Jews it *can't* be a Jewish holiday? Then I absolutely disagree with that. Things become Jewish when Jews *decide* to do them. Costumes on Purim are something Italian Jews *decided* to copy from Carnivale. And now that's Jewish. Pickled herring is a thing Polish Jews *decided* to borrow from the traditional Polish Christmas Eve meal. And now it's Jewish. Bagels were a monastery bread, and *that's* Jewish now too. 'Akiva' is an Aramaic name. 'Mordechai' is Babylonian. And those are both *Jewish* names now."

"Yeah, but there wasn't a *movement* to make those things happen. They just happened *naturally*. You can't just *decide* that something is gonna be a thing now."

"And why not?"

And Jake just couldn't with the conversation anymore. There was just no talking to Ariel sometimes, especially when he already had Liora on his side.

"Like, honestly," Jake told me, when we were out for drinks just after his divorce. "I love Ariel, but it's like talking to my father. And that is *so* damn irritating. I mean, I admit that I'm stubborn," he reiterated, to my amused expression. "But there *is* a difference between dogmatic and being stubborn."

"Look dude," I told him. "I know you've got a problem with your pops. And fair enough, maybe stubborn *is* different from dogmatic. But 'honestly?' You've got some stuff to work out with yourself. Because the more you deny the even the *possibility* that you might be like your dad in ways you don't like, the more likely youre gonna become all those things about him you don't like. And you've gotta figure that shit out."

Jake...didn't really like that.

In fact, it's been years since we'd had that conversation, and I haven't really spoken to him since, because honestly man, I can't be everywhere.

Sometimes I need some time to myself to just, y'know, *think*. Or take a leak. Or *sleep*.

But, as much as it'd upset him, it hit home, that conversation.

Because after that, Jake decided that he needed to "find himself." With all the usual trope-stops of India, Japan, and backpacking through Tibet and Malaysia with his 34-year old black ass like he was some 20-something year old white girl after college.

But none of that worked, obviously.

Going to the Far East to "find yourself" doesn't work for black people, because the Far East only hides the souls of *white* folk.

So after a year of that, Jake decided to try that *other* lifestyle choice anathema to black people.

No, not kale, the *other* anathema.

Therapy.

And it actually *worked*.

Although, for what it's worth, for all the time it takes to get to "acceptance," it sure doesn't seem like much of a destination once you get there.

More like an empty train stop where nobody gets on or off because, *duh*, everyone's already two stops ahead of you. It's your own fault that you have to sit through, 18th, and 23rd, and 28th because you decided to not get your shit together and leave Union Square before the train went local to Penn Station.

But Jake was okay with all that now. Enough, at least.

Taking his bowl of cereal with him, Jake meandered over to his couch and started flipping through channels the same way he'd been swiping and clicking through profiles on the million dating apps and websites he'd been on recently.

It was hard dating as a divorcee. Being so used to that feeling of comfortability and predictability, and seeming so needy to fast forward any new relationship into that familiar space that you actually ended up scaring people away.

ARIEL SAMSON: FREELANCE RABBI

It probably wasn't any different from what widows or widowers felt, but with a lot less tragic baggage.

After all, they hadn't really had a choice in their situation.

It was during these musings when the name "Ariel Samson" incidentally stumbled into Jake's aural periphery, startling him into pausing his channel-surfing as Chuck O'Halloran's balding scalp glistened under the studio lights of Stage 32 at Constitution Studios.

"—past few weeks a feud has been playing out between them in the Brooklyn Orthodox Jewish community, with undertones and accusations of cronyism, insurrection, absolutism, irreverence, and even race. The shockwaves from the fallout have been felt as far as here at Constitution Studios and our rising star *Late Late Night Night with Wes Valentine*. I'm Chuck O'Halloran, and last night *The O'Halloran Outlook* hosted a very special town meeting, to see if we could bring people together by bringing them face to face. And, well...here's how that went."

Jake sat his bowl down with narrowed eyes as the segment began—set in an uncomfortably intimate studio with ominously dramatic lighting. A round conference table served as the main stage for the evening, with Ariel at one end of the horseshoe seating, Rosenstern and Guildencrantz teaming up at the other, and O'Halloran seated in the middle, flanked by a newly middle-aged woman with feline eyes and earthy-brown skin, and a portly older man in Benjamin Franklin glasses who was the living embodiment of every kindly black grandfather ever.

Two rows deep of stadium seating lined the perimeter of the space, populated by the morally outraged of Midwood, the irritated denizens of Park Slope, and nearly all of CAY.

Ilan, of course. But also Jerome. Phyllis. Blair. Sruli. Keith. Nahum the Husband and Chedva the Wife. The old couple. The thirty somethings. The elder stateswoman. The once-in-a-whilers. Chani Guildencrantz and the Hillel contingent. The tattooed lady (whose name was Lydia, appropriately). Even Kalman and Dassi had come with Tamar and Benjamin.

And obviously Ellis. Because when she'd said she was rallying the troops, she'd meant it.

Of course, Jake didn't know—had no way of knowing—any of that.

Manishtana

All he saw, as he sat furiously grinding his teeth for the next twenty minutes, was his baby brother, alone, weathering a kangaroo trial against Rosenstern and Guildencrantz's fevered efforts to drag him through the mud.

✡ ✡ ✡

"Firstly," O'Halloran began, addressing the politicians to his right and left. "I'd like to thank District Leader Darren Richardson and State Assemblywoman Gina Dorlus for agreeing to moderate this town hall with me, and for you gentlemen for agreeing to participate. So let's get to it. The immediate reason we're here tonight is because of the fallout following the DUI arrest of your son, Assemblyman Rosenstern. As it turned out, the establishment that he got intoxicated at was a lounge under your rabbinical supervision, Rabbi Samson, and that seems to have escalated the general ire of Rabbi Guildencrantz, who not only heads his *own* kosher certification agency, but also has been disapproving of your 'Freelance Rabbi' persona since nearly its inception—a sentiment shared by Assemblyman Rosenstern, particularly concerning the campaign over the Purim holiday of 'Hamantaschen Not Hate'— which dredged up yet *another* politically embarrassing moment for you, Assemblyman. Tempers and accusations have only been flaring since then, so I'd like to, let's just clear the air, and try to unpack all of what's happening here."

"Well Chuck," Ariel started. "Much like you just said, a friend of mine was trying to start up this lounge—a hookah lounge—and he was getting the runaround because kosher certification agencies wouldn't certify an establishment that was open very late and served alcohol. And it's never really made sense to me why if you're out after 11:00, good luck finding someplace kosher that's open. So I decided that I'd just certify my friend's place myself. I didn't really think much of it at the time, and if Rabbi Guildencrantz had a problem with it he never reached out to me about it at any point before this incident. And I think he's written enough op-eds for us all to know that he's more than capable of voicing his opinions, particularly when it comes to me."

Shots fired.

370

Gentle laughter tittered in the room while Guidencrantz puffed himself up like a sanctimonious bird of some kind, inflated with high-minded religious rhetoric.

"The problem, as I understand it," he began. "And as dozens of kosher certification agencies across the country understand it, is that Rabbi Samson seems to think that kosher agencies should certify just the food and that's it. And that simply isn't true, because that misses the whole point of what *kashrus* is. *Kashrus* is *not* just about the food. It's about the total picture. As I'm sure you know, Rabbi Samson, the scholar Nachmanides has an entire commentary about not eating kosher food gluttenously, and not drinking kosher wine to excess, and not overindulging in physical matters. To keep the letter of the law without the spirit of the law is not acceptable. And a dangerous precedent is what your *hechsher* to Holy Smokes represents."

"With all due respect," Ariel replied. "That seems to be a specious argument. When was the last time you denied a *hechsher* to a restaurant because they underpaid their workers? Or didn't pay them on time? Or treated them disrespectfully? Those are all commandments, so isn't that part of the 'whole picture' too? Also, as you've correctly assumed, I'm well aware of that stance of Nachmanides. But if we're establishing that there's a well-known directive to not overindulge, then what's the problem with granting certifications to *any* establishment, regardless of the hours and environment? And conversely, what about *any* environment inherently prevents someone from overindulging? I can overeat just as easily in a burger joint that closes at 4 in the afternoon as in a hookah bar at 4 at night. And I can presumably get just as drunk in a classy restaurant in the city as I can in any dive bar in Red Hook."

"You're playing at semantics, Mr. Samson," Guildencrantz waved his hand dismissively.

"I think Rabbi Samson makes a fair point though, Rabbi Guildencrantz," O'Halloran interjected. "Also that mandate of 'not drinking to excess' would seem to be something that patrons like Pinny Rosenstern need to bear in mind, not the owners of hookah lounges or the rabbis who certify them."

Rosenstern bristled.

"Look let's stop beating around the bush," he barked. "Our community has certain standards. *Any* community does. In the 80's I fought for how far away from schools that bars and sex shops should be. Why? Because that was a community standard to protect our young children from certain influences. For ALL my district schools. Now here, just because the community is Jewish—and even moreso, Orthodox—it doesn't get to protect its own standards? Now, should my son have been out drinking and driving that late? Or at all? No, that was stupid and irresponsible. Would he have still done it even if you *hadn't* created a so-called kosher oasis for such an incident to ferment? Who knows? All we *do* know is that he *did* go to your place because you *did* create the environment. This incident is exactly *why* certifications aren't given to certain places, but *you* decided to flaunt that and you're here playing the victim. I suppose next you'll say we're coming after you because you're black!"

Oh no. Oh no, he didn't just—

"I mean," Ariel answered with a rueful smirk as the room held its breath. "Now that you mention it, that's not *entirely* out of the realm of possibility. There's plenty of restaurants with certification from a local community rabbi. So..."

"See? *See?*" Rosenstern shouted back. "None of this is even about the *hechsher*. This is just *him*. You just run around with your little show dressed like some 40's gangster wailing about how the community does you wrong when all you really care about is tearing it down and making it look bad!"

"I'm sorry, saying we can do better as Jews is trying to tear everything down?"

"It's very easy for anyone create problems that don't exist and then capitalize on that by pretending to have all the answers."

"Are you *ser—*"

"Rabbi Samson," O'Halloran interjected. "Can you maybe give an example of what you mean about Jews 'doing better'?"

"...Well for one, as a community, Jews in this country love to be offended when we're not invited to the table on certain issues. But whenever a table needs to be built, we often don't show up to help build it. Like—since we're talking about race—take Black Lives Matter. We could've been there on the ground floor in Ferguson. I mean there's the OU, there's the RCA, there's the Federation, there's the ADL. We *have* the resources. We just need the leadership to *use* them, and not just on 'Jewish' issues. Because Jews are a multiethnic, multiracial people. *Every* social issue affects Jews, from immigration to racial profiling to police brutality."

"Oh, *of course* you're on board with Black Lives Matter," Rosenstern snorted dismissively. "The big bad Jews are all racist, but who cares about being anti-Israel because it's ok because they're black."

"When it comes to BLM, ideological purity isn't necessarily a factor for me. Because if I can show up to *shul* despite repeated racial macro and microaggressions, if I can glean religious insights from rabbis even while ignoring that they revile blackness, if I'm expected to abide by the Israeli Rabbinate despite *both* of its Chief Rabbis making racially inflammatory remarks just weeks into their tenure...then I can stomach a lil bit of BDS-sympathizing by folk actively trying to make sure I don't go home dead in the country that I *actually* live in...And that *too* is a reality that Jewish leadership needs to stop closing its eyes to."

"And you're saying *you're* that leadership, I'll bet."

"I'm not saying that. I—"

"Are you saying he's *not*?" Assemblywoman Dorlus piped up, her lips pursed in a smirk like a cat watching a mouse that's wandered into its reach.

Rosenstern froze mid-outrage, realizing he was trapped—or at least being baited—and continued somewhat more subdued.

"*He's not*," he asserted, trying to gracefully tone down the crescendo that the momentum of his tirade had been rushing headlong into. "He's just riding on the backs of other people's names, and using them t—"

"So when it comes to 'authentic' Jewish leadership...you mean *yourself*, I'm assuming," she suggested mildly enough, but with a grin that was more "lion baring its teeth" than "Cheshire cat."

Which wasn't too far from the truth. Assemblywoman Dorlus was one of the many African American politicians who'd called for Rosenstern to resign after his debacle. So, for that matter, was District Leader Richardson.

Neither one of them were particularly on Ariel's side. But they were out for blood, and Ariel's crusade was a good enough opportunity to bury Rosenstern. Guildencrantz, too.

Meanwhile, O'Halloran—whether actually incompetent or deliberately letting more blood get stirred into the water—acted as a moderator in name only, letting all kinds of wild accusations and tangents enter the discussion unchecked.

"Look, assemblyman," Rosenstern started, wise to the game and trying to preempt it. "I know what you're going to say with the whole blackface thing. And sure I've made some missteps. I'm human, and who hasn't? But my record and the work I've done for my community—*all* the communities in my constituency—more than speaks for itself."

"Oh, it most certainly does," Dorlus grinned even more widely, tapping the manila folder full of receipts that had been resting benignly under her hand until this moment. She opened it and began flipping through the papers inside. "Your constituency includes Afro-Carribbean Americans and Muslims, yet you've advocated both for Stop-and-Frisk and covert surveillance into mosques and Islamic community centers."

"I—"

"But when it comes to 'your' community—of which you're so zealous to protect from pretend messiahs—you've voted against every sex crime bill presented to the Assembly that would extend the statue of limitations for victims of child molestation to come forward, on the basis that, and I quote, 'reputations could get dragged through the mud and civil settlements could potentially bankrupt Jewish schools and institutions,' end quote."

"Well that's—"

"You've also had extensive ties to Shaarei Yerushalayim, an organization that seeks to transform Jerusalem neighborhoods by pushing out Palestinian residents. Your wife serves as executive director of the organization, and mysteriously is the only officer listed as being compensated. One which you made gifts to of around $45,000 from your campaign coffers and who officers of have been caught on tape offering prostitutes to entice prospective home sellers, in violation of IRS regulations and Board of Elections policies."

"Look, *that* is a—I just happen to—"

"Not to mention that according to tax filings and government documents, for at least three years you quietly helped steer millions of dollars in government funds toward a group that employed your brother. In one case, the payment was traced directly from a grant you sponsored into your brother's pockets to co-found a *yeshiva* for at-risk teens."

"Assemblywoman Dorlus," District Leader Richardson interjected, playing kindly diplomatic black grandfatherly good cop. "I'm not sure of the relevance of—"

"Oh, I'm just trying to see, trying to establish a baseline of what exactly Assemblyman Rosenstern considers a Jewish community leader. Because what *I'm* seeing," she gestured to Ariel. "Is a young man responsible for revujenating a historic synagogue and creating resources for his community. Surely those are desirable qualities and accomplishments in a community leader? I was a high school principal for twelve years, and what I see in this young man I would've killed to have teaching in my classrooms...Speaking of schools," she returned her focus to Rosenstern again. "What happened to your brother's yeshiva?" She consulted her notes again. "Yeshivas Ateres Chaim?"

"I—what do you mean?"

"Well your brother has repeatedy touted his work at the school, and claimed he was its program director from 2009 to 2012. But somehow it's not registered with the State Education Department or the New York Department of State. It's also absent from any tax filings or audit documents from its supposed parent organization. It still has a website presence online, but many of its links are dead and it doesn't seem to have been updated in at least a year."

"Well, it, uh, it became an online campus for a while, I'd heard. Then it closed. That's what I've heard."

"Ah, I see," she peered past Rosenstern to his cohort. "Is that true Rabbi Guildencrantz?"

"I can't—"

"Well, before you answer that, I'd just like to point out that you are still currently listed online as being part of its staff."

"I—" Guildencrantz stammered, caught off guard for the first time that evening. "I haven't been involved with Ateres Chaim for quite some time. And when I was, it was only in an advisory capacity. Otherwise I was fairly hands off in the yeshiva's operation."

"So when it comes to educating children," Richardson furrowed his brows. "You're willing to let a school operate carte blanche with your rubberstamped blessing, but for food you need to be intimately involved in any establishment that opens in your vicinity?"

Manishtana

"Actually," Dorlus rejoined, seemingly recanting. "I think it's a little unfair of me to ask you about Assemblyman Rosenstern's under-the-counter dealings, Rabbi. After all, 'community leader' or no, you can't know what people may or may not be doing in you name. Especially since there's more than enough that you've said in your *own* name. As I understand it, you've been suspended from your position of Chief Rabbi of Eindhoven for signing onto a letter declaring that homosexuality is 'curable illness'?"

"That, ah, that's a complicated situation, and I've since recanted in acknowledgment of the sensitivity that exists around the topic. But that doesn't change traditional Judaism's admittedly uncomfortable stance on—"

"Ah, yes, those 'community standards' the assemblyman was referencing, correct? Which is curious, because the certification you oversee, the...Octagaon K? It seems that several prominent rabbis and other community members don't abide by its seal because it's not considered to adhere to the accepted standards?"

"Well, that's also complicated. Octagon K relies on some leniencies that make—"

"So then it would appear you're a tad selective about which 'community standards' are imperative to be upheld. And maybe that you too, are just going by the 'letter of the law,' you said? Which makes your rejection of Rabbi Samson's certification a little...hypocritical, no?"

"I—"

"Ah, and what about these comments here? Weighing in on the same bill that the assemblyman voted against? You said, and I quote, 'To say to a child, "You have a right not to be abused, you have the right not to be touched by someone you don't want touching you," is absurd. What about the child who *wants* to be touched? It's a nonsense myth in our society that children are so innocent that they cannot arouse sexual attraction.'"

Guildencrantz fell silent.

"No reply? I understand. That's probably also 'complicated'. Perhaps then you can clarify this statement of yours made during a radio interview a few years ago, when a caller asked if you considered Abraham Lincoln a 'righteous gentile'. Your reply, and I quote again, 'That's not for me to judge, but I hold it against him that he set free the blacks.'"

ARIEL SAMSON: FREELANCE RABBI

A gasp arose from the audience while Rosenstern and Guildencrantz stiffened up.

"'I'm not being prejudiced," Dorlus continued, with equal parts measured glee and anger. "'The blacks were thriving under slavery. They couldn't steal, they couldn't kill, they couldn't take drugs, they couldn't be immoral, they read the Bible of their white masters. Blacks were learning to be decent and civilized. They were making progress! If Lincoln had waited maybe another 30, 40, 50 years, that'd would've been better. He set them free too soon. He—'" she paused, looking up at Guildencrantz with a facetiously quizzical expression. "Should I continue?"

The room held its breath again. In the deathly silence, O'Halloran cleared his throat.

"I'd like us to get back to something you said ealier, Rabbi Samson..."

✿ ✿ ✿

It was just a quick glare from Guildencrantz. One that happened during the break and got cut from the broadcast. It was so pronounced and venomous that it caught Ariel's attention, even though it wasn't even being aimed at him.

In fact, if he hadn't looked up to try and catch Ellis' attention, Ariel would've completely missed Guildencrantz's scowl, would never had followed his line of sight into the crowd, and never have had a possibility—a crazy possibility—slammed him in the stomach like a cement block.

At first he thought it was directed at Chani.

She'd met him in the hall just before the segment had started filming, looking distraught and apologizing. Then it hit him why the Guildencrantz name sounded so extra familiar.

Because Chani *Guildencrantz.*

"I guess your dad is pretty upset, huh?" Ariel had joked mildly, minutes before filming was to start.

"Not my dad," Chani'd shaken her head. "My uncle. Our families don't talk anymore."

It seemed that she had more to say after that bombshell, but at that exact moment Ariel was being torn away by the studio to start the debate.

But just now? He had a hunch.

One that was compounded by the quick, probably inadvertent glance Guildencrantz had shot over Ariel's shoulder as Assemblywoman Dorlus was recounting the good rabbi's problematic racial views.

And then came that glare. And so something clicked into place for Ariel.

Pulling his phone out of his jacket pocket, Ariel quickly texted Ellis.

He saw her react to the vibration in her pocket. Check her phone. Look back up at him, stunned. Shaking her head and miming to Ariel that she didn't know, she looked into the audience rows and started walking up one of the aisles just as the studio manager began counting the cameras down, signaling the break's end.

"Alright," O'Halloran resumed. "So let's..."

The rest of whatever O'Hallorhan had been saying started sounding faraway as Ariel watched Ellis walk back down the aisle and toward her seat, with a face like a ghost.

She nodded yes.

Unbefuckingleivable, Ariel shook his head as a snort and a chuckle unintentionally escaped, interrupting whatever it was that Guildencrantz was saying.

"Are you finding something amusing, Rabbi? Please share."

"Amusing...? I...Not really, no," Ariel continued to chuckle, shaking his head at the obviousness of it all and waving Guildencrantz on. "But please, continue."

"That is to say," Guildencrantz resumed his thought. "Th—"

"Actually," Ariel interrupted again, still chuckling, but feeling something growing steadily stronger in his gut as he spoke. "Y'know, 'amusing' isn't really the accurate word here. Um... '*comedic*,' maybe. Depending on the definition, I mean. Aristotle defines 'comedy' as, um, an imitation of men worse than the average. That could work here."

It got so quiet in the studio you could hear the temperature drop.

"Shakespearean comedy," Ariel continued, his delivery becoming less and less mirthful as he went along. "Now *that* generally involves a happy ending with marriage between unmarried characters, but I, uh, I suspect Rabbi Guildencrantz *might* have a little issue with that."

ARIEL SAMSON: FREELANCE RABBI

Guildencrantz sat completely still, seemingly not even daring to breathe, even as the two **chossids** sitting in the closest row behind him stiffened up.

"And then there's Northrop Frye," Ariel's cadence had finally arrived at the fathomless depths of the disgust that swelled in his chest. "Now *he* defines comedy as a struggle between a relatively powerless youth and the obstacle of societal conventions...And I think we might be onto something there with that one. Kind of. I mean, that seems to be your gripe here, right? That I'm flaunting 'conventions' and 'community standards' and whatnot? And everything would be fine if I just 'respected' them? Except that's not really accurate is it?...Because you don't really want my respect. *You* want my fear. You don't *care* if I respect you or not, so long as I just fall in line like a good little Jewtomaton. You. Want. My. *Fear.* You want me to stay in the little box you think I belong in. Because that's how you stay in *power*. That's how you keep *control*. You set yourselves up as holding the keys to the kingdom and keep everyone else too afraid to realize that the door isn't even locked. The Tree of Knowledge is standing in the garden, and there you are, feeding off its shade, twisting its branches and coiled around its trunk like the poisonous snakes that you are, because without its fruit? You're too bankrupt of character and integrity to even convince your *shadow* that you're worth being followed. You wrap yourselves in Torah scrolls and Israeli flags, parading around like you love Jews and Judaism *so* much. That you're these selfless champions who only want to protect it and us. But only the 'right' ones and the 'right' kind. Because what *you* love is the corruption of rules that *you* call being 'religious.' That *you* call 'Orthodoxy.' And the only thing you want to protect? Is your place in it. So you and your ilk spend an inordinate amount of time talking about me and people like me. Trying to dog-whistle implications of what kind of less-than Jews we are, because we upset the hill of bodies and minds you build your thrones on. Well, I'm done defending myself to you and people like you. You are bullies. You are hoodlums. You are bigots. And you are cowards. And I am *disappointed* in the way you've hijacked the Judaism and the observance that *I* love...So no, I don't suppose 'amusing' is a very accurate description at all, is it?"

The studio was as silent as the tomb that Ariel had just laid Rosenstern and Guildencrantz to rest in.

Manishtana

From the back row, Jumaane uttered an impressed *"Damn"* louder than he'd intended—a sentiment echoed by everyone watching the exchange at home (and eliciting a fist-pumped *"YES!"* from Jake)—and a studio burst into thunderous applause and incredulous roars of *"What the hell did I just see happen?! Whaaat??""* from the pro-Ariel side of the room as the anti-Ariel side began to quietly slink towards the exits and O'Halloran tried to wrap up the segment over the din.

Without any hiccup of doubt, Ariel had drawn—shit, *carved*—an unmistakable line in the sand. And there was *no question* that he had just triumphed in the court of public opinion.

But somehow the look on Guildencrantz's face wasn't particularly assuring in the way of victory.

Of course it wouldn't.

Because Rabbi Ariel Samson had committed the cardinal sin of officiating the wedding of Tamar Watkins...

"Can you find out what Tamar's maiden name is?" Ariel had texted Ellis during that earlier break.

...nee Denebeim...

"Not Denebeim. She was married before. Her original maiden name."

...nee Guildencrantz...

"I think she might be a Guildencrantz."

...cousin to Chani Guildencrantz...

"And so this might be a HUGE personal thing."

...estranged daughter of Rabbi Dov Ber Guildencrantz.

ARIEL SAMSON: FREELANCE RABBI

Monday, June 13, 2016
8 Sivan 5776

Ariel and his brother had never really gotten along. I mean, they didn't *not* get along with each other, but they just never clicked really.

It wasn't a value judgment or anything, just a fact. They were two very different people.

Where Ariel was affectionate and wore his heart on his sleeve, Jake was harsh and stern.

Cold.

But not cruel.

Jake, for better or for worse, was the most fiercely overprotective oldest brother any sibling could hope for.

"For better" on those days when he would pick up or drop off his little siblings at school, making his presence menacingly known to any would-be troublemakers as to who exactly they'd have to deal with.

"For worse" during those maddening times when he acted like none of his siblings knew how to do anything on their own.

This, Ariel and his sisters suspected, was something their father Avigdor had implanted in him. That, as firstborn to firstborn, their father had programmed Jake with the prime directive of defending his little brother and sisters against harm above all else.

Manishtana

As a concept, it was a noble enough ideal, but in imparting it Avigdor'd ended up treating Jake like a little adult from far too young an age, filling him with way too much information about how the world worked, and laying weighty worries on his firstborn son that were too heavy for a child's shoulders to have to bear.

Of course, once Jake hit his teens, Avigdor tried to course-correct—*over*correct, really—attempting to rein Jake in like the child he should've been treated as in the first place.

The end results were disastrous, to say the least, and Jake couldn't *wait* to escape his family and their shackles on his life, running headfirst into his own mistakes. (Although by "escaping his family," he really just meant "his parents." And even *then*, he really only meant his father. It was an open secret to all the Samson siblings that Jake was just a Batsignal away if they ever needed him.)

By the time Ariel had come along, their father had mellowed out on trying to mold his sons into weapons of mass protection, but there was still something...lacking...in his and Ariel's relationship.

As a father, Avigdor did pretty much nothing but work all the time.

Working at his job teaching. Working on lesson plans and grading tests when he got home. Working at fixing up the house, fixing leaks, mowing the lawn. Working, working, working.

Always doing something.

He was a strict father, though fair, despite the detachment that was there. And also a weird kind of awkwardness.

Once in a while, the mask would slip—when he laughed or smiled—like someone goofy was trapped inside an adult suit and was being forced to read from a script in the role of "Parent."

But those moments weren't terribly often, and when they did happen, it was usually while watching his favorite old movies, or somehow connected to either Liora or Aviva, Ariel and Jake's sisters.

The boys never got the laughs. They got stilted "I'm proud of you, kid"s and "Good job"s and "Keep it up, young man"s instead.

"I'm not sure Aba really knows what to do with us," Jake said to Ariel once.

Ariel was inclined to agree. Personally, he never really got the feeling that his father even liked him. Just that he was being civil enough, maintaining a polite interest in his life.

It didn't take a genius to suspect that all that had something to do with Saba, Avigdor's father.

Save for a yearly birthday phone call, none of the Samson kids had seen or even talked to their grandfather since Savalava's divorce, just after Jake's *bar mitzvah*. Since then, Saba hadn't showed up to any family gathering, celebration, holiday, called for a birthday, sent a card—nothing. And, after the first few snubs, the invitations eventually stopped being extended.

After the first few years of being quietly shushed by his mother, and cautioned against bringing it up with his father or grandmother, Ariel eventually stopped asking about his grandfather or why no one really talked about him or why he didn't come around anymore.

And then, at the end of Ariel's junior year of high school, after eleven years of being the elephant in the room, Saba died.

It'd happened a couple of hours after **Shavuot** ended.

Ariel's mother had taken the call, and she'd passed the news to his father. After a few minutes of hushed whispers, Ariel's father emerged from their bedroom, already on the phone. Within the hour, siblings, aunts, and uncles were informed, *chevra kadisha* sent, rabbi contacted, funeral home called, and burial arrangements prepared.

It was all very clinical and efficient.

Unemotional.

And not just on Avigdor's part.

There wasn't much in the way of an emotional reaction on *anyone's* part to hearing the news. Except for maybe Savalava, who Ariel overheard through his mother's phone, telling her that *of course* she was coming to the funeral.

Just to make sure Saba was dead.

Eager to be on the safe side, AviandAri tiptoed around their father for the rest of the night. He seemed to handle the news very coolly—*too* coolly—in a matter-of-fact sort of way that put everyone on edge, unsure if there was another shoe waiting to drop or if this was all there was for him to give.

Even their mother gingerly interacted with him, with all the caution of trying to coax a grizzly to eat from her hand.

"I'm fine," was Avigdor's simple reply.

And, apparently, he was.

But that next morning, the day of the funeral, Ariel's father had managed to acquire a masterful facsimile of grief.

Knowing his father, however, Ariel could tell that he was merely wearing it as if it were an overcoat.

Heavy, but something he could easily slip off, hang up, and likely never have any intention of wearing again. A perfect picture of composed mourning, his father delivered a stunning eulogy, full of ruminations and reminisces, of scholarly quotes and sources, and it was eloquent, overwhelming, and it touched the heartstrings of everyone who heard it.

Ariel was floored, even as he noticed how it did nothing to penetrate the stony, exactly appropriately bereaved visages of his aunts and uncle, the knowing look that passed between his father and grandmother, and the curt nod of approval she gave in return.

After the burial, after everyone returned to the Samson home to begin sitting *shiva*, and after all the guests had offered their condolences and left, Ariel found his father out on the back porch, looking out into the night.

Quietly, Ariel settled next to him, full of so many questions that had been bubbling for over a decade. But wordlessly he sat there with his father in velvety silence, their shoulders almost touching.

That was the rule of sitting *shiva* after all, right?

You sat and you waited for the grieving to make the first move. To say the first thing. If they ever decided to. Because sometimes there aren't any words.

After a few moments of the stars twinkling into view, Avigdor cleared his throat, and began talking into the darkness. Ariel's ears perked up, attentively listening to the closest thing he was ever going to get to answers, and hearing all the things his father hadn't gotten to *really* say.

You see, Avigdor had been three.

It was literally the first memory he had.

There hadn't been any logic to the argument, that was apparent from the bewildered cadences in his mother's tone, answering his father's vicious snarls.

Sadly, his father's venomous timbre didn't particularly resonate as significant to little Avigdor, as it wasn't anything new. Even at that tender age, Avigdor couldn't recall a time when any of their names—his, his mother's, his sister's—had been spoken by his father with warmth or affection.

Except for when there were other people around, that is.

And even then, the more genuine it sounded, the more hollow it echoed in their ears, a brazen lie told against the rest of their existence full of Shmuel's annoyance of how much space his wife and children took up and how much food and money they consumed out of his pocket.

But it wasn't the sound of their fighting—exhausted and perfunctory, wearily retreading old bitterness from countless arguments before—that etched itself into Avigdor's memory.

No, it was that sound of his father's fist hitting his mother's jaw, that thud of meat against bone, that seared itself into Avigdor's brain.

That visual of his father's hands wound into the fingers of his mother's hair, the sneer on his lips that extending into his eyes, lighting up with wicked glee every time he tasted the sting on his gnarled knuckles as her face and ribs crumpled around them, pummeling her wet screams short with blow after blow. And then the words of hatred that spewed forth with every pause in his assault.

Avigdor supposed that this was the moment when he first began to detach from the world around him.

It became a simple equation at that point, a collection of unemotional variables:

Parental Unit 1 was under attack from Parental Unit 2.

Parental Unit 2 required no assistance.

Focus aid on Parental Unit 1.

And so into action Avigdor sprung. He might've been playing with Aliza when it started.

That part he didn't remember.

He *did* remember thinking that Aliza was safe, and he *did* remember being concerned about the little brother or sister his mother was currently three months pregnant with—the unborn sibling that would become his brother Raphael—and so it was time to turn his attention to the matter at hand.

The hallway in the apartment was narrow, so narrow that two people could barely walk side by side down it. His parents were standing again, facing each other from opposite ends of the hallway. His father, proud, cruel, and sweaty, chest heaving with ragged breaths. His mother, battered, with a tear-streaked and swollen face, holding her protruding belly, her always-covered hair scandalously exposed and disheveled, her *sheitel* ripped from her head and on the floor, while teeth from her shattered dentures lay scattered like pearls from a broken necklace.

Verbal warfare had now commenced, the first of many melees that Avigdor and his siblings would endure throughout the years, weathering both the humiliation of the beastly vitriol shouted through paper thin walls, and of having to face the pity of neighbors the next day who had no idea where to put their eyes.

But, here, at hurling words like rocks from a slingshot, Avigdor's mother was far more skilled than his father, even with her lack of dentures lisping her words. Because she actually cared. Because she actually loved. She tore into her husband in only the ways a lover can, stabbing at his weakest spots and deepest pains and most shameful of truths, bringing his anger to a boil. Like a feral animal, Avigdor's father began stalking towards Avigdor's mother again, intent on unleashing his fury a second time.

To the right of the hallway was the bathroom. Quickly, Avigdor dashed inside, and grabbed his training potty. He waited. Timing was everything. He'd seen this happen a hundred times in the cartoons he watched on Sundays when his father decided to wear the skin of being a good human person, shapeshifter that he was. All Avigdor needed to do was wait. His father would raise his leg to walk forward, and that's when he'd toss the potty into his path, causing his father to slip and fall, rendering him unconscious with birds and stars floating around his head, thereby ending the fight.

It'd be ridiculously funny were it not so horribly sad, watching a three-year old apply *Looney Tunes* cartoon physics to a domestic dispute.

But that's what Avigdor was. A three-year old. It was all he had. And to that three-year old, it was an airtight plan.

His dad advanced, Avigdor tossed the potty through the door—with perfect timing no less—watching with despair and a crushing sense of failure as it was kicked aside.

His father was on his mother again. He batted at her head, thumping it against the wall. Dazed and disoriented, she fell.

Little Avigdor dove from the bathroom and caught his mother as she slid, or at least as well as three-year old arms can catch anything, at any rate. He felt his head throb as he drew himself up to his full height and shielded his mother from the deluge of venom that washed over him from his father, denigrating every facet of his mother's personality, glaring at her with eyes laced with contempt—the same eyes he used on his children, at least until they grew old enough to fix his face for him—as he declared her as something with even less worth than an object to be used. And not at all helping the pounding headache Avigdor was forming, were the retorts his mother shrieked on the other side of his head.

Avigdor couldn't remember the specific talking points of that particular fight, but it was the introduction to the same instances he'd hear over and over, time and again, and before he'd learn to, well, maybe not *hate*—never *hate*—but at least *resent* his mother for not having any kind of concept of a filter as to what children should and shouldn't hear from and about their parents. A lesson he'd promptly forget, and promptly regret forgetting, when raising his own firstborn twenty-three years later.

At any rate, the fight eventually stopped with his father storming out of the apartment to go who-knows-where, perhaps to one of the many women who assisted his Herculean dedication to violating his marriage vows of fidelity, leaving Avigdor—for the first of many times to come—to comfort his sobbing mother as she apologized through her tears for her choices in life and for their situation, filling his ears with "her side" of the story, as if he hadn't been traumatically present for it all.

And that's when the Avigdor He Could've Been died before it even had a chance to live. He was Other Avigdor now. The Protector. The Hero. The Inspiration. The Beacon.

For everyone but himself.

He was three.

And suddenly, with Avigdor's raw disclosure, everything about him became crystal clear to Ariel.

He was able to see his father now in a way that Jake was too resentful to ever be able to.

Ariel could see now why his father got along better with their sisters than he did with him and his brother.

Why he took the girls to martial arts practices, and on hikes, and watched swashbuckling films with them, and taught them how to fix cars, and complimented them and constantly *constantly* let no opportunity pass to build them up and make them fiercely aware of their worth.

Manishtana

Because he knew what kind of daughters he wanted to raise.

He knew the kind of confidence and skills and esteem he wanted to sew into every fiber of their being, so that they would never—*ever*—find themselves in the kind of relationship that his mother did. (Of course, all that esteem building was exactly what made Aviva too embarrassed to tell her father when she came to find herself in an abusive relationship of her own.)

But Avigdor's boys? They scared him.

He didn't know how to connect with them because he'd spent his entire life vowing to himself what kind of man and father he *didn't* want to be.

He never thought to consider the kind that he *did* want to be.

And by the time he realized that, he was looking down into his arms at a newborn son, terrified by the realization that he'd never figured out how to be the kind of man that would be sure to *raise* the kind of man who would be the kind of father he wished *he'd* had.

That was it, Ariel realized.

Their father was just scared.

Scared of being the kind of father his father was.

Scared that his kids wouldn't be able to protect themselves against him if he ever turned out to be.

And that's when Ariel knew, beyond a doubt, that it wasn't—that it never *had* been—about his father liking him or not.

That Avigdor loved his kids. All of them.

Even the boys. He just hadn't a clue about how to show it.

Ariel supposed that's where their mother came into the picture.

To fill in those emotional gaps that their father not only couldn't fill, but was just plain *missing*. She was used to it after all.

She'd had plenty of practice filling in those same gaps in Avigdor himself, because she loved and saw the man he was supposed to be, not the one his world had made him become.

"I'm not going to pretend that I liked him," Avigdor continued, as an orchestra of crickets began to swell, speaking more for himself than to Ariel. "And I won't pretend that I'm such a good Jew that all the respectful 'good son' things I've done over the years were ever me being selflessly **kivud av**. The truth is a lot of those things—and they were the right things to do—but I would've never done any of them if your mother hadn't forced me and pushed me to do them.

Because she was damned if my soul was gonna get any more spiritually wounded on account of him. And I now...with him gone...I appreciate that now. A lot."

Avigdor turned and looked directly at Ariel now. Directly into his eyes. Which was not a thing Avigdor was really prone to doing with people.

"You're a good kid. And I'm proud of you, kid. And I have no idea what I did to make that happen. Or if I even played any part. You go through the world just...you just always look for the best in people. And you're so patient with them. Them, us, humankind, whatever...Never—*ever*—change that about yourself. You hear me?" he said fiercely. "It is *who you are*...Because I can't do what you do. It doesn't matter what the Talmud says about being *dan l'kaf zechut*, I don't believe it. *Never* will. Some people just aren't inherently good. Some people, like your grandfather...***alav hashalom***," Ariel saw him twist his mouth around the words wishing this particular deceased a likely undeserved eternal rest. "...Actually, I won't say that....Yeah, I won't say that...But I will say be careful. Don't change who you are, but be careful. Because some people just want to twist everything you love up and then watch it burn."

"Some people just want to watch what you love burn."

It was curious timing that tonight, eleven years later, those particular words of his father's popped into Ariel's head.

Well, not *that* curious, actually. After all, tonight *was* his grandfather's *yahrtzeit*—dammit, *nachala*—same time it always was, a couple of hours after the holiday of Shavuot ended.

This year, in fact, it fell on almost the exact same Gregorian calendar day as it was all that time ago.

No, the curious thing, as Ariel leaned against a stranger's car, limply clutching the one Torah scroll he was able to rescue to his chest, was that just over a decade later, as firemen bustled around, and sirens blared and blazed into the night, true to his father's word, Ariel was watching his hard work burn.

Mushroom clouds of black smoked billowed almost invisibly into the gloom of eventide, permeating the air with its distinctive pungency. Orange and bright-yellow flames blew out the windows, and tongues of fire flickered, flared, and spat showers of sparks, licking their way up the facade of the building, straining to reach higher and higher into heaven.

389

Manishtana

The firefighters could only watch the synagogue burn, the idea of them rushing into that inferno being thoroughly ludicrous.

They could only shake their heads as they tossed the words "accelerant" and "accelerated fire" amongst themselves as they did they best they could to protect the apartment building next door, spraying foam on the sides and roof.

Someone lamented that with all the prayerbooks and religious texts and prayer shawls kept inside, the internal blaze was easily the temperature of a kiln. Even from across the street the heat was oppressive, and onlookers could still feel it radiating against their skin from yards away. Glowing embers leapt and twirled into the swirling hot black of night, while everything that was ever Congregation Ahavath Yisroel was scorched away, fading on the winds to join its long since passed colleagues, the last *shul* of Avon Gardens.

It burned majestically in that good night, and in quiet dignity.

Ariel's fingers found themselves entwined in the threadbare velvet casing of the Torah scroll he clutched, gripping it as if pinching the faded material would wake him from this nightmare.

Absentmindedly, he looked down at it, noticing that the covering was now stretched out of shape and pierced with finger holes, with a singed portion blackening its once crimson color. He felt a gloved hand on his shoulder, and a gruff but concerned voice, but the words just weren't sinking in or connecting.

It looked like he was in shock.

He *was* in shock.

But it wasn't the shock of loss at seeing his beloved pulpit and the community he had built around it smoldering before his eyes.

No, Ariel was in shock because he was still processing that someone had tried to kill him that night.

"*ARIEL!*" came a scream.

He heard the screech and barely registered as Ellis hopped off her motorcycle before it even came to a full stop, letting it fall on its side as she ran over to her friend.

"Omig'd *what happened*?" She threw her arms around him, then started patting his body down. "Are you okay? What happened? I *just* left!"

"Well, funny thing," he began, attempting a jokey voice. "I guess I should've listened to you a *lot* more Because I'm pretty sure Rosenstern and Guildencrantz just tried to kill me."

"*What?!*"

"Well, they," he started again, then felt the burn of tears starting to well up. Someone had tried to *fucking kill him*. "They, uh—"

"Hey, hey, whoa, it's okay. It's okay," Ellis quickly soothed, immediately reading him. "Look, look I'm right here. Let's, y'know, let's just talk about it."

She took out her flask and unscrewed it, handing it to him.

He started to protest that he didn't want to unlace his fingers. That holding on to that Torah scroll was the only thing keeping him as together as he was at the moment.

They'd both survived together, y'know?

And Ellis read that too. She pressed her flask to his lips, and he drank.

After he took a gulp, swallowing down the knots growing in his throat with it, he began to speak.

It'd been a long day, as Ellis already knew. She'd been there for it.

The last day of classes over at Brooklyn College had been almost a month ago, so the day's crowd, assembled for the last day of Shavuot, had been considerably smaller, absent nearly all of the college-age students who'd been boosting the congregation the whole year through.

Tonight's **havdalah** service had doubled as an end-of-year farewell party, bittersweetly wishing success to those who'd graduated that May in their future lifeplans, reminding those kids taking summer session courses that services would still be regularly held and to stop by, and telling everyone how much CAY would be looking forward to seeing them again when the next semester started up for the fall.

It was an emotional, yet fun time had by all.

Nearly two hours later, after the last of the congregants had left, Ariel was left alone to do some minor straightening up in the sanctuary and *kiddish* area downstairs.

Trudging upstairs into his office when he was done, Ariel closed the door behind him as he absentmindedly rifled through the synagogue's mail that had accumulated over the last couple of days.

Manishtana

Sorting through junk mail after junk mail while he sat at his desk, an envelope thicker and heavier than the others caught his attention.

On the back, sealing the envelope closed, was a large gold seal embossed with a six-branched *menorah* and the words "Jewish Leadership Union" circumscribed around the edge.

On the front it was addressed, specifically, to Ariel.

Curious, he tossed the remaining mail aside and peeled open this mysterious parcel, its inside revealing two tickets and a letter:

"Dear Rabbi Ariel Samson,

Since 2002, the Jewish Leadership Union has honored four Tri-State area-based rabbis and/or cantors who demonstrate extraordinary commitment to progressing social justice, passion for improving interdenominational dialogue, or tireless leadership concerning intercultural community engagement in the Greater New York Area.

This year, it is with great pride that we inform you that you have been nominated to be among those honored in person as an honoree for the 2016 Dreidel Leadership Award at the Jewish Leadership Union's 33rd Annual Gala on Tuesday, September 27, 2016 in New York City, as a guest of the JLU.

As one of the four honorees for this award, you will be asked to give a short speech about the work you do and the community you serve. Join us for a special cocktail reception to honor and celebrate our tireless Jewish community heroes, followed by dinner and ceremonies.

Please RSVP by Wednesday, August 10th, and we look forward to seeing you to celebrate this momentous occassion. Festive, cocktail attire. Kashrut will be observed.

Jewish Museum of Midtown
134 W 30th St, New York City
7:30-9:30 PM
7:00 PM Sharp: VIP Reception

Mazal Tov!
Rabbi Angela Abrams, President

ARIEL SAMSON: FREELANCE RABBI

Rachel Stein, Executive Director"

Wait, what?

Puzzled, Ariel found himself re-reading the letter several times, feeling strangely lightheaded.

Clearly there was some kind of mistake, right?

But no, as Ariel scanned the list of biographies included along with the invitation letter, there he was—"Rabbi Ariel Samson, Congregation Ahavath Yisroel, Brooklyn, New York"—sandwiched in-between a former Freedom Rider rabbi emeritus, an LGBTQI rabbi with multiple appearances on *Newsweek*'s "50 Most Influential Rabbis in America" list, and a Chicago-born rabbi of a Mahwah, NJ congregation and advocate for gun violence prevention.

Ariel leaned back in his chair, momentarily blown away.

He couldn't believe it, he thought, feeling a mixture of pride and giddiness rise in his chest.

After all the struggle and opposition and antagonism, it was all starting to be worth it, he grinned to himself. His hard work was about to be recognized.

It was a familiar grin that he grinned.

Suspiciously familiar. One he distinctly remembered wearing only when he was enjoying particularly good magic moss.

But he distinctly remembered that he hadn't partaken of any magic moss.

Just as Ariel was noticing that the odd scent on the air that was only faint a few minutes ago had gradually increased, there was an urgent pounding on the front door of the synagogue that echoed through the empty building.

Which was weird, seeing as how the front door wasn't locked and there wasn't any need for anyone to knock.

Two crashes of splintering glass followed—one in the foyer and one in the stairwell, from the sound of it—and, alarmed, Ariel rushed to the window and looked down, just in time to see two black-clad figures hop into a nondescript black van, their tires screeching as they tore off into the night.

Stuffing the envelope into his pocket and rushing toward the door to investigate, Ariel yanked on his unnaturally warm doorknob and was greeted by a wall of smoke and heat.

Manishtana

In the empty space outside the doors of the sanctuary, the fire spread with ease, leaping from the wooden box holding satin *yarmulkes*—for those men who arrived without headcoverings of their own—to the wooden chest of lace doilies—for married women who lacked the same—converting the partially carpeted linoleum floor into a maze of mischievously playful flame. Plumes of black smoke vomited up the stairwell, cutting off any access to the safety that lie outside the building and choking the air. The amber-and crimson flares were garish against the faded bright-turquoise sanctuary doors, their paint bubbling in the intense gasoline-fueled heat.

Locked in by fire, Ariel's only option at this point was to retreat to his office, negotiate the twenty-foot drop to the unforgiving concrete below, and pray that he didn't overshoot the jump and impale himself on the spearheaded wrought-iron gate enclosing the *shul*.

Or, more accurately, that would be any sane person's only option.

However, true to form as the filthy Super Jew that he was, Ariel had only one overriding thought: He had to rescue the Torah scrolls from the ark.

It was a stupidly insane thought, and, quite honestly, it just might've been the one to save his life.

Whipping off his jacket, Ariel kicked over the water cooler that sat in his office and took a deep breath while he let the water soak the cloth. Quickly tying the wet jacket around his face, covering his nose and mouth, Ariel took four or five steps back into his increasingly ablaze office, then made a running leap over crackling lashes of fire and columns of smoke, grateful that tonight he hadn't locked the sanctuary doors first before heading to his office—as he usually did—instead leaving them wide open in an uncharacteristic show of laziness.

Landing in the sanctuary, where humble flames were just beginning to lick at the wooden beams, he crashed into a row of pews, stabbing the funny bone of his left arm.

Counting his blessings where he could grab them, Ariel noted that, for whatever reason—whether the arsonists didn't dare to actually directly douse the ark and sanctuary, or whether they never anticipated that Ariel would delay trying to save his own life by braving the flames in an attempt to rescue CAY's sixty-year old scrolls—the sanctuary was far less ablaze. Nonetheless—as the first of the stained-glass windows blew out, sending multicolored shards of hot glass into the night—the fire was rapidly surging into the room, as if it it were actively attempting to consume Ariel and the building with him.

Running down the aisle as the dry, grey-green carpet began to sizzle and crackle beneath his feet, Ariel reached the ark, throwing aside the blood-red velvet drapes, fiddling with the warming combination lock, and tossing it aside to pry open the cold, hard-oak doors. Inside, the two Torah scrolls sat, huddled against each other like frightened children.

Behind him, flickering little orange light bulbs, sitting in neat little rows next to bronze placards engraved in Hebrew and English, exploded in tinkling bursts of glass and light, leaving behind wispy trails of bone-white smoke that rose in the air, as if released souls were ascending to heaven like the whispered prayers of old Jews. Leather seats roasted and popped, the scent of broiling processed animal skin mingling with the acrid smoke. The blaze advanced, now only three rows of pews away, and smoke inhalation creeping even closer.

Grabbing the smaller of the two scrolls, Ariel rushed over to the window as his eyes started stinging and watering, rolled it open as far as it would allow, then tossed the scroll into the unkempt grass in the narrow alley between the synagogue and the railway tracks.

A translucent salad bowl chandelier snapped free from its red-hot bronze chain, shattering as it crashed into the waiting maw of fire below that greedily lapped it up.

Blindly snatching up the second, larger scroll, Ariel forced the both of them through the narrow window, just as the flames at last reached the front of the sanctuary, boyishly dancing around the *bimah*, leaping in excitement, its crackling sounding like so much haunting giggling.

Ariel army-crawled down the grassy alley, still holding the one scroll with one arm. The other scroll he'd thrown too far, and it lay below on the tracks beside the *shul*, torn and shredded. Soon the usual freight trains would rumble by on schedule, trampling it under tons of steel.

Sweating from the fiery blaze erupting overhead, Ariel climbed over the fence at the end of the alleyway and spilled onto the street on front of the *shul*. As he backed away from the heartbreaking sight, pulling his jacket away from his face, he heard the faraway squeals of sirens growing louder from several blocks away.

From that point it was oxygen checks and a blur of police statements and the beginning of the almost three-hour war that over 100 firefighters would fight with the blaze.

Kalman had been the first to show up, first to check on his friend and second to gaze at the ruins of his grandfather's legacy.

At least the physical ruins anyway.

Kalman would always carry the guilt of having already otherwise defiled it. Maybe, Kalman thought as he watched the blaze, this would serve as some kind of penance. A literal burnt offering. If this was legal currency in exchange for his baby's life, then he'd gladly pay that price. A thousand times over.

Many of the regular congregants arrived later, with moist eyes and beside themselves with grief. The younger crowds and the newer crowds showed up later, some of them beginning to hold hands and sing songs. First of mourning, then of hope.

Streams of texts and missed calls came pouring through Ariel's phone, and he left them all unanswered. He'd get to them tomorrow.

And then came Ellis.

"Oh my G'd," she'd exclaimed once Ariel had finished his tale. "Are you okay? Do you need me to take you home? Do you need to go to the hospital? I rode my bike over, but I can head back and come get you with the car, just—"

"I'm okay, Ellis," he managed a weak smile.

"No. You're fucking not. But okay," she grabbed his face. "Alright, there's some press hovering over there. You stay here, I'll go take care of it, okay?"

He nodded, mutely, and Ellis took off in the direction of the reporters circling like vultures among the crowd.

"In these old houses of worship, synagogues, churches," a fireman was telling one. "The fire starts very rapidly in the void areas. This place is almost a century old."

Which was true. The building that Congregation Ahavath Yisroel had moved into and renovated in 1951 had first been built in 1917 to house a budding Conservative community that ended up largely decimated as a result of the first World War.

For the next almost four decades it sat vacant, until—considered a worthless venture by most—it was purchased by an enterprising young real estate mogul, one Abe Katz, as a favor for his former classmate and fellow Army vet, Samuel Gellerman. Together they would build a new font of Jewish life for their families, in nose-thumbing defiance of the shadow of the Holocaust.

And they'd had a good run.

Although honestly, I didn't really care about them at the moment.

I was more worried about Ariel.

Sitting there, staring up at the thick beams of blackened and charred wood, the smoking ruins with the faintest glow of embers around its edges, seeing both the literal and metaphorical fulfilment of his father's words from a decade ago, and finally understanding. Finally getting what his father meant but still unable to believe what his senses told him was true.

And right then, right there, I could see the thought forming in his brain:

"Sorry Abba...But *fuck dan l'kaf zechut*."

And I couldn't let that happen. I couldn't just watch that irritatingly saccharine optimism of his die. He needed some real comfort, platitudes however empty. But there wasn't anyone to give them to him. Because he was the rabbi, and giving people those words to others was *his* job.

So I was gonna do it for him.

I made my way through the crowd, bumping against shoulders, everyone being so enthralled in the spectacle that they didn't really notice. And finally, I reached him.

"Rabbi Samson?" I said.

"Yes?" he perked up immediately, already sliding into rabbi-mode, bless his heart. Even now, feeling like his heart had been ripped out of him, there he was tossing it all aside just at the hint of someone else needing help. Only this time, the person was here to help *him*.

"I just want to say that I'm so so sorry about this. This place and the work that you did here meant so much to me. I...well, I dunno what I'm gonna do now. But I just want to thank you so much for being here and doing everything that you've done for me and for so many others who've learned to call this home."

397

"Well, thanks so much," he said, warmly, hiding that he didn't recognize me at all. That was okay, though. "And, yeah..." he looked wistfully up at the bonfire. "This really does suck. But, y'know..." he shrugged. "*Gam zu l'tovah*. This too is for the good, y'know? It'll all be alright in the end."

I nodded, watching as his own words—words he really needed to hear—penetrated him. How, having heard them, he began to realize that he believed them. And even if he didn't, that now wasn't the time to mope.

There were people who were in need.

He'd only lost a job. Others had lost a home.

"What are you gonna do?" I asked.

"Rebuild," he said, confidently. Realizing it more to himself than saying it to me. "There's no other choice but to. So that's what we're gonna do. Rebuild."

As if my presence had painted a neon sign over Ariel's head, everyone suddenly came rushing over, congregants, bystanders and press alike, and I was engulfed and swept away into a mass of people questioning, asking, worrying, wondering.

"What are we going to do?" asked different versions of the same anxiety.

"Glad you're all here," Ariel answered them collectively, grinning, full of newfound confidence and defiance, his eyes searching the crowd for me, but the gulf between us was too much for me to be seen. "I hope to see a turnout this huge for services this week."

"Services? But where?" came the murmurs.

"My apartment," came the answer. Proud. Undaunted. "Contact the CAY website for more information, and I hope to see you there. Friday night Kabbalat Shabbat is at 8:30. Saturday morning **Shacharit** is at 9."

"Rabbi Samson," a reporter asked. "The intensity of the fire has lead to suspicion of arson being at play here. Can you comment on any of that?"

"Sure," Ariel shrugged, lifting himself off from the car and walking towards the camera.

The crowd hushed to hear him speak. Looking directly into the light and lens, he gave his steeliest gaze and said simply, "You missed."

Attaboy, Ariel.

ARIEL SAMSON: FREELANCE RABBI

You show 'em.

"*On June 13th, 2016, shortly after the holiday of Shavuot, malicious tragedy struck Congregation Ahavath Yisrael. Our beloved sanctuary was set ablaze by unknown conspirators, leaving our half-century old synagogue in ruins.*

But not our community.

We at CAY are sure that we know how our ancestors felt on Tisha b'Av when our holy Temple was decimated. But we will rebuild and we will restore. And we need your help.

All things happen according to the Divine plan, and instead of accepting defeat, we are looking forward to the bright future that will rise from this tragedy. The story that began in October of 1951 will not end on June 13th of 2016.

Please share so that this message of hope spreads just as quickly as the fire of destruction did. We are grateful for all donations, kind words, prayers and support."

By midnight Ariel and Blair had created and posted the Go Fund Me page, and by the next morning donations had already started pouring in by the hundreds.

From that Monday night until Friday morning had been a whirlwind of logistics, networking, and, for Ariel, making his apartment presentable for the thirty or so people who had RSVP'd to show up.

Overall, even in the face of the tragedy, everyone was feeling invigorated, excited about how well the Go Fund Me petition was going, and energized with the infectious electricity of building their Defiance Minyan.

It was a zeal that touched everyone. Except for Jerome.

Jerome was not happy.

No, he was somewhere between feeling disrespected and...obsolete.

See, since Halloween 1972, Jerome Litwak had been Congregation Ahavath Yisroel's guardian angel in human form. Its zealous protector.

For someone to have attacked *his* shul?

More importantly, for *him* to have failed to keep his people at CAY safe? It was a feeling of failure more painful than if he'd been trapped in those flames himself.

Oh, how the mighty had fallen. Obviously the name and reputation of "Mt. Sinai" had been long forgotten.

"Mount Sinai."

That's what Rabbi Gellerman used to call him.

It was a well-earned nickname, after all Jerome towered head and shoulders above the other CAY congregants and was as wide as a tank.

Jerome wasn't sure what Rabbi Gellerman would find more heartbreaking: Jerome's failure to keep CAY safe, or that the order to burn it down had likely come from Rabbi Shimon Guildencrantz's son.

Rabbi Guildencrantz the elder, back in his day, was the spiritual leader of Avon Gardens' Beis Hakeneses Hagodol Hachodosh, and Rabbi Gellerman's Orthodox opposite number. (Or catty-cornered number, if you factored in Rabbi Victor Jaffe and Temple Shaarei Tikvah.)

And Jerome would never forget the shock that he—and likely all who witnessed it—felt when one Sunday morning during Sunday school, Orthodox Rabbi Guildencrantz crossed the then Conservative threshold of Congregation Ahavath Yisroel, to speak with Rabbi Gellerman.

Manishtana

To understand, Rabbi Guildencrantz was quite an amicable fellow, and had warm relations with the other rabbis of Avon Gardens and their communities.

He was even well liked by the church clergies of the various Christian denominations sprinkled throughout Avon Gardens' boundaries.

But there were two things Rabbi Shimon Guildencrantz firmly did not do: enter churches, or enter non-Orthodox Jewish prayer buildings.

The reason for both was a Talmudic edict, forbidding Jews from entering prayer structures designated for people with theologies antithetical or heretical to any of the fundmentals of traditional Judaism, famously codified by Maimonides as the Thirteen Principles of Faith.

For Christians, the questions of G'd's indivisibility and incorporeality were obviously no gos. There wasn't any real dispute about that. There have literally been centuries of debate around that incompatibility.

And we were winning.

But the Christians called "Inquisition" first, so they took home all the points.

But for Rabbi Guildencrantz's fellow Jews—given how in just two centuries the emerging new denominations had defrocked the Torah of its divinity, abolished the timeless immutability of its edicts, and introduced the concept of roomfuls of barely pubescent 12 and 13 year-olds garbling the lyrics to 90's hip-hop whilst running around in socks on a dance floor—it made for a helluva elephant in the room.

An elephant that, at first glance, appeared to be pretty disdainful at best, or disrespectful at worst, of other faiths and observances.

Besides, it was just a *building*, right?

Which, *wrong*.

Because Judaism—the Judaism that Rabbi Guildencrantz believed in—saw faith, *any* faith and *any* form of observance, as something very powerful, as palpable, as an energy that transformed the very walls of the space it took place in.

And it was not an atmosphere to be trivialized.

No church or synagogue or temple or mosque or ashram was *ever* "just a building" any more than a *tallit* was "just a scarf" or a rosary was "just jewelry."

There were many other ways for interfaith and interdenominational understanding to be achieved. But crucial to that, as Rabbi Guildencrantz saw it, was standing firm in one's beliefs, and being confident enough to delineate religious boundaries.

The dialogue that grew from that honesty could lead to far more greater respect and understanding than cowardly bowing out from the uncomfortable messiness of faith.

All that having been said, you could imagine the impact of seeing Rabbi Guildencrantz enter CAY that Sunday morning.

The classroom had frozen.

Even Rabbi Gellerman sat with mouth agape mid-word for a moment, then he quickly recovered himself, signaling for the teacher to resume the regular lesson while he abruptly ended his sermon to cross the room and greet Rabbi Guildencrantz.

The two men shuffled into the hall, and as the door closed behind them, Jerome heard the briefest snippet of a conversation, as Rabbi Guildencrantz, with furrowed brows, said in hushed tones to his fellow clergyman, "I need a *torat m'Sinai.*"

It was a clever play on words.

"*Torat m'Sinai*" generally meant the edicts (*torat*) taught to the Jewish people by Moses, who in turn had brought them down from Mt. Sinai (*m'Sinai*).

But literally it meant "an edict from Mt. Sinai." And that was exactly what Rabbi Guildenstern had come for, on behalf of his daughter.

See, traditional Jewish law is...Well, it's a lot different than it was back in my day. But—at least according to today's society—it often manifests in ways that aren't the friendliest when it comes to "gender equality" as everyone insists the definition of "gender equality" is.

Like divorce.

Almost everyone knows about the *ketubah*, the Jewish marriage document.

But not so many people know that there's also a Jewish divorce document, the *get*.

Manishtana

Without a *get*, regardless of whether there's a civil divorce or not, a couple is still considered to be 100% Jewishly married.

Which is slightly problematic for a couple of reasons.

Reason One: If a woman with a civil divorce, but not a *get*, gets involved/married to someone else, she is actually Jewishly an adultress and her children are the legal category of *mamzer*, which, while often translated as "bastard," is actually not synonymous with illegitimacy, and just means a Jewish child born from any of the forbidden sexual relationships in Leviticus 18.

It's like squares and rhombuses. Not every bastard is a *mamzer*, but every *mamzer* is probably a bastard. Maybe.

(Fun fact: Any child born to a married woman, even if she is known to be outchea, is presumed to be her husband's, unless she publicly has a side piece, or if she's so promiscuous that even Rahab is sideeying her all the way from Joshua 2, like *"You're 'just friends'? Forreal? That's what we're doing? Aight."*)

Reason Two: Only men can initiate the *get* process.

But with Reason Two there's a little caveat. Let's say there's a woman who wants to get out of her marriage, but her husband is decidedly against that. The husband, according to Jewish law, can be...coerced into giving her a *get*.

In a physical "How many fingers to you want left?" kinda way.

Rabbi Guildencrantz' daughter was in such a position.

And he needed a little Luca Brazi-esque muscle to help nudge the situation to a resolution. His errant son-in-law was being recalcitrant and ignoring the rabbi's more civil pleas, so, Rabbi Guildencrantz was in need of an edict to be presented from "Mt. Sinai" to his undesirable current family member.

And as a favor to Rabbi Gellerman, Jerome complied, putting his ill-begotten skills of persuasion to holy use.

It was a one-time deal, Jerome figured. How often did that kind of thing happen, anyway?

In the Orthodox world? As it turned out, there were tens, hundreds even, of women who often found themselves stuck in that same predicament. And on and off, Jerome was often tapped to deliver a *"torat m'Sinai"* to some very unfortunate and vindictive husbands in Rabbi Guildencrantz' community.

So, when the elder Rabbi Shimon Guildencrantz had died, and his son, Dov Ber Guildencrantz took over his reins, Jerome thought nothing of it when he was called into duty on a case yet again, if only as courtesy to Dov's father and the long since passed Rabbi Gellerman.

The younger Guildencrantz, however, had inherited none his departed father's grace or diplomacy.

Where the elder Gildencrantz had embraced the technicality of *praying* in non-Orthodox spaces being the only no-no in times of great need, the younger Guildencrantz had unequivocally slammed that door shut, wasting no time in selling his father's Beis Hakeneses Hagodol Hachodosh and transplanting the congregation to the newly-built Congregation Orach Chayyim of Flatbush, nestled in one of the mushrooming right-wing religious enclaves of 1990's Midwood.

Sure, Guildencrantz Jr. rubbed Jerome the wrong way, and sure, there was some distaste around the fact that—unlike his father—the younger Guildecrantz charged unhappy wives for his aid in releasing them from their domestic hells.

But still, helping women trapped in bad marriages was bigger than the both of them, so Jerome continued to answer the call whenever it came.

That is, until David and Hadar Fierman came along.

Hadar wanted out of a marriage rotted through with abuse, gambling, and infidelity. But David had gotten used to the life of luxury that comes part and parcel of marrying into substantial money, and he wasn't quite keen on giving that up.

And so, when attempts to reconcile proved fruitless, David decided on a different tactic: a bit of arcane Judaica known as the *heter meah rabanim*, the decree of 100 Rabbis.

An obscure and contentious edict, the *heter* called back to Judaism's pre-11th century polygamous allowances, enabling remarriage without a *get* for a husband whose wife was recalcitrant or otherwise incapacitated and unable to participate in divorce proceedings. It was a measure so drastic—requiring the signatures of 100 Rabbis culled from three different countries—that there was substantial controversy as to whether the document should be employed at *all*, under *any* circumstances.

And yet—despite Hadar being neither reluctant to divorce *or* incapacitated—David Fierman had somehow managed to secure one, from a certain **beit din**.

Beis Din Shaarei Tzedek.

Whose head judge was none other than Rabbi Dov Ber Guildencrantz, who, luckily enough, happened to inexplicably come into $50,000 later in the same week that the *heter* was issued.

It was probably also a lucky coincidence that court depositions revealed that exactly $50,000 in cash, cashier's check and money orders had been withdrawn from David Fierman's accounts that same week.

When the news buzzed through the community, that was the moment Jerome realized that the younger Guildencrantz didn't want, wasn't interested, in having zealous Jews to call on, eager to help those in *halachic* need but fell outside the parameters of what the jurisdiction of American law could provide.

No. No what Dov Ber Guildencrantz wanted a squad of enforcers to impose his will wherever he saw fit. And Jerome vowed he would never answer that call again.

That was also the moment when Jerome decided that he could never identify as "Orthodox," no matter *how* observant he became.

He might've had problems with Orthodoxy before, might've been reluctant of the shift towards more observance that CAY had taken after Rabbi Gellerman's death.

But he knew he definitely didn't like the new brand of Orthodoxy that the younger Guildencrantz represented.

If *these* were the people who said they were doing it "right," who were better Jews than people who went to the beach on Shabbat but gave immensely to charity, better than Jews whose children fed the homeless in *mitzvah* projects, even as they served shrimp at the *bar mitzvah*...If Guildencrantz could wear that title with no shame or irony, then Jerome wanted no parts of that label.

That's why Jerome appreciated and respected Ariel so much.

Because Ariel proved that being Orthodox didn't have to mean that you were a bag of Orthodicks.

And yet, Jerome lamented, he'd let Ariel get almost killed on his watch. And that was just...

Cate.

Jerome knew she'd had *something* to do with this.

And he'd never really liked her, ever. From even before his suspicions that she was cuckolding her husband.

He had no proof, but it seemed obvious enough.

In fact, he was baffled how Howie didn't see it. Everyone *else* seemed to, even if they didn't say it. Jerome figured there had to be *something* that Cate had on Howie for him to turn such a blind eye.

(And, of course, she did. Because, Cate. After all, there was a reason for Howie's curiously prominent lips. And why his father's side of the family was conspicuously absent from Cate and Howie's wedding.)

At any rate, Jerome had never trusted her. And it seemed to him that Ariel had never, either.

He had no idea what had transpired in that meeting a few months back, but Jerome had never seen Cate as quietly furious as she'd been after she'd left Ariel's office that last Shabbat *kiddish* the week before she and Kalman resigned from the board.

And as disappointed as he was to see Kalman gone—distressed at both the loss of Kalman's enthusiastic leadership and the likelihood of him being the latest fly ensnared in Cate's adulterous web—Jerome was relieved to see Ariel demonstrate his integrity, quietly, discreetly, and resolutely.

But no one went up against Cate Finklestein and emerged unscathed. Again, he had no proof, but Jerome's gut told him it was Cate who'd planted the seeds of CAY's destruction.

That's why he'd had words with her just a few days after CAY's fire, warning her in no uncertain terms that the remaining congregants of Congregation Ahavath Yisroel—and *especially* Ariel and his circle—were off limits, for now and all time.

Or there would be...consequences.

Of course, Jerome would never lay his hands on a woman, even one as Machiavellian as Cate.

He damn sure made it *seem* like he would, though.

But no, Jerome was saving his hands for the two people he *could* put hands on: the two *chossids* that never left Guildencrantz's side.

That too was a hunch.

But he'd been around enough shady people—and been one himself—to recognize the scent of another predator on the air.

And he'd noticed the suspicious pair at the town hall, sitting behind Guildencrantz in the closest row to him. They'd walked in with the rabbi, flanking him on either side, and they'd left with him once the segment had finished filming, not speaking a word the entire time.

Manishtana

These new kids on the block were probably Guildencrantz's current goon squad, getting *gets* for a nominal extortion fee from desperate wives while Guildenstern dodged federal kidnapping charges by scoring plea deals ratting out other Rabbis in the same racket.

Jerome kicked himself for not being more alert before.

But he was ready now, he thought as he stood with arms crossed outside of Ariel's apartment, as congregants began to trickle in for Friday night services.

If that duo showed up tonight—if *anyone* showed up looking for trouble—they'd have to go through *him*.

So spoke Mt. Sinai.

✡ ✡ ✡

Attacking the ludicrous unrealism of our favorite TV sitcoms with real-world facts might be considered low-hanging fruits as pretentiously pseudo-deconstructionist as referencing something as being "Kafkaesque" or insisting that "Frankenstein" is the name of the *scientist* and the name of the *character* is "Frankenstein's monster," but I still think it bears saying that the only thing more improbable about any New York-based sitcom—from the conspicuous lack of black people, to the fact that car and apartment doors are *never* locked, to the conspicuous lack of black people—is how unaffordable the main characters' apartments would be given their lifestyles and occupations.

For Carrie Bradshaw, on a writer salary of $4,500/month, to be able to afford her $3,000/month Upper West Side rent—plus the $4,200 monthly bacchanals of Manolos, taxis, and nightlife—the show could technically *still* be called *Sex in the City*, but it'd take a decidedly more *Secret Diary of a Call Girl*-turn somewhere along Season 2.

In that venerated tradition, Ariel's 2 bed/1bath, 1300 sq ft, $2100 a month apartment was likewise ludicrously beyond his actual $3313K monthly takehome, even *with* the kickbacks he got from Ilan.

Luckily, there was Ariel's Great-Aunt Devora, sitcom character come to life in her own right.

Artsy, childless eccentric that she was (because, just stop "pet moms") Devora had led a checkered journey of an adventurous life, ending up well-enough off to have picked up some inexpensive properties in the 70's all over Brooklyn, including the terraced, second-floor Midwood spot Ariel had called home ever since his great-aunt had gifted it to him as a graduation present, subletted for a nominal fee.

All very fortuitous if you're planning on hosting 30+ people in your living room, no doubt.

But Ariel was more concerned with the urgent mission of fumigating his apartment of geekdom.

No one really needed to see his archive quality double-sided framed theatrical poster of all three *Lord of the Rings* movies. Or the Triforce lamp that illuminated his living room. Or his Starship Enterprise pizza cutter. And probably not the Gryffindor pennant mounted above his kitchen, either.

I mean, everyone pretty much figured he was a virgin. No need for the orgy of evidence to prove the point.

In other crises, Ariel was slowly realizing that, in his kneejerk zeal to stick it to the man, he hadn't thought this endeavor all the way through. After all, this was a glorified house party, and the worst kind of house party is the kind when you're the host.

Twice the stress and social awkwardness, but minus the safety parachute of bailing whenever you were done.

Because, y'know, you kinda live there.

At least he didn't have to buy all the food and booze for *kiddish*, courtesy of Blair's treasural machinations, Ilan's donation of beer and spirits from Holy Smokes, and the general generosity of CAY regulars and casuals, whether they were showing up or not.

Because cooking was not one of Ariel's fortes.

When he'd first been out on his own after college, he'd tried baking a whole chicken once. It...it didn't work out.

Luckily, again, there were enough deli platters and packaged desserts stacked like Tetris blocks on his kitchen counter that he could spend his time hiding his Bleach shower curtain and clearing the 4th edition D&D books from his living room floor, forced from their usual cabinet home to make space for the lone refugee Torah scroll Ariel had managed to rescue, still smelling faintly of smoke.

As for the rest of the living room space, it had already been outfitted with his couch, some folding chairs—donated by a certain well-tailored pastor of a Brooklyn Baptist church out of begrudging respect, professional courtesy, and an emotional resonance concerning firebombed houses of worship—and three or four white criss-cross patterned garden trellises that served as a makeshift *mechitza.*

Although technically—seeing as how Ariel's living room wasn't a permanent prayer space—a *mechitza* wasn't really necessary, making it just as much of a skeuomorph as the copper-plating on pennies or the rivets on a pair of jeans or that shutter-clicking sound your iPhone camera makes.

But Ariel's rabbinical legitimacy had been under siege for too long, so everything was being done above and beyond the book.

As the old African-American proverb went, "You have to be twice as good to get half as much."

And something, something "crackers."

✡ ✡ ✡

Ariel was just setting up the candle-lighting station with Ellis when people started trickling in.

Actualy, correction: People started trickling in just as Ariel was setting up the candle-lighting station with Ellis, *after* Ariel's quick jaunt into the kitchen to break up the mini-brawl between Sruli and Phyllis.

"You should *thank G'd* for my gentle nature," Phyllis hissed over Blair's restraining shoulders, getting her last barbs in. "Because I'd get out of *jail* before you got out of the hospital!"

"Oh *yeah?*" Sruli shouted back, as Ariel fought to separate the two. "Well I thank G'd for you *all the time,* Phyllis! I thank G'd you're not my *mother,* I thank G'd you're not my *sister,* I thank G'd you're not my *girlfriend,* I thank—"

"*Yeah?*" Phyllis shot back as Blair and Ellis pulled her from the room. "Well thank Him that I'm not your nurse *either!* Because I'd check your prostate with a *shark* on my hand!"

"Geez," Ellis commented after the fracas had died down and the fighters had retreated to their separate corners in the kitchen. "The way those two go at each other you'd almost think they had a thing for each other. Give or take about twenty years on either side."

"Ugh. Please not again," Ariel reflexively blurted out.

Ellis arched a questioning eyebrow.

"Nothing," Ariel said quickly. "Wait," he turned on Blair. "Why'd you think it was a good idea to put those two on kitchen duty again?"

Blair shrugged.

"They're always at each other's throats anyway. Figured they could get their blowout done and out of the way *now*, so smooth sailing for the rest us of us for the rest of the night."

It was a decent enough plan that—unlike Ariel's roast chicken—*actually* ended up working out.

While Phyllis and Sruli paced back and forth on the opposite sides of the room during services, Ariel was able to direct his attention to actually conducting them. Although he found their death glares over the *mechitza* a tad distracting while he was trying to cultivate an atmosphere of togetherness and solidarity.

In fact, Ariel was so pre-occupied with the behind-the-scenes drama not leaking into the general arena that he didn't even notice half-goat beard Chabad guy was there.

Not until services were done, and everyone had begun meandering into the dining room where Sruli and Phyllis had passive-aggressively set up *kiddish* under Blair's mediating eye.

Ariel had begun heading over to greet the chabadnik—he hadn't seen him in a few months, after all, and we haven't seen him since page 121—when suddenly he stopped in his tracks, frozen.

It wasn't because of Half-Goat Beard.

It was because of his guest.

That was unusual enough on its own, mostly because tonight's gathering had a caveat of no new faces, unless they came attached to a congregant in good standing.

That rule had been at Jerome's vigilant insistence.

"Are you okay?" came Ellis' voice at Ariel's shoulder as she sidled up next to him. "You look like you've seen a ghost."

"Maybe I *am* seeing one," was Ariel's shellshocked reply as he walked towards the apparition.

I smirked a little as I watched him creep closer. He didn't notice me, of course. There were too many people in the room for that, even if he *had* been looking in my direction.

The ghost was dressed in the standard Chabad uniform of black polyester frock-coat and fedora, with polished black shoes on improbably tiny feet.

And was the spitting image of I.I. "Cap'n" Herschel.

411

Manishtana

Not as Ariel remembered him—after all, he'd only been about four when the rabbi had passed—but as he'd seen him in pictures with Saba, thirty years younger, with bright red hair like orange marmalade and vanilla ice cream skin.

"*Shalom aleichem*," Ariel greeted once he'd reached the temporal anomaly, cautiously extending his hand.

"*Aleichem sholom*, Rav Samson," it replied with a wide and toothy grin, shaking Ariel's hand with a grip too warm to be one of the undead.

Their handclasp ended, with Ariel still gaping only slightly less than before.

"You don't remember me," the not-ghost said knowingly, judging from Ariel's general bewilderment. "Your family used to *daven* at my grandfather's *shul* in East Flatbush. Rabbi I.I. Herschel. I'm his grandson Mendy."

"Oh *wow*," Ariel gushed. "You looked *so* familiar but in a weird kind of way. I guess I was too young to remember you from back then."

"Yeah, I was ten and you were maybe one, one and a half when I last saw you? But your family was pretty hard to miss," Mendy chuckled with a mischievous glint in his eye not unlike his grandfather.

"I imagine," Ariel laughed. "What even brings you here?"

"I'm usually running the Chabad in New Haven, but I'm visiting Crown Heights for a *simcha*," he gestured to Half-Goat Beard. "Chaim actually told me about this *minyan*, although you've been pretty hard to miss in the news these days. I've been watching. You're popularly unpopular in some circles."

Half-Goat Beard, aka Chaim, gaped in wonder at the exchange, glancing back and forth between Mendel and Ariel with a look of wonder as his worlds were improbably colliding.

Or, more accurately, with that look that white Jews give when a Jew of Color proves to have spades more legitimacy than they were *graciously* being granted by patronizing well-meaning post-racial progressive white Jews.

"Please wait for the rabbi to make *kiddish*," came Balir's pointed rallying cry, snapping Ariel out of his reverie.

"Well," Ariel regained his composure, answering the call. "Actually, do you mind giving a few words before *kiddish*?"

Mendy opened his mouth to protest and Ariel shrugged.

"I'm feeling a little bit Pagliachi with all this right now," he explained. "Consider it a family favor?"

Mendy smiled and nodded, understanding the request. In the vein of who watches the watchmen, sometimes even a rabbi needed a rabbi. Also, no, I'm not gonna sit here and explain the Pagliachi reference.

Because Google is a thing, you philistines.

Ariel and Mendy walked into the dining room to the expectant and marginally hungry particpants.

"Thanks for coming out everybody," Ariel began. "Before we make *kiddish* I'd like to welcome a guest joining us tonight, Rabbi Mendy Herschel. Our families have known each other a long time, and it's really an honor to have him with us, so I'd like him to say a few words first. Rabbi?"

"*Good Shabbos, good Shabbos,*" Mendy began, swaying with the customary Chabad full-body rock, like one of those bobbing drinking bird toys. "Thank you all for welcoming me here, and thanks to Rabbi Samson for inviting me to speak. Like the rabbi said, our families have known each other a long time. My grandfather converted your grandfather almost, what, forty years ago now? Anyway, I'm not here to talk about why we're all here. There's enough talk about all that, and I don't wanna get political. I'm just here to offer a little bit of **chizuk** that everyone here should continue pursuing Torah and *mitzvos* with the same zeal and dedication that we're gathered here tonight with."

"It was said," Mendy continued after a pause and some scattered *"amen"*s. "That Reb Simcha Bunem of Pershyscha would carry two slips of paper, one in each pocket. On one said '*Bishvili nivra ha-olam,*' 'For my sake the world was created.' On the other was '*V'anokhi afar v'efer,*' 'I am but dust and ashes.' And that he would take out each slip of paper as necessary, as a reminder to himself. These quotes, it was said, reminded him that to live in tension is a natural state. To always be both humble and simultaneously believe in the infinite power God places in each of our souls...But in today's world things are a little more complicated. We deal with more people and more complex issues. And *chassidus* has sayings for that, too. Reb Menachem Mendel of Vitebsk, *chossid* of the Maggid of Mezritch, used to say that just as we accept that our neighbor's face does not resemble ours, so must we accept that our neighbor's views do not resemble ours. And just like our faces and views do not resemble our neigbor's, neither does our realities or our experiences. Reb Menachem Mendel of Kotzk, the Kotzker Rebbe, once said that if *I* am who I am because I am who *I* am, and *you* are who you are because you are who *you* are, then *I* am who *I* am and *you* are who *you* are. But if *I* am who I am because *you* are who *you* are, and *you* are who you are because *I* am who *I* am, then I am not I nor are you, you. With that in mind, I'd like to offer that we keep two more slips of paper in our pockets. In one, we should keep the saying of the Rebbe, 'If you see what needs to be repaired and how to repair it, then you have found a piece of the world that G'd has left for you to complete.' And in the other pocket, we should keep the second half of the Rebbe's thought, 'But if you only see what is wrong and how ugly it is, then it is *you* yourself that needs repair.' And I bless everyone here that they forge forward to repair the piece of the world that has been given to them to fix, regardless of the naysayers that fight against them. *Good Shabbos.*"

"*Good Shabbos*," came the communal response, with "*Shabbat shalom*" sprinkled in.

And, with a validiating weight lifted from his shoukders, Ariel made *kiddish*.

✡ ✡ ✡

The *kiddish* wasn't the usual CAY *Oneg* level of food, just enough to fill bellies enough to fuel people's walk home, and so after about twenty-five minutes of eating, everyone had begun their forty-five minute Jewish Goodbye Tour, with encores.

For Ariel, that meant a deluge of last-minute inquiries about the CAY fire and Go Fund Me progress.

Was it really arson? Yes. It was a gasoline-fed fire. The two glass crashes Ariel'd remembered hearing had apparently been the two large Molotov cocktails that had sparked the blaze.

Did they know who did it? Not yet. But the description of the black van Ariel had spied speeding off had matched the description of a similar van, one allegedly involved in a case the FBI was investigating around kidnapping charges of *get*-recalcitrant husbands.

Were the Katz brothers involved somehow? Probably not, despite all appearances and how swiftly and tastelessly the Katz brothers had sold off the ruined property in just two days. And to the selfsame Washington firm that had begun Ariel's involvement in this adventure in the first place.

What now?

"Now?" Ariel had answered Nahum the Husband and Chedva the Wife. "Now we show up for Shacharit tomorrow at nine. And then for **Mincha** at 7:30, followed by *seudah shlishit*. And then, if **Mashiach** doesn't show up *motzei Shabbat*, we figure it out again next week."

"But..." Chedva had started.

"Look," Ariel admitted. "I'm not gonna pretend to have a crystal ball. What happens next? I have no idea. There's *bitachon* and then there's *hishtadlut*," he continued, referencing the Hebrew terms for trust in the Divine plan and personal human effort, respectively. "The only control any of us have is over our actions, not their outcomes. And all I know is that I'm gonna keep moving forward and keep *us* moving forward. *That's* what's next."

Nahum the Husband and Chedva the Wife absorbed this, contemplatively nodding as they bid Ariel their goodbyes, promising to show up for the next day's services, and freeing Ariel's time up to be tagged in the next round of goodbyes as an elderly couple shuffled up next in line.

It was the old couple, the one that usually sat alone together at *kiddish*, earnestly bent over their meals because—between rising medical bills and shrinking social security—more often than not they didn't have one at home.

"Mr. and Mrs. Aronson!" Ariel's face lit up. "I haven't seen you in a few weeks now! I was worried! So glad you could come!"

"We were glad to be able to make it," Mr. Aronson replied with a gummy grin and a quivering chuckle.

"We'll be seeing you tomorrow?"

Mr. Aronson paused, vibrating in place as he mulled over his answer.

"No...No we just came to say goodbye."

"...Goodbye? Why?"

"Well," Mrs. Aronson spoke up. "We figured we'd see the last of all this before we parted ways."

"Are you moving or—" Ariel halted as it struck him what the Aronsons were saying. "But, wait, no, we're still gonna have a *minyan* going, the Go Fund Me we have up is—"

Mr. Aronson held up a tremulous hand and stopped him.

"I know you do, rabbi. And I know you will. We trust you will. And there is no denying the dedicated and determined young man you are to continuing this congregation...But it won't...," he seemed to falter for words, then reached out his hand to clasp his wife's. "My wife and I, we met at CAY back in 1947," he looked at her with shining reminiscing eyes. "It was only families back then. We were the only singles in the *shul* at the time. Met during erev Shabbat *oneg*, actually. We married at CAY, raised kids there, grandkids, great-grandkids, even..."

"Those were good times," Mrs. Aronson replied, smiling back into her husband's eyes. She broke away from his gaze to meet Ariel's eyes. "You are building a beautiful thing here. And we wish you all the best. But it's not CAY."

Ariel began to protest.

"We're not saying that's a bad thing," she insisted. "In fact, we couldn't be any prouder leaving behind you amazing young people to create something special into the next generation. But it's time we moved on. Both CAY's and our time is done here."

Mr. Aronson stretched his hand out.

"Goodbye, rabbi," he grinned again, clenching Ariel's hand with strong bony fingers in an unexpectedly strong vise-like grip.

"*Tzetchem l'shalom*," Ariel smiled back, despite a heavy heart. "And *Shabbat shalom.*"

Ariel watched the old couple shuffle toward the door, hand in hand with each other and the Ghost of Congregation Ahavath Yisroel Past, closing that chapter and the door behind them, bittersweet and poignant.

"Ariel, honey," Phyllis' trademark rasp trampled through any thoughts Ariel was beginning to form as she marched over to him. "*Good shabbos.* Great night. You did good. I'm gonna head out now."

"Thanks *so* much Phyllis for—"

"Oh, you're leaving?" Sruil cut in, eagerly appearing out of thin air to get in one last snipe. "I guess all the booze is gone then?"

Phyllis lowered her sunglasses and stared bloodshot eyes at Sruli from over the top of the dark lenses.

"Let me tell you something, honey. You're not special. There's *hundreds* of Sruli Kleins in the world. And you're not even the popular one."

"Oh," Ariel stopped at the entrance to his bedroom. "Well this isn't awkward."

"Yeah, sorry," Ellis shrugged, sitting cross-legged on his bed and thumbing through on old yearbook of his. "I was waiting for the bathroom and what's her name tried to rope into some conversation I really have no interest in."

"*'What's her name'?*"

"Yeah, y'know. The one with the eyes. Anyway, I distracted her and ducked in here. I figured no one would think to go poking around into the rabbi's bedroom."

"I mean, except you," Ariel smirked.

"I mean, except me. Because I have no home training. Are they gone yet?"

"Literally everyone is gone now."

"Gasp!" Ellis reacted in feigned shock. "So you're alone in your flat and have a girl in your room! How scandalous! What about **yichud**?"

"Oh no, you're right! I gues since we're alone we're obviously going to have all the sexes with each other! And probably mixed dancing!"

"*Chas veshalom!*"

"Well, y'know, the door *is* open. So we're prolly good."

"Ah, yes," Ellis nodded sagely. "Air pressure. *Yichud's* mortal weakness."

They shared a knowing laugh.

Sure *yichud* had its place, but sometimes even Ariel secretly thought the paranoia around it was slightly extra.

Don't tell anyone. They'd take away his rabbi-card.

"By the way," Ellis continued, holding up Ariel's high school yearbook and tapping his class picture in all its awkward glory. "I had no idea you were able to surpass the level of dorkiness you currently inhabit. But I stand greatly corrected."

"Yeah, well..."

"Also," She turned the book around to peer more closely at it. "Interesting *kippah* choice. Bukharian?"

"Yeah, that happened," Ariel confessed, referencing the colorfully embroidered kufi-resembling head covering that he'd worn for most of his youth. "Then in college I got tired of answering people's assumptions that I was Muslim. So I entered beanie-land," he gestured to the smaller, more Jewishly recognized coaster-sized circle of suede he'd been wearing since sophomore year.

The style, that is. Not the actual one he was wearing.

"So you swapped out one set of questions for another, essentially."

"Pretty much."

Ellis chuckled, starting to uncross her legs.

"Welp, if everyone else is gone I suppose I should head out too. Let you get some rest for shindig Number Two tomorrow, rabbi."

"I...sure."

Ellis paused.

"What?"

"Nothing. I mean...well, I've still got some stuff to clean up. Company, y'know, would be nice. Also I didn't actually eat yet and there's a ton of dessert that never even came out. And I have enough *challah* for the both of, so..."

"I...I dunno, maybe I should just..." she paused, mulling her options over, then goodnaturedly narrowed her eyes at Ariel. "Are you gonna be trash like you were the last time just the two of us hung out?"

"Yeah," Ariel admitted with some well-earned shame. "I *was* kinda trash. But I'm learning to be recyclable."

"Well, good. Just keep in mind that humans are still biodegradable either way."

"That is the most straightforward veiled threat I think I've ever heard. And gotcha. And also there's a bottle of Patron that no one's touched yet."

Ellis put her hand to her heart.

"Why, Rabbi Samson, are you trying to seduce me?"

"No!" Ariel said quickly, starting to flush. "I'm just say—"

"Relax. I'm sold. Besides it's only 10:40 or something. There's nothing really for me to do back home but hope that Emily and her new dubious life choice remember that the living room couch isn't communal space for *everything*."

"Everyth—oh. *Oh.*"

"I've seen things, Ariel," she shuddered. "Terrible things."

"20 ccs of tequila, stat," Ariel nodded, heading to the kitchen.

"Ariel," Ellis asked, leaning back in her chair and lazily staring up at the ceiling. "Why do my feet feel like octopuses? I want to swim up the wall."

"Dude," Ariel rolled his head up from the table, heavy from a tad too much Monkey Shoulder. And something slightly more herbivorous. "I dunno, man. You're halfway through the Patron. I—oh, wait, did you have the brownie platter?"

"*Yuup.*"

"*Ohhhh.* Those were the ones Ilan brought."

Ellis dropped her head down to look at Ariel with wide eyes as high as a kite that was smoking another kite that was also high.

"*No.*"

"Don't worry," he giggled. "It was baked under rabbinical supervision."

"Oh shit."

"Shabbos Mouth©."

"Sorry. Oh...shuckles."

That set off a good ten minutes of delirious peals of laughter.

"I've never done edibles before, though," Ellis admitted, precariously clutching her shot glass as she lurched forward in her seat. She finished the glass then added, with just a dash of sultry, "This is my first time. Will it be gentle?"

"Y'know, you are really enjoying our awkward sexual tension way too much."

"I *am*," she sighed. "It's a character flaw. I have many. Would you like some?"

"*Hah!* You don't think I have enough already? Did you *see* my bedroom?"

"I was choosing to kindly not judge your Steven Universe slippers."

"Those are *so warm*, though."

"*Pfft.* Between that, your Stormtrooper footie pajamas, and your Justice League sheets, I feel like you go to bed every night wrapped in a turducken of sadness and failure."

"Why are you so *mean*?" Ariel whined through tears of resigned laughter.

"Because I'm a horrible person. Holy sh—I mean, gee whilikers I need some air."

"Let's, I mean, I *do* have a terrace."

"Yes, pleasely."

Clumsily grabbing their respective bottles from a dining room table crowded with plates, half-eaten food scraps, and an empty brownie pan, Ariel and Ellis heaved themselves up and shuffled through the living room out onto the refreshingly cool air of the balcony. There weren't any chairs, so they both sat on the concrete terrace floor. Or more like comically slid down the wall in slow motion like descending hot-air balloons until they settled into something resembling a seated position.

"So say stuff," Ellis said once they'd landed.

"Stuff? Like, what kinda stuff?"

"I dunno. You say interesting things. And your life, and stuff. That."

"I mean, I guess...? Like, discovering this whole Aspberger's thing is being wonderful and horrible."

Ariel took a shot and Ellis tilted her head, studying him.

"Like how?"

"I mean, it's...like...*So* much more makes sense now? Like I've been discovering that I've been sorta pretending this whole time? And been feeling for so long that I was wasting my life trying too hard, or maybe not enough? And it's like *'Is that really a true thing? Am I just feeling not really feeling at home in black or Jewish spaces?'* And it's like, nope, this is a totally different thing."

"And also those other places are rubbish too."

"*Right!* Exactly! But then it makes things, like, easier? Like, seeing a lot of signs that should've made me or my family realize it sooner? But then knowing that there was just *so much* identity stuff on our plates that there wasn't really room for it? And, like, people just always thought of me as a geeky introverted kid, and I just got so good at pretending to be 'normal'—or 'neurotypical,' I guess— that I was able to fool everyone. And me too. And people were just so hard to relate to. Like, sure, a lot of that was probably the race and religion thing. But then on top of that I just didn't 'get it.' I tried so hard to make friends—maybe *too* hard, I think. And I didn't really get those couple of good buddies until Jumaane and Colin. That was, like, *college.* But they, I dunno, they *got* me. Y'know?"

Ellis nodded, looking out distantly over the terrace railing.

"Yeah. Yeah I get it...I had a friend who really got me...Was pretty cute, too. *Beautiful eyes.*"

"Is he the one that got away," Ariel smirked, with just a teasing hint of jealousy.

"They all got away. I'm a 'catch-and-release' kinda girl. But yeah. He...he actually just died a couple of weeks ago."

"Oh. I'm—I'm sorry."

"Me too. Our birthdays were the other one's half-birthday. It was one of those cute things. I knew him from my first summer jobs back home at Tesco. I guess it's like a Shop Rite here in the States?"

Ariel sat quietly as Ellis went on.

"Anyway, he'd had a drug problem in high school. A lot of stuff, but definitely heroin. But he was getting over it. And he was doing well, too. Like, he was supposed to live forever, just because he'd made it as far as he did. But then he didn't. And...I mean, when the cops found him, he was just another dead junkie to them. And they probably clocked out after, and went home just fine. But everyone else who knew him was never the same...He, he used to ask if there are minutes on the clock that we've never seen. Like, have you ever actually seen 2:14 in the morning or 8:10 at night? Like that. And...I guess I've just been thinking that you never know who people are in the minutes we never see, y'know?" she turned to Ariel. "Does that make sense?"

Ariel nodded, partially understanding, and partially understanding that the weight of the conversation was beyond his impaired capacity to digest in the moment.

"I get it," is what he said.

"Yeah, well...anyway...*That* was a random morbid tangent," Ellis laughed away some of the pain. "So, like, how are *you* doing? Like, *really* doing?"

"I'm, y'know, I'm doing," he replied, focusing on the scotch in his glass. "I—"

Ellis plucked the drink out of his hand and downed it.

"Hey! Th—"

"You drink too much," she scolded. "And you're not a drinker. *I'm* a drinker. You're a stoner. And I am *not*. So you be a stoner."

"You sound like my grandmother."

"Frell you. Also, so you mean you've been ignoring *generations* of good advice."

421

Ariel shook his head indignantly, despite the grin spreading across his face.

"Whatever, you. Anyhoo...I guess I'm...I dunno. I feel like everyone's looking at me to be some voice or something. But I'm really just being, y'know, *me*. And I'm just...trying to do the right thing, y'know? Or at least faking it until I know what I'm doing."

Ariel's admission sat on the silence of the night air.

"Well...," Ellis replied, breaking the lull. "*I* think you're doing a good job. And a real job."

"I...thanks, Ellis. Really. That means a lot. Especially coming from you."

"Well I don't say things just to make people feel warm and fuzzy. I mean it. And...," Ellis lingered, as some emotion starting swelling up in her beyond her control. A visceral swell of intoxicated truth that overwhelmed her usual reservation and restraint. "It's just not fucking fair."

"Shabbos Mouth©," Ariel reminded.

"With all due respect, I don't give a shit. Because it *isn't* fucking fair."

"I...What isn't?"

"Like, pretty much your entire fucking life. Like, you've been here the entire time, stayed the entire time, flown the Orthodox flag the entire time, and there's...theres so many *shitty* and rapey and culty rabbis out there. And you're here just trying to do the right thing by everybody, and people are trying to *kill* you. I mean...I used to *daven* at a *shul* with my parents back home. Every week, every Shabbat, every *chag*. And *still* no one knew my name. And *still* everyone mixed me and my sister up with each other. And we're *three* years apart. I mean, at first, sure, but after *eighteen* years? *Who* doesn't know the name of someone they've prayed with for *eighteen* years? *Seriously*? But sure, our congregation is 'accepting.' Sure, we're 'welcoming.' Fuck. You. I have *never* felt welcomed in a *shul*. *Ever*. I've showed up in *spite* of not feeling welcomed. But sure, pat yourselves on the back that you're soooo 'inclusive.'"

Ariel reached out a comforting hand towards Ellis, and she slapped it away.

"*Don't* touch me. I'm so *fucking* mad at you."

"Mad at *me*? But why?"

"Because *you* almost got yourself *killed*," she roared, tottering to her feet, and Ariel staggered up with her, confused.

"People *hope* in you, Ariel," Ellis fumed, jabbing at his chest with her finger. "You actually *do* all the things that Judaism and observance and Orthodoxy and *frumkeit* and *whatever* actually *should* be. You...You made me feel *actually* welcomed in a *shul* for the first time. *Ever.* And...and then you went and had to play some naïve, stubbornly principled Boy Scout and got yourself *almost killed,* Ariel! You almost fucking *died.* And you would've taken all of that good with you, all of that, and I...I just..."

Eliis had reached the high of her fever pitch, the peak of her vulnerability laying bare secrets she would've never revealed, *ever.* But it just wasn't enough. It still ate at her chest in words she was still too guarded to form.

If she were American, or just a touch more intoxicated, she might've just then screamed it all out, all of her confusing, conflicting, furious, sad, upset, heartbroken, wordless frustration at *everything,* right over the side of that terrace, until her throat was raw and her lungs were burning and empty and heaving in the otherwise quiet night.

But stiff upper lip and all that. Keep Calm and Repress.

So instead it all just flared up to a crescendo, hovered at the height of its trajectory, then sputtered out like a spent firecracker fizzling away.

She closed her eyes, swaying a bit as she exhaled her stress off, and then looked at Ariel with eyes he'd never seen before, just as a grumble of thunder lowed in the distance.

"Look, I just...," she started anew, in a strangely measured tone, so calm that it was unnerving. "You really just piss me the fuck off. And...and have you ever had a weird sort of crush on one of your friends where you're not sure if it's a crush or not? *'Do I want to kiss them? Do I just really enjoy their company? Who knows? Not me!'*"

Before Ariel could register the question, Ellis' arm was suddenly around his waist pulling his body closer to hers, and she arched up into his chest on her tiptoes, her other hand tenderly cradling the back of his neck, tilting his head and lowering it, drawing their mouths together in a long, languid kiss.

Another tremble of thunder murmured overhead, and a slight rain began to mist. But the lightning came from their kiss, electric and white-hot, crackling outward from where their lips met,

423

radiating throughout every inch of their bodies from there. And Ariel had no other choice, no other desire, but to kiss Ellis back, mirroring her, bringing his hand to rest below her ear, his thumb caressing her cheek as his other hand drifted to the dip of her waist.

As if orchestrated by some divine choreographer, the rain began to pick up just as the soulful croonings of "Stand By Me" could be heard floating on the night air from somewhere in the neighborhood. And Ariel and Ellis leaned into each other and swayed in time to the swelling strings and harmonies as if everything in the world that night was happening just for them.

Lips were soft. So soft. His. Hers. Neither of them could tell anymore where one of them ended and the other one began. Ariel could feel Ellis' body go rigid then shudder under the pressure of his fingertips as the hand he rested on her waist began tracing a gentle but firm path up her spine, pulling her closer until there was no space left between them. Ellis' hand migrated from the back of Ariel's neck to the crook of his jaw, coaxing a shudder out of him as she softly traced the outline of his ear. Her other hand found a new home pressed against Ariel's chest, feeling his heart beat under her palm, but only for a few seconds, before the sensation made her clench her hand into a fist, clutching his shirt in her fingers as she leaned deeper into him.

As abruptly as it had begun, the kiss ended equally as slowly, with Ellis reluctantly drawing her lips away from Ariel's, sliding her hand up from his chest to touch her fingers to his open mouth as she lowered herself back down on her heels.

"We probably shouldn't have done that," Ellis acquiesced softly, moving backwards from Ariel, both of them suddenly more sober, and beautifully flustered, their skin and hair beaded with rain droplets that glistened under the dim orange glow of the streetlights, a different kind of thunder growling between them.

And *that*, kids, is why *yichud* is a thing.

"Well," Ariel offered, clearing his throat and trying to keep the gravity as light as possible. "We've, y'know, we've probably done worse with other people before."

"Yeah. Except this time I think we both know that this is very different. And that it really matters."

Ariel was silent, because there was no debating that. Not as Ariel replayed that perfect kiss in his head across unending seconds.

Ellis smiled a tiny smile, then exited the terrace back into the apartment.

"Goodnight, Rabbi Samson," she smiled at him, enigmatically. *"Shabbat shalom."*

"Shabbat shalom, Ellis Green."

mincha

"Wow. Whoever did the seating chart just did *not* give a fuck, amirite?" came the British-ish voice.

Ladies and gentlemen, Ellis had at last entered the building, finally joining a still-fairly-high Ariel isolated at his roundtable of enemies.

And she, as always, looked amazing, as she did in her own way.

Well, maybe just a *little* bit more than usual, actually.

She—as evidenced by Ariel temporarily forgetting that you can't chew water or drink salmon, and also that breathing was a thing to do to keep living—was being a little bit extra tonight.

Tonight, she was the most dressed up Ariel had ever seen her, and likely as normal as she was ever capable of getting.

A gothic black-and-cobalt dress with a lace-up corset bodice that descended into layer upon layer of asymmetrical black taffeta peplums was the centerpiece of the ensemble. Over that, she wore a black bolero with bell-sleeves covered in scrawls of black Venetian lace, its pearl-buttoned collar left open to show off a black lace choker, adorned with an antiqued bronze Star-of-David and onyx faux-pearl drops.

A braided leather belt hung slack around her waist, adorned with her everpresent keys, hanging from a sky-blue carabiner off her left side. And finally, there was the pair of almost knee-high black combat boots that looked like they walked off the stage of a KISS concert, complete with leather purple flames that licked at the toe and heel, metal plates bolted on the front and sides of the soles, five buckles on one side, a zipper on the other, and skull-tipped neon-pink shoelaces running up their entire length.

Because, Ellis.

(I'd also mention her hair—a side-braided fro-hawk updo, dyed an electric-blue—and maybe even the makeup—lavender glitter smokey eyes, accented with a fierce double-winged metallic-blue eyeliner, and syrupy golden lipstick that made her lips look wet enough to slide right off her face—but, y'know, I literally *just* said "Because, Ellis.")

"Gentlemen," she smirked at the rounded eyeballs of the entire table, and promptly took her seat in the empty chair next to Ariel, who, by the way—in a burgundy sharkskin 3-piece, navy-blue shirt, grey plaid tie and pocket square, burnt amber wingtips, and a black leather *kippah* with a floral silver-foil arabesque print—wasn't looking too shabby himself.

They made quite the odd couple, Ariel and Ellis.

James Bond from *Skyfall* and Lydia from *Beetlejuice*.

"'*Ms. Liba Sheindel Green,*'" she cheerfully read her name off the card, written in equally as swoopy penmanship as everyone else's. "Ooooh. Isn't that classy?" she asked Ariel, sliding the card into her black leather clutch, covered in tiny skull studs.

"It's *so* classy."

"I'm practically catching the vapors. Anything good?"

"These lemon-artichoke chicken pockets are *amazing*," he slid the plate toward her and she picked one off and bit into it.

"Omig'd you're right," Ellis exclaimed. "Have you tried one of these Rabbi Guildencrantz? No? Assemblyman Rosenstern?"

Her tongue-in-cheek inquiries were met with stonefaced silence from the table as if she hadn't said a word.

"*Oh*-kay, not artichoke fans. Understandable. It's an acquired taste," Ellis shrugged. "And—Wait. Have you guys been sitting here this whole time and not talking about the thing?"

"That's what *I* said!" Ariel agreed. "How rude is that?"

"*So* rude."

"I know, right?"

"Wow guys," Ellis looked around at the table as no one met her eyes. "If you're gonna try to kill a man, you can at least have the courtesy to like, I dunno, have some vaguely threatening movie-villain dinner banter. Twirl a mustache. *Something.* C'mon people. Lean in. Claim it."

Ariel snorted, and as Ellis caught his eye and gave him a sly smirk, it suddenly struck him that he'd never really looked at her before.

Like *looked* at her looked at her.

He'd grown so used to her just being around—day-in and day-out at work, every Shabbat in *shul*—that he hadn't really *seen* her. And he didn't mean the gold flecks in her tawny, almond-shaped eyes, or the beauty mark tucked in the cupid's bow of her lip, or the softness at the waist of her callipygian frame.

No, he meant those little imperfections. The ones that were just now drawing him in. The small scar on her left cheek. The pinpricks of skin tags that peppered her neck. Her slight underbite. Her—had that kiss really been three months ago?

It amusedly dawned on Ariel, still surfing the out of body haze courtesy of the night's earlier Easter grass, that he and Ellis were being *highly* hypocritical. Because they definitely had *not* talked about their "the thing." Not even once since it happened.

Ariel'd been too busy rabbi-ing to get a chance to talk when Ellis came to services that next morning, then she'd skipped coming to the *seudah shlishit*, and even though she came to the musical *havdalah* that evening, as soon as it'd finished, Ellis was gone.

The weeks after that had been a dizzying rollercoaster of police questionings and press conferences, television appearances, weddings of friends and family, Ellis' eight-week European vacation while *Late Late* was on its summer hiatus, and numerous other excuses for missed connections.

Sure, the past few weeks since Labor Day had found Ariel and Ellis falling back into their familiar work and *shul* routines, but that tension, that spark, or *whatever* had been there and exploded out of them on Ariel's terrace that night?

It seemed like it'd just faded away on its own, like a song ending on the radio.

And maybe that was just...fine?

I *did* say that not every pleasant exchange with a stranger foreshadows a romance lying in wait, remember?

But it *can* herald a friendship.

431

And that's better than a whirlwind romance any day of the week. I mean, that's love too, right? When your friend has a piece of your heart and you swear to protect the piece you have of theirs? Also, they pay for their *own* damn food when you go out, and isn't that the greatest love of all?

He and Ellis were just friends, Ariel realized. And without her—without her finding and chastising and coaxing and prodding and, well, *listening* to and *supporting* the person he was inside, the real him even *he* didn't realize he was—he knew he'd never have figured out how to become the perfectly imperfect person he was supposed to be.

Maybe *now* he just might find that person who was his perfectly imperfect match.

Some friends are for a reason, some friends are for a season, and some friends are for life.

Ellis was for life. He knew that now.

As one of Guildencrantz's *chossids*—the huskier of his everpresent duo—rose from the table, checking his phone, an idea blinked into Ariel's head. An amazingly brilliant idea. Or maybe just a really high one. (Spoiler alert: It *was* just a really high one.)

With a huge smile threatening to split his face open, Ariel shot up from his seat and scanned the room.

He caught Busboy Seth's eye and tried to flag him down.

Then laughed when Busboy Seth flagged another server down and sent them in Ariel's direction.

✡ ✡ ✡

Ellis was casually helping herself to the salmon on Ariel's plate, smirking like the cat who ate the canary, and mildly curious why Ariel was pacing back and forth about a foot away from the table, as eager as a cat *trying* to eat a canary.

She figured it had something to do with whatever he'd just talked to the little brunette server about, because he was clearly bursting at the seams with anticipation, anxiously awaiting for the server's return from the kitchen.

Speaking of returns, Guildencrantz's missing *chossid* reappeared, sliding back into his seat next to the rabbi.

"*Zey zaynen shoyn do,*" the *chossid* said in an undertone, just loud enough to be heard.

"Zey zoln vartn biz er heybt zikh on mit der rede," Guildencrantz nodded in acknowledgment. His tone was casual, a sleight-of-hand masking the sinister intent of his words. *"Ven men makht der onzog vegn im, geyn mir avek un azoy vet zaynen do a sakh leydike zitserter—"*

"Bist zikher az dos vet arbetn?" Rosenstern interrupted, frowning. *"Bald vet forkumen di valn un mer tsores felt mir nit—!"*

"Zorg zikh nisht, er iz a bokher a tsedrikter, gring vet er farfirn gevorn," Guildencrantz reassured, calmly rocking his hand in Rosenstern's direction. *"Zey zaynen sheyne meydlekh, dokh veln zey koketirn mit im, vegn vi vunderlekh iz geven zayn rede un vi zey haltn in zukhn a naye shul mit a rebe a progresiver vi er un vu gefint men zikh zayn shul. Un azoy vayter..."*

"Un ven zey kumen bay im shabes bay nacht..." Rosenstern grinned cruelly. *"Vos den? Geyt di mayse az er iz zey meanes geven? Oder zey zaynen getribn in znus mit im?"*

Guildencrantz shrugged enigmatically, turning his hands up.

"Abi me basheft di rikhtike rayes, gib ikh zey a fraye hant."

"A toyve!" Ellis commented in seeming approval, nonchalantly engrossed in slicing up the wedge of salmon on her plate. *"A groyse yasher-koyech, dir far shitsn sheferish farkayt."*

Guildencrantz, Rosenstern, and their respective entourages all jumped in their seats, startled. Stunned gazes bore down on the woman named "Liba Sheindel"—*LIBA SHEINDEL,* for Tevye's sake—that somehow *no one* was expecting to understand, let alone *speak,* the secret Jew-language of Yiddish.

On account of all of the black, you see. Because apparently language families have racial-specific comprehension-locking features.

"Ir veyst," Ellis continued, ignoring the stares as she cut into her fish. *"Ven ikh geven a dervaskene, di bobe hot geflegt mir ufgeregt. Keyn mol nit geredt mit mir af English. Nor oder Daytsh oder Yiddish. Un ikh hob gevust az zi ken gut English. Ir tate iz geven a Amerikaner, un ir man iz geven a Yamayker, s'iz dokh klor az zi ken a fleysik English. Nu, far vos? Farvos hot zi mir geredt nor af yede nit-Englishe sprakhn vos zi ken ven ikh kum bar ir far a bazukh? Sof kol sof, ven ikh bin geven nayn yor alt, un hot shoyn umgern oysgelernt a shtikl Yiddish, hob ikh zi gefregt af Yiddish: 'Bobe, far vos redtsu mit mir nor af Daytsh oder nor af Yiddish? Ikh veys shoyn az du kenst git English. Far vos redtsu nit mir mir af English?' Veyst ir vos zi hot mir*

gezogt? 'Tayere, du host a shverer veg. Es vet zayn a sakh mentshn vos vet dir zogn vos du kenst un vos du kenst nit, vos du bist af emes un vos du bist nisht. Ober zey kenen nit dir leykenen vos gehert tsu dir, di vos iz dayn geboryn-rekhts, dayn yerushe. Es lign dir in blut shprakhn, Liba. Halt zey mit koved un derekh-eretz. Halt zey vi an oytser.' Azoy hot zi mir gezogt. Af English, di eyn un eyntsik mol af ir gants leben. Un ikh hob zikh tsugehert. Un ikh hob oysgelernt. Ikh hob oysgelernt Hakka un Mandarin Khinezish. Ikh hob oysegelertn Yamayker redenish. Ikh hob oysgelernt Daytsh. Ikh hob oysgelernt Hebreish. Un ikh hob oysgelert Yiddish. Vayl zey zaynen mayns."

The table sat frozen in silence, almost as if everyone else was afraid to breathe, the only sounds being the clinking of Ellis' fork and knife, the background chatter of the ballroom, and the chipper high-pitched voice of the speaker at the podium.

"Anyway," Ellis looked up finally, smiling as she popped a jagged square of off-pink fish into her mouth. "All that having been said, how bad of an idea do you think your little conversation was just now? On a scale of say, zero to 'one of Ariel Samson's best friends is one of the nicest *arsim* you'll ever meet. But he's still an *ars*. And when you know *arsim*, sometimes they happen to know a guy who knows a guy. Sometimes that guy is a pimp. And sometimes that pimp recognizes the name of the john that a client is asking his girls to set up. So then that pimp may or may not give a head's up to a fellow *ars* that someone has it out for their homeboy. In fact," Ellis said, producing her phone from her clutch, holding it up for the table to see. There was an eighth note icon visible on its screen, indicating a music file. Or, perhaps, a *different* kind of sound file. "That pimp might even record the transaction as proof.'"

Ellis blithely kept the phone aloft for a moment longer, as what little remaining color that was left in everyone's faces drained away faster than black artists out of black music.

"So yeah," she continued, putting her phone away. "Where on that scale do you think your little **farbrengen** falls?"

"Ellis," Ariel suddenly reappeared at the table, excited and oblivious to the ashen faces and gallows atmosphere at the table, but *very* animated about what he held clutched hidden in his pocket. "Um, can I talk to you outside for a quick second?"

"Sure," Ellis smiled cheerfully as she rose from the table. "This better be good though, because this salmon is phenomenal. *Derekh-*

agev," she added in a deceptively light voice. *"Es volt nit gegangen loytn plan. Nisht mit* mayn *rebn. Khas-ve-sholem loz ikh geyn azoy."*

Motionless, the gentlemen at the table watched Ariel and Ellis disappear through the ballroom's double doors and out of sight, and for a loaded moment, no one said anything.

Then Rosenstern and Guildencrantz turned, meeting each other's eyes and seeing the same fury and trepidation being mirrored back.

Just as wordlessly, Guildencrantz glanced at each of his *chossids* and they both rose from the table, responding to some unspoken command.

New plan.

✡ ✡ ✡

Meyer Sherman and Velvel Goldwasser always knew exactly what Rabbi Guildencrantz was saying.

Even with just a look. A raised eyebrow. A shrug.

There was a reason why they were both his right-hand men. You didn't become the *rebbe's* enforcers by needing things spelled out for you.

So when he'd glanced at them at the table, they knew to get to work. And, as always, they were prepared.

The brass knuckles in Meyer's pocket felt cool against his leg, and Velvel's taser slapped against his chest as his jacket flapped with each step.

That would just be the warm-up, of course. Just to soften Ariel and Ellis up. Once they were in the van, the cattle prod would come out.

It was a well-rehearsed routine that the two *chossids* executed like clockwork. They'd done countless jobs for the rabbi, but *this* one...*this* one was personal for him.

Which made it personal for *them*.

In all the years they'd worked for him, Meyer and Velvel had *never* seen someone twist the rabbi up so much, had never seen the need for revenge gnaw at his soul so badly as it did for this Ariel Samson, the rabbi who married his daughter to a *schvartze.*

A fucking schvartze!

For that, they would make this hurt.

435

They were gonna do it eventually, anyway. Even if he *did* cancel his show and rescind his *hechsher* from Holy Smokes.

Because some things were just unforgivable, and when Rabbi Guildencrantz got revenge in his head, he didn't serve it cold, he served it at absolute zero.

Zero compassion. Zero negotiation. And absolutely zero remorse.

It had rained earlier, so the streets were fairly deserted.

Perfect, the *chossids* thought as they exited the building.

They spotted Ariel and Ellis halfway down the block, and were just beginning to trail them, when two heavy hands came crashing down from behind, one on each of their shoulders.

"*Shalem Aleichem, yidden*," Jerome smiled. He closed his eyes, inhaling deeply, opening them as he exhaled. "Such a beautiful night!"

"*Aleichem shulem, Aleichem shulem*," the *chossids* greeted back, bobbing obsequiously with false piety to this man-mountain, anxious to attend to their duty.

"Come," Jerome said taking a step with them back towards the gala entrance. "Have a *l'chaim* with me inside!"

"Reb Yid," Meyer began, eager to cut the pleasantries short in the least suspicious way possible. "We would love to but we really have to get going—"

"You can't stop for a *l'chaim*?"

"We're late for a *shiur*," Velvel embellished, his tone pitch-perfect in its apologetic compromise even as he began moving in the opposite direction. "Can you be **moichel** us and we can make it up to you the next time?"

But Jerome's grip kept them held fast.

"You should have the *l'chaim* with me," Jerome continued genially, the *chossids'* struggle to escape not making any dent or difference to the strength of his hold. "It'll keep you from doing something very unwise that you really don't want to be doing. Regardless of *whatever* Rabbi Guildencrantz says," he added knowingly, and with just a hint of menace to his otherwise jovial tone.

Meyer and Velvel looked at each other, then sized-up the large, but still *old*, man. And there were two of them and only one of him.

Jerome read their looks and smiled even more broadly.

He took a step back—as Meyer reached into his pants pocket and Velvel reached inside his jacket—and settled into his old fighting stance like someone easing into their favorite lounge chair. But it'd been awhile since he'd been in the thick of things like he used to be back in his rougher days.

Did his 64-year-old bones still have it?

Who knows.

But he was excited, and just a tad hungry, to taste the thrill of it again, eager to see what these two young whippersnappers—younger than he was, even with their ages *combined*—had to offer.

But, as it turned out, a deliberate cough in the night interrupted Jerome's chance at nostalgia.

Meyer, Velvel, and Jerome turned towards the curb, where they hadn't noticed the figure exit his parked car. He stood there leaning up against it, with all the casual threat of a bored panther reclining on a tree branch.

He was dressed business casual under a light jacket that strained against his body, almost as if he'd enjoyed a steady diet of dumbbells since he was a toddler.

"*Shalom aleichem, chaverim,*" he began in a pleasant but clipped tone, wearing a smile that didn't quite reach his eyes. "I was just sitting here in my car, hoping someone could help me out tonight, and it seems like I've run into just the right gentlemen."

Meyer and Velvel's eyes darted to each other, then warily back to the possible new threat of the stranger, while Jerome—still keeping his eye on Meyer and Velvel—wondered why this newcomer seemed so...familiar.

"See, I'm—" the new player hesitated. "Well, I'm not really supposed to be here. *None* of us are," he added, as the front passenger's side and back driver's side doors opened up, and two female figures emerged—one smoking a cigarette, as cool as a pocketknife dressed in a business suit, the other, a chestnut-brown-skinned woman with short-cropped hair, stretching out kinks in her neck. "And we'd be in *soo* much trouble if anyone ever found out. But, y'know," he shrugged. "Big siblings just can't help themselves sometimes."

Meyer and Velvel stared blankly, confused and now afraid, while Jerome slowly nodded and backed away, amused, as it suddenly clicked why the newcomer seemed so familiar.

The women with him, too.

Maꟼishtana

After all, the family resemblance was uncanny.

"But, y'know. Sometimes your baby sibling needs some cavalry, whether they know it or not. His name's Ariel. Ariel Samson. He's a rabbi. Maybe you've heard of him?"

✡ ✡ ✡

"Whoa, Ellis!" Ariel held his hands up defensively. "I get it! But why are you so—"

"Why aren't *you*?" she yelled back at him. "*Call girls*, Ariel! Ladies of the night! They were gonna hire a couple of call girls to pose as fans or admirers or whatever to weasel their way into the *minyan* in your flat and then make it look like you hired them, or Carlebached them, or *whatever*. You need to be *careful*! If Guildencrantz's contact hadn't ran with Ilan back in the day—which, by the way, *why* does Guildencrantz have a call girl contact, but never mind that, they, just, I mean, *wow*—"

"Ellis..."

"We need to hit back. Hard, and fast. Now look, Ilan sent me the recording of Guildencrantz trying to set this all up—"

"Ellis..."

"The arson case on CAY is still open, but Rosenstern is putting pressure on it, so it's losing heat. But if we bring this file with—"

"Ellis..."

"What! Why do you keep saying my name? What?"

"Just, like, relax."

"What do you mean 'relax'? We've got to move qui—"

"We're not doing any of that."

"We, what? *What*? What do you mean we're not—"

"We have dirt on them. *We* know that. And *they* know we know that. And they know we *know* they know we know."

"Ok, I'm gonna need you to focus here, Dr. Seuss."

"I *am* focused. And I'm saying no, we're not doing any of that. I refuse t—look, I know you want to plow ahead guns ablazing into all that. And doing that would be so easy. But I can't. I won't. I won't because if I do—if I turn around and walk through those doors, kicking asses and taking names the way you do—Then they'd win. They'd win because I'd lose myself. Because that's *not* who *I* am. And hey, I get it, *you* are. And that works for you Ellis, it really does, but that's not me."

Ellis opened her mouth to protest.

"Don't!" Ariel stopped her. "Please don't say one of those kickass, no-nonsense things that you say, because if I don't get this out now then I never will, because I'm not this self-aware everyday."

Ellis begrudgingly held her piece and let Ariel continue.

"You go in everywhere expecting the worst," Ariel explained. "And that keeps you and those around you safe. It sure as hell's kept *me* safe. But I go into places hoping for the *best*. And that lets me open doors and build bridges. For me and, hopefully, for the people around *me*. That's just my side of the coin. And even if it weren't, I...Y'know, I've been thinking about a lot of things. And relationships. And how good and evil is one of those things. It's a relationship. And relationships aren't about the big moments. It's *not* about the big moments, it's about creating and fighting and living through the little ones. Not about the boomboxes in the rain or the cupcakes in elevators. It's putting toothpaste on each other's toothbrushes in the morning and, and wearing that shirt that you know is their favorite color. And it's taken me an embarrassingly long time to figure that out. And this right here? With Rosenstern and Guildencrantz? This would be a big moment. And I don't want to do those anymore. Because there'll always be another Big Bad. Another Rosenstern and Guildencrantz after these two get whatever's coming to them whenever that comes. And I'm not burning myself out on big moments anymore."

"Well that's great and all, but, with all due respect, it's just a really stupid idea. To just throw all this evidence away."

"Oh no, we're *definitely* gonna hold on to it. Make them scared and wonder when we'll hit them with it. *They* don't need to know that we're not gonna do it."

"And, why the hell is this your plan again?"

"Well...Because this," Ariel beamed, pulling out a whole lemon from his pocket.

"Because of a lemon? What—Ari, are you, *high*? *Here*? *Tonight?*—Dammit, I'm *so* gonna kick a hole through Ilan's whole ass when I—"

"No, I'm not! I mean, yeah I am, but no that's not why I'm saying this. Or holding a lemon. Ok, maybe it's both, but—anyway, the *point* is this is a metaphor. Rosenstern and Guildencrantz? They're throwing lemons at me. And I'm gonna go back in there, and sit down at that table, and look them right the fuck in their eyes. And I'm not gonna blink. And I'm gonna dare them to be assholes, because I'm done dicking around with them. I'm *done* dicking around with them," he repeated, emphatically.

A smile crept at the edges of Ellis' lips in spite of herself.

She dropped her head and shook it, chuckling, then looked back up at Ariel, smirking.

"And then what? Tequila?"

"Oh, hell no. Tequila is a *terrible* life choice. Tequila is like *'Welp, I'm done caring about making cogent life decisions for the day, so here goes nothing!'*"

"Oh, go to hell," Ellis laughed. "Tequila is amazeballs."

"No," Ariel shook his head, beaming at her, weirdly jovially solemn. "*You're* amazeballs, Ellis."

"It's ok, I know. And you're being weird now."

"No, seriously. It's a true fact. Sorry, not sorry, you are one of the most amazing people I've ever met, and one of the best friends I've ever had, and I—well, there's no way I'd be the who and the what I am without any of the ass-kickings you've given me. So, this is for you."

And with that, Ariel bit into the lemon, tore off a chunk of skin, and started chewing.

"Ariel—What the—*Stop!* What the hell are you doing!"

"I'm showing you I—" he stopped, keeping himself from gagging as he chewed. This, he was realizing, was a very *not* good idea. This was a horrible idea. "I'm showing I appreciate our friendship! And the things I've—I've learned—"

"By—*What?* No! Can you—" Ellis shrieked in a combination of horror and amusement, trying to pull the fruit form his hands. "Omig'd Ariel *stop eating a whole fucking lemon—*I just—"

"NO!" Ariel roared, leaping back out of her arm's reach, gulping down the chunk of skin and biting into the flesh again. "I need to do this!"

"YOU DO NOT NEED TO EAT A WHOLE RAW LEMON ON THE STREET ARIEL," she shook her hands at him, laughing even as she was furious with him.

"I'M GONNA EAT THIS—oh gosh," he started to heave, then caught himself. "I'M GONNA EAT THIS LITTLE YELLOW BITCH WHOLE! THE SKIN, THE—THE—," he lurched again. Held his hand out as he waited. Rallied. Then swallowed the acrid mush of chewed up lemon pulp and crunched seeds. "THE PULP, THE SEEDS, *EVERYTHING!*"

Ellis held her hands to her forehead, shaking her head and flabbergasted at what she was witnessing.

"Omig'd, you are, you are really gonna..." she laughed with incredulous resignation, and threw her hands up. "I can't..." Ellis turned and took a couple of steps away, then turned back around. "Alright, *fine*, you can take me on a date tonight."

Ariel froze mid-third bite.

"Wait, what?"

"We can date. Or at least we can have one date. Tonight. Which I think *definitely* needs to include tequila now."

"But I thought—I mean, I didn't think we, like—after the," he lowered voice and whispered, "*the kiss*, and when nothing really after that, I thought we were just, y'know, we were just doing the friend thing then."

"So did I. So you were right. For then. But now I'm thinking something different."

"You're thinking something different."

"Yes."

"So, like...what did I do?"

"You didn't 'do' anything. I just decided that I wanted to date you. Pretty much just now. Trust me, I'm just as surprised by this plot twist as you are."

"You...But why?"

"Well, one, because I'm not a side character in *your* story, Ariel. I've been thinking thoughts and going through an entire character arc this whole time *too*, y'know."

"I,uh...I mean...And two?"

"Two is...Ugh...Two is *because*, Ariel Samson, part of me adores you right now, and another part wants to punch you in the face. And...and you give me caterpillars, alright?"

"I give you caterpillars."

"Well, they're not *butterflies*. But, y'know. Room for growth. Or maybe I just have a tapeworm...?"

"Ok...ok I can do caterpillars. Caterpillars is fine."

"Oh, but not the tapeworm? I see how it is."

"I mean, I can do tapeworm too, bu—wait, stop, you don't even *have* a tapeworm. Why are we talking about tapeworms?"

"I *could* have a tapeworm."

"Omigosh," Ariel put his head back in an exasperated laugh. "You are the *most* infuriating per—can I at least stop eating this lemon?"

"Why was eating a whole lemon any part of any plan?"

"Such a horrible idea," he agreed as he threw the half-eaten lemon away. They watched it bounce twice in the street, then roll into a gutter.

Ariel turned to Ellis, and noticed there was an uncharacteristic shyness radiating from her, an awkwardness in her that he'd never seen before. They took a couple of steps toward each other.

"Okay look," Ellis held up a finger, stopping both of their advances. "This is how this is gonna go. We're gonna do the flirty flirty thing and get close, and then that's gonna freak me the *fuck* out and I'm gonna either shut down or run away, or both. And I can promise to try my best not to hurt you when that happens, because I'm only *mostly* a monster. Then, after I calm down about it and stop being afraid—yes, *afraid* of getting hurt, because, again, only *mostly* monster—then I'll come back guilty as shit and worried that I've fucked something really good up. And look...not a lot of people stick with me. I can be hard to handle. I admit that. I can totally own up to not even *secretly* being a shitshow...But I'm worth holding on to. And I *will* walk through fire for people that I let in here," she tapped her chest. "In my heartplace. So, uh. Yep, that's my elevator pitch."

"Deal," Ariel said with a grateful smile.

They stood directly across from one another.

The perfect distance for a kiss.

Ariel took a step closer, but Ellis shook her head.

"Shomer. Nigga."

"I'm never living that down, am I?"

"Nooo. Ne-*heh*-ver. Besides, you, Rabbi Samson, have a speech to give. In about five minutes or so."

"I—yeah, I suppose I should probably do that."

"Yes, probably. So," she stepped aside and gestured that his path was clear to get moving.

Ariel laughed, shook his head, and began the journey back to the gala. Ellis fell into step alongside him, shaking her head at herself.

They walked the wet streets in bemused silence, casually bumping arms as they drifted into each other's paths. Tentatively declaring with not undeliberate bumps just how fucking weird they though the other one was...and that they liked them anyway.

Not just the parts of each other that made sense, either. But even the parts they didn't yet understand.

"You realize," Ellis pointed out. "That Rosh Hashana is next week, right?"

"Yep."

"And that we can't exactly hold High Holiday services out of your flat?"

"Nope. But we've got a good chunk of change in the Go Fund Me, right?"

"Yep."

"So we should be able to rent a space for Rosh Hashana and Yom Kippur?"

"I guess. We'd have to ask Blair to get on that. But after that? We still won't have a *shul*."

"After that...After that, we'll just figure it out, I guess."

He had no idea how. Neither did she. And at the moment, it meant surprisingly little to either one of them. The future was bound to be a weird uncertain place.

But in that moment, it was just the two of them, and the night was beautiful.

Ellis shook her head again, telling the one butterfly she felt starting to quiver in its chrysalis to shut the fuck up, because it didn't know shit.

Pulling her flask out of her clutch, she unscrewed it and took a swig, because feelings are scary.

She passed it to Ariel.

He knocked back a gulp, and was surprised to taste apple juice.

"Wha—?" he exclaimed.

"You didn't *seriously* think I was coming to work sipping on *booze* all day long, did you?"

Ariel's shocked expression melted into a grin at Ellis' golden-lipped smirk, and it was his turn to shake his head.

Performative theatricality.

Of course.

✡ ✡ ✡

Manishtana

The rest of Ariel's speech wrote itself, the last pieces falling into place even as the emcee announced his name, introducing him as the final nominee of the evening to speak.

Ariel rose from the table to the applause of the audience—leaving Ellis and Jerome behind to keep company with an uncharacteristically skittish Rosenstern, his spooked aides, and a shaken and *chossid*-less Guildencrantz—composing the crowning touches in his head as he walked to the podium.

Inside, he'd continue, *I felt like I was getting arrested for trespassing while walking around in my own home.*

And that just seems a little bit backwards to me. As Jews, we as a people have learned to become very congratulatory in our initiatives to affirm the humanity of people "over there." But what about acknowledging the dignity of our fellow Jews in our own backyards?

Many of us fight tirelessly for social justice against institutionalized discrimination in this country, yet operate as vehicles perpetuating those same systems of marginalization upon the Jews that don't look like us in our own pews. Or aren't married the way we are. Or don't believe precisely as we believe.

We win awards for pursuing intercultural engagement with other communities, yet we neglect to dialogue with the multiculturalism present in our synagogues and temples and day schools and summer camps.

We tout the Jewish value of every human being created in the same reflection of the Divine Image, but we label other Jews as not being "really" Jewish because they aren't what we see when we look in the mirror.

But then there are those of us who don't.

And I am glad to count them as colleagues, both present here and beyond this room, and among my fellow nominees.

"Atem nitzavim hayom koolchem," says the opening verse of this week's Torah portion of **Nitzavim**.

"Today, you are all still standing."

To those who of us who push back, who don't listen to the accusations of political correctness or a liberal agenda. Those of us who weather the attacks from the forces that champion misogyny, racism, homophobia, xenophobia, Islamophobia, and still endure. I say thank you. I say keep your chin up.

Today, you are all still standing.

ARIEL SAMSON: FREELANCE RABBI

To those of us who feel discouraged and battered. Tired and weary of suffering the slings and arrows of life, just to say that we are here and that we exist and that we matter. I say don't lose hope. And you are not alone.

Today, you are all still standing.

And to those—here, Ariel would look directly at Guildencrantz and Rosenstern—who would discourage us, who would use every agency in their power to silence and intimidate us. To paint us as misguided and our efforts at not having any worth. To them I would say...'thank you.' Thank you. For forging us. For testing us. For molding us into the best us we can be. For smelting us into the best possible weapon to defeat you and dismantle everything you stand for.

Haynt zaynen mir ale geshtanen.

Aujourd'hui, nous sommes tous debout.

Wareware wa, imakoko ni iru.

Hoy, todos estamos parados

Ngayon, lahat tayo ay nakatayo.

Joudi nou tout kampe' ensemble.

Jīntiān, wǒmen dōu zhànlì.

Sevodnya vse mi stoyim.

Anachnu nitzavim hayom koolanu.

Despite your best efforts, today, **we** *are all still standing.*

ABOUT THE AUTHOR

MaNishtana is a writer, playwright, speaker, and rabbi, whose work takes prejudice, bias, and ignorance head on with a humorous and often irreverent voice that shatters the misconceptions of Orthodox Judaism, American Jewish racial identity, and African-American religious identity, with gut-punching insights and gut-busting sarcasm. And just a touch of bourbon. And then another touch after that. He currently lives in New York with his wife Shoshana and daughter Gadiélla. In a perfect world, he can be summoned by placing a bottle of Woodford Reserve, the full Koren Talmud Bavli Noé Edition set, the Sword of Omens, a lock of Squall Leonheart's hair, a dry-aged 2" bone-in ribeye steak, and a 5-piece pinstripe suit (with matching tie and pocket square, pocket watch, and wingtips with brogues, *obviously*) at each of the six points of a Star of David, inside a circle drawn with white Jewish tears. As per scripture, the ritual must be completed while chanting to Danny Elfman's 1989 musical score to *Batman*. Under less than optimal conditions, MaNishtana can otherwise be reached via email at manishtana@manishtana.net.
Ignore the general cauldron-like shape of this bio.
It is where I buried all my darlings. Obviously.